A STONE FORGOTTEN

MÓRDHA STONE CHRONICLES, BOOK 4

KIM ALLRED

STORM COAST PUBLISHING, LLC

A STONE FORGOTTEN
Mórdha Stone Chronicles, Book 4
KIM ALLRED

Published by Storm Coast Publishing, LLC
Copyright © 2019 by Kim Allred
Cover Design by Amanda Kelsey of Razzle Dazzle Design

Print edition
978-1-7322411-7-6
Large Print edition
978-1-953832-08-5

For all the young girls and women who have yet to find their place...
dig for the courage to follow your heart.

You can't go home again.

1

Baywood, Oregon - Present Day

The red 1972 Oldsmobile Cutlass circled the block, slowing every few feet before darting ahead. Horns honked, and the driver did the one thing he'd learned to do well. He flipped a middle finger in his rearview mirror, which earned him another honk. The driver grinned with satisfaction before turning his concentration back to his mission, trying to find a damn place to park. Street parking was out. He'd mastered many things in the last three months, but the ability to finesse this behemoth of a vehicle between two others still eluded him.

He slowed again as he gave one last thought to a larger parking space on the street. A glance in his rearview mirror confirmed a long line of traffic behind him. Any other day, he'd let the mongrels wait. He cursed and stomped on the gas pedal, forcing the steel machine to burst forward. A man in a business suit, trying to cross the street, jumped back, juggling his coffee cup. This earned the driver a finger flipped in his direction, and he laughed. Some things truly brightened his day.

After finding a suitable spot in a lot three blocks from his target, the driver leaned his tall, athletic frame against the car, crossed one boot in front of the other, and surveyed the lot. Every building, car, and person fell under his scrutiny. He ran his fingers through his close-cropped, ash-blond hair and raised his face to the sun. This was going to be his lucky day.

He pushed off and swaggered down the street, now quite familiar with downtown Baywood, but he remained diligent. Every street corner required a pause in his stride as he scanned the area. One never knew who one might run into in such a small city. His days in London had proved how tiny even the largest city could be.

After twenty minutes of surveillance during his three-block walk, he reached his destination. The brick buildings on this street were well maintained and quieter than the main thoroughfare. Rainbows of flowers burst from baskets hanging from street posts, and depending on the direction of the breeze, their subtle scent tickled his nose, reminding him of his gardens back home. The memory elicited a stab of melancholy that he shook off.

He turned his focus to the equally colorful banners waving along the street, marked with information about farmers' markets and art fairs. The overstimulation to his senses jabbed at the back of his eyes, and he stopped to lower his head as the ache returned. He reached for the bottle of pills in his pocket, but after shutting his eyes and waiting several seconds with his head bent against the wall of a building, the ache receded.

He blew out a long, slow breath, then refocused on each person as they passed. The crowds were similar to London in full season, yet the colors and sounds could still overwhelm him. This particular street restricted cars, and people strode down the middle of the street, laughing with friends or stuffing food in their mouths. Tourists with shopping bags peered into the windowed storefronts, deciding on whether to enter the store or move on. He inspected each face for a sign of recognition but received only an occasional blank glance in return.

Halfway down the block, he stopped near an antique store. He stepped next to the storefront window, which gave him a partial view of the interior of the store without entirely exposing himself to anyone who might be inside. An aged and marred rolltop desk sat stuffed between an oak-framed standing mirror and a two-drawer dresser. Rows of shelves filled with junk, or antiquities as the store referred to them, blocked the rest of the store from his view. He stepped closer to the window to gain a different perspective. One customer stood in front of a bookshelf and two others roamed the aisles.

He glanced up and down the street before opening the door. Cool air greeted him, and he wrinkled his nose at the mechanized air, mustiness and a cloying sweet smell he couldn't place.

He'd only stepped in a few feet when a feminine, high-pitched voice called out, "Feel free to look around. I'll be with you in a minute."

The driver perused the store for the second time in the last two days, waiting for the customers to leave. If he didn't have success today, he would need a safe place to watch the store without entering. He didn't want someone becoming suspicious of his activities. After spending enough time to appear interested in the old junk, and with only one remaining customer still staring at books, he strolled to the counter in the middle of the store.

The same young woman he'd spoken with before worked behind the counter, talking on the phone and staring at the computer. He waited, and when the clerk glanced up at her new customer, a full smile lit her dull brown eyes with a look of dreamy longing. The driver repressed a shiver and did what he always did when needing information: he matched her smile with his own as he tugged at the sleeves of his long-sleeved tee.

It took several more minutes before she wrapped up the call and rushed out from behind the counter.

"I'm so sorry to keep you waiting." She blushed to her roots and batted her eyes.

He sighed. At least this was something he knew how to respond to. He gave her a slight bow, and his responding grin crinkled the corners of his cornflower-blue eyes. "I'm sorry to intrude on you again so soon."

The clerk lowered her gaze, and her fingers worked at the edges of her sweater. A tug here and a pull there. "Oh, it's not a problem. Are you still looking for Ms. Moore?" Her eagerness to please was so overwhelming, he wanted to take a step back.

He stood his ground and nodded. One thing he'd noticed in his short time in Oregon was how infatuated women seemed with his accent, and he found he could use that to his advantage. The less he spoke, the more the other person did, hoping to engage him in full conversation. The more they told him, the more he'd respond as if quietly rewarding the speaker for their information. If his situation weren't so bizarre, he'd find it all fascinating.

"She never came by yesterday, but I think she'll be in today. No promises, of course. Even our most active clients have their own schedules. But I know she's interested in reviewing the provenance of a new armoire that just arrived. She has a client who has been searching for something similar. If not today, it should definitely be tomorrow."

He nodded. The poor thing couldn't seem to stop blathering.

"All right, love. I appreciate your assistance. I really can't believe I lost her card in the first place."

She twisted her hands. "I'm sorry I'm not able to give you any information on how to contact her. I'd be happy to leave her another message."

He studied her, wondering if she'd end up being a problem. His sigh was protracted. "I'd rather just try to catch her when she comes in. If not here, I'm sure she'll be at the antiques market next week."

The clerk frowned. "Yes, I supposed she will be." She pulled at her lip and peeked at him from under her lashes. Her head popped up. "Why don't I call her one more time? Just to remind her of the item."

When he raised an eyebrow, she rushed on. "It's not like we can hold the piece. We do have other customers, and though it's usually slow on Tuesday mornings, traffic really picks up in the afternoons. The tourist season has been quite active this summer."

He turned on his most charming grin and held out his hand. "I can't thank you enough for your hospitality and assistance." When she reached for his hand, he whispered a kiss over it and felt a shimmer of excitement from her. "If I could ask one more thing?" His grasp tightened ever so gently, his thumb rubbing along the fleshy part of her palm. "If you could not mention me when you speak with her."

She started to pull her hand back until he increased the movements of his thumb and forced a brighter smile. She relaxed as her half-dreamy expression returned.

"It's really nothing, love. I'd just like it to be a surprise."

2

Pound. Pound. Pound.

Silence for a blissful five seconds.

Pound. Pound. Pound.

"Damn." She couldn't take it anymore. AJ Moore slammed the lid of her laptop closed and leaned back in her chair. She ran fingers through her short chestnut locks and stared out the bay window to the ocean below. The fog had dissipated an hour ago, leaving behind blinding reflections cast from a lazy sea. The view could mesmerize her for hours if she let it.

Pound. Pound. Pound.

There was little hope she would win the battle against the noise. She pocketed her cell phone and ran down the stairs to the main floor to face the increased sound of hammering. She pulled up short when she reached the door to the newly expanded kitchen. Suddenly the pounding didn't seem as bad when seen from this vantage point. The person swinging the hammer with such repetitive expertise stood over six feet tall with a muscled chest and arms that bulged against the constraints of his T-shirt. Sweat shimmered along his arms as Finn Murphy lined up his next nail.

Over the three months since they'd returned from their time jump, she'd had to pinch herself. Her few weeks living in 1802 Europe had seemed like years as she traveled from Ireland through England and on to France. At first, those weeks had been fraught with fear, anger, betrayal, and loss. Then she had discovered the profoundness of loyalty, courage, and trust with strangers who had given their lives to help her come home. Her heart ached at leaving Ethan Hughes and Maire, Finn's sister, behind, but they had been right. They didn't belong in this time, and it was her one remaining fret with the beautiful man before her. He wasn't of this time either, though he claimed not to care.

She shook herself as Stella's favorite expression floated in with the soft breeze from the window—don't borrow trouble. She stared at the shambles of their kitchen. The construction was partially completed. The plumbing worked and the appliances were in place so they could reduce their trips to town for takeout, but everything had to be covered in heavy tarps while Finn and Jackson finished the carpentry.

AJ stepped lightly as she closed in on Finn. He ran a hand over a joint, then began measuring something or other. Carpentry wasn't her thing, but this particular carpenter was another matter. She ran her hands over his biceps as she leaned into him, standing on tiptoes and stretching her neck to plant a soft kiss on the back of his neck. The action startled him, and he dropped the measuring tape and pencil.

Finn spun and picked her up, eliciting a brief squeal before he silenced it with a deep kiss, his tongue driving deeper than she had anticipated, but she returned the passion as she wrapped her arms around his neck. When he lifted his head, his emerald-green eyes darkened, and his wicked, slanted grin forced his eyebrow up.

"I was thinking of taking a break." His warm lips grazed over hers.

She tried to push away so she could stand, but he gripped her tighter and carried her through the opened french doors to the deck. They dropped into a chaise lounge with a loud whoosh.

"I didn't mean to interrupt your work." She curled into him and ran a hand over his face, still marveling at the love reflected in his gaze.

"Aye, you are a distraction. I'll never hear the end of it when Jackson returns with supplies, but I can't seem to help myself." He leaned down for another kiss.

AJ savored it for as long as she dared before they both forgot about Jackson's imminent return. She resettled in his lap to give her some distance from his persuasive lips. "You're making great progress. The two of you don't have to push so hard."

"Your mother is looking forward to celebrating her birthday here. Jackson and I have agreed on a timetable, at least for the first floor."

AJ sighed. Helen Moore, her mother, had been tickled pink when she'd met Finn and discovered he owned the Westcliffe. It had surprised AJ as well. The old inn had been a favorite haunt of her father's, and he'd brought AJ to play in the tidal pools as soon as she took her first steps. It became a special place for the two of them as her father wove tales of faraway lands with fierce queens, courageous knights, and daring pirates.

The inn was where she had first met Finn when his ship had appeared out of the mist, a traveler from another century, though she hadn't known it at the time. The Westcliffe had also become one of her stories for the *Baywood Herald*, but she preferred to ignore all she had learned about the Ramseys, the original builders of the house, and their unfortunate legacy of madness.

AJ and Finn had been home from their jump for two weeks before Finn had casually mentioned at dinner that he was the sole owner of the Westcliffe. He had purchased the inn, creating the illusive corporation with the Hensley name, during a previous time jump, when it became apparent the stone necklace he was chasing kept showing up in the area. The property included a dock with a private bay deep enough for his eighteenth-century sloop, the *Daphne Marie*.

Finn didn't talk about his time traveling through the centuries, but he shared bits and pieces when they seemed relevant. He had a healthy bank account he insisted came from gambling through his jumps. After her several attempts at casual questioning, Finn had clammed up. He always ended those conversations with a squeeze of her hand, a kiss on her forehead, and a distant look in his eyes that convinced her there were things from his past he wasn't ready to discuss. It bothered her he wouldn't talk about it, but they had time, and with everything else that had happened, she wouldn't push.

The revelation about his ownership of the Westcliffe had created a whirlwind of activity. AJ and Finn had lived in her apartment until basic necessities had been restored in the turn-of-the-century inn. The place was in surprisingly good shape after sitting vacant since the seventies. Leonard Jackson, a local property manager, had seen to its upkeep, though most of his care had been performed on the exterior. The inside was dated and most of the rooms were too small.

They'd spent a month making plans. After deciding to ignore all the extra bedrooms, they'd focused on refinishing the first floor and creating a master bedroom on the second floor with a private office for AJ. Finn preferred his office on the first floor next to the library they had both instantly agreed was a necessity.

As soon as Helen had heard about the library, she'd insisted that AJ take all of her father's books. Helen had no need for them, and no one would appreciate them more than AJ. Now her father would always be close, just down the hall.

AJ gazed at the ocean, Finn's arms around her, his steady breathing the one thing that kept her grounded. She turned her face up to his. "You know my mom would be just as happy with the tarps and plastic still down. We only need to portion off a section for the food."

"Stop worrying. Isaiah just finished his extra course work and has the rest of the summer to help us."

AJ snorted. "We've had more of Jackson's family working on the place than I can count."

"It's a good thing he has so many grandsons." Finn entwined her fingers in his. "Did I interrupt your work again?"

She brought their hands up and kissed his knuckles before rubbing them against her cheek. "It's not your fault. I don't know why I thought I could work here while construction was going on."

"Are you going to your apartment?"

She shook her head. "Not today. I'm not sure my mind is where it needs to be for writing."

"You haven't climbed in a few days."

"Maybe we could go tomorrow, before Jackson gets here."

The silence stretched.

AJ released his hand and shifted so she could face him straight on. "You don't like climbing."

Finn grinned and kissed the tip of her nose. "I love climbing with you now that I have a feel for it. I guess all those years climbing rigging taught me a thing or two, but I know it's a special time for you. I don't want to intrude."

She studied him and had to admit it was obvious he enjoyed the climbs. His energy was almost palpable each time they arrived at the cove. He had been a quick study, intuitively finding the best holds and edges, and his muscular frame seemed to be a natural fit for the activity. While she appreciated his understanding of her needing time alone, a little stab touched her heart. There were times he needed his own space, and that was all right. But how much of it was him trying to find a place in this new life? Little doubts nagged at her whenever she caught him staring off at the sea. He was staying busy with remodeling the Westcliffe, but then what?

She kissed him hard and fast, as if her kiss were enough to clear the demons that lurked beneath his surface, ones she hadn't been able to reach. When she released him, his eyes softened, and he hugged her tightly.

"We'll work through this, AJ. We just need time."

"Are you two love birds going to spend all morning out there, or do you think we might get some work done today?"

Both heads turned to find Jackson standing at the french doors, a cardboard tray filled with paper cups in his strong, ageless hands. Jackson was an African-American man of indeterminate years. He wouldn't share his age, and he doled out other information only when he felt it necessary. He had to be in his sixties with the number of grown grandchildren they'd met, with one of them ready to give him his second great-grandchild.

"Sorry, my fault. I thought Finn could use a break before you returned." AJ jumped off Finn, her new focus on the cardboard tray.

"Uh-huh." He leaned down so she could plant a kiss on his cheek before she took the tray from him. "He had an assignment while I was gone. You keep giving him breaks, and we'll never make that date for your party."

AJ cooed over the coffee as she handed one to Jackson and then Finn. Jackson had gone out of his way to stop at her favorite coffee house. "I hear we're going to be saved with Isaiah's return."

Jackson grinned. "I don't know how it happened, but my sons done found themselves marvelous women who raised their boys right. Isaiah will definitely get us back on our timetable." He turned serious as he stared at AJ, pointing with one long, bony finger. "But that doesn't give you license to add additional breaks. We agreed on that."

AJ tried to hold back a grin with little success. "Absolutely."

Finn and AJ had had to beg Jackson to be the project manager for the reconstruction of the Westcliffe. After they had asked several local businesses about contractors, they'd discovered Jackson had owned the best construction company in town before he'd switched to property management. Isaiah said it was easier on his bones, and Jackson, after giving his grandson a withering glance, said he had been tired of dealing with wise-cracking employees. Even with that, AJ doubted it had required the concessions they'd agreed to before Jackson took the job. She had caught the glimmer in his eyes when Finn had made the first offer. Jackson had wanted to work on this building since the day he'd started managing the property, but he was a stickler for details. And owners or not, he expected AJ and Finn to follow the tasks assigned to them.

Somewhat pacified, Jackson turned to go inside and Finn stood to follow.

Before he walked through the door, Finn skimmed a hand along her arm. "And where will you be?"

AJ shrugged. "I'm having a late lunch with Stella. She thinks she has another client for me, and I got a call from an antique shop in town. I promised to look at a new piece for another client." She kissed his cheek. "I won't be long."

3

Hours later, sitting on the back deck of the inn, Finn watched two hummingbirds fight over an oversized feeder as he sipped from a tall glass of iced tea, the tinkling of the ice the only other sound between him and the reserved man across from him.

Jackson clenched an empty pipe between his teeth as he stared out to sea, his own glass held tightly in his hand. Detritus from their lunch sprawled across the table, a light breeze stirring the used napkins.

The day had started early, like every other day since returning with AJ. Finn ran a hand through his untamed hair and stretched back in his chair. His days were becoming a pattern that both assured and unnerved him. He had developed a routine, something he hadn't done for more years than he could remember. The closest he'd come to a habitual schedule before had been preparing his ship for sail, or berthing it when the sail was done.

Complete renovation of the Westcliffe would take months, even if they'd have most of the first floor in shape for Helen's party. There would still be finishing work on the first floor before tackling the two upper floors, and they would have to dedicate some time to preparing the outer structure for winter while the weather held.

He'd never imagined finding a home, a secure place that was truly his where he could stop looking over his shoulder. Then AJ had stumbled into his life, a headstrong woman who had stirred his blood to reckless behavior until they'd found safety and a place to build a future.

Yet he couldn't put his finger on what unsettled him.

"You never said what happened to your ship."

The question startled Finn and iced tea spilled on his jeans. He brushed at the wet spot before shrugging. "I gave her to my crew to take home to Ireland." It was enough of the truth.

"That's a shame. She was a real beauty. You could have made money giving tours."

Finn laughed. "And deal with tourists every day?"

Jackson scowled, then chuckled in return. "You have a point."

The men returned to their quiet contemplations. The hummingbirds had taken their battle to a different part of the garden, and now the raucous sounds of birds at a platform feeder mounted twenty feet away filled the air. Finn had set the post and mounted the feeder near an old, bent fir tree the week they moved in. AJ had added other hanging feeders around the yard, followed by the hummingbird feeders. As if the gulls didn't put up enough of a racket, the sounds of songbirds fighting for their share of food were the first thing he heard each morning. And while they shouldn't bother him, they seemed to chip away at his nerves.

"Why do you always pull out that pipe of yours? It doesn't look like it ever held tobacco."

Jackson gave his own one-shouldered shrug, and when he didn't respond, Finn figured it was just one of many topics Jackson felt undeserving of further comment. Then he surprised Finn.

"I was a mean drunk. Many, many years ago. After the war."

Finn thought back, trying to remember which war that would have been. He hadn't paid attention to national events during his jumps searching for the necklace. The local climate for whatever town he found himself in was all that was necessary, and beyond that, it was whatever snippets might be talked about in the local bars. Fortunately, Jackson's comment was either the end of their discussion or his to continue. And Jackson surprised Finn again when he dropped his hand to his knee, the ebony-colored wood pipe clenched in his fingers as he continued his tale.

"Vietnam was a hell-hole. Not the country itself. There were mornings—ah man," Jackson leaned back as he turned his face toward the sea, but his eyes glazed over with other memories. "First thing in the morning, when the mist hung over the rice paddies, the thick, primal jungle in the distance, and the sky a deep hazy blue, it could be the most beautiful place in the world. I think those small moments were the only things that kept me sane."

Finn nodded. "There's nothing pretty about war, or what it does to those who survive the battlefield."

"I wouldn't talk to anyone about it. Still don't for the most part. I used the bottle to help me sleep. Then I used it to help me through the afternoons. I don't know what made Olivia stick with me through it all. But she found some local war widows and eventually talked me into a program before it took me for good."

"She's a fine woman."

Jackson snorted. "One of the best. And if I hadn't gone to that program, she would have kicked me out the house, and I don't know if I'd have ever seen the kids again." He shook his head and drained his iced tea until the remaining chunks of ice clattered against the glass. "My old man died a couple of years after I got out. Olivia went through the boxes my mother sent over and found his collection of pipes." Jackson laughed, and he looked down at the pipe, running his fingers over the detailed etchings. "One of my earliest memories was seeing him on the back porch. Sometimes all you could see was the glow from his pipe, smell that sweet, pungent scent floating through the yard." He closed his eyes, his lips curving into a quick smile, his hand continuing to rub the pipe.

After several quiet minutes, Finn asked, "Did you ever smoke?"

He shook his head. "I somehow got through the war without smoking or doing drugs. It was all alcohol. Now I wish I had smoked a little weed rather than picked up the bottle." He held up his pipe. "This was the only pipe in his collection that hadn't been used. Never figured out why. It was one of his oldest ones. One day I tested it out, just getting the feel of it between my teeth, and it just seemed to fit."

Finn turned his gaze back to the ocean, thinking about Jackson and feeling sorry he hadn't met the man in his earlier jumps. Three of his jumps had been in this area. It had been his second jump to Baywood when he'd purchased the Westcliffe and had the realtor set up a management company. If he had met Jackson back then, what would the man have thought when Finn returned decades later looking no older than when he had left?

Something clenched in his gut, and he pushed it away.

"You're not going to turn into Ramsey, are you?"

The question startled Finn, at first not recognizing the name. Ramsey had built the Westcliffe in the early 1900s. His son had gone crazy during World War II, eventually driving his family away. Finn shuddered to think that could happen to him. Then he remembered AJ's other article about the McDowell house that Ethan had rented while he had been in Baywood.

McDowell had been another man driven to madness by his obsession with the sea.

Finn's laugh was stilted. "What would make you say that?" He felt Jackson's gaze but refused to meet it.

"You have a good life here. A good woman who adores you, and a beautiful new home." Jackson turned the pipe over in his hands. "Sometimes that's not enough." He tucked the pipe into the shirt pocket under his stained and weathered overalls, then leaned toward Finn, hands on his knees. "It's not my business, but you have that look about you. Like something ain't finished."

A cold chill crawled up Finn's spine, and he shook it off. He gulped his tea and began to gather the remnants from lunch. He tried a grin. "And what's your answer for a restless soul?"

Jackson stared at him for a moment, and this time Finn did meet the dark brown eyes that seemed wiser than his years. "Either finish it or let it go. Don't let it fester." Jackson stood and helped Finn pick up plates. "Now enough with the women's talk. You're behind schedule."

Finn's usual grin finally fit into place as Jackson headed inside, but then the grin slid away. It was finished. Wasn't it? He missed his sister, and he missed his ship, but that would all pass in time. Then what was it that nagged?

Two blue jays hovered nearby, waiting for scraps of food. He shook his head. They'd soon be taking over the place. What had AJ been thinking, feeding them? What he needed was time alone with her, something their current schedule hadn't allowed. He considered his options. Perhaps a special dinner with wine and candles. Then maybe a long soak in that over-sized tub he'd insisted on. And for a little while, he'd bury that bothersome itch.

4

AJ's first stop had been the print shop. She opened the box while still in the parking lot and pulled out one of the freshly printed business cards. The soft cream finish was simple and elegant. It bore her name and contact information. She rubbed her thumb over the title underneath her name—*Antiquities Broker*. Something settled inside her, a distant memory of her father squeezing her shoulders in excitement over finding a new treasure in an out-of-the-way thrift store. This was right. It would take some work to get established, and she was grateful for the odd consignment jobs she'd done in the past. Now it was time to knock on those doors to pick up more business.

She pulled out several cards, sliding them into her new business-card holder. As an afterthought, she tucked a couple more in her pocket. She drove toward the tourist section of town and found a parking spot two blocks from her main destination. Still early for her lunch date with Stella, she stopped at a coffeehouse before going to the antique store.

The day too beautiful to ignore, AJ watched the tourists as she drank her coffee at an outside table. After a few sips, she pulled out her tablet and perused her calendar. Her mother's party was a month away, and though it would only be family and a few friends, the tasks sometimes appeared daunting. At some point, she'd thought organizing a party during construction on the house while trying to build a new career had made sense.

It was during these quiet moments that the daily plans she'd made seemed so insignificant.

She leaned her head against the brick of the building. Some days, she seemed to just go through the motions. Live the everyday life. She remembered docking in Portishead, the first time she'd seen England after their harrowing journey across the Irish Sea. People had trudged through the streets, and she had thought their life dull: going to work, going home, with little else in between. She wasn't one of those people.

After returning from their time jump, the nightmares had begun. Most stemmed from those last days at the monastery and the bloody battle. Finn had been tortured, and she'd never been so scared of losing him. At times, a feeling of déjà vu came over her, but she could never put her finger on what triggered it. Her brother, Adam, said she suffered from PTSD, but what would she tell a therapist? Besides, it didn't fully explain her melancholy.

At first, she'd thought her bouts of depression were trauma related but had pushed that aside. She missed the friends she'd left behind, friends who were now long dead. Ethan had been more than a friend. He'd been a mentor, a big brother. A role Adam had never found an interest in accepting. And what could one say about Maire? She'd been an oasis in the middle of AJ's despair after being left behind at Waverly. In the end, she'd been so much more—a beacon of strength that had made AJ a better person.

Brushing a tear from her cheek, AJ sat straighter. That was the problem. She was grieving. Why hadn't that occurred to her before? She'd spent so much time keeping busy, doing anything she could to avoid remembering the friends she'd left behind. Now it all made sense. And though her thoughts of Ethan and Maire made her sad, she had to consider her life now. It was far from mundane. And she had Finn.

They weren't only building a new home together, they were creating a fresh start without blueprints. It might be a rocky start, but they'd been through so much worse. This next part should be a cakewalk. Finn needed to find his place, and she'd help him. The Westcliffe would keep him busy for the next year, and by then, everything would have settled into place. Feeling better, AJ drained her cup and headed for the antique shop before the clerk could call to nag again.

She window-shopped along the way, always on the lookout for something unique for her customers. After her third stop, the hairs on her neck rose. She froze. It had been a while since anything had triggered her Spidey sense. Her hand instinctively reached for her pocket, and finding it empty, a cold sweat broke down her spine, sending alarm signals along her nerves.

It wasn't legal to conceal her dagger, but she could legally wear it visibly displayed without a problem. She snorted. Daggers weren't exactly a fashion statement, especially while trying to grow her business. What sane person would hire a dagger-toting antiques broker? The thought of jumping to someone's mortal defense on the placid streets of Baywood made her chuckle. Yet something had set off her warning bells.

She continued looking at the displays but only to use the reflection of the glass panes to check her surroundings. Nothing. She turned back the way she had come.

There.

Someone ducking into a shop.

She waited but nothing else happened. Nothing more than the crowds picking up as the tourists started their serious shopping.

Feeling foolish, she stopped her browsing and increased her pace to the antique store. She looked forward to seeing Stella after her business was done. If anyone could steer AJ back on course, it was her best friend. Her steps had lightened by the time she opened the door to her destination.

5

Stella Caldwell tossed her gardening gloves on the patio table, fell into the chaise lounge, and snatched up a chilled glass of pinot gris. Nothing felt better than finishing the last of her weekly gardening chores before stretching out to enjoy her accomplishments. She checked her phone for messages and noted she had a full hour before meeting AJ for lunch.

She sipped her wine and thought about her friend. It had been one thing to work with Adam, AJ's brother, to find her. It was quite the leap of faith to believe the growing evidence, if you could call sheer speculation evidence, of the possibility that AJ had been lost in time. So why was it so difficult to believe AJ's story of where she'd been, 1802 England? Or had it been Ireland?

She sighed, set down her wineglass, and closed her eyes. A light breeze rustled her auburn hair, and she rubbed her temples. She was happy for AJ. She was. The love AJ had for Finn sparkled in her eyes every time she mentioned his name, and the way Finn watched AJ when she wasn't looking made it clear those feelings were reciprocated. Yet, AJ had changed in the week she'd been gone, which, for AJ, had somehow been three months. There was a restlessness about her she tried to hide, but Stella didn't buy it.

"Honestly, Stella, I'm the same person," AJ had claimed the first week she'd been back, and they'd finally had time to themselves. "I'm just not ready to go back to the paper."

"But you love being a reporter." Stella had driven them down the coast, and they wandered the waterfront of a local tourist trap, buying taffy and cheap sweatshirts. "Sam went nuts when you didn't show up for work. He called me five times."

"I know. I sent him my last article on the historical building series. Robert or Clara can pick up the slack until they find a replacement."

Stella stopped mid-step. "You're not going back?" She tried not to look stupid as her jaw dropped to her chest, which was no easy feat even in her fabulous, orange polka dot dress.

AJ shrugged and grabbed Stella out of the way of a skateboarder. "Not for a while. I think I found something else."

Stella rolled her eyes. "Don't tell me. Tour guide for 'Time Travel Vacations.'"

"Not funny."

"It's a little funny."

AJ smiled. "I suppose it is." She shook her head. "You wouldn't believe all the amazing antiques I saw. Well, many pieces weren't antiques yet. I actually touched a brand-new Chippendale. But there were tapestries that had to be a couple centuries old." A small grin curved AJ's lips, and the crinkles around her eyes relaxed. "It gave me new purpose. A rekindling of my love of history and antiques. I think I could be an antiques consultant. I've done a bit of that off and on the last couple of years and built up a small client base. With a bit of persistence, I think I could make a go of it. I'd have to manage a larger region, not just Baywood, but I could help match sellers and buyers with the regional antique shops."

Stella glanced away. A mother chased two unruly toddlers down the short sidewalk into the open arms of their father, who had squatted to catch them. The toddlers giggled with enthusiasm. No worries, Stella thought. At least not today. No one could say what tomorrow would bring.

She swiveled back to AJ and tilted her head, giving AJ a once-over, then nodded. "I can see it. It suits. And now with Finn, you're becoming quite the millennial."

AJ snorted. "Yeah, not sure that's quite fitting."

After a few more minutes of silence, AJ turned to Stella. "What do you think of Finn?"

Stella hadn't been expecting that, and she waited another minute before answering. "I don't know him that well. You've only been back a week, and Ethan did a good job of getting me to completely distrust Finn. So it's going to take a bit."

AJ reached out and grasped Stella's hand. "That's okay. It took Ethan time to trust Finn." She turned her big brown eyes on Stella and gave her a slow smile. "But he eventually did. They saved each other's lives."

And that was as much as Stella had wanted to hear. Something horrible had happened during AJ's travels. Finn's still-healing injuries had been proof enough of that, and there was the way he always kept an eye on AJ. There was more than love that ran deep between them, as if there was something left unfinished. The strangest part? After all the hassle of tracking down the stone necklace, neither AJ nor Finn would discuss what had happened to it.

Stella picked up her wine and drained most of it, wishing she'd either opened a red or made coffee. Not that she didn't like a good white, and the temperature was perfect for it, but all this worry over her friend was making her nauseated. She leaned back and closed her eyes when the doorbell rang, followed by a knock.

Damn. Couldn't the solicitors read the signs and stop knocking on her door? When the knock came again, this time with the doorbell as an afterthought, she sighed and heaved herself out of the lounge. She was still mumbling when she opened the door. Her face drained of color.

"Hey, Stella. I wasn't sure I'd catch you at home, but your office was closed." Adam Moore wore a grand smile as if he always stopped by for a chat.

She glanced down and saw the suitcase at his feet. When she raised her gaze, Adam wore a sheepish grin she was getting ready to hate all over again. "Oh, hell no."

6

"Oh, hell no." Stella backed up a step, her words replaying over and over in her head as she decided whether to let him explain or just slam the door in his face. The latter would be more satisfying.

"Just give me a minute to explain. You're the only one I can talk to about this." Adam spread his arms out in a pleading gesture, imploring and somehow a bit sad. His expression shifted from remorseful to slightly panicked.

She tapped her foot, breathed in a lungful of the tangy coastal air floating in through the open door, and sighed out a long moan. "I'm going to be forever punished. I spend one week helping you out and this is my reward."

Adam didn't say a word. It may have been three months since they worked together, but he seemed to have remembered his best argument was to keep his mouth shut.

"Fine. Come in." She looked down at the suitcase. "That stays by the door. We can talk on the patio." She turned and stopped in the kitchen to start a pot of coffee.

By the time she'd carried the tray of coffee pot and mugs to the patio, Adam had settled into the large rattan chair, his head back, eyes closed. He looked like crap. The dark circles under his eyes were one indicator he hadn't been getting any sleep. The rest of his physical appearance hammered the point home. His hair looked like he'd been running his hands through it all day, or perhaps he'd walked through a mini tornado. His clothes were rumpled, and his skin was pale. Had he been sleeping on a park bench? The only thing missing was a shopping cart and a couple layers of dirt.

She dropped the tray on the table, rattling the cups, and Adam popped up, eyes darting around.

"Sorry. I didn't mean to startle you." Stella fluffed a chair pillow before sitting across from him.

Adam stared at her. "Really?"

She shrugged. "Well, not that badly. Shit. What has you on edge?" Then she couldn't help herself. "You haven't seen strange fog again, have you?"

"That's not funny."

"Yeah, I get that a lot. But it actually is." Stella poured two cups, doctored hers, and handed the plain dark brew to Adam.

She sipped and waited. Remembering that Adam, who was a trial lawyer, could wait her out indefinitely, Stella ran through scenarios that would land him at her door. Her mug hit the table with a loud thump, making Adam jump again.

"Madelyn found out." Three simple words were all she needed to say, and Adam slumped against the chair. "Did you tell her, or did she figure it out herself?"

Adam had told her about his gambling debt while they'd searched for AJ. A fact he'd been hiding from his wife for weeks. Stella had warned him to come clean and tell her, even after he'd come to that conclusion on his own. Yet here they were.

"I was going to tell her." Adam squeaked out his reply, and he winced at the hollowness of his own words.

"Oh, for Christ's sake, Adam. You've had all the time in the world. Be honest. You thought you could get away without saying anything."

He gulped his coffee, grimacing at the scalding brew, and slipped her a quick glance before dropping his gaze. "The debt was paid months ago, and I haven't gone near a poker table since long before that. Everything at home seemed back to normal."

"Then what happened?"

He pushed his hands through his hair, and Stella almost laughed. With a lot of gel, maybe some dark blue highlights, Adam would make a good-looking punk star. Adam caught her smile and scowled. "Glad you find it amusing."

"Sorry. I'm listening."

"It was a bit rocky at first, you know, when AJ came back. Madelyn knew there was more to AJ's disappearance, but I kept to AJ's story about her and Finn's weeklong romantic getaway. With all the end-of-school stuff at home, and getting the kids ready for summer camp, well, things normalized."

Stella half listened as she gazed at her bed of yarrow. Damn. She'd missed an entire section that required deadheading. "Have the kids left?"

"What?"

"The kids. You said they were going to camp. Have they left?"

"Yeah. Day before yesterday." Adam grew still. His gaze shot to hers, his expression turned to one of horrible understanding as he whispered, "She was waiting for the kids to leave."

The old Stella, the one that didn't know Adam, might have gloated a bit at his dilemma. Though it was difficult to admit, and she would never volunteer the information, the new Stella had learned to respect Adam, and maybe, just a little, sort of liked him. He had been so worried when AJ had disappeared and had been dogged in his efforts to find out what had happened to her. She knew part of his motivation had been a bit self-centered. He'd thought he was going mad and needed to find a reason behind the strange fog that had made AJ, Finn, Ethan, and a huge-ass sailing ship vanish into thin air. But she had also seen his genuine happiness when AJ had come home.

She also understood the decision he and AJ had made not to share the real story with their mother or Madelyn. Of course, both women may have eventually been convinced of the real story, especially with four people witnessing the whole event. In the end, it wasn't her call, and she'd acquiesced to AJ's gut. And now, here was Adam, trying to do the right thing in all the wrong ways. She couldn't help but feel sorry for him. Damn it.

"Did she know about the gambling?"

Adam breathed out a heavy sigh and refilled both mugs. "No. But right after AJ and Finn came home, Finn learned what we did to try to find AJ. He paid the last portion of what he owed me for finding the necklace." He shrugged. "I told him it wasn't necessary, but he insisted on paying his own debts, and he wanted me to clear mine." He scowled again. "I hate that I might like him."

Stella hid another smile behind her mug. She knew that feeling. "AJ told me."

"Finn slipped me an envelope after a family dinner, and I kept it in my jacket pocket overnight until I could give it to the loan shark the next day."

Stella nodded. "And Madelyn found the envelope."

Adam's head shot up. "Really? Is it just a woman thing or what? Where else should I have put it?"

Stella patted his hand. "It's not a woman thing, I've just watched too many movies. It was just bad timing. She was probably looking for something, or maybe she thought it was time for the jacket to be cleaned. Maybe it was just fate catching up with you."

"You're right on two scores. She was going to take the jacket to the cleaners, and it was definitely fate ready to take a big bite out of my ass."

"I've got to give it to her. She was cool about it with all the waiting and planning." Stella laughed out loud, which made Adam scowl. "You don't see it." She laughed harder.

"No. Sorry. Your amusement at my hardship escapes me."

"It's not that." She snorted. "You two are so much alike. She should have been a lawyer."

Adam sat back and blinked before releasing a snort. "And I was oblivious to her entire plan. She hid it so well." He propped his elbows on the table and held his head in his hands. "What am I going to do?"

"You're going to give her time and space."

His head popped up. "No. I think I need to show her how sorry I am. We need to make this right."

"How many times did you say you were sorry as she was kicking you out the door?"

His head went back into his hands as he stared at the table.

"Give her some space."

"I need a place to stay."

"There's a lot of hotels in town."

"And all the good ones are booked."

Stella shook her head. Tourist season.

"What about your mom?"

Adam gave her a sneer from under his hands.

"You are not staying here."

Adam glanced up, eyes pleading in a sick puppy-dog way.

Stella looked away and picked up her phone to check the time. "Shit. I have to get going. I'm meeting AJ for lunch." She stood and stared down at the sad man, wondering if they were fated to be strange bedfellows. "You can hang here for the afternoon while we figure something out." She raced to her room, changed clothes, fixed her makeup, and ran out to the hall to grab her purse as a thought struck.

AJ still had a few months left on her apartment lease. Maybe. She reached for the door, then sighed. Damn. She spared a few moments to retrace her steps to the patio.

Adam had leaned back in the chair, staring into nothingness.

"I'll be gone for a couple of hours. I have an idea but need to check it out. Just stay here until I get back. Watch TV, listen to music, do whatever. Just wait. Okay?"

He had turned listless again but somehow found the energy to look up at her. "Thanks."

She wanted to give him encouragement but there was nothing worse than false hope. She didn't know Madelyn and had no idea if kicking Adam out had been her way of proving a point or if she had contacted a lawyer. Best to keep her mouth shut until she spoke with AJ.

7

The antique store smelled of mildew, furniture polish, and, of all things, bubble gum. AJ scanned the place before venturing past the front door. It had been years since she'd stepped into this shop, and from her recollection, not much had changed—except for the bubble gum. Antiques of all sizes, from large furniture pieces to the smallest of household trinkets, vied for attention. The store was crammed with so many items, they overflowed into the aisles, giving her a sense of claustrophobia.

Most of the collection focused on the fifties, give or take a decade, which made the items vintage rather than antique, but they would still make nice additions to homes with the right décor. She checked the tags on the nearest items. All overpriced. She didn't expect anything less from a shop in the middle of the tourist district. She hoped her client hadn't purchased the armoire yet. There were other stores that focused on larger antiques with better prices.

AJ picked her way through the clutter as she moved to the middle of the store where she discovered the source of both the mildew and the bubble gum. One side of the aisle held three poorly crafted bookcases stuffed with old books. After a quick perusal, she grudgingly admitted there were some interesting titles stuck between the old weathered cookbooks, history books, and two incomplete sets of Encyclopedias Britannica.

The other side of the aisle displayed racks of nostalgic retro candy. Large bins of, yep, bubble gum explained the sweet scent. This section would make up for a good portion of daily tourist sales along with the smaller antiques.

She turned back to the books, her hand reaching for a thin children's book, when she heard the footsteps behind her.

"Can I help you, miss?"

AJ turned to find a slightly plump blonde woman, barely old enough to drink standing behind her. The woman's hands fidgeted behind her back.

AJ pushed the book back onto the shelf and wiped her hands on her pants before reaching out a hand. "I'm AJ Moore. I think we spoke on the phone earlier."

The clerk instantly brightened and grabbed AJ's hand with a limp grip before tucking it behind her back. "Oh yes, we've been expecting you."

AJ glanced around the store but didn't see anyone else and assumed the "we" must have meant the owner and this young clerk. She nodded. "Sorry it took me so long to get here. My calendar is a bit of a mess these days after moving."

"Oh, I can imagine. I still have boxes from my last move." She turned, and AJ followed her deeper into the store. "The piece is just over here."

For the next twenty minutes, AJ gave the walnut armoire a thorough inspection. It had a few mars but nothing unexpected for a piece this old. At first, her heart pumped, thinking she had found a John Swicegood piece. But after locating the maker's mark, she discovered it was an excellent replica from a furniture maker who had lived in Astoria. It was still a worthy antique and as overpriced as the other items in the shop.

Satisfied she'd accomplished her task, she turned to find the clerk hovering an aisle away, darting glances toward the door.

"It's a nice piece, late 1800s," AJ said, hoping to retain the clerk's attention.

"Oh." The young woman's eyes grew large. "I had no idea it was that old. Most everything else here is mid-twentieth century. Or that's what the owners tell me."

"Yes, they're correct from what I've seen. Do you know where they got this particular piece?"

The clerk nodded. "There should be a record of it in inventory."

When she continued to stare, AJ prompted, "Could you look it up?"

The young woman blushed. "Oh, sorry. Of course." She straightened and rushed behind the counter, plopping in front of the computer. In between typing, she glanced at the door as if waiting for someone to arrive.

AJ stood at the counter and waited, casually checking the time on her cell phone without seeming impatient. She had five minutes to get to the restaurant. Stella wouldn't mind if she was late, but the clerk was starting to make AJ uncomfortable. She could retrieve the information faster if she'd stop glancing at the door every two seconds.

"Will it be much longer? I have another appointment, and I'm running a bit late." AJ wondered why the information hadn't been ready for her since they had just spoken that morning.

"I'm so sorry, Ms. Moore. It's printing now." The young woman's head lowered and when a bell rang, her head popped up.

AJ turned and heard the squeal before she saw the heads of

two young moms, both holding squirming babies. When she turned back, the clerk seemed to deflate, almost as if she'd been expecting someone else.

"Has it printed yet?" AJ strummed her fingers along the counter, suddenly understanding some of her brother's impatience with people. She straightened and smiled as the clerk handed her a single page. AJ scanned it, pleased to find useful information, a practice usually lacking from this particular store. "This is great. It should help my buyer make her decision."

"That's, uh, great." Her eyes were fastened on the door again.

"Well, thank you for your time. I'm sure my client will be in touch."

The girl raced from around the counter. "Are you sure there isn't anything else I could show you? We have a new rolltop desk that just came in. Or maybe the collection of Waterford from a recent estate sale?"

AJ shook her head. "Sorry. This isn't a buying trip. I only made enough time to look at the armoire. I'll try to stop by again in the next few weeks."

She made a quick dash for the door, putting the moms between her and the clerk. She understood the reason to glom on to an antiques broker, but the clerk couldn't seem to decide who was more important, AJ or whoever she had been expecting to walk through the door.

She sucked in a lungful of fresh ocean air to dispel the cloying stench of bubble gum. Checking her phone one more time, AJ turned to get her bearings. The restaurant was new, and she couldn't remember if she was supposed to turn right or left. She was glancing around one last time, starting to turn right, when a man striding across the street jarred her to a stop.

He was average height, an athletic build with lean muscles and short ash-blond hair. He was similar to dozens of other men, yet something about him seemed familiar. His head was down so she couldn't make out his face. He tugged at the sleeves of his shirt and the world tilted. *No.* Just a bad memory.

"AJ." Her name was bellowed out over the growing crowd of tourists.

The man's head came up for an instant before lowering, his stride increasing, his hands continuing to tug at his sleeves. *Beckworth?* No. That wasn't possible. He was long dead.

"AJ, over here." Stella's voice pierced AJ's trance.

AJ spun toward Stella, thankful for a friendly face, then turned back toward the street. The man was gone. AJ stepped forward, peering around tourists, glancing in both directions and across the street. How could he have disappeared so quickly?

"For God's sake, AJ. I'm right here." Stella panted as she reached AJ. "I saw you from a few shops down. The restaurant is back this way."

AJ stared at the spot she had seen him. "Did you see that man crossing the street?" She turned hopeful eyes toward Stella.

Stella glanced at the street and shook her head. "What man?"

AJ's shoulders slumped. "Never mind. I guess I'm seeing things." The tremors started at her fingertips and coursed through her body, running down her legs and leaving them as weak as if she had run a marathon. She reached for Stella.

"Good God, AJ. You're not pregnant, are you?"

That jolted AJ out of her growing panic attack, and though she was still shaken by her vision, she burst out laughing.

Stella relaxed. "Well, you still have your sense of humor. I think you need some food."

"And maybe a little wine?"

"That goes without saying. And you'll never guess who showed up at my front door."

AJ took a last long glance around before letting Stella guide her down the street. Food. That must be it. She'd forgotten to eat breakfast. Before she stepped inside the restaurant, AJ scanned the street and sidewalk, watching for a blond-haired man. Though she didn't see anyone, the hairs on her neck rose as the door closed behind her.

8

Finn ran his hand down the long, lean leg, testing for soundness. Satisfied with what he felt, he stood and patted the mare's soft gray neck as she nuzzled his hand. He laughed and reached into his pocket for an oat-and-molasses treat.

"What do you think?"

Finn turned to the woman holding a leather bridle. She stood almost as tall as him, her tanned, muscled arms revealed by a worn, black tank top that bore the name of something called Dead Head. Her lanky frame ended in faded blue jeans and weathered, dirt-crusted boots. She tilted her head and a long, chestnut-brown braid streaked with bits of gray swung to one side. Her refined cheekbones emphasized her shrewd hazel eyes, which watched his every movement as he interacted with the mare.

"Do you want to take her for a ride?" The woman, Maxine— but he was to call her Mac—continued to lean against the fence railing, sizing him up as if he were the one for sale rather than the horse.

"That won't be necessary." He held her gaze and caught the quick flash of disappointment before it was gone. She held her grim smile. AJ was going to like her. "I've a fair sense for horses. She seems gentle enough. I'll take her and the Friesian gelding."

The woman stood straighter and blinked before her eyes narrowed with suspicion. "That was rather quick. And you don't want to ride either one?"

Finn shook his head. "I don't have the time today, but if it's okay with you, I'd like to come back in a couple of days. I believe your ad said you board animals."

She nodded.

"Great. I'd like to keep them here, possibly for a few months until I can make other arrangements closer to home."

She ground the toe of her boot into the dirt as she considered his request. "I'm not one to squash a sale, but you've only been here thirty minutes."

Finn grinned his charming, slanted smile. "Aye, and you're worried what type of owner I'll make. I understand. I've spent my entire life around horses, on that you'll have to trust. I've also spent the last month visiting other horse farms, and while they all seem to know their horses, your name kept coming up." Finn ran a hand down the mare's flank, then patted her on the rump before turning back to Mac. "You keep your farm clean, the horses are sound and well-cared for. All except those two horses in the far barn. They've had a rough go, but I suspect you've taken them in to care for them."

Mac's expression softened as she looked him over again before settling back against the railing. "If you'll give me your contact information, I'll email you their lineage, health records, and contracts. And I'll want to be here when you take them for their first ride."

"Fair enough."

He shook her hand, thanked her for her time, and spent another ten minutes talking to both horses before jumping into an old green Chevy pickup to drive home.

He whistled the entire way, windows down, the wind rustling his brown, sun-streaked hair, feeling like his old self for the first time in weeks. He had lucked out. The farm was only forty-five minutes from home, and he had instinctively known the minute he'd met Mac that she would have what he was looking for. He'd still like to find a way to get the horses closer to Baywood, but he had plenty of time to find another arrangement. He hoped AJ would enjoy the surprise. If he could go climbing with her, she could ride with him. He chuckled. He knew one way to break the news to her.

A J forced herself to stay within the speed limit on her drive home, but her foot wanted to slam the pedal down and drive the coastal highway until she ran out of gas. She had forgotten about seeing the man that looked like Beckworth as soon as she slid into the booth for lunch, but that had more to do with the bombshell Stella dropped before AJ had a chance to sip her first glass of wine.

She shook her head, still not believing Adam had shown up on Stella's doorstep looking for a place to stay. She had to give Madelyn points. The woman had played her hand well, waiting for the kids to go to camp. So much had changed with her brother since coming home and finding him on the dock, worried and way too helpful.

Stella had woven quite the tale about the week she and Adam had searched for AJ—how Adam had been hysterical, for which she couldn't blame him, and how guilty he had felt, for which he did bear some responsibility. And he'd never given up, but kept pushing, even when the leads had led them to places no sane person would have gone.

She snorted. Adam had been obsessed with AJ's journey,

soaking in every nuance of experiences. After careful deliberation, she'd let him read her journal, though she wouldn't let him leave with it. It wasn't that she didn't trust him, it had simply become too precious to leave with someone.

Adam had spent an entire afternoon sitting on the back deck reading it from cover to cover. When he handed the journal back to her, something passed between them. No words, but a mutual respect and understanding, and the dam AJ had built around Adam broke. He still needled her at family dinners, but after witnessing the relationship between Finn and his sister, Maire, she saw it for what it was. Simple brother and sister razzing. Her nagging rejoinders seemed to bring them closer.

She had been dumbfounded to learn of Adam's gambling debt and understood more than anyone else his irrational need to keep it hidden. Adam took his familial responsibilities seriously, more so after their father had died. It would have been difficult to swallow his pride and tell Madelyn, but she had agreed with Stella that he needed to come clean, the sooner the better. Yet here they were. She doubted Madelyn would divorce Adam over this, no matter how mad she was. AJ had spent little time around Madelyn, but after all the years the woman had been part of the family, it was obvious how important her family was to her. No. Madelyn was making Adam sweat, and AJ reasoned he deserved some time to consider his actions until Stella shared her plan.

"It's not that I have a problem with Adam bunking in my spare room, but you know what I'm like in the mornings. I like my own space. Even for a couple of weeks, we'd kill each other."

AJ laughed. "I don't think it would be that bad. He'll be at work before you open an eye in the morning. And he'll be on the computer or have his head in a book by the time you get home. You'll be like ships passing in the night."

Stella nodded as if in agreement, but AJ knew she was only

doing it for appearance. She waited for whatever Stella had cooked up.

"I was thinking. Now that you're all moved in at the Westcliffe, your apartment is just sitting empty while you ride out the lease."

AJ almost choked on her bite of salad, and she washed it down first with water, then with a gulp of wine. "You've got to be kidding."

"What? It's empty with the exception of a few pieces of furniture and a couple of bookcases."

AJ didn't know why it felt wrong. It just did.

"I know you're probably still upset with him for rampaging through your bedroom, but he could use the spare room now that you've moved all the furniture to your new office."

Was that why it bothered her? She had forgiven Adam for his crazed search for the necklace. Hadn't she? She blew out a breath and shrugged. "I guess it's just an apartment now. And God knows, the two of you spent almost an entire week there while I was gone. It makes sense."

Stella's relieved expression made AJ laugh. "Though I would have loved to have seen how the two of you made it through a week together."

Stella flashed her a pointed look. "Now that's just plain mean."

After lunch, safely ensconced in the silent warmth of her car, Adam's plight disappeared. The ash-blond male that had been tugging at his sleeves produced an immediate achy feeling in the pit of her stomach. She hadn't been sleeping well and that tended to muddle her brain for the first few hours of the day. Was it possible she had hallucinated the entire thing?

The question she conveniently ignored was whether to tell Finn. As much as she worried about him settling in, she caught his occasional side glances when she'd had a particularly sleepless night. It hardly seemed worth bothering him about a stranger who bore an uncanny likeness to someone long dead. Everyone had at least one doppelganger. The truth was, it wasn't the first time she'd thought she'd seen someone from the past.

If she analyzed it, who could blame her for hallucinating Beckworth? He'd kidnapped her and dragged her across the channel to France, and in a turn of fortune, she'd stabbed him. It hadn't killed him, but surely two hundred years had finished the job.

She pulled into the driveway to find the sun sparkling on the ocean, brushing her new home in soft strokes of burnished golds and dusky coppers. The comfortable setting loosened the muscles in her shoulders. She was surprised to see Jackson's truck gone. The two men usually worked until five and it wasn't quite four. Maybe Jackson had left for another lumber run.

The old Chevy truck Jackson had found for Finn was parked in its usual spot. Seeing it, and knowing Finn was home, continued to erase her unease, though her fingers remained ice cold.

She climbed the few steps to the porch, her legs still a bit shaky, and stopped to smile at the rattan chairs and table on the front porch. The inn was truly becoming a home. When she entered the house, the utter stillness made her second-guess Finn's whereabouts. He should be hammering, sanding, or sawing something. She dropped her purse in the hall before continuing to the kitchen. The dusty tarps had been folded and stored next to freshly sanded pieces of wood trim stacked against the dining area wall. The toolbox was shut, a clear sign that Finn was done for the day. So where was he?

She walked to the staircase and listened. Faint music she hadn't heard earlier filtered down from the second floor. "Finn? Are you home?"

"Up here."

Curious as to what he was up to, she bounced up the stairs and stopped cold when she arrived at the door to the bedroom. Something red spotted the carpet leading to their room. She stepped closer and stared. Rose petals?

Her body swayed as a small tingle ran down her spine. The rest of her tormented day disappeared, and she picked up a handful of petals, breathing in their earthy, floral scent. She followed the trail into the bedroom and toward their bathroom. A silent laugh bubbled up, and she shook her head. She thought Finn had dozed off during those old romantic movies she'd made him watch. He appeared to have learned a few tricks.

She kicked off her shoes and picked up more petals on her way to the bathroom, the heady scent leaving her giddy. She recognized the fragrance. These flowers were from the roses planted along the side of the house.

When she entered the bathroom, she could only stare as she licked her bottom lip.

The sunshade had been pulled down. Several candles cast the darkened room in a soft glow, their fragrance blending with the stream of petals. Two glasses of bubbly perched next to the tub alongside a bucket holding the rest of the icy bottle. She noted it all within seconds, which was all the time she had before her gaze was fully consumed by the man in the tub.

Finn leaned back, soap bubbles lapping against his broad, bare, wet chest. A lock of brown hair, its streaks of gold lit by candlelight, hung over his brow, and his deep emerald eyes sparkled as he flashed that grin that made her knees go weak.

"Welcome home. I think you'll find the bath to your liking, sweet lass."

9

AJ slowly stripped. The earlier tingle spread through her as Finn watched her every move. After tossing her bra and panties, she slid her foot into the warm, silky water. As she stepped all the way in, Finn pulled her down so her back rested against him. He kissed her temple and entwined their fingers. She closed her eyes and released a sigh. He was right, the bath was perfect.

"What a nice surprise." She stretched out her legs and tangled them with his. "What's the occasion?"

He ran a hand through her hair and whispered, "I missed you."

Her throaty laugh made him squeeze her tighter, and she felt his hardness growing beneath her. "I missed you, too." She kissed his hand. "I think it's been four hours."

He laughed with her. "But we've spent too much time on the inn and very little on us."

"I think we have Jackson to blame. I've never seen anyone with such dogged dedication to timetables."

"He is an evil taskmaster to be sure." He nibbled her ear. "But I think he was grateful to have the afternoon off."

His kisses moved down her neck, and he licked the skin

where it met her collarbone, forcing a bolt of heat down her spine, and she arched her back. She tried to turn around, wanting to taste him, but he held her in place, seemingly unfinished with his own exploring.

"Relax. There will be plenty of time for both of us." His hands moved along her body before reaching for their glasses of bubbly. He handed her one and they sipped as the warm water cocooned them.

He was right. They needed to slow down, if only for a day or two to catch their breaths. Her mom's party was important, but no one was going to say anything if the place wasn't perfect. It was close enough.

"Do we have plans for Saturday?" He nibbled her other ear.

"Hmm. I don't think so."

"I have someplace I want to take you."

"Where?"

"Think of it as a surprise."

"What have you cooked up?"

He chuckled. "Shall I ask you to trust me?"

AJ hesitated before responding to his teasing question. He'd asked the same thing that last fateful day on the ship. Her simple answer had somehow been perceived as permission to launch her back in time. As much as she had hated him for it at the time, she couldn't imagine her life any other way. She felt him tense at her silence and that wasn't acceptable. She sat up, took the glasses from their hands, and set them aside.

She twisted around to face him and cupped his face in her hands, her eyes never leaving his. Then she wrapped a hand around the back of his neck and pulled him down. "I'll always trust you." Her kiss was anything but gentle. Urgent passion raced through her as her tongue searched for his, and the water splashed as he repositioned her so she straddled his lap.

He traced his lips down her neck again, continuing to her

breasts. After he suckled each one, he lifted her onto him, and they took their time. They hadn't finished with each other by the time the water cooled, so he lifted her as she laughed, carrying her dripping wet to the bed. Neither cared as they spent the rest of the fading afternoon wrapped in each other's arms.

By the time the shadows lengthened along the bedroom's thick saxony carpet, Finn held AJ against him, both of them sipping champagne.

"How was Stella?"

AJ laughed. "You won't believe this. Adam showed up on her doorstep with a suitcase."

Finn let out a breath. "So everything caught up with him. Do you think it's permanent?"

"I don't think so. I told Stella he could use the apartment until Madelyn allows him back home."

He kissed the top of her head. "You are a wonderful sister."

"Yeah, well. No one else is using it."

The rest of her day rushed back, breaking the spell of the moment, and she stilled. The brief glimpse of the man, seen hours ago, seemed more vague than before. After all these months, why would Beckworth be the one person she imagined? It was the sleeves. The man had tugged at them just like Beckworth. A mannerism that had become a point of annoyance with AJ. It was nothing more than a crazy fluke.

She sat up, kissed him, and slid out of bed. "I'm starving. What were you going to make for dinner?"

An eyebrow curved up. "I prepared the bath."

She pouted. "I was looking forward to one of your pasta dishes."

"Really? And do I get something special for cooking as well?"

Her head tilted to one side as she thought about it. "I'll wash the dishes."

He lunged for her and caught her before she could take a step, her laugh reverberating through the room. "Is that all?"

She turned and tightened her hold on him, her face resting against his chest. "After dinner, we'll go out and look for Boötes."

"The constellation?"

She nodded. "You do remember what happened the last time we looked?"

"Aye." He gave her a long, heated kiss. "That memory will never fade."

They stumbled down the stairs together and parted company when they reached the foyer. Finn headed for the kitchen, and as soon she heard him rummaging for pots, she stepped into the library.

The library had been patterned after her father's study. Floor-to-ceiling bookcases filled most of the room. A window looked out to the front porch, but other than a bit of morning light, the room stayed in shadow the rest of the day. AJ found it fitting. The room had been painted a deep, rich burgundy, though most of it was hidden behind the dark cherry cabinetry. Her father's desk now resided in Finn's study, and his leather chair was positioned in front of the fireplace, right next to AJ's favorite stuffed chair from her apartment. They spent hours sitting side by side in the library either reading or making plans for the house.

She opened a closet half hidden next to a bookcase. It was a walk-in closet that had been expanded to accommodate a small armory. Finn refused to be without his firearms. They might live in the twenty-first century where lawlessness was more regulated, but Finn's life had taught him caution, and he didn't hesitate filling the room. Through AJ's connections, Finn had quickly acquired an impressive arsenal.

In addition to the filigreed, flintlock pistol he'd brought with him from their time jump, the one he'd used to rescue Maire and her from Beckworth, he'd added four additional handguns, two suitable for AJ. A shotgun and two scoped rifles filled a rack on one wall. A case on the other side of the room held two crossbows and two traditional bows. Swords and short blades filled the rest of the wall space. An oversized desk sprawled in the middle of the room where the handguns were stored, along with drawers full of ammunition. It also held the one item she'd come for.

When she returned to the entryway, she tucked the sheathed dagger into her purse.

When she smelled Finn's cooking, she followed the scent of sizzling garlic to the kitchen, where he had already set the table, candles and all. Maybe there was nothing to worry about, but one thing she'd learned from her time jump: don't waste precious time. She would resume the training Lando had started on that knoll in France, and then she'd ask Finn to teach her the crossbow. If he had plans for their Saturday, then she had plans for their Sunday.

Training day.

It might be all in her head, but nothing would come between her and Finn. Not if she had anything to say about it.

10

Beckworth dropped his keys in a bowl by the front door and stormed down the narrow hall of the cottage-style house. The oppressive smell of overcooked bacon, cats, and something called "lemon-fresh scent" smothered him, adding to his irritation. He'd only succeeded in part of his mission and it could take days to find her again. He was reaching for the door of his bedroom when he heard his name bellowed from the kitchen. Luck wasn't with him today.

"Teddy? Is that you?"

He bent his head until it touched the door to his room, a muscle ticking along his jaw. These women were going to drive him crazier than he already felt.

"We can make you a snack. Did you get lunch?"

He shook his head. Edith and Louise had been good to him, and as many times as he wanted to lock them away until he found a way home, they kept proving useful. He calmed himself, pulled his sleeves down, and turned for the kitchen.

He cringed when one of the blasted cats walked across the kitchen counter before sitting at the edge. It turned its green all-knowing eyes on him and stared without blinking. Murphy's eyes. Taunting him. He strode toward the cat, but it leaped away before he could reach it, as it did every time.

"There you are. Did you have a nice trip to the museum?" Edith set a plate on the table and turned for a pitcher of iced tea.

"I didn't quite make it to the museum." Beckworth sat in front of the plate and pulled a linen napkin across his lap.

"Well, that's a shame." Edith took the chair across from him, her plump frame forcing a creak out of the oak chair. She opened her book of crossword puzzles while studying him with a grim smile and sharp brown eyes, hawk like in her round face. Her short, steely-gray hair curled around her head like a halo, which seemed apropos after saving him from his first weeks in this dreaded century.

He stared down at his plate. The sandwich—called a BLT—made his stomach growl. He had grown attached to it, and Edith made it for him almost every day. A pile of potato chips and a pickle shared the plate. Once Edith had discovered his favorite meals, she rarely wavered.

Neither she nor her sister, Louise, who had found him in their driveway, could figure out why he was so different, but they seemed to excuse it for his being English. That, and the apparent amnesia that had made him forget where he was, how he'd gotten there, and pretty much everything else of the time period he was in.

As soon as he took his first bite and nodded his approval, Edith's lips twitched in satisfaction as she picked up her pencil to work her puzzle. At least the sisters didn't talk a great deal, though they did tend to hover. Sometimes it seemed as if they were warders ensuring their prisoner didn't get out of line.

Edith's head snapped up at the sound of clattering at the back door. The noise grew louder as it moved down the hall.

"Louise, what the hell are you doing?" Edith yelled as if Louise were in the next county.

"Nothing."

Beckworth stuffed another bite in his mouth and lowered his head. He wasn't going to get in the middle of this.

The shuffling of feet made him glance over to see Louise, her long, gray hair falling out of its purple ribbon, butterfly hairpins barely holding it from falling in her face. She toted a plastic tub and dragged a green plastic bag behind her.

"What the hell is all that?" Edith frowned as Louise dumped the tub on the table.

"Hi, Teddy. Did you have a nice time at the museum?" Louise's cheerful tone didn't diminish as she pushed the green bag against the wall and grabbed a cookie from the plate in the center of the table. There was always a plate of cookies in the middle of the table.

"He didn't go." Edith closed her puzzle book and stared at the tub.

Beckworth finished the first half of his sandwich, bit into the pickle, then peered into the tub filled with wires and hard plastic boxes. *Always something with these two.*

"Well, there's always next time." Louise pulled a small folder from the box and sat in her usual chair in between them. "Where's the iced tea?"

Edith sighed and got up. "On the counter. Two feet away." She retrieved two glasses and the pitcher. She refilled Beckworth's glass first before filling the other two glasses.

"Teddy, do you know anything about surveillance?" Louise shuffled through the papers in the folder.

He wished he hadn't told them his first name, but he had been delirious when they'd first found him shortly after the time jump. He had been injured, a knife wound in his shoulder from that Moore woman. The wound had been slightly infected, but the whirlwind that dragged him from his time to this one had drained him. He shuddered to think what might have happened if he hadn't landed here. At some point during his delirium, he had given them his name and probably more than he cared to remember. Every time they used his nickname, he felt like slitting his throat. Or theirs.

He used his napkin to tap the corners of his mouth and gave Louise his most charming smile. "I am somewhat familiar with surveillance, but as you know, your technology has me at a disadvantage."

The sisters looked at each other and giggled.

"Oh, Teddy, you sound like someone out of a Jane Austen novel." Louise patted his arm.

He'd lost count of how many times they told him that. When he'd discovered the Austen books in the sisters' overstuffed bookshelves, he'd read them all several times. They reminded him of home.

"What is all this crap?" Edith pushed stuff around in the tub.

"Stop that. You'll tangle the cables. Ernie assured me everything in here worked. He also agreed to help if we need it."

Edith rolled her eyes and nodded a knowing look at Beckworth.

Beckworth played his part and forced a smile. "As long as you make him a peach cobbler."

Both women giggled again before Louise went back to the papers in the folder. "Well, he might get that cobbler this time. This looks more complicated than I thought."

Beckworth wolfed down the last half of his sandwich and ate a potato chip. "What is all this supposed to do?"

Edith flipped through the pages in the folder, then perked up. "We can track someone with all of this?"

Beckworth stopped mid-chew, clutching his iced tea to wash down the food stuck in his throat. He barely breathed, waiting for the answer.

"That's the idea." Louise grabbed the folder from Edith and

pushed it toward Beckworth. "I know you can't seem to remember how a lot of things work. Well, hell, you don't seem to remember what most things are, but you always seem to figure it out after reading the instructions."

"If Teddy figured out the cable box, he should be able to get this to work." Edith pulled out a lump of wires. "Everything has a label. That should help."

Beckworth had been more surprised than the sisters by how well he had acclimated. A man two hundred years in the future, how could he possibly know anything? The fact they hadn't locked him in an asylum when he regained consciousness amazed him. Convalescing in bed, watching a large rectangular object called a TV, where people walked around and talked, had required several liberal shots of whiskey. That had been followed by two weeks of a drug-induced haze.

Louise and Edith broke out in high-pitched squeals, and Beckworth pinched the bridge of his nose. He hadn't been paying attention and wasn't overly sorry he'd missed whatever inane thing one of them had said.

"You're not getting one of your headaches again, are you, Teddy?" Edith's look of concern made him want to shake his head. These two women had picked him up like some bird with a broken wing, naïve and trusting, careless of who or what he might truly be.

"No, Edith." He patted her hand until she blushed. "Sometimes I try too hard to remember."

Louise sat down, her hand reaching for his arm. "We don't mean to push you. That isn't what this is. I just thought, you know, since you were trying to find that friend of yours, maybe this might help." She peered into the tub, her eyes glazing over, perhaps realizing how overwhelming it appeared. "I didn't want to make a peach cobbler anyway."

Edith gave Beckworth a conspiratorial wink and whispered, "Louise isn't particularly fond of peaches."

"Ah." Beckworth nodded and considered the tub. "Well, maybe you don't have to buy those peaches. Show me what you have." He might not know anything of this time period other than the most obvious of notions, but he'd always been smart, as irritated as it had made his father. With bits of information and some time, he figured out most things. The car had taken the most time, not with the driving but with all the blasted rules. What he'd give for a good horse or carriage, but neither of those could replace the speed of the car, which, as it turned out, intrigued him the most.

"What was Ernie doing with all this stuff?" Edith pulled out a plastic box the size of a deck of cards and tried to pry a piece of metal from it. "You must attach this to something. It has a pretty strong magnet."

"I think it's a GPS system. You remember that party last month at the rec center?"

Edith nodded as she pulled out more cables and another plastic box.

"Ernie and that old man who lives in the orange house. I can't remember his name."

"Burnt sunset."

"What?"

"The color. It's called burnt sunset, not orange."

"Well, it looks orange to me. Anyway, they couldn't stop talking about GPS this and GPS that. I was bored to tears."

"Nothing made you sit there and listen. I think you like spending time with Ernie."

Edith winked at Beckworth, and he nodded his usual response. "Go on, Louise," he coaxed before they got sidetracked any further.

"Well, Teddy, you had mentioned you thought you were here

to find someone. And, well," the sisters exchanged a glance, "you seem to be going about it a bit differently than most." Louise hesitated, blushed a bit, then said, "You seem to want to know where they are instead of just finding them to say hello."

Beckworth didn't say anything. What could he say? He knew his story wouldn't hold, it made no sense to him, and while these two women might seem crazy, they were more intelligent than most would think upon first meeting them.

"There you go, Louise, you're making him uncomfortable. Don't fret, Teddy. Take your time. You'll figure out who you are and why you're here. In the meantime, what harm could it do to just find out where this person may live?"

He studied Edith for any sense of duplicity, but her eyes shone bright with encouragement, and it froze him for an instant. A long-ago memory of someone else believing in him, someone with his same cornflower-blue eyes. They smiled as they handed him a meat and potato pie. The memory snapped like a rubber band, and he was back in the cheery yellow kitchen overrun by pictures of kittens and chicken figurines.

"I just hope it triggers a memory." Beckworth peered into the tub, pushing cables around to get a better look.

"I suppose it won't hurt to just follow someone." Louise reached for another cookie.

Beckworth stood, hands on the tub. "I hate to ask, Louise, but do you think we could use your quilting table?"

He caught Louise's wink at Edith. Their constant winking and giggling annoyed him, but as long as they kept doing it, he knew he was safe.

Louise jumped up and grabbed the tub from him. "Let's go lay it out. The windows should give you plenty of light. If I move that stool over, it might give you better reach over the table." She bustled down the hall, giddy with a new project.

Edith followed them, her voice quivering. "Our very own James Bond."

Beckworth smiled. That was a name he remembered well. He'd learned more about this century through TV than any amount of reading could have provided in the last three months. When they'd introduced him to James Bond movies, well, there was no other word for it. He had been fascinated.

Particularly when the bombs went off.

11

AJ spent the next day running errands. On the way home, she stopped by the hardware store to buy spray paint. On impulse, she drove back to the antique shop, slowing as she scanned the men loitering nearby. It wasn't as though she expected to catch a glimpse of the man she'd seen the day before, but the shop drew her like a magnet. She circled the block twice before finding a parking spot where she could watch the store without being noticed.

She watched tourists for an hour, and though a couple men were close in appearance, there was always something not quite right. They didn't have that certain saunter to their step or their hair was too long. The more she identified the wrongness of the men walking by, the more she remembered the nuances of the man she'd seen and how much his behavior had resembled Beckworth's mannerisms, but it had all happened so quickly.

AJ knew from her years as a reporter that people's recollection of events changed over time. Sometimes people remembered what they actually witnessed, bits and pieces finally forming and solidifying. But just as often, those memories became warped with fabrications and their minds created their own connections.

The question came down to the reliability of her own recall. Was she beginning to remember those fine details, or, as both Finn and Stella would probably suggest, was she still recovering? Frustrated, she slammed the steering wheel, wincing as she gave the antique shop one last stare before starting the car and heading home.

Jackson's rusted old truck and a sleek, dark-green luxury car were parked next to Finn's truck. Curious, AJ walked around the shiny, new vehicle, peering inside, but found no clue to its owner. Once inside the house, she stashed the can of spray paint in her climbing bag before heading for the kitchen.

Finn and Jackson stood next to each other in the dining room, staring up at the corner of the ceiling where two short pieces of crown molding had been nailed in place.

A third man in his early twenties leaned against the counter, a self-satisfied grin on his face and a glass of iced tea in his hands as he watched Finn and Jackson murmuring. He was African-American, his hair cut close, and dressed in jeans and a faded Bob Marley T-shirt that fit so tightly, his biceps bulged. AJ could almost count the washboard abs.

He turned his head when she approached, and his smile dazzled. Other than his eyes being a light amber rather than a chestnut brown, there was no doubt she was staring at the spitting image of Jackson when he had been this young.

Isaiah winked at her. "They're trying to decide if they like the crown molding."

AJ joined him at the counter as she glanced up. "I think it's perfect, but we'll have to wait for them to figure it out on their own."

"Yeah, but I could've had the rest of the molding finished by the time they agree on anything."

She laughed. "You should be used to your grandfather by now."

"He's only like this with a few people." When AJ raised an eyebrow he explained, "You know my grandfather is a man of few words. When he's on a job, he does what he's told, makes suggestions as needed, and gets the work done."

"He seems to do the same here."

Isaiah shook his head. "Not quite." He nodded toward Jackson and Finn. "They're like two peas. They discuss each decision in detail, laying out the pros and cons. Then, if they still can't decide, they go out on the deck. Sometimes they both just stare out to sea for a while, or they talk for an hour about anything other than the house. When they come back in, somehow, without ever having talked about it, they seemed to have made a silent agreement on their next steps."

She'd never paid attention to how the two men worked together. Now that Isaiah mentioned it, she remembered all the times she'd find them on the deck, either sitting in silence or chatting away. She assumed they were work breaks, but the two of them had truly bonded. A string of tension released, so minor she barely recognized it for what it was—relief that Finn had found a friend.

It didn't relieve her from her other worries—would he get bored? Did he miss his home, his century? But a solid friend was a good start.

She turned to study Isaiah. "That's a pretty nice ride you have out there."

He laughed. "You know the measure of the man is his car."

"I think you know better than that."

His smile turned shy. "Well, the women seem to like it."

"What does Jackson think?"

"He thinks if I'm in the construction business, an old truck would have been a wiser choice. But after spending last summer on the crab boats, I made enough money to splurge a little."

"I think it's a gorgeous chick magnet."

Their laughter interrupted Finn and Jackson's musings. Finn broke away to place a kiss on her cheek. "We hadn't planned on the molding, but Isaiah thought we should put up a test strip."

"And what did the two of you decide?" AJ tried for a serious face.

"I suppose the kid has an eye, and the craftsmanship is passable." Jackson scratched his chin as he stared at Isaiah. "I didn't know you'd been working on your finishing techniques."

Isaiah grinned, seeming to recognize high praise from his grandfather. "I've been playing around with it."

"Well, you've had enough of a break. The rest of it isn't going up by itself." Jackson nodded at AJ and turned to pick up a two-by-four. "We'll finish the last of the pantry and storage cabinets, then you can show us more of that fancy finishing work." His last words were mumbled as he took the board out to the miter saw on the deck.

Finn slapped Isaiah on the back. "Good job. Before you leave today, I'd like to show you some ideas I have for finishing the rest of the kitchen."

After Isaiah went back to work on the molding, Finn grabbed AJ's arm and led her down the hall to the library, where he closed the door.

"What's wrong?" Before AJ could say another word, Finn pulled her into his arms and kissed her. Not a quick peck, but a long, hard, passionate kiss. His tongue parted her lips, and as he began to explore, her earlier anxieties about Beckworth and what she should tell Finn melted away, right along with the rest of the world.

12

AJ woke early, slipping from bed while Finn slept, and dressed in jeans, sweatshirt, and sneakers. Mornings on the coast were chilly even in summer. Downstairs, she set the coffee to brew while she poked through the lumber piled against the wall in the dining area. After finding the target-sized, half-inch two-by-two board, she went in search of a marker. She drew three concentric circles on the board and placed it on the front porch.

Her next stop was the entryway, where she retrieved the dagger from her purse. She studied the sheath and the two small leather loops on the back. The sheath had been made for a strap. Grabbing her climbing bag, she searched the pockets. The nylon straps were in the third pocket. She didn't use them very often, but as her father always lamented, there's a use for everything. The straps were in varying lengths, and she wrapped each around her thigh until she found the perfect fit. She spent the next few minutes weaving the strap through the leather loops.

After strapping the sheath to her thigh, she stared at it and a slight thrill ran through her as an image of some daring female pirate came to mind. Then reality replaced the image when it morphed to a gloating Beckworth, then a grieving Thorn returning to the inn with Dodger, his surviving bodyguard, and finally Peele, dead with the others left behind at the monastery. As gruesome as it was, the memory restored her sense of purpose. She walked back and forth down the hall, testing the placement of the sheath. The nylon strap worked well enough over her jeans. If she had to wear it hidden under a dress, the strap might chafe. She'd have to give that some consideration, but for now, it fit her needs.

She glanced at the stairs. Finn would wake soon, and she wanted to be gone, just another morning off for a climb. She hurried to the kitchen and poured coffee in a large thermos. She stuck the thermos and a banana in her climbing bag before swinging it over her shoulders. After closing the front door silently behind her, she picked up the board and made her way down the path to the tidal pools.

The tiny cove was mostly rocks with pockets of sand. Small pools of seawater formed in the rocks when the tide was out, but the pools disappeared when the tide was in. She could never remember when the tide was in, but Finn paid attention. He missed the sea. He never said it in so many words, but she would catch him staring at the horizon, and while everybody gazed at the sea, most people were soothed by the view.

When Finn scanned the open waters, he was equally calm, but there were many times AJ noticed the clenching of his jaw or his tight grip on the back deck railing. She didn't know if he itched to be on the water, or if he was thinking of Maire, his men, or the *Daphne Marie*. Finn still owned the sixteen-foot sailboat he had bought when they first met. He'd bought the boat to take her sailing, and a warm glow filled her each time she remembered him confessing the purchase after their return. Even then, having only spoken with her twice, he had felt their connection. It had taken her longer to admit to the attraction.

Finn hadn't set foot on the boat since they'd returned. One

more thing that gnawed at her. He loved the sea, yet for as often as he stared at it, he refused to sail. Whenever she mentioned how perfect the weather was to take the boat out, he guided the conversation elsewhere. Another topic they didn't discuss.

She walked the narrow path around the tidal pools to a patch of sand on the far side. The walls of the cove were solid rock with boulders of varying sizes running along the base. She found one such boulder that sat close to the wall and placed the board on top of it. The surface of the boulder wasn't level and required several attempts before finding the best angle. The board tilted slightly to the right but that didn't matter. She shook the can of paint, then sprayed over the lighter marked circles she'd drawn earlier.

Standing back, AJ eyed the board. Satisfied it would suffice, she grabbed the thermos and poured herself a cup. She found a place to sit, peeled her banana, and ate breakfast while watching the birds attack the pools. Each time the waves receded, they scurried from pool to pool, hopping and poking, finding who knew what in their shallow depths. With the banana gone, she placed the peel by the thermos, refilled the cup and savored it, turning her attention to the dagger.

She visualized each lesson Lando had taught her about throwing the dagger—how to set her feet, which leg to put her weight on, the different positions for holding it. That day on the knoll in France had been the only time she'd tried knife throwing, and it had been surprisingly difficult. Learning to climb had been challenging, but she'd conquered that. If she focused on practicing what she'd learned from Lando, then she'd be ready to broach the subject of further training with Finn.

Of course, she'd have to tell him why she felt the need to improve her skills. After another day or two she might drop the whole idea. Her sighting might have been nothing. Was probably nothing. The more she thought about that one minute on the street, the more she questioned her memory. Was she recalling the finer details of the moment, or had her addled brain added in pieces from her last altercation with Beckworth? The entire episode might fade like her nightmares. Then she'd feel foolish.

As she finished her second cup of coffee, another image from the knoll came to mind. On the day she'd jumped back home, when they had reached the knoll, AJ had thought she'd seen something in the bushes. At the time, she'd assumed an animal or bird. The thermos cup slipped from her hand. After AJ had read the incantation, and the fog had appeared, there had been a shadow of something, an unrecognizable shape out of the corner of her eye. She had thought it must have been something in the fog, tendrils reaching out, but...

She shook her head, ignoring the odd sensation in her gut. She replaced the cup on the thermos and raised her arms to stretch her muscles. If there had been someone there, why hadn't Finn seen it? His attention might have been focused elsewhere, splintered between his desire to return with her and leaving his sister and everything he knew behind. Dwelling on what might or might not have been hiding behind the fog would drive her mad. She finished her stretching, the muscles in her arms nice and warm, and strode to the board. After giving the board a determined look, she turned and walked twenty paces.

She retrieved the dagger from its sheath, then replaced it. The action was repeated several times until it came out cleanly and she could replace it quickly. She'd improve with time. Next, she concentrated on the dagger's weight, testing it in both her right and left hands. It felt heavier and unwieldy in her left hand, which gave her one more thing to practice. She wouldn't be as proficient with her left, but it would still be an advantage. With the dagger back in her right hand, she wielded it as if she were in a fight. First to the right, then the left, she twirled and stabbed, underhanded and overhanded. She was slow and sloppy, but after several months of never touching the dagger, she was satisfied with her baseline abilities.

Her next test was the board. She placed her feet as Lando had taught her, focused, lined up the target, thought about her arm movements, and threw the dagger. It hit the board before falling to the sand. She stared at the board and smiled. It didn't stick, and while that was mildly disappointing, she would have been amazed if it had. The fact it hit the board was a small success she marked in the plus column.

Over and over she threw, walked to the board, dug the dagger out of the sand, and trudged back. In the half hour she'd been practicing, the knife had stuck three times. The first time had been left of center, almost off the board. The second time had been in the lower right hand quadrant, and the last had been high to the left. The knife placement didn't bother her yet. What interested her was why the dagger stuck and the wide variance of where it hit. The fact that it was happening she understood. She was a novice. But to get better, she had to know what she did differently with each throw, and that was where an instructor would help. Over time, she'd figure it out, but she'd prefer to get there faster.

She retrieved her blade and faced the board, deciding if her arm was up for one last throw. Her nerve ends tingled from overuse, and her arm could be used as a paperweight it was so tired.

"So this is where my board went."

AJ twirled, dagger pointed out as she faced Finn.

An eyebrow went up as he folded his arms. "Jackson spent the last thirty minutes looking for that board."

AJ glanced at the board, then at the dagger, which she slid into its sheath, and blew out a curse. "I thought it was scrap."

"It wasn't."

"Sorry."

He stepped to the thermos, poured a cup of coffee, and drank. He wiped his mouth and gave her a long look, his emerald eyes narrowed.

"Are you going to tell me why you've decided to practice with your dagger?"

She shrugged with one shoulder and walked to him, taking the cup from his hand to sip before handing it back. "It helps to think."

He drained the cup and replaced it on the thermos. "I see." He pulled her close, tucking her back to him so they could watch the tide wash in. "And it's nothing else?"

The question should have been expected. He'd eventually discover her training, but she hadn't prepared an answer. She blew out a breath and pressed her body to his, closing her eyes as his grip tightened. "Sometimes all I think about is how useless I was. How I spent so much time depressed and distracted when I could have been learning things that could have made me stronger."

He brushed her hair away from her neck and kissed her, and she shivered with pleasure as his lips trailed to her collarbone. "I don't think we'll find a skirmish anytime soon."

Her laugh was shaky. "Probably not, but it still makes me feel better." After a moment of silence, Finn's chin resting on her head, birds racing from the waves, she asked, "Is Jackson mad?"

Finn chuckled. "You'll owe him something. He spent all yesterday cutting those boards to size."

She wilted. "I guess I should have asked."

"Now you know better. It's not like we can't get more lumber." He turned her around and found her lips before she could respond. Then all she did was give in to the pleasure of his kiss, his arms holding her in their private cove. "I was going to wait until Saturday, but I think we should take the afternoon. Just the two of us. Isaiah is back full-time so he can help Jackson with any heavy lifting."

"What do you have in mind?"

"A surprise."

AJ smiled. "What kind of surprise?"

He shook his head. "You'll get nothing out of me. Except for one thing."

"And what is that?"

His lips captured hers again, and if Jackson weren't waiting for Finn, the heat between them could have turned to something more. AJ made a mental note to check the tides for the next warm afternoon. Then she'd plan a private picnic in her favorite place in the world.

AJ tucked the board behind a boulder where it would be safe from the incoming tide, and they walked hand in hand back to the house. Halfway up the path, she tugged at his hand.

"Can you show me how to use the crossbow?"

She didn't meet his gaze, but she caught him studying her.

It took him a few seconds to reply, and she felt his grip tighten. "You should know how to use all the weapons in the safe, but I think you should start with the traditional bow to truly understand its relationship with the arrow. If you're going to continue practicing with the dagger, I suggest you alternate with the bow to use different muscles. The rifles and pistols will be easier for target practice. If you're going to learn to shoot them, you'll also have to learn how to care for them."

AJ swallowed hard. He approved of her wanting to learn, but his mood had shifted. She reconsidered her plans. Maybe she should tell him about her visions and worries. It wasn't like he hadn't dealt with so much more, but wasn't that the point? She didn't want to burden him when this was their time to heal. And they needed time to learn more about each other. They'd known each other for six months, but most of it had been under suspicion and danger—then recovery. They'd had little time for the normal get-to-know-you pleasantries.

He understood her need for security, and she was thankful for that, but his casual acceptance bothered her. In fact, it made her feel horrible, but she stuffed it back, convincing herself there was nothing more to tell him. Nothing but her own imagination.

When they reached the porch, she stopped and kissed his cheek. "Thank you." She pulled away to race up the steps and through the hall, not stopping until she reached their bedroom. She turned on the shower, stripped off her clothes, and stepped into the scalding heat.

13

The road curved around green pastures, the ocean a thin ribbon in the distance when the road curved west. Then it disappeared, leaving nothing but thinning trees and fencing. Finn had said nothing when they'd left the inn, giving her a quick kiss and a wave to Jackson and Isaiah, who had been arguing over the final touches to the kitchen cabinetry.

AJ smiled and leaned back to listen to hard-bop jazz while Finn drove them north. Forty minutes after they'd left, he turned down a tree-lined drive. The sign at the drive read *Two Oaks Farm*. She glanced at Finn but, other than a curve to his lips, he kept his eyes on the driveway.

Then she saw the horses. Several of them grazed in a pasture, their tails swishing in the afternoon sun, two foals lying off to one side. She sat straighter as they drove around a modern, two-story farmhouse and parked next to an equally sizable barn.

Excitement and worry filled her. Were they going riding? Finn hadn't told her how to dress, though she typically wore jeans. He had mentioned once or twice about missing his horses, and she knew they should do something about it, but with the inn and her new budding career, it had fallen off her radar.

After shutting off his truck, he grasped her hand, kissed it, and smiled his rakish grin.

"Are we going riding? I don't think I'm wearing the right shoes."

He kissed her hand again, his green eyes twinkling with mischief. "Not necessary." He opened the door and left her sitting there.

She released her seat belt and followed. When she met him at the back of the truck, a lean, dark-haired woman walked out of the barn. Her long braid swung behind her, and her tank top showed off her buff arms. Everything about her shouted accomplished horsewoman, but nothing said it better than her mud-encrusted boots. As the woman drew closer, AJ noticed the streaks of gray in her hair. She was a good two inches taller than AJ.

The woman smiled warmly. "I'm glad you called. You're doing me a favor by coming today." She reached out to shake Finn's hand.

"It must be the luck of the Irish." Finn's brogue fell easily from his lips, and the woman smiled wider.

Then she turned her hazel-eyed gaze on AJ. "You must be AJ." The woman seemed to be sizing her up, and somehow AJ felt lacking.

AJ forced a smile. "Yes."

"I'm Mac. Let's take you around back." She turned and headed back to the barn.

Finn took AJ's hand, squeezed it, and trailed behind Mac as she walked them through the dark barn. Stalls lined both sides of the aisle, all of them empty except for the last one, where a gigantic horse kicked at the wall.

"Don't mind Ajax. We tried a breeding today, and he needs quiet time before he goes back out."

"I understand AI is used more frequently these days."

AJ stared at Finn as if she didn't know him. She knew AI meant artificial insemination, the more popular approach for many breeding farms, but how did Finn know that? Like missing a baby's first steps, she chastised herself for not noticing how quickly Finn was adapting to technology.

"We use AI quite often, but if I own the stud, I'd just as soon do it the way mother nature intended. There are risks, but I think the boys need to be boys." She winked at AJ. "If you know what I mean."

AJ laughed. "Absolutely,"

Mac walked them out the backside of the barn and turned them down a path that led to another smaller barn attached to a secondary fenced pasture. Two horses, with a fence separating them, grazed in leisurely companionship. AJ's gaze locked on the huge black horse. What a magnificent beast. He lifted his head as they approached and, chuffing once, trotted to the fence line. Finn released her hand as he strode to the fence and stroked its neck. The horse nodded his head up and down until Finn reached into his pocket for something that looked like a small cookie. He fed it to the horse, who munched on it before nuzzling Finn.

"Well, that didn't take long. I guess you do have a way with horses." Mac scratched the side of her face.

"You have no idea," AJ said. "He's had horses since he was a child."

Finn glanced at her and grinned. "Come over and meet yours."

She gaped at him, then stared at the other horse. Smaller and dappled in gray, she couldn't take her eyes off it. Her voice sounded strangled. "Mine?"

"Yes. I bought them both earlier this week. It's been too long since we've ridden."

She hesitated and then walked down the fence line to stare at her new horse. She gulped. She'd owned cats before but this was a whole new level she hadn't been prepared for. Finn knew her inexperience with horses, even if her riding skills had improved. Her eyes burned, and she blinked, stretching a tentative hand to the horse who had walked over and pushed her nose against the fence before looking AJ in the eye. AJ stared back, and as she searched the depths of those black eyes, she felt two things simultaneously—how deeply she loved Finn, and how guilty she felt for her inability to share her doubts.

She was so involved in her own thoughts that his warmth surrounded her before she heard his approach. Her voice cracked. "What made you buy me one?" She reached out her hand to stroke the horse's incredibly soft nose.

He wrapped his arms around her as they watched her horse. "We do everything together. That doesn't mean I won't come out and spend time with the horses while you're off on your business. But there will be times for long rides and picnics. There are several trails that leave from here." He kissed the side of her head. "Do you like her? Her name is Seraphina."

The mare had moved closer, lifting her head above the rail to give AJ more access to stroke her neck.

She giggled. "Seraphina. She's beautiful, and I love her." She turned to look back at Finn's new horse as it moved closer, either interested in the companionship or jealous for attention. "He's so big, but he's just as gorgeous. What's his name?"

"Hagan."

She tilted her head, considering both the horse and Finn. "He suits you.

Finn handed her two horse cookies. She laid one on the palm of her hand and reached out. The soft nuzzling tickled her hand as the mare took the proffered cookie. The horse moved closer to the fence, waiting to see what AJ would do.

AJ laughed. "All right, girl. You have my number already." She offered the last cookie, and the horse snapped it up. The mare seemed to know that was the last treat and trotted away, the black gelding turning to follow her down the shared fence line.

"Mac wants to show you where everything is. Then we should get back to check in with Jackson."

AJ turned and hugged him. She gazed up and pulled his head down to plant a soft kiss on his lips. "I know this was more for you, but I so appreciate you including me."

His expression took on a guarded look before relaxing, and AJ felt a small stab at his reticence. Soon, his grin replaced her misgivings. "We're in this together, AJ. Always."

14

Finn didn't stop talking and planning the whole drive home. AJ didn't know how he had kept quiet on the drive up, then reminded herself of all the secrets he'd kept in the past. She didn't need a horse, but his plans for rides through the local parks and picnics by streams sounded delightful. Time for the two of them would be perfect to temporarily forget about the inn, Adam living in her apartment, and her burgeoning career in antiquing. Most importantly, this might help Finn fit in while he discovered his niche.

She wanted to help him, but he needed to find his own way. All she could do was be there for him.

When they pulled into the lot, Jackson and Isaiah stood next to Jackson's lumber-filled truck. Jackson waved his hands, and Isaiah, just as stubborn as his grandfather, hovered over him by a good six inches and shook his head.

"Uh-oh." AJ wished Finn would park on the other side of the lot so she could escape the argument.

"Aye." He sighed. "I thought I could get away for a bit. They had plenty to do with the instructions I left."

AJ almost laughed but thought better of it. "I think they changed plans."

"It would seem so. I'll take care of it."

They exited the truck, but before Finn could intercede with the family squabble, AJ pulled him back and gave him another quick peck on the cheek. "Thank you for the afternoon. I love the horse."

He pulled her closer and kissed her lips, deeply and passionately, until AJ didn't care who was in the parking lot. He lifted his head, a sparkle in his eyes that promised more to come.

AJ stepped back and calmed the tingle coursing through her. Her voice came out husky, "I have a few things to do upstairs. Then I think I'll run into town to get us something special for dinner. I imagine we'll want to stay home tonight."

"Aye. And you might want to make sure we have something for a hearty breakfast. You'll need to restore your energy." He gave her another quick kiss, then turned toward the two men who were now both waving their arms.

AJ leaned against the truck and watched Finn walk away, her gaze moving from his wind-tousled brown waves to his broad shoulders, then lower to his lean body before resting on that fine ass. She sighed. How lucky a girl was she?

She skirted the skirmish and darted up the steps to the house, dropping her bag and running up the stairs to her office. A new client had asked her to track down an old stationary desk, and she knew of two places in town she could investigate. She placed a call to an out-of-town shop before texting Stella.

You there?

Yep.

Drinks?

Joe's. One hour?

Done.

She changed her clothes and waved to Finn on her way out

the door. Jackson and Isaiah were back to work, problem resolved. She shook her head as she opened her car door. Finn could negotiate a truce between heaven and hell.

The first antique store was a bust—not a surprise. That was why she'd gone there first. She hadn't been to the store since it had changed hands, and it was still overpriced. The second store delighted her. They didn't have what she was looking for, but she found items for two other clients and worked out an arrangement as a broker. Pleased with how well her day was going, she pulled into Joe's small parking lot, her mind still working through whether to call the clients now or wait until Monday.

She was halfway to Joe's front door when something made her turn. She caught movement to her left as a man strode off, head bent, shoulders hunched. He was lean with ash-blond hair. The hairs on her arms rose, and before he disappeared around a building, he tugged at his sleeves.

AJ hesitated a moment, not sure if she should follow, but she had to know, one way or another. She sprinted after the man. Stella would wait. She slowed as she came to the edge of the building where the man had turned mere seconds ago. It led to another busy street. She poked her head around the corner, then sagged against the building after searching the crowd of tourists. She had been too slow. He could lose himself easily in this throng. Damn.

Next time she wouldn't hesitate like some rookie. Catching her breath, she noticed her whole body shook. It wasn't fear— not really. She considered her emotions. Okay, she was a bit scared, but also pissed. She didn't know if it was truly Beckworth, she knew how crazy that was. But this wasn't a coincidence. She could be losing her mind. It was probably her PTSD materializing into some bizarre reality, but for now she'd go with the first option—this wasn't her imagination.

She pushed back her hair and shook herself. It was time to share this with Stella. She'd know what to do.

When AJ plopped into the booth, Stella's eyebrow rose. She said nothing while AJ settled and ordered a beer.

"Okay. You're not leaving until you tell me what's wrong." Stella pulled her glass of wine closer.

"That obvious?"

"If the heavy breathing isn't enough, you ordered a beer."

"I drink beer."

Stella nodded. "At barbecues and when still recovering from a hangover, but those are rare these days. Thank God."

AJ raised the mug of beer placed in front of her, and they toasted to the infrequent hangovers.

"I think someone's following me."

Stella sat back and appraised her. AJ recognized that look. She'd seen it way too often these last few weeks. Stella had been terrified the week AJ had been gone. She'd understood that the first day she'd been back, but she hadn't understood the depth until a week or so later when Stella had been hovering. It had tapered off until AJ had announced she would not be returning to the *Baywood Herald*, giving Stella another reason to question AJ's mental health.

Sometimes AJ felt like she stood on a sand bar, and every time a new wave washed out, a little bit of sand moved with it, forcing her to find a new balance. Stella watched like a new mom, waiting to see if her toddler would stumble, ready to pick her up when she banged her head. She might as well let Stella get her money's worth.

"Do you remember the guy I told you about called Beckworth?"

Stella shivered. "Yeah, not as scary as that big scarred-faced guy, or as dangerous as the duke, but still pretty bad. He had a title, didn't he?"

"Viscount, but I think it was more a title he bought than anything he'd earned."

"Wasn't everyone still looking for him when you left? Or came back? I'm not sure how to say it."

"Jumped."

Stella slurped her wine. "Okay, jumped."

Stella wasn't comfortable with the time jumping. Hell, who would be? It wasn't anything she planned on doing again. "I was the last one to see him, which was right after I stabbed him."

"I was trying not to remember that part."

AJ grinned. "This is going to sound weird, but after everything else, and after I calmed down from being scared to death, I felt empowered. I don't know. The ability to defend myself, the adrenaline was a rush."

"Says the rock climber."

"Fair enough." She pushed a finger through the water ring from her mug, pulling out long strands. "Just before we jumped home, when we first arrived on that knoll, I thought I saw something in the trees."

"I don't remember you mentioning that before."

AJ shook her head. "I didn't really remember it. Maybe a bit after we returned, but I was so worried about Finn and his injuries, it faded. Then I didn't want to think about Ethan and Maire, how hard it was to leave everyone behind." AJ stopped and hitched a breath. She continued to pull strands away from the ring until it resembled a multipointed star. Stella touched AJ's finger.

"So what made you think of it now?"

AJ blinked and the long, slim line of her lips curved into a frown. "When the fog came in to bring me home, I thought I saw a figure running toward us. It happened so quickly, and the mist was so dense, but I swear I saw something."

Stella squirmed in her seat, and her hands grabbed a napkin, already forming the origami shapes she was fond of making while thinking or nervous. AJ assumed both reasons were viable for today's shapes.

"There could be several explanations," Stella reasoned. "The obvious is what we talked about long ago. The fog can twist things, make you think something is there that isn't."

"And I believe after that talk, I discovered the *Daphne Marie* at the dock of the Westcliffe."

"Okay, bad example. It might also have been one of your friends. You had several you had to say goodbye to. Perhaps one of them followed to see you off."

AJ nodded. "I hadn't thought of that. It's a possibility, though I'm not sure why they'd hide."

"You're assuming the figure you saw and whatever was in the trees were the same thing."

AJ laughed nervously. She wasn't sure where it came from, and she could tell Stella didn't either. "Sorry." She swallowed a gulp of beer. "I think you may have spent too much time with Adam."

"Seriously. You have no idea, but what are you getting at?"

"Don't get me wrong. You've always been smart, but now you're thinking like an investigator."

Stella paused, then sat straighter. "I was, wasn't I." She clinked her wineglass against AJ's mug before drinking. "Here's to my newfound talents, thanks to your crazy-ass brother."

"Poor Adam."

They both paused as if remembering someone who had died, though if Madelyn didn't take him back soon, AJ figured he'd feel like he was dead.

"So, what sparked these memories? Wait. You said you thought you were being followed." Stella's brow creased. Her eyes widened, and she leaned over the table. "You can't possibly believe this Beckworth guy is following you?"

AJ grimaced. "Adam really has rubbed off on you." She hunched in her seat. "It's driving me crazy, but I thought I saw him in the parking lot again."

"Again?"

AJ nodded. "The first time was when we met for lunch after my trip to the antique shop."

Stella whispered, "When I kept calling, and you just stood there, staring as if you didn't know where you were?" When AJ nodded, Stella blew out a breath. "For heaven's sake, why didn't you say something? Wait. You did." Her gaze became unfocused. "You asked about a man."

"His hair was cut short, but that's easy enough to do. It was the same color, and he had the same build, though the clothes were so different. I keep trying to imagine what he'd look like in today's clothing. He always dressed like a dandy."

"So he had the same build. That could be thousands of people."

"I know, but it was more than that." She leaned toward the table. "It was the way he pulled at his sleeves."

Stella shot her a quizzical look.

"Beckworth had this affectation that annoyed me. He played with the edges of his sleeves, always tugging them down. When I walked out of the antique store, I couldn't remember which direction the restaurant was in. As I turned around, I caught sight of the man walking across the street. He wasn't just walking, he had a target in mind. Then he pulled at his sleeves, and it was like I dropped into a vacuum."

When she stopped, Stella held AJ's hands, and they were shaking. She squeezed before pulling them back to run them through her hair. "I know I sound crazy, but I thought I saw him again in the parking lot just now. I ran after him, but he disappeared down Park Street."

"Good luck finding him through all the tourists."

"I know."

"Do you think it was a coincidence he spotted you in front of the antique shop?"

"I don't know."

"Maybe he was headed for the shop, then changed his mind, and he just happened to look like this Beckworth guy."

AJ thought back to the antique shop. There wasn't anything strange about the visit. Wait. That wasn't entirely true. The clerk had wanted her to stay, finding excuses to keep her around. And how many times had the girl called to confirm an appointment?

"Well, shit."

Stella drained her wine glass. "This isn't going to be good."

"I think the clerk at the antique store might have set me up."

"What do you mean?"

AJ recapped her visit to the shop, and how the clerk kept watching the door as if waiting for someone, finally trying to keep AJ from leaving.

"It's possible the two things aren't connected, but it might be worth a visit." Stella finished her origami swan and placed it on the table. Their waitress had a daughter that was fascinated with the little shapes. "What does Finn think?"

AJ's head dropped as she rummaged in her purse for money.

"AJ, you're not keeping this from him, are you?"

She shrugged as she laid a twenty on the table. "I wanted to make sure of what I was seeing." Her voice wavered.

Stella huffed. "I'm only going to say two words. Remember Adam?"

AJ blanched, and her voice lowered. "I know."

"Let's go."

"Where?"

"I'll drive you over to the antique store. Let's find out one way or another. Then you'll go home and tell Finn."

AJ followed Stella out of Joe's, eager to have her friend at her side. How she would explain this to Finn could wait until she knew for sure. She was beginning to understand Adam's dilemma with his gambling debt. While her decision to wait seemed to bring her closer to understanding her brother, it moved her a step away from Finn and left her cold.

15

Beckworth leaned against the brick wall and watched the women emerge from the restaurant. Though he was half a block away, surrounded by the tourists the sisters always complained about, he imagined the sound of AJ's laughter. She had always been a tempting minx, though his baser dreams were always of Maire. What could he expect with the woman underfoot for almost two years? It had been a burden in the beginning. Then he had seen Maire's internal fire, one that burned almost as hot as his.

While Maire touched something in him long ago destroyed, AJ gave him purpose. He rubbed his shoulder where the small scar remained, something of her he would always carry. He grinned as they moved toward the red sports car. Edith was right —if you can't find the one you seek, you can always try her friends. And this Stella Caldwell had her picture posted all over town as an estate agent. Louise's forethought to bring home the GPS system had given him the break he needed.

His luck had improved when he'd dumped out the box of metal objects and wiring to discover there was more than one tracking device. There had been two. After determining how they worked, he had given one tracker to each sister and they had gone their separate ways. Using the prepaid cell phone they had bought him, he'd called and given them instructions on where to travel while he figured out the software. Most of it was beyond his knowledge, but the instructions were clear once Edith helped with the words he didn't understand. He grudgingly gave Finn a nod of respect for surviving all those long months traveling through time.

Finn had it easier, at least from what little Beckworth had gleaned from the man. His jumps had been in shorter time shifts, so his ability to transition to each new time period became easier. Two hundred years at one time might have forced others into an asylum, and with the infection from his knife wound, he'd felt crazy enough. Fortunately, the luck that had carried him through most of his life remained, this time in the form of two lonely sisters, and while they usually drove him mad, they had proved themselves useful a dozen times over.

Beckworth straightened as the women got in the sports car. He could wait for them to return. AJ would need her car, but they piqued his curiosity. He raced to the small moped the sisters had borrowed from their neighbor. The machine had seen better days, and it had taken time for Beckworth to gain his balance, but it worked better through the busy streets of Baywood. It wasn't fast enough to keep up with cars on the coastal highway, but in town with crowded streets and stoplights, it was perfect. He didn't have any trouble following the red sports car, which seemed to get caught at each light. If they left town, he'd turn around and wait at AJ's car, but after several blocks and a couple of turns, his stomach clenched. He knew this neighborhood well, and when the sports car pulled into a parking spot just a few doors down from the antique shop, his gut twisted tighter.

Swallowing a deep breath, Beckworth considered their

actions. If they went to the antique shop, it might have to do with that piece of furniture AJ wanted to inspect. Or, as he truly suspected, she had recognized him. She hadn't gotten more than a glimpse the couple of times she'd spotted him, but she was smart, and it may have been just enough to ignite her own curiosity.

When the two women emerged from the car, they walked directly to the antique shop. Now he had a dilemma. Did he wait until they left, then go in and confirm his suspicions? Or did he assume the worst and wait at AJ's car? Could he trust this GPS gadget not to fail? Louise and Edith had both assured him as long as the tracking device was on the vehicle, and as long as the battery lasted, the tracker was foolproof.

It wouldn't hurt to wait and see how long they stayed inside. He had nothing but time on his side.

AJ hesitated before opening the door.

"Have you decided what you're going to ask her?" Stella hovered behind her, scanning the street.

"No, but I'll find a way to bring it up. She may not even be working today."

"I hadn't thought of that. That would be anticlimactic."

AJ snorted. "And as horrible as that may be, we can at least find out what days she does work."

"You know I prefer my instant gratification."

AJ took the time to turn and smile at Stella. "Thanks for not thinking I'm nuts."

"Oh, honey, I never said you're not nuts. I'm just more open to the fact that the universe is whack."

AJ laughed and stepped inside, the bubble-gum scent smacking her in the face. She turned down the first aisle, then slowed her pace when she heard multiple voices and spotted the blonde clerk. She spoke with three ladies as she rung up their sale. AJ turned back to find Stella staring at a wall hanging.

"It's the same clerk. She's finishing a sale."

Stella tore her gaze away from the picture, but glanced back again. "This is the creepiest place I think I've ever been in." She moved toward AJ but stopped to pick up a vintage Woody Woodpecker lunch box.

AJ took a double take. "We're not here to shop."

"I know, but this could work on my patio to hold my clippers." She stepped away but gave it a last look, almost walking into another display.

"I'll find you a better one later. Let's see if there's anyone else in the store. I'll take the back."

"Ah, stealth mode. I'll take the candy aisle." Stella walked a few paces, her head swiveling before she stopped to pick something up. To AJ, Stella's subtle nuances screamed boredom, but to anyone else she appeared to be an interested shopper. Stella's experience came from years of following her real estate clients through hundreds of homes, pretending to be interested in the same house she'd shown dozens of times. And she was an expert at it.

It didn't take long to confirm the place was empty of other customers. When she heard the other women move toward the door to leave, AJ circled around to where Stella had stationed herself, staring at a curio cabinet of angel figurines. AJ almost laughed out loud. Stella appeared so fascinated, any clerk worth their mettle would be hovering.

AJ was surprised to find this clerk had an instinct for it. She scurried over to Stella.

"Is there a particular one you'd like to look at? These are really quite incredible." The blonde's hands were tucked into the pockets of a light sweater, and AJ would bet a month of her nonexistent salary she had a key to the cabinet in her hand. The woman was good at her job, but she was young. Could Beckworth charm her?

Stella smiled at the clerk and then turned to AJ. "Am I interested in angels?"

"Not hardly." AJ waited for the young woman to turn her attention to her, and when she did, she caught the clerk's surprise.

Something flickered in the girl's expression before her attention wandered briefly toward the door. After a second, she found her smile. "Ms. Moore. I'm glad you came back."

There were several ways AJ could handle the situation. The clerk had given her plenty of reasons to return and ask about the store's collection. She could make up a story about searching for a particular item, or see if her client had decided to buy the armoire. AJ still had her reporter skills, rusty as they might be, but there was something about the way the clerk studied her that set her teeth on edge.

"I was hoping you could tell me who the man is that was asking about me?"

Stella coughed as the clerk's brown muddled eyes widened. "Well, that was subtle."

The girl's gaze darted around the room, either looking for an escape or trying to come up with a story. After a few seconds, her shoulders sagged. "I don't know his name." Then she perked up. "He said he knew you but had lost your card. He just wanted to reconnect. We're very careful. We would never give out your information." She straightened a bit, her arms now wrapped around her middle, her chin raised a notch. "It didn't seem inappropriate to tell him when you might be here."

AJ couldn't fault her logic. The antique business relied on networking, connecting buyers and sellers, and getting to know the players. The clerk was right. People asked about other antique collectors and brokers all the time. She hadn't done anything wrong, but AJ needed a name, something to confirm who was following her.

"I'm sorry. I didn't mean it to come out like it did. Of course you didn't do anything wrong."

The clerk appeared relieved, and Stella, who rolled her eyes, leaned back against a large bookcase, arms folded as she watched AJ work.

"He's only been in a couple of times. I haven't seen him since you were last here."

Of course not, AJ thought. He had seen AJ when she'd come out of the shop. If she hadn't given out AJ's personal information, how had Beckworth found her at the restaurant? That was too large of a coincidence. "Can you tell me anything about him?"

The clerk perked up. "Oh, yes. He was gorgeous, blond hair, darker than mine, styled in a longer brush cut. He was taller than me, but not real tall. He has an athletic build, like a runner's. He had that day's worth of beard that looks horrid on some men, but on others..." Her eyes softened, and when AJ glanced at Stella, her friend had the same glazed look. Okay, she had to admit, she understood where these two women had momentarily wandered. If she didn't have her own man who could wear a day's growth of beard and stop women in their tracks, she'd be drooling too. So she patiently waited for the young girl to finish her fantasy.

"Sorry, well, you know the type," the clerk finished.

Everyone nodded and sighed.

"And he was so sweet."

AJ's brows furrowed. She hadn't expected that, and suddenly she wasn't sure. She remembered Beckworth snarling at her and Maire at the breakfast table at Waverly Manor, his explosive nature on the ship when they reached France, and the murderous look in his eyes when she'd stabbed him before he could drag her back to the ship. Could she have been wrong and this was nothing more than her imagination? She was glad she hadn't said anything to Finn.

"But I think it was the English accent that really did me in."

16

AJ stumbled out of the shop. She glanced around, her brain somersaulting as the clerk's words repeated over and over in her head. English accent. Blond hair. She reached out to steady herself on a lamppost and turned to lean against it. The warmth of the sun calmed the tremors, and she drew in a deep breath, picking up the subtle smells of ocean, exhaust from the passing cars, and candle wax from the store next door. At least it wasn't bubble gum.

The man could be anyone. Blond hair and an accent weren't anything to go on. What disturbed her the most was the clerk's infatuation with this mystery man. Memories flooded over her like an old film reel—Beckworth's handsome, smiling face at their first meeting at Waverly Manor, his grace as a host when he entertained Dame Ellingsworth and the obnoxious Lady Osborne, and his wit when speaking about books and travel. There was no doubt the man was duplicitous.

"Honey, are you okay? Do you need a paper bag?" Stella laid an arm on AJ's shoulder.

She gave her friend an exasperated shake of the head.

"I'd say you look like you've seen a ghost but it seems pointless. It's him, isn't it?"

AJ lifted a shoulder. "It could be anyone by that description, but yes, I think it's him." She closed her eyes and shook her head. "I don't know how, but every fiber in me says it's him."

When AJ opened her eyes, concerned by Stella's silence, she almost laughed. "Stop looking at me like that. It's not the end of the world."

Stella seemed a shade paler, but she wore that stubborn mother-hen expression. If AJ weren't shaky herself, she'd be awed by the fact she'd finally brought Stella to the point of speechlessness.

"This was supposed to be over." Stella wiped beads of sweat from her forehead and squeaked out a snort. "To be honest, if I hadn't heard the words from the clerk's mouth, I would have thought you were still suffering a little PTSD."

AJ forced a smile. "That's what I thought when I first spotted him here, but the feeling of being watched wouldn't go away. It wasn't his face because I never got a clear look. It was his mannerisms, the way he walked." AJ shivered and wrapped her arms around herself.

Stella scanned the vicinity. "He could be watching us right now."

AJ lifted her head and followed Stella's gaze. She had a good point. AJ scanned the street, turning as she did so, waiting to see if anyone would run, but after completing her circle twice, she stopped. "If he was here, he's gone now."

"Let's go. I feel exposed around all these tourists."

Once back in the car, Stella gripped the wheel, her reactions to the traffic reminding AJ of a first-time driver. She gave herself a mental slap. Since returning, her worries had focused on Finn and herself. She snickered. She'd even worried about Adam, but not once had she thought about what Stella had gone through. Not really.

The first days back from the jump, Stella had hovered over AJ as if she might disappear in front of her. Then she'd truly shocked AJ by admitting she'd teamed up with Adam to find her, even after listening to Adam's unbelievable tale of a vanishing ship. The thought of working with him had set Stella's teeth on edge, but she had been convinced that AJ wouldn't have left without telling anyone.

Then Adam had shared their week's adventure about tracking the stone necklace back to the house where AJ had bought it. Two sisters, Sarah and Martha, had inherited the Heart Stone and journals from their grandmother, Lily Travers. Lily had been a keeper of the stones, a lineage of women who'd protected the stone through the centuries. AJ hadn't been sure what that all meant and had stored it away for future study.

Adam and Stella's trip to the university, which Martha had suggested, had led them to Professor Emory at Antiques & Lore in Eugene. AJ marveled at how much Adam and Stella had discovered about the stones—how the Druids had used glass beads, a silver tray and an unexpected bolt of lightning to create magical stones that could travel through time. They just hadn't been able to piece together how the stones worked, but no one could have without *The Book of Stones*.

Finn had been eager to learn more. He'd wanted to visit the sisters and go to Eugene, but AJ wasn't ready. It wasn't that she didn't want to know. She'd itched to investigate it, but her first thought had been Finn. Though she hadn't recognized it as grief at the time, she'd known their research of the past was a way to stay connected to Maire. They needed to wait and come to terms with their loss: otherwise, their investigations would focus more on Maire than the stone.

Once the first phase of remodeling the inn was completed,

they would have time to revisit the past. When they spoke with the sisters and the professor, it would be from a better place, and if they learned more of Maire's fate along the way, it wouldn't sting as much—or so she'd told herself. If Beckworth had really found a way into the future, that discovery would change everything.

Stella's silence pressed on AJ. Her friend should be chatting nonstop, tossing out all the reasons why it couldn't have been Beckworth. Even in her most stressed times, Stella had something to say. Guilt filled AJ. She should have spent more time with her friend. They'd all been traumatized by the unnatural events.

"Are you okay?" AJ asked.

Stella spared her a glance before turning back to the road. "I don't know what I was thinking driving through this part of town. I should have taken the long way around. It would have been faster."

"We're not on a schedule."

"I just feel like slamming on the pedal and driving until I run out of gas."

"I'm sorry you got involved."

Stella spun her head toward AJ and then swore when she had to hit her brakes for a jaywalking tourist. "Damn. I think it should be perfectly legal to hit these people."

AJ laughed. That sounded more like the old Stella. "Seriously. I've been so worried about Finn and my own shit, I haven't made sure you're okay."

Stella relaxed her grip on the wheel and blew out a sigh. "Well, honey, I have to agree the whole thing has turned my world upside down. But you were a victim in this, and I suppose Finn as well." She waited until they stopped at a light before turning a more thoughtful look at AJ. "Hell, we were all victims, and now we're trying to find the right pace in this new world.

Though I will state for the record we've been missing too many happy hours."

AJ laughed. "I think I can remedy that."

"That's the best medicine. Getting back to normal routines." Stella inched the car past the green light and intersection, the traffic still holding them to a crawl. "But I think that bubble just burst."

"If it's really him, I can't figure out how he could be following me. Why would he be going to antique stores?"

"Did he know you liked antiques?"

AJ considered the question. "Yeah, maybe. He knew I loved the books."

"So he's traveled here from two hundred years ago. It would have taken time to acclimate, right?"

"The original incantations Finn and Ethan were given on their first jump weren't translated properly. Their continued jumps were unpredictable, creating scattered lapses in time and location. Each time the Heart Stone moved out of reach, they seemed to be dragged with it. I'm not really clear how it worked. Finn and Ethan never spoke of the time they followed the stone. All I know is that eighteen months in their own century had passed before Finn took me back with him."

She ran a hand through her hair, then pulled at her bottom lip, considering how Beckworth might have jumped. "Maire corrected the incantations which made our jump home more accurate. Beckworth must have gotten his hands on the more current translation. But even if the timing was more precise, he would still be facing a two-hundred-year shift into a foreign country, assuming he didn't go mad like that first Druid."

"He seems to be adapting, so let's assume he only went slightly mad. How do you catch up on history and figure out how to find someone?"

"He would have to solicit help from someone."

"Maybe. I'm not quite sure how that discussion would have gone, and I doubt he searched the internet."

AJ tapped her fingers on her knee. "I'm so stupid."

"What?"

"Newspapers."

"I'm not following."

"A man from two hundred years ago would know about newspapers. It only makes sense that he would read them, and maybe learn how to locate older ones. What if he found me through the newspaper?"

"Isn't that a long shot?"

"Beckworth might be disoriented, but he is smart and devious."

"He would still need to find you."

"I've had an article in almost every edition of the *Herald* for the last four years. As soon as he sees my byline, he'll know I worked at the paper. He could have tracked me from there."

"They wouldn't have told him anything, would they?"

AJ shook her head. "Not intentionally." Her gaze turned to watch the tourists and passing stores. "He's calculating and patient. He crafted a good enough story to convince the store clerk. All it would take is someone mentioning I'm brokering antiques. The staff at the paper would think they were doing me a favor by steering clients to me."

They remained silent until they arrived at AJ's car. Before getting out, she turned and grabbed Stella's hands. They were as cold as hers.

"What am I going to do?" AJ kept her voice calm, and Stella pulled her in for a hug.

"You're going to tell Finn."

Beckworth slowed the moped before pulling to the side of the road. He surveyed the area, then scratched his head as he studied the screen. It didn't make sense. If the GPS was working, then AJ should be close, but he didn't see her car or any house. There weren't any other streets she could have turned down. He pocketed the tracking device and continued for a quarter of a mile before stopping to check the screen again.

The unit clearly showed she was behind him now. Turning around, he drove back to his original stop, parking next to a mailbox. He stared at it. Of course, mail was delivered by a deliveryman into these boxes.

He strode to the mailbox, looked over his shoulder, and peeked inside.

Empty.

He walked a few paces until he found the edge of an aged, gravel driveway obscured by the tall grasses that grew along its edges. When he checked the GPS, the red dot blinked motionless where he stood. The driveway was tree lined, and he crept a few feet, peering through the trees until he caught a glimpse of what might be a roof. He shifted to the other side of the drive, inching past a couple of trees. *Yes, a roofline.* After a quick glance back to the road, he spied the moped. He'd only be a few minutes, but it was probably worth the time to hide it.

It was doubtful anyone would think anything of it, but if AJ had become suspicious, the unattended vehicle might draw unwanted attention. He drove the moped a quarter mile away and pushed it behind a tree. Instead of walking back on the road, he snaked his way through the woods until he came to the driveway. He bent his head, listening for vehicles, voices, anything that might shed light on what he was walking into. Nothing but birds and the sound of the ocean greeted him.

The trees thinned along the driveway but still provided enough cover. He crossed the driveway and eased his way toward the coast, keeping the driveway on his left. His footing faltered when a shrill whine broke the stillness, and he dropped to a knee. Within seconds, it was gone.

There was something familiar about the sound, but he couldn't place it. He continued his slow approach until the trees came to an end. A wide expanse of grass and a paved parking lot lay beyond. He squatted against a tree and smiled. AJ's car shimmered in the midday light. The sisters had been right: the GPS had been a brilliant idea.

Along with AJ's car, three other cars parked in front of a three-story house that looked out over the ocean. Two of the vehicles were trucks, one with lumber sticking out of the back. Once again, the whiny sound disturbed the silence, lasting only a few seconds. Then Beckworth remembered. One of the sisters' next-door neighbors worked with wood and used an electric saw. It made the same sound. Someone was building something.

Is this your home, my lovely, or are you just visiting?

He surveyed the area with a critical eye. The trees had been cleared around the property. He couldn't go any farther without being spotted, at least not in daylight. After twenty minutes, he stood. If he was going to stay out here, he needed to be properly supplied. Louise had given him binoculars to watch whales along the coast. He hadn't grasped why one would want to do that but had found the glasses of interest. They would come in handy now. He had a clear view of windows and might get a look inside.

A sketchy plan began to form, and he refined it as he hiked back to the moped. He stopped at the mailbox, removed a scrap of paper and pen from his pocket, and wrote down the numbers. Back on the moped, he stopped again where the street connected with the coast highway. He wrote down the name of the street before turning onto the coast highway, whistling a show tune from one of Edith's favorite movies.

This had been a good day after all. The sisters had shown him how to find an address on the computer map, which displayed streets, trees and other terrain. With the address in his pocket, and the sisters' computer, the property could be studied until he learned every inch of it. He only needed to confirm AJ lived there. His laugh burst free, fading into the wind as he wove through the back roads to town. Where AJ lived, Finn lived. Of that he had no doubt. And now, with the sisters' help, his prey was within reach.

17

On the way home from lunch with Stella, AJ ran through various scenarios of how to tell Finn about Beckworth—if it was him. She could ask Finn for help with dagger practice and casually mention someone might be following her. She shook her head. It might be better to wait until this evening while they relaxed on the deck, where the sea would calm his anger. The longer she went without saying something, the more his irritation would increase.

When she pulled up to the house, the sight of Jackson's truck brought a sigh of relief that eased the tension along her spine, confirming what a chickenshit she was. With the weight of what she'd kept from Finn, it would be best to wait until they were alone.

She lingered in the car for several minutes, pushing back her irrational fears. Regardless of the slim evidence that Beckworth might be out there, she should tell Finn everything, but then they'd have to face their past. They'd been so good at avoiding it.

She leaned her head against the steering wheel. She didn't need a medical degree to know avoiding the past was unhealthy. Why did it scare her? She'd been so sure it was PTSD, and there was some truth to that. Then she'd finally realized she'd been grieving as well. When she accepted that, her mixed-up emotions seemed less crazy. It explained why they only spoke of the future and never the past.

Her head snapped up and a trickle of wetness rolled down her cheek. She knew the truth of the matter—the heart of it all. A harsh and painful laugh burst out. She worried that, deep down, Finn wanted to go back, that she wouldn't be enough to hold him here, that all their talk of the future was a lame attempt to bring him peace. She rubbed her face, pushing the tears and fear away, marshaling the courage to march into the house and lay it all on the table.

She'd barely stepped into the house when shouting broke out. Her shoulders slumped. She was suddenly irritated she'd have to wait and screw up her courage all over again. She tiptoed to the kitchen and peered around the doorframe. Jackson was waving his arms, never a good sign, and Isaiah was nose to nose with him, arms relaxed by his side, his face reflecting his exasperation. Finn stood a few feet away, hands on hips as he watched the two, occasionally shaking his head and saying something that was too low to be heard over Jackson and Isaiah's heated exchange.

AJ backed up before anyone noticed her and sprang up the stairs. Any other time, she would have laughed at the situation. Life had become livelier since Isaiah had shown up. He and his grandfather were both sticklers for the details. Unfortunately, they had very different ideas on what details were important. It usually fell to Finn to break the tie without hurting either of the men's feelings. And that was Finn's specialty, his expertise in negotiation tactics.

Given another short reprieve, AJ stared out their bedroom window. While she didn't doubt Finn would resolve the issue between grandfather and grandson, the question was how long that would take. Unwilling to wait, she changed into shorts and a tank top, grabbed her dagger, and escaped out of the house. She strapped on the dragger as soon as she hit the path to the tidal pools.

She practiced for an hour, her focus spent on training her left arm. By the time her muscles refused to cooperate, she still hadn't hit the board throwing left handed, but there was noticeable improvement. Close enough for now. Practicing with the dagger had empowered her, and hiking back up to the inn, her resolve hardened. The sun wouldn't set with Beckworth hanging over her head. She had given him too much control and that was no longer acceptable.

The house was eerily silent, and she cocked her head. The soft tapping of a hammer on a nail pierced the quiet, followed by sanding, and then the quick buzz of a saw. At least they hadn't killed each other. When she walked into the kitchen, the three men were working in different areas. Jackson stepped through the french doors with a piece of newly cut trim for the bench seat. Isaiah stood on a ladder, nailing a strip of molding to the ceiling in the dining area, and Finn stood with his back to her, sanding the new storage cabinet doors in the dining area.

The three of them were so quiet, each one focused on the task at hand, it seemed a bad time to interrupt, especially after the squabble. She backed away once again, this time fleeing to her office. She made three calls, setting up two client appointments and introducing herself to an antique store up the coast she'd not visited before.

When a truck door slammed and an engine started up, she pushed away from her desk. She gazed at the fading light over the horizon as she stretched, forming her opening statement to Finn. Now that they were alone, there would be no more distractions. She ran down the stairs before her courage disappeared.

She found Finn on the back deck, remains of a beer still held in his hand.

"I see you worked through another disagreement." She kissed him before sitting next to him on the bench.

He put his arm around her shoulder and pulled her close. "They're worse than two bickering hens." He chuckled. "But I'm beginning to think Jackson starts the arguments on purpose."

"Why would he do that?"

"Isaiah is a craftsman with an intuitive talent. He has an eye for detail and the skill to match it. But he's quiet, doesn't want to make a ruckus, so he tends to keep his ideas to himself. I think the arguments are Jackson's way of teaching Isaiah to stand up for what he knows is a better option."

AJ laughed. "Seems like there should be a more rational approach."

Finn leaned in and kissed the top of her head. "That would mean Jackson would have to tell Isaiah how skilled he is."

"Ah. Well, all I know is that you have your own talents for dealing with their disagreements."

"Those two are nothing. Try managing thirty men on a long voyage with bad weather and even worse luck. This was child's play."

Finn's nostalgic words were the first he'd spoken of his old life since their return home. Now her own words were burning to burst out. She wrapped her arms around him, hugging him fiercely.

"Hey, now, what's all this about? Not that I'm complaining." He plucked at her arms, trying to push her back, but she held on tighter, not ready to look him in the eyes.

"I need to tell you something."

"Hey, boss. I have a question on this last piece of molding." Isaiah stopped in the doorway. "Oh, sorry, AJ. I didn't know you were back."

AJ blushed and sat back, distancing herself from Finn. She hadn't bothered to listen for the sounds of the second car leaving. "You were all working so quietly, I didn't want to disturb you."

"We shouldn't be much longer." Finn's questioning gaze searched her face.

She nodded and sucked in a deep breath—and her phone rang. The ring tone said it was her mom calling, and thankful for another reprieve, she answered. "Hey, Mom, what's up?"

Her mother's hysterical words were so loud, AJ had no doubt Finn heard them. "Did you know Madelyn kicked Adam out of the house?"

18

Beckworth stared at the upheaval of Louise's closet. He wasn't quite sure where to start.

Edith's closet had been neat and orderly, everything in its place. Her clothes had either hung in organized rows by color or been folded and stored in plastic bags. Shoes had lined the wall, also by color, regardless of the type of shoe. In the back of the closet, a small dresser had held sweaters, gloves, and assorted wraps. Labeled boxes of hats and belts had sat atop the dresser. Across the top of the closet, additional boxes had been stored on shelves that ran along three sides. These had been filled with letters, photographs, and remnants of items that belonged to a man.

Beckworth had assumed the items were from Edith's dead husband, but when he'd perused the letters, he'd discovered they'd been written by two different men. He'd raised an eyebrow at that discovery. Edith either had had a lost love before she married, or she'd had a dalliance while married. He didn't pay attention to the dates of the letters: he didn't care about her past. What he searched for wasn't in Edith's closet.

Now staring into Louise's closet, he was completely

dismayed. It was a surprise the closet door could shut at all. Louise must have three times as many clothes and they hung in haphazard clumps. Coats were interspersed with summer dresses, winter clothes mingled with summer blouses, and all dotted with pieces of men's clothing. Shoes, although piled in mounds, were surprisingly separated by function. Winter boots in the back, dressy flats in a corner, and laid out front and center, an array of brightly colored tennis shoes—dreadful lime green, an eye-bleeding hot pink, and bright cherry red.

Boxes of various colors and shapes were crammed between the stacks of shoes on the floor and filled the upper shelves to the ceiling. There had to be dozens of boxes, twice as many as in Edith's closet. His search would take all day, and he didn't know how much time he had before the sisters returned.

Edith and Louise didn't leave the house together very often. At first, Beckworth had assumed it was because they wanted to keep an eye on him, but after the first month, he'd realized that wasn't it at all. While the sister's may live together, they led completely separate lives.

Louise went to church on Sundays and her knitting circle on Wednesdays, and she volunteered at the homeless shelter Monday and Thursday mornings. Edith bird-watched on Saturdays, went to bingo on Tuesday nights, played bridge every other Thursday, and took classes at the community center when something struck her fancy. Beckworth had been shocked when Edith had come home with grease marks on her plaid shirt one Monday afternoon after spending two hours learning to change oil in the car.

If nothing else, the sisters were self-reliant, and he had to admire that. It was the same fortitude that had sustained him, keeping him alive since the early years when he shouldn't have survived. Yet he had. And he would endure this time period as well until he found his way home.

He had woken that morning in a sour mood. Even the possible discovery of that Moore woman's home couldn't improve his spirits. Until breakfast.

"Teddy, Edith and I were thinking of going down to Newport to see the new exhibit at the aquarium. Would you be interested in going with us?" Louise read the paper as she asked, and Beckworth knew from experience she didn't care if he joined them or not. If she had, she would have pushed the paper aside and played with the edge of the place mat.

He sighed in relief. This day trip presented the perfect opportunity. He couldn't remember how far Newport was, but if it was an exhibit, it should require a good portion of the sister's day. He delayed his response, pretending to consider the offer, then rubbed his head. "It sounds marvelous, but I'm afraid I woke in a bit of a foul mood this morning."

"I thought so," Edith said as she reached for another biscuit.

Beckworth glanced at her, unsettled by her statement.

"Yes, I thought the same thing." Louise squeezed his arm.

God's blood. How had they come to know him so well?

Edith nodded. "It's in your eyes. You squint when you're out of sorts, but it's not the same squint when you get your headaches. Then your brows scrunch up, and you tend to stumble a bit."

"Like when Edith has one too many after a night of bridge."

Edith glared at her sister before rising to remove a plate from the oven. "That's why Louise made extra bacon. We put some away for your BLT this afternoon, but there's some extra for this morning too. Maybe that, some orange juice, and a cinnamon roll will get you squared away."

Louise held on to his arm, and though he didn't like to be touched, he didn't move. Somehow, events were turning his way again, and he wasn't about to squander this opportunity.

"Edith and I have both been dying to see this exhibit, and as much as we hate the crowds, today is the first day we've been able to match our calendars."

"We didn't think you'd be interested," Edith said. "And maybe with us out of the house, you can have some peace and quiet, take a walk on the beach, or take the scooter downtown."

Or scour the house for whatever you did with my blunderbuss pistol.

Beckworth forced his most charming smile and patted Louise's hand while nodding at Edith. "I'm truly a lucky man to have fallen in your driveway." He paused for effect, rubbing his forehead. "This has been more trying that you can imagine."

Both women hovered over him, giving him gentle hugs.

"Don't worry. It will all come back to you. You just need the right trigger."

He almost laughed out loud as they smothered him with more hugs, their heavy perfume pricking his eyes.

Before they left, they made sure he had the keys to the moped their neighbor had all but forgotten.

"We'll stop and bring back that clam chowder you like so much," Louise mentioned before leaving.

"If you feel up to it, practice with that GPS again. Don't give up too quickly." Edith pushed Louise out the door, and they were gone.

Beckworth hadn't told the sisters how well the GPS had worked. They didn't know he'd found his target and attached the tracker to her car or that it had led him to what was presumably her house. And before he did anything about that, he needed his blasted pistol.

Louise's closet loomed in front of him. He heaved a sigh, pushed off the bed, and dove into the chaos. He began with a methodical approach, starting on the left and working clockwise. In the end, he worked from the top down, searching every box on the upper shelf. As in Edith's closets, some boxes he ignored—they were too light to hold his pistol. Once the top shelf earned him nothing, he worked across the floor, diving into anything large enough to hold the blunderbuss.

His last pass was through the clothes, checking pockets and ensuring there weren't any hidden doors along the wall. After two hours, he dug his way back out. He gave the closet a last look to assure himself it looked as disorderly as he'd originally found it, then heaved his body against the door to shut it.

Wiping the sweat from his brow, he strode to the kitchen, grabbed one of the beers Louise had bought for him, strode out to the back patio, and collapsed into a lounger.

A blasted waste of time. What could they have done with it? The sisters either had a secret hiding place he'd never find regardless of how long he lived here or they had sold it. He shuddered at either prospect. He closed his eyes and listened to the waves hit the shore a block away. Perhaps a walk would do him good, but he was comfortable where he was. A light coastal breeze blew over him, the briny smell of the ocean easing the tension in his shoulders.

When he woke from the unplanned nap, he listened for any sounds of the sisters. He wasn't sure how long he'd slept, but his beer was still cool to his touch. He finished it off and stared at the small yard, missing the expansive gardens of Waverly Manor. Even without involvement in the duke's sordid plans for the stones, Beckworth had made inroads in reestablishing Waverly as a strong house. He'd been prospering with his new title of viscount and had no longer required financial support from the duke. Everything he'd endured to gain his father's approval, to make a name for himself, and to garner a title would all be for naught if he didn't find a way home.

He wouldn't survive in this time period, and the calmness he had achieved moments before vanished.

After staring glumly at his empty beer bottle, he'd begun to get up when a movement and a slight slapping sound caught his attention. The wind had picked up and brushed at a loose tarp on the far side of the yard. His gaze fell on a small shed tucked behind overgrown vines and shrubs. He'd ignored it the dozen times he'd spent time in the backyard, disregarding its weathered wood and the single-pane window in the door. This time, something pricked at the back of his neck and a reluctant hope seized him.

He strode around three sides of the tiny shack. The fourth side perched against an equally old wooden fence separating the properties. The outbuilding was no more than twelve feet wide and ten deep. Besides the small window on the door, an additional window on the far side was covered with years of dirt and grime.

Stepping to the door, he gathered a last vestige of hope and tested the handle. It resisted at first, and Beckworth assumed it was locked, but then wood gave way.

A musty, earthy smell hit him when he pried the door open. He waited for his eyes to adjust to the darkness. The shed held a wall of gardening tools, a push mower, more storage boxes, and a few bags of fertilizer. And along one side of the shed, sitting on top of a sturdy wooden table, underneath the dimly lit window, sat a metal box.

A wave of excitement shot through him. *Could this be it?* He pushed his way past the bags of fertilizer and ran his hands over the box. It was well constructed of sturdy metal with a door that wouldn't open. It must be a safe, yet it was so small. One more thing two hundred years had changed. He stared at the digital display and keypad. *Well, hell.*

The safe was large enough to hold the blunderbuss, but he'd need a code. He ran through his options. Other than beating the sisters senseless until they talked, which would be a problem since they were still proving themselves useful, he wasn't sure what to do. He closed the door, retrieved a second beer, and returned to the lounger.

Twenty minutes later, he set the empty bottle on the table next to him and laughed. He'd listened to the sisters grumble in the past about passwords. Edith complained to Louise that she was careless with them, always using the same one. Edith had been quite patronizing, discussing her method of creating different passwords for every account. He hadn't originally understood the importance of it, but pieces of the weekly diatribe suddenly made sense.

The sisters typed passwords into the computer each time they showed him something on the internet. Would the safe work the same way? He didn't know for sure, but he assumed Edith would be in charge of the safe. With all her gloating over Louise, she'd mentioned how she kept all her passwords recorded and stored in a secret place.

He'd have to start his search over again, but a lightness spread through him, and he flexed his fingers. He could almost feel the hard wood of his pistol grip resting comfortably in his hands.

19

AJ spent two hours with her mom, listening to her go on and on about Adam. What had he been thinking? Why hadn't he said anything or come to her? AJ thought about defending Adam. She understood his fear about coming clean, but that might have been from the guilt of her own little secret about Beckworth. In the end, she let her mother get it out, adding supportive nods of the head and a strategically placed "I totally agree, Mom."

Exhausted from listening, AJ was thankful she got out of there before her mother remembered the part about Adam living at her old apartment. Then her mom would really be upset, everyone keeping stuff from her. AJ remembered all too well how that had felt when Finn had kept things from her.

She shook her head as she sat in her car and thought about her next step. She should go straight home and come clean to Finn. Secrets did nothing to make the other person safer. It didn't keep away the hurt feelings or repercussions. Secrets only delayed the inevitable, making everything worse. Yet instead of driving home, she checked her messages.

Adam had called five times. She leaned her head back and sighed. What had she expected? She listened to his last message and deleted the four previous ones. He was at the apartment and he sounded like he was having a meltdown.

It appeared her own comeuppance would have to wait a little longer.

She'd barely reached her old apartment door when it burst open. He must have been watching through the peephole for the fifteen minutes it had taken her to drive over.

"How's Mom?" Adam bounced on his toes as he waited for AJ to enter.

"How do you think?" AJ dropped her purse on the new sofa Adam had added since the last time she was there. She looked around. He'd added another stuffed chair, a small dinette, which was covered with what appeared to be Adam's work papers, and, when she walked to the kitchen—yep, that had to be largest espresso machine she'd ever seen outside a coffeehouse. It took up half of the usable counter space.

"Seems you're settling in." AJ perched at the counter, still staring at the espresso machine.

"I haven't been able to think much while at the office. I work better here."

AJ didn't have a response. She understood his feelings. She rubbed her forehead. Stella was right. The more time she spent around Adam, the more she began to understand what made him tick. And what Stella had hinted at was correct as well. She had more in common with her brother than she cared to admit.

She watched him as he continued to bounce, this time standing in the kitchen, hands in pockets, eyes darting around the apartment. She couldn't take his anxiety on top of her own.

She nodded at the coffee machine. "I hear you make an awesome espresso."

Adam settled down, seemingly happy for a distraction. "Stella seems to like them. Can I make you one?"

"I'd love that."

Adam busied himself at the machine, and AJ marveled at how serious he became when handling the instruments, carefully cleaning as he worked.

"I can see you, twenty years from now. Retired in some small beachside community, owning your own local coffeehouse, and people from miles away coming in for your espresso and one of Madelyn's famous croissants."

Adam's shoulders sagged at AJ's comment and she smirked. "Stop being a defeatist. You know this is only temporary."

Adam placed a cup of espresso in front of her and turned to make another one. "Easy for you to say from the sidelines."

AJ sipped the espresso and closed her eyes. Damn that was good. "I suppose it is. But sometimes it's those who aren't so close to the problem who can see it better."

She waited for Adam to finish his own espresso and finally take a seat at the counter with her.

"How angry is she?" Adam turned his espresso cup, not yet taking a sip.

AJ sipped hers again. "This is truly an amazing espresso, Adam."

When she glanced at him, she was surprised by the pain she saw in his expression and she caved, reaching her hand out to squeeze his. "She's not angry, she's hurt. I tried to explain your side but she wasn't listening to me."

Adam nodded. He knew their mom better than she did. Helen always needed to vent before she could sit and take time to think about the situation.

"She'll come around, but you should call her before then."

"I'll go see her this afternoon. I'm sorry for making you come over. I guess you're seeing firsthand what happens when you're not honest with those around you."

The comment brought AJ up, staring at Adam, and she felt the blood leave her face. "Are you referring to anything specific?" Her words were flat, toneless.

Adam watched her, his own misery set aside in order to look more closely at hers. She squirmed under his intense stare and cursed him for using his trial tactics on her.

"Tell me about this Beckworth fellow."

Stella. Had she truly been spending so little time with her friend that Stella felt the need to spend more time with Adam? They were like two old gossip hounds and AJ was the topic du jour.

AJ pushed her hair back and leaned against the chair, folding her arms across her chest. "What has Stella told you?"

If Adam knew he'd hit a sensitive topic, he didn't show it. "Just that someone from the 1800s followed you back and is now trying to track you down. And that he isn't someone we'd invite to a family dinner."

"At this point, it's speculation. I haven't gotten a good look at him."

"And that's why you haven't told Finn?"

"Good grief, Adam. How often do you and Stella get together and talk about me?" How easy it was to transfer her own guilt to bashing Adam. She couldn't believe she'd actually voiced that sentiment out loud and couldn't quite look Adam in the eye.

"You told Stella this man was smart. Even lost in a future world, isn't it possible he could be just as dangerous here as he was in his own time?"

AJ stared at the espresso cup, still refusing to meet Adam's steady gaze. She hadn't considered the fact Beckworth could be dangerous. Wouldn't he want to go home, just as she had? Was that why he was following her? A shiver ran through her. She had been so worried about what Finn would do, she hadn't given Beckworth's adaptability full consideration. He'd kidnapped Maire, dragged them both to France without their consent and then kidnapped AJ again at the monastery.

"I was going to tell Finn today, then Mom called in a panic."

Adam stood and picked up the coffee cups and carried them to the sink before turning back to her. "Let me walk you out."

AJ stared up at him. "You're kicking me out?"

"I'm going to do for you what both you and Stella tried to do for me. I wouldn't listen. I can only hope you'll be the wiser of us. Go home and talk to Finn. Then I'd love to hear the rest of the story and how I can help." He held up his hand before AJ could open her mouth. "Don't say it. I've been around too many people, both guilty and innocent, who try to hide things. I don't think you're hiding anything other than what may or may not be happening with this Beckworth fellow. But you lived through a trauma that you're not talking about. That's your business, but sometimes talking about it can help. I'm just saying I'm willing to listen if you ever need it."

AJ sighed. She was going to hate what she did next. She stood and hugged Adam. It caught him off guard, but then his arms tightened around her. "Who would have thought I'd feel closest to you when hiding things from the person I love?"

"No one ever said the Moore kids were the brightest bulbs when it comes to family."

AJ laughed. "No. I suppose not." She grabbed her purse and opened the door to leave. Before she stepped into the hall, she turned back to Adam. "Keep your eyes open for a tall thin man with short, ash-blond hair. He tends to tug at his sleeves a lot. This apartment is still listed in my name."

Adam held her gaze, his expression serious, then he nodded. "Good to know."

As AJ drove home, Adam's comments started to fester. How

dangerous was Beckworth? If he was here, he had to be alone, right? He'd obviously scared her enough to carry her dagger with her, but she had never considered the danger to her family and friends. What had she been thinking, not telling Finn? PTSD be damned. She needed to get her head on straight.

20

Finn waited for AJ on the back deck. He'd changed into an emerald-green shirt he knew drove her wild, and with the strong breeze, his tousled hair reminded her of that arrogant Irishman she'd first met. He held out a glass of wine to her.

"What's the occasion?" She slipped next to him. The wine tasted like a balmy salve to her weary bones, and she hoped it would embolden her for their talk about Beckworth.

"I didn't mention earlier that Jackson completed the cabinetry work. It just needs Isaiah's finishing touches."

She clinked her wine glass with Finn's. "That is cause for celebration. Does that mean we can put the tarps away?"

"Not yet. Isaiah's trim work will still create dust, and we'll start painting soon."

"It sounds like we've jumped ahead of schedule."

"Not entirely, but things are moving faster with Isaiah's help." Finn held her hand and stared at the ocean. A light mist settled over the far horizon, promising a foggy night. "How's your mother?"

"She'll be fine. I waited until she was past the screaming and crying stage and had moved on to anger. I stopped by Adam's to encourage him to visit."

Finn chuckled. "Just in time to catch the tail end of her anger stage. Sometimes you can be an evil sister."

She shrugged. "Maybe I think he's due a little karma for not telling her by now. Mom doesn't like being kept in the dark."

"No one does."

He squeezed her hand, and she averted her gaze. The casual statement carried a dual meaning. Finn still found times to gently apologize for having kept so many secrets from her. It was also his way of easing her into sharing her own worries, while acknowledging the difficulty she had in telling him. He knew so well how tenuous that line was—trying to shelter others. Just as he and Adam had tried to do.

"Jackson brought us a salmon from one of his fishing buddies. Shall we cook it up and then spend a wicked evening cuddled together?" His grin promised more than just cuddling.

"I'd hate to see a good salmon go to waste." She leaned over and kissed him. They'd have all night. "Start the grill. Let's put it on a plank."

AJ sat at the counter, sipping wine, while Finn navigated the kitchen. He enjoyed cooking, and she loved watching him. Surrounded by all the shiny modern conveniences, she could still picture Finn in their Irish cottage, peeling carrots and plucking chickens. An eighteenth-century man polished through his time jumps into the most amazing man she'd ever hope to know. And he loved her. Of that, she had no doubt.

They ate dinner in the library. The wind had grown stronger, making the back deck undesirable, and Finn needed a change of pace from the kitchen and dining area. AJ started the gas fireplace, and they cleared off the small desk. He shared tales from his youth through dinner, and by dessert he had her laughing at his recollection of her first time on a horse. After their meal, AJ cuddled with him in his chair by the fire.

They spoke of trivial things. Were they sure about the colors for the kitchen and dining area? What did AJ think of Jackson's suggestion for a small walkout deck off their bedroom? How was Adam handling the separation? And then came the moment AJ knew would come.

Time to talk about Beckworth.

As if he'd read her thoughts, Finn shifted in the chair. "Why don't you get a bath ready for us? It's time you shared what you've been unable to tell me."

AJ sighed and got up. His expression held nothing but his love for her. No judgment, no recriminations, just the darkening of his emerald gaze that promised it would all be okay. She kissed him gently, but she sensed his tension riding just below the surface.

"I'll get it started."

"I'll straighten up the library and be there soon."

AJ took the stairs slowly, running through the best options for explaining Beckworth. She could just blurt it out. That somehow, inexplicably, Beckworth might be here. Or maybe walk through the first time she'd seen him, explaining the odd experience, and how she thought it was more of her PTSD. Then Finn might understand why she hadn't said anything right away.

Before going to the bathroom, AJ laid out a nightgown, then smiled, not sure she'd need it. She shook scented salt pellets into the tub, started the water, then sat to stare out the window. The sky had darkened but a light band of orange sparkled between the ocean and the low-hanging clouds. No fog after all.

Once the tub was filled, she picked up the paperwork she had left strewn on the bed and dropped it in her office. As she turned to leave, something caught her attention out the window. It came from the south—where the bay was. No. She rubbed her eyes and looked again, not believing what she saw. Or not wanting to.

A thick fog moved out. Long tendrils of mist curled lazily as the fog began to lift. It was going away. That was a good thing, right? It must have been what she'd seen on the horizon earlier —the wind easing it out of the bay. That had to be it. They'd been in the library so they hadn't been aware of it.

A loud knock sounded from below, followed by the rapid succession of someone hitting the doorbell over and over. She raced out of her office. *Now what?*

She was halfway down the stairs when Finn walked into the foyer, his expression as surprised as she was.

The fog.

"Wait!" AJ called as Finn reached for the door.

He gave her a quizzical look, and they both jumped at the next round of pounding.

AJ wasn't sure what she had wanted to say. Maybe nothing. She just wanted to be next to him before he opened the door. She didn't know why, it was just important that she was near him.

Finn seemed to understand, and he waited, pulling her close to him.

She held her breath as Finn opened the door. Pleasure, then wild panic seized her, and Finn's grip tightened around her.

Ethan.

She laughed, but it came out partially strangled. Her stomach churned, and she rubbed her arms against the sudden chill.

His expression was inscrutable—except for his eyes. His silvery-gray gaze held the look of someone haunted.

Finn was the first to break the eerie silence. His whispered voice carried a hint of warning and despair. "What happened to Maire?"

21

"You're saying Maire has been kidnapped?" Finn asked for the second time.

Ethan responded with the same tired reply. "There's no other possibility."

AJ had been fighting off the shakes since Finn had opened the door. She sucked down her glass of wine, and while her vision might have been getting hazier, her brain was clearing, her trembles residing.

The three of them crowded around the library's gas fireplace. Ethan leaned back in AJ's overstuffed chair, one leg crossed over his knee, a glass of Irish whiskey rolling back and forth in his hands. He hadn't changed much since the last time AJ had seen him. His tall, lanky form seemed a bit thinner. His black hair had grown longer, held back in a thin leather strap. His weight loss showed in his carved cheekbones and hooded eyes, but his smile was the same. She fought the urge to sit next to him, wrap her arms around him, and bring him comfort, but this wasn't the time. Not yet.

AJ perched on the arm of the other chair, her arm wrapped around Finn, who sipped his Jameson as he studied Ethan. The whiskey was doing nothing to release the tight muscles still bunched in his shoulders.

"Let's go over it once more." Finn's voice held a calm, steady tone. He could have been discussing the weather instead of the fate of his sister.

Ethan's response was rote, as if he'd already told the story ten times and not just the once after the quick and emotional greeting at the front door. "After you left, we stayed at the inn for a few more days. Maire and Sebastian continued to work on deciphering *The Book of Stones*. They started from the beginning, making changes in their interpretations as they discovered minute errors from their original transcriptions."

AJ smiled when she heard Sebastian's name. He was the monk who had lived at the French monastery for decades. He knew the history of the Torc of Stone, a silver Celtic neck ornament that held the large Heart Stone, also called the Mórdha Stone, and its five smaller stones. Any one of them could transport people through time. *The Book of Stones* explained how the stones worked and how they came to be. The only requirement was the ability to read and decipher the ancient Druid language. Fortunately, Sebastian had been studying and protecting relics for years and had a working knowledge of the language. Maire, being Irish and raised in Ireland, understood a fair amount of old Celtic. Unfortunately, there were several Celtic languages, so Maire and Sebastian had joined forces to decipher the book whose Druid language was quite similar to old Breton Celtic. Nothing was easy where the stones were concerned.

"Once Thomas and the men had cleared the monastery of the last remnants of the duke, we decided to move back there." His eyes flitted to AJ and Finn. "The monastery would be more secure from outside forces. And if any threat came, Sebastian could quickly hide the book and stones in the lower levels."

AJ retrieved a pad of paper and pen from the desk, then

returned to her place next to Finn. "Who stayed at the monastery with you?" She remembered from the first time Ethan had shared his tale, but she decided it was better to record the details and understand where all the players were.

"Thomas and all the earl's men minus one. Walters and a couple of his men who weren't ready to return to England. Thorn and Dodger remained as well." Ethan downed half his glass and rubbed a hand over his face. "Thorn was still grieving the loss of Peele. As you know, his two bodyguards had been with him for ten years. Maire convinced them to stay and wait with them for Jamie's return."

Finn nodded and turned his attention to the fire. "You said Jamie sailed back to England. Who exactly left with him on the *Daphne Marie*?"

"The rest of Walters's men who broke from the duke. One of the earl's men who was sent to deliver an update to the earl and request new orders. And Lando went as well. I think he wanted to keep a watch over Jamie and the ship." Ethan gave them a wistful smile before staring into the dregs of his scotch. "We expected Jamie to be gone for a fortnight. It was almost two before he returned, and he sailed under the cover of night. The French patrols had increased."

"And when did Sebastian receive a response from Napoleon's second consul?"

AJ scratched notes, trying to keep everything in some order, but her gaze kept shifting between Finn and Ethan, worry for them forming creases on her forehead. She ran a hand over Finn's arm, but lost in his thoughts, he didn't seem to notice.

Ethan shifted in his seat. "The missive came shortly after Jamie's return. The peace between England and France had begun to erode. Maire completed her translations of the more critical passages. She would have copied the whole text if we'd given her time, but Sebastian was convinced they had uncovered all they could."

"I assume Napoleon sent someone with military training to the monastery." Finn tapped his fingers on the top of his whiskey glass, his focus turned from the fire to wait for Ethan's acknowledgment.

Ethan nodded. "A retired general would be arriving in several days. The Brittany coast is too critical to let a port go unprotected. We immediately began preparation for departure. Maire proved difficult to get on the ship."

Seeing his haunted smile, AJ stood to refill her wineglass, somewhat irritated that her vision had cleared. She poured a little more wine.

Ethan waited for AJ to return to Finn's side before continuing. "She didn't want to leave the book or the torc, but the safest place for them was at the monastery. Sebastian had learned his lesson with the duke. Someone would have to raze the place to find where the monk hid everything."

His gruff chuckle made AJ wince.

"Before I boarded the ship, Sebastian handed me the stone he had originally given the earl, the one I wore through the earlier time jumps. He told me to hold on to it, just in case. Two of the stones were still missing, and we had no idea who might have them. Hell, they could be at the bottom of the sea for all we knew. But the monk thought someone he trusted should keep one. Without the Heart Stone, the torc was useless."

The three of them sat silently, each staring off into their own thoughts, misgivings, and choices.

Ethan was the first to stir, and he stood to glance around the library as if seeing it for the first time. "I have to admit. When I arrived on the dock and saw lights on in the inn, I was concerned I'd find a thriving business with nosy guests. I can't tell you how relieved I was to see AJ's car."

AJ forced a smile, happy for a change in topic. "It seems our captain had the foresight to purchase the inn during one of your previous jumps."

"Because the bay was a perfect fit for the *Daphne Marie*?" Ethan turned to Finn.

"Aye, and the jumps kept returning us here."

"We were on the East Coast just as often."

He shrugged. "Something about the place, I suppose."

The silence returned as everyone turned back to the fire. AJ wished they had put in a real fireplace. She missed the crackling sound of the burning wood.

After several minutes passed, Ethan turned to them, his expression grave. "Enough with the catch up. We're skirting the most important question."

AJ jerked the same time Finn's shoulders bunched. What more was there? But she knew Finn wanted to hear the rest of the story again. The part where Maire went missing. Was Maire's life always to be in jeopardy? AJ was so focused on her concern for her old friend, she almost missed Ethan's next question.

"What the bloody hell did you do with Beckworth?"

22

The temperature in the room grew stifling, forming beads of sweat along AJ's hairline. Overwhelmed with an urgent need for fresh air, she inched toward the door, but when Finn glanced her way—she froze. Other than his gaze, which flicked between her and Ethan, he seemed carved of granite. Every muscle rigid, his face a blank expression chiseled on hard features, his eyes iced shards of emerald. This was the man Adam had been scared of.

He didn't frighten her, but her gut clenched. He'd known she wanted to tell him something. Irritation tugged at her. It wasn't as if she'd been positive it was Beckworth. She wanted Ethan to disappear for the rest of the evening. She wanted to explain why she had taken so long to tell him. Well, almost tell him.

Finn's jaw clenched, the muscles along his bare forearms tightening as he grasped the chair. With one last glance at her, he stood, collected his glass, and grabbed Ethan's on his way to the decanters on the antique sidebar. He poured two glasses and held one out to Ethan, who took it without saying a word.

Ethan glanced at AJ before returning to his chair. His expression clearly showed he wanted to be anywhere else but here. It was also clear he wasn't going to get in the middle of this. She was on her own.

AJ held her ground, though she dropped her gaze, searching the floor as if it held some clue on the best way to dig herself out of this dilemma. *Don't be angry, don't be angry.* The phrase became a chant in her head while the silence grew.

Finn remained standing on the far side of the library next to the fireplace, which he thankfully shut off. He turned his attention to Ethan. "What makes you think Beckworth would be here?" His voice was flat, but AJ caught the tone in his words, and they sent a cold shiver through her. Yep. He was really mad.

Ethan had the good grace to ignore her. He inched up in his seat, settling his elbows on the armrests, both hands on his drink. "On the knoll, after AJ read the incantation and the fog rolled in, a figure popped out of the bushes from behind you. I don't know what the man intended, and at first, I wasn't sure who it was, not until the two of you had disappeared and the fog began to fade."

He drank half the whiskey before continuing, his focus on the amber liquid sliding along the glass as he twirled it in his hands. "Maire was the first to recognize him. She called his name and when he turned toward us, there was no mistaking it was Beckworth. But before the fog disappeared, it built up again, the tendrils reforming. That's when I knew he had one of the missing stones. There was no other explanation. I'll never forget the fear in his eyes. And just as the fog had taken me moments after you whisked AJ back in time, Beckworth vanished in the mist.

"Maire was terrified at first, knowing neither of you would know he'd followed. But I still remembered the very first jump, how unsettled I was, how long it took to acclimate. And you know as well as I from the many times we've jumped, if Beckworth wasn't close enough to disappear at the exact time as you and AJ, then his arrival, while in the same time period, could be miles away from where you landed. We've seen it happen before, and that's why I ended up in Ireland when you first jumped back with AJ. I was caught in the wake of the fog. The stones always seek the Heart Stone."

He sat back, took another sip of whiskey, his next words almost soothing. "We had no idea if you'd made it home. I knew Beckworth, even as crafty as he was, would be disoriented for some time. I think part of Maire's reason for wanting to stay at the monastery was more than just to transcribe the book. She wanted to be close should you or Beckworth return."

Finn stared into the empty fireplace before glancing at AJ. "And how long did you know Beckworth was here?" His scalding gaze and the tightening of his jaw told her exactly what he was thinking. The same thing she had thought standing in the conservatory at Waverly Manor. Betrayed. And she could now empathize with his feelings at the time, all those months ago when she had questioned him about his meeting with Hensley or his need to go to London, leaving her with Beckworth. And she felt like crap, just as he must have.

"I've only seen glimpses of him." She meant to respond with strength and confidence. No real secrets here. Yet her words barely registered above a whisper. When no one spoke, she cleared her throat and changed tactics. "I remember when we first walked onto the knoll. I thought I saw something behind the bushes, but it was a quick movement, then nothing. At the time, I didn't know you were planning on returning with me. All I could think about was how to say goodbye, and how I had wasted time not finding more time for the two of us." Her voice quavered. She stopped to suck in a breath and run through a silent ten count.

Once settled, she tried again. "I thought the movement must have been an animal. Then, just as Ethan said, when the fog came for us, I thought I'd seen a figure move from the bushes. Then the fog took us and there was nothing but white. I had been worried for Ethan and Maire, but Lando had been close."

She glanced at Finn, and the new storm in his eyes told her she'd made another mistake. She had just admitted a second tidbit she hadn't bothered to share. *Good grief.* How easy it was to get sucked into a web of deceit. And how does one pull one's self out? She suddenly felt a stronger kinship with her brother. Maybe it ran in the family. Had her parents ever held secrets from each other?

After another silent moment, she went straight for the truth, but without the begging for forgiveness. He'd either understand or he wouldn't. "When we arrived back, you were unconscious. All I could think about was how grateful I was that we had gotten home. Then I needed to get you someplace to heal." Her voice dropped. "Then with my family around us, you on the mend, and neither of us wanting to talk about what had happened, I forgot about what I'd seen on the knoll." AJ hitched a breath and laid out the rest. "Until I thought I saw Beckworth last week, and then the shadowy figure I'd seen on the knoll started to make sense. I just wasn't sure how."

"And it didn't seem prudent to tell me any of this?" Finn stood straighter but didn't move from his spot across the room.

"I was going to." Her words came out as a squeak.

His silence was worse than yelling. And the quiet hung between them like an estranged lover trying to push its way between them.

Ethan coughed, finished his whiskey, and stood to place the empty glass on the sidebar. He strode to the desk and cleared a spot in the middle. He pulled something from his pocket and spread it over the newly emptied space. "When word of Maire being taken reached us, we sent search parties, trying to determine where she might have gone. The problem was, we had no idea who had captured her."

AJ almost cried for joy when Ethan changed the subject, but Finn wasn't letting her off the hook. His hooded gaze reflected nothing of his feelings—not anger, not understanding, not concern, nothing. He gave her one last hard glance before striding to the desk to see what Ethan had laid out.

Suddenly, a great fatigue settled over her. An all-consuming tiredness that seduced her like a siren's call from Morpheus. She watched Finn as he listened to Ethan, asked a question, then nodded as if in agreement with his response. She should be there, adding her own thoughts, but she felt like an outsider watching through a glass shield.

What had she expected? She'd created this problem from her own insecurities, and she had to step away before her escalating fears of Finn's reaction crushed her. She finally admitted one thing to herself, something she should have known from the get-go. One can't hide from the past. It had to be faced head-on. Nothing like hindsight to kick her square in the backside.

All those months, unable to share her true fears with Stella and refusing to answer Adam's innocent questions. Maybe she had kept Finn at a distance, always knowing the pull from his past would force him back.

She needed air.

AJ backed out of the library, but she doubted either Finn or Ethan noticed her leave. She stumbled to the front porch and down the steps, stopping at the path to suck in a deep breath. Right or left? The simplest of decisions were beyond her reach. She turned back to the porch, dropping down on the top step to stare across the parking lot to the nest of trees, dark sentinels that were meant to hide them from the world. Now she looked at the trees as strangers. Did they hide more than they protected?

Was Beckworth out there somewhere? Had he discovered where she lived?

She sprang up and dashed into the house, racing up the stairs to the bedroom. Her clothes flew where she threw them as she stripped. After donning one of Finn's T-shirts, comforted by his lingering scent, she opened the windows to the waves and crawled into bed, pulling the covers tight about her.

Thoughts competed for attention as she sorted through ways to make this right. Finn was angry, probably confused as to why she hadn't confided in him. She had been so angry with him when he had refused to share his secrets. Would she have listened if he had told her the truth at Hensley's or at Waverly? Would she have seen his side or continued to be petulant about her own dilemma?

She didn't know. Or maybe she simply didn't want to admit that she wouldn't like the answer.

AJ wasn't sure at what point she fell asleep, or what time it was when she felt Finn's arms fold around her and pull her close. She remembered grabbing his arms, holding him in place as he pressed his body against hers—warm and safe. And she fully released herself into the waiting hands of the god of dreams, hoping he would share a glimpse of a future where everything would be set right.

23

Beckworth couldn't believe his luck. For the second day in a row, the sisters' itineraries took them away from the house, leaving him alone for several hours. After he heard both cars leave the driveway, he waited patiently at the kitchen table. It wasn't unusual for one of them to return to the house five minutes after they'd left because they'd forgotten something.

He tapped his fingers on the table with one hand while his other hand grasped the slip of paper in his pocket, gently rubbing it as if waiting for a genie to appear to grant him three wishes. If only it was that easy. After fifteen minutes had trickled by, he popped up and ventured out to the shed, sticking to a calm and steady pace. Who knew what nosy neighbors might be watching?

The acrid smell of fertilizer smacked into him as he pulled back the door of the shed. Once inside and standing in front of the safe, beads of sweat broke out on his forehead and a slight dampness grew under his shirt. The keypad was all that stood between him and going home. There was more to it than that, but for one long evening and well into the morning, all his hopes had come down to this moment. He couldn't walk into the lion's den without an advantage. He closed his eyes, sucked in a rattling breath, wiped the moisture collecting on his brow, and punched in the first number.

Finding the password had been easier than he could have anticipated. If he'd had to find something that Louise had squirreled away, it might have taken weeks to find it. But Edith was organized and that was her one failing. Since his youth, Beckworth had begrudgingly learned discipline, his own survival depending on it too often to count. This hadn't been the first time he'd studied a target to understand their motives and patterns.

After he discovered the safe, he'd driven the moped out to the house where he'd followed AJ, but her car wasn't there. Her missing car didn't mean she didn't live there, but it had soured his mood. When he'd returned home, he'd found Edith and Louise in the kitchen, making dinner. His stomach growled, and he realized he'd forgotten to eat the BLT they'd left for him.

"Did you have a nice ride, Teddy?" Louise filled a glass with tea and handed it to him.

Beckworth sipped, grimaced internally, but forced a smile and a nod. "Yes, it was good to get about."

"I couldn't agree more." Edith stirred something at the stove. "Dinner will be another twenty minutes or so. Why don't you relax until then?"

His mood lifted. The gods had thrown him keys to unlock the doors to the magic kingdom. Should he dare another search with the sisters in the house?

He strode into the living room, where the television was tuned to an old black and white movie. He set his iced tea next to a chair so it appeared he was watching. After peering into the kitchen to make sure the sisters were busy, Beckworth slid down the hall to the study. He started with the desk, the most obvious place for secrets. The desk in his personal library held many secrets, and he closed his eyes. All the wishing in the world wouldn't magically transport him home. It would require his wit and nerves of steel. And a weapon.

He searched the top drawer not really knowing what he was looking for, but if there was more than one password, it should be some sort of list. Not finding anything of importance, he moved on to the middle drawer, which was filled with nothing more than writing paper, envelopes, and empty folders. As he reached for the bottom drawer, Edith's voice sounded closer.

He held his breath.

After a second, he released a slow, quiet sigh as her voice faded away.

The bottom drawer held multiple folders. His spirits rose as he read through the neatly scrawled handwriting that labeled each file—water bills, electric bills, cable bills, grocery receipts, and so on. His high hopes began to fade until he reached the back of the drawer. To be thorough, he peeked in the last folder, which had no label. A thin notebook had been tucked into the file. He snickered, and his fingers trembled as he pulled it out. He paused to listen. Muffled voices in the kitchen. The sisters must be grumbling at each other.

He set the notebook on the desk and opened it. There weren't many pages but everything was written in Edith's meticulous script. The first few pages were informational—when bills were due, where the main water shut-off was located, and when the water heater had been purchased. As he quickly moved through each page, his optimism diminished, until he reached the end.

The second to last page contained two columns. On the left was a list of single words—checking, savings, loan, social security, cable, and on it went. The second column reflected single words he assumed were passwords, some with letters, some letters and numbers. Very few were only numbers. He scanned the list but what he needed wasn't there. He'd just turned the page when someone bellowed his name.

Moving quickly to the hallway, he yelled, "What was that?"

"Five minutes," Louise called from the kitchen.

"All right." Beckworth returned to the desk.

He was halfway down the second page when the word jumped out at him—safe.

His mouth went slack as he stared at the number. Now that he'd found it, he couldn't believe it. In the second column were six numbers—121752. The numbers were followed by what appeared to be the number eleven crossed through twice.

His hands shook. This was it.

Scanning the desk, he searched for a piece of paper and pen. A small square pad of yellow paper almost made him laugh. Edith filled the front of the refrigerator with what the sisters called sticky notes to remember appointments. Louise preferred pink sticky notes, and they showed up in various places throughout the house. He grabbed the yellow pad and wrote down the number. He had memorized it, but he didn't want to take any chances.

He slid the notebook back in its folder, shut the drawer, and tucked the note in his pocket just as Edith's voice made him jump.

"What are you doing in here?" Edith's voice didn't hold its normal charm. She sounded suspicious.

He'd been caught. He ran a hand through his short-cropped hair, the ache returning to his head. Then an idea sparked. He ignored Edith, grabbed the pen and pad, and jotted down a few words.

"Teddy? Did you hear me?" Edith stepped closer.

Beckworth turned his head toward her, lowered his voice, and choked out, "Sorry. What did you say?"

Edith glanced at his face, then raced the next few steps to the desk. "Are you okay?" She stared down at the pad of sticky notes and Beckworth's trembling hand. "You're shaking. What's wrong?"

"The biscuits are getting cold. What's taking you two so long?" Louise's head popped around the door.

He turned to Louise and forced his eyes wide but said nothing.

"Teddy, you're scaring me. What happened?" Edith asked.

Both sisters peered over his shoulder at the pad, but it was Louise who spoke first. " 'Brown hair, curls, AJ.' "

"What is this?" Edith laid a hand on his arm.

He let another few seconds tick by as his eyes danced between the two sisters. "I think I remembered something."

Louise gasped and held her hands over her mouth.

Edith squeezed his arm. "We told you. It just takes time. These words seem to be describing someone. Do you know who?"

Beckworth shook his head. "I was going to my room to get my book. I thought I would read while you finished dinner. I was in the hall when my headache came back and then something flashed. A memory I think."

"Oh my," Louise exclaimed, and she reached for his shoulder, giving it a light squeeze. "Who do you think it is?" She read the words on the pad. "AJ. Are those initials?"

"I'm not sure." Beckworth said little, allowing the women to fill in the gaps.

"Is it a woman?" Edith asked.

Beckworth waited a beat. "Yes."

"Oh, Lord." Louise rubbed her hands together. "This is so amazing. Who is she?"

He held back a laugh, but a slight grin escaped. "I think she was my betrothed."

After that, the sisters carried on the dinner conversation

almost without him. He occasionally nodded or provided single-word answers. Mentioning a possibly failed betrothal had been a brilliant maneuver on his part. He should have realized some time ago, with the books and movies they'd smothered him with, that the sisters would take a single thought and create an entire story of their own imagination. He'd simply steered them one way or another to fit his evolving plan.

Now, alone in the shed, he blew out a breath he hadn't realized he'd been holding. His heart hammered when he saw the digital display above the keyboard light up with the first number. He punched in the rest of the code and waited.

Nothing. The display went dark.

No.

He punched the number again and tried the handle. Nothing.

He ran his hands through his hair, cursed, and turned to kick the mower. *Think.* It had to be the right number. It was impossible Edith would have changed it without making note of it in her journal. Louise maybe. Not Edith.

Turning back to the safe, he studied the keypad. That was strange. He flipped open his phone and, yes, that symbol was on one of the buttons. It was two horizontal bars crossed through with two vertical bars. He burst out laughing at his own ignorance. Edith's journal reflected the six-digit code, and she'd followed it with this symbol. At the time, Beckworth thought she had written down the number eleven and then crossed through it twice, but she had actually meant this hatched figure. That had to be it.

He sucked in a deep breath, letting it seep out slowly before punching in the six digits and the final symbol. A green light appeared, followed by a soft click as the door squeaked open. He wanted to shout but remained cautious, though a relief-filled laugh echoed in the shadowy outbuilding. His laugh stopped abruptly. What if his pistol wasn't inside?

Opening the door wide, he bent to stare into the dark recess. The seconds ticked by as he tried to assimilate what he was looking at. Then his laughter broke out again, doubling him over in sweet joy.

He retrieved his blunderbuss and ran a loving hand over it. "Now what do you suppose the sisters thought of you when they found you in my pocket?" A question he'd asked himself a hundred times with no real explanation other than the sisters had always been a bit peculiar. As soon as he pocketed it, the intense flood of once more being in control of his own destiny overwhelmed him.

But it didn't compare to the feeling when his hand grasped the butt end of a second gun.

24

To anyone else, the screeching gulls so early in the morning would force heads under pillows as late sleepers begged for a few more minutes of quiet slumber. Many people ignored that intangible time of dawn, when the sun, still hidden behind the trees, cast its ethereal glow capturing the essence of life. Everything was sharper, clearer.

The moment invigorated AJ, the call of the gulls driving her upward. She loved climbing with the birds. They lived their life without apology for the raucousness they created. They celebrated their existence at the top of their lungs, almost making her want to scream with them.

Instead, AJ laughed as a gull flew close before banking away. She grabbed the next hold and continued her ascent. It had been two days since she'd climbed, and she needed it more today than any other, unable to recall when she'd been this out of sorts.

Finn had been gone when she'd woken. He hadn't left a message, and wherever he'd gone, it seemed Ethan had gone too. Panic had overtaken her when she'd found both gone. Fear had clamped her heart as she'd raced through the house searching for any signs that he hadn't left for good. That he and Ethan hadn't jumped back to their own time.

Had he been saying goodbye to her when he held her in his arms last night, kissing her forehead as she drifted to sleep? No. It wouldn't matter how angry he was, he would never leave without telling her. The three of them had decided they needed to be patient, smart. It wasn't until she found the note, something he had no problem leaving for Jackson, that her chest stopped pounding and the nausea subsided. The note had been brief. Something had come up, he'd be gone all day, Jackson knew what to do.

She'd almost cried with relief when she'd read it. He just needed guy time with Ethan to talk things through, catch up. She understood. She did. Pushing off from a small ledge in the cliff, she inched her way to the top. The gulls stayed with her until she reached for that well-known rock that signaled the finish of her climb. After pulling herself up and rolling to her back, a light sheen of sweat coating her, AJ stared into the crisp blue sky and listened to the gulls as they moved down the coast. As always, they had seen her safely to her goal.

She unclipped her harness from the rope and crawled over to her favorite tree, leaning against it to watch a salmon trawler glide over the calm sea. A light breeze ruffled her hair and dried her tanned skin. Her thoughts strayed to Finn as they often did, but she pushed them aside, not ready to analyze how to make things right.

The snap of a twig brought AJ around in a flash. Her hand pulled the dagger from its sheath on her thigh, but she relaxed when the friendly figure held his hands up in defense.

"I didn't want to startle you, but it appears you came prepared." Ethan nodded at her blade.

AJ blew out a breath. "For heaven's sake, Ethan. Next time

call out." She slid the dagger into place and walked over to hug him.

The climb at her favorite cliff ended in the yard of the old McDowell place. The turn-of-the-century eyesore had been for sale for years until Ethan had rented the house months ago. It had been his idea for AJ to write a story on its history, ending her reporter's dry spell. The story had developed into a series of articles that had led to her investigation of the Westcliffe Inn, partially as a ruse to get a story on Finn's ship, the *Daphne Marie*. Such innocent and simple lives at the time, given all they had been through since. And here he was, as if they'd never left.

Ethan groaned. "You've gotten stronger since I last saw you. Any tighter and you'll bruise the ribs that were still on the mend the last time you saw me."

She gasped and stepped back. "I'm so sorry."

Ethan laughed and put an arm around her. "Nonsense. I needed that crushing hug." He kissed the top of her head. "I'd sit out here with you, but wouldn't you prefer a cup of coffee? I'm trying to remember how to use the espresso maker I left behind."

"You bought an espresso machine?"

"I'm afraid it was Adam's fault."

"How did that happen? I didn't think you two were that close."

"We weren't, but he had this immense machine in his office, and he brewed an excellent cup."

"That explains the new machine in my apartment." When Ethan gave her a curious glance, she added, "He's living there temporarily."

He nodded. "Adam seems to have a love affair with coffee that goes beyond either you or Stella."

"Hush. That can't be possible."

They laughed as they strolled toward the house, arms around each other's waists.

Ethan poured coffee, and they sat at the kitchen table overlooking the ocean. The two hovered close, like any two friends catching up since their last visit, even if it had been three months and two hundred years ago.

"Why are you here?" AJ studied him. He didn't look as if he'd slept well.

"I thought I covered that last night."

She shook her head. "I mean here, at the McDowell house. I know the Westcliffe is a bit of a mess, but it's not like we don't have the room."

He shrugged. "This house suits me. I was relieved to find the two of you caring for it. I asked Finn to bring me over this morning. Besides, it's easier if I have my own vehicle. Finn thinks of everything."

"The two of you must have left early."

Ethan eyed her, performing his own steady perusal, his silver gaze full of a concern she'd seen too many times. She sipped her coffee, trying to avoid his glances, not wanting him to see the depth of her fears, but she couldn't stop looking at him. They would make a strange sight to anyone who didn't know them, thinking them estranged lovers rather than the inseparable friends they had become. They'd been through so much together, and he'd been a solid presence, always protecting her. She'd thought she'd never see him again.

"Shall we get to it and tell me how often you've seen Beckworth? I assume he is the reason for the dagger."

She blew out a sigh. "Only twice, and they were merely glances, perceptions."

"And it never occurred to you to tell Finn?"

She turned away, suddenly finding the view more interesting. What could she tell him? That her nightmares had followed her into her waking moments? That she feared Finn would grow restless and want to go home? Or that she feared she had begun hallucinating when she'd discovered someone following her? It all made her so tired.

"Not to pry, but wasn't it secrets that created the rift between the two of you at Hensley's?"

"I don't need reminding."

"Some could argue that point. Tell me why Adam is living in your old apartment. If memory serves, I caught him ransacking your bedroom when I was last here."

AJ snorted and settled back, the muscles in her shoulders relaxing. Ethan had found Adam turning her room upside down, searching for the necklace that held the Heart Stone. "Looking at it that way, I suppose it was inevitable." She turned her coffee cup in her hands and pushed her hair back, becoming more animated now that the focus was on someone else. "When you were here last, Adam had been struggling with a gambling debt he'd hid from Madelyn."

Ethan nodded. "Now it all makes sense. I never understood why he took a job with Finn. He was trying to make money to pay the debt." He chuckled. "So what happened?"

AJ shrugged and pushed her empty cup toward him. "Madelyn found out, waited for the kids to go to summer camp, and kicked him out."

Ethan grimaced as he picked up her cup and returned to the espresso machine. "Poor chap," he yelled over the sound of the machine. "He seemed truly infatuated with her, and it was clear his family meant everything to him."

"Oh, there's no doubt he's not in a happy place right now. Karma can be a bitch." She took the refilled cup from his hands, lowered her head to the cup to inhale the rich aroma, and took a sip. "Don't worry about my brother. Madelyn and I aren't close, certainly not enough for me to talk to her about it, but I doubt she has any plans to make it permanent."

"Making him squirm?"

"Absolutely."

"You women are proving to be more devious than men. The earl said as much when I was younger though I didn't believe him, but you and Maire drove that point home."

At the mention of Maire, a sad smile touched his lips, and he glanced away.

She squeezed his hand, feeling completely helpless. "We'll find her."

"I know." He rubbed his face, then ran his hands through his hair. I don't know how Finn lasted the weeks he was away from you, knowing how angry and hurt you were, terrified for your safety. At times, it seems it will break me."

AJ moved behind him and wrapped her arms around him, laying her head against his back. She could hear the rough pounding of his heart, and she struggled to hold back her tears. "It was horrible thinking he'd betrayed me, lied about his feelings for me. Then believing you had died." She shivered as she remembered Ethan being pierced with a sword before falling in that glade.

Ethan turned, enfolding her into an almost unbearable hug before settling into a comfortable embrace. Two friends who weren't sure how to help the other but somehow able to find a moment's peace.

AJ pulled back until she could look him in the eye. She gripped his arms tightly, almost wanting to shake him to ensure he listened. "Maire endured eighteen months in Beckworth's captivity while waiting for Finn to return. The two of us survived well enough evading his henchmen. She's tough. She'll be all right until we find her."

"She's my heart, AJ. I don't know what I'll do if I lose her."

25

After leaving Ethan, AJ drove to the *Baywood Herald*. She had left her boss, Samuel, believing she might return, but that chapter of her life was over. She had to stop leaving doors open when she knew she'd never walk through them again. It was time to face the past, retrieve her backbone, and stick to her decisions.

Samuel didn't disappoint. He cursed her and then attempted sweet talk, anything to get her to stay. She patted his hand, murmuring words of thanks and "you'll be fine" before walking out. She exited the building into the cool coastal air and turned her face to the cloud-filtered sun. A massive stone had lifted from her, the weight of yesterday.

Spotting the bench under a sprawling maple tree, the place where she'd spent hours planning her stories, she sat and people watched. She didn't know if her new broker gig would pan out, but it was the right direction, assuming she'd have the chance.

With Ethan's unexpected arrival, the game had changed again. The unknown should have scared her, and maybe it did, but as she considered the situation, she realized she wasn't the same person she had been in the spring. Not by a long shot. She was stronger, smarter, and better trained. Something released in her again, another string that ground her—she had friends who had her back. She simply needed to ask.

Then a band tightened around her chest, her earlier giddiness dissipating quickly as if someone had encased her in a bubble and sucked out all the air. Finn's angry face flashed in her mind, followed closely by his hurt expression before all his emotions had completely shut down. She had done that to him. Just as surely as she had when they were at Hensley's and she'd eavesdropped, catching words out of context. Instead of asking him about the conversation like a rational person, her fear of never finding her way home had overridden her common sense. She had put distance between them, causing them both grief and agony. Had it been luck or fate that had brought them together again?

She called Stella, hanging up when her voice mail answered. When she tried calling Adam, his assistant, Joyce, said he was in court. She ate a quiet lunch at a tourist trap, preferring the safety of the crowds, one eye over her shoulder. Now that Beckworth's arrival had been confirmed, she kept a hand near her purse, where she'd illegally stashed the dagger. After lunch, she strolled through the various shops, discovering a quaint new antique shop down a back alley. It was a sliver of a shop filled with books and small antiques like timepieces, china, and personal accessories. She left with a new contact to add to her fledgling business.

Having run out of things to keep her away, AJ drove home. She wasn't sure what worried her most, finding a still-angry Finn or, worse, discovering he hadn't returned. The best possibility was to come home to a house full of working men and Finn sanding a cabinet. She would be able to sense his mood with others in the house, maybe allowing for some soothing of feathers before they were alone.

She wasn't so lucky, and those mixed feelings amplified when she pulled into the lot of the Westcliffe. Finn's truck was back but Jackson's and Isaiah's vehicles were gone. She parked and leaned her forehead on the steering wheel, forcing deep breaths as she worked through how to make him understand why she'd kept Beckworth from him. It wasn't that she didn't know what to say, it was determining how many of her fears she was willing to expose.

The house was quiet except for the soft tinkle of wind chimes on the back deck and the occasional twitter of a bird. Then she heard a melodic sound and turned toward it. She followed the music to Finn's study. Bach, one of Finn's favorite composers. She remembered their trip to Portland to attend the Oregon Symphony and the night they had spent at the hotel, and her cheeks warmed. Would memories of their nights together always bring on a blush? She took a deep breath and stepped inside.

Finn leaned over his desk, his focus pinned on what appeared to be a map. It was the folded paper Ethan had given him the night before. Images of him at the navigation table on the *Daphne Marie* shot pains of regret through her. How much did he miss his ship?

She waited just inside the door, unsure whether to interrupt him. Before she could take a tentative step backward, the map rustled.

"Come look at this." He didn't look up, and his tone gave no indication of his mood.

AJ swallowed the lump in her throat and stepped to the desk. It was an antiquated map of the British Isles.

"Come around and look at it from this side. It will make more sense to you."

Any other time, she would have easily moved within his reach, either to sit on his lap or feel his embrace. She hated that she hesitated, her guilt stifling her. And where had he run off to?

As soon as she stepped next to him, her question was answered. He'd been riding. She could smell the horse on him, and she breathed a heavy sigh. Of course, where else would he go when he needed to think? How could she have forgotten the horses?

"This is Ethan's map." AJ touched a finger to its edges, her instincts for preserving the old hardwired into her.

"Aye."

"What are the circles?" As soon as she asked, she figured it out but wanted to hear Finn's voice.

"This marks our path since arriving back in Ireland. The blue marks the path you and I took. The green reflects Ethan's path."

"Which is why they cross over here," AJ said as she pointed to a spot on the road to Southampton where Ethan had rescued her from Dugan, one of Beckworth's men. She paused as she studied the map. "They cross again here, a little farther south." She drew in a breath. "The glade where you found Ethan."

"Very good." He put an arm around her waist and drew her closer as he bent over the map.

She should be paying attention. Whatever he was showing her was important, but all she could think about was how naturally he'd pulled her toward him. She leaned into him and his embrace tightened, forcing her to blink to clear her vision, but the map remained blurry.

"Are you paying attention?" He squeezed her, and she sensed him watching her.

She refused to look at him, not wanting him to see how relieved she was. She trained her focus on the map. "I'm sorry. What did you say these red lines are?"

There was a moment's hesitation before he responded. "This

was Ethan and Maire's journey after we left. Up until here." Finn pointed to a spot on the map where the red trail met another circle and paths changed to purple and black.

She studied the locations and then smiled. "Hereford. They went to the earl."

"Aye." His soft whisper trailed along her neck, and she redoubled her efforts to pay attention. "The purple was the direction Maire and her guards traveled, apparently in what may have turned out to be a search for the first Druid's book. The black was Ethan's path to find her when the earl's guards returned to say she'd been kidnapped. Again."

AJ ran her finger along the various lines marking her travel, first with Finn, followed by her escape with Ethan and their backtracking to find Maire, and finally to Southampton, where they'd boarded ships for France. The journey she and Maire had taken when they'd escaped Dugan and run into the Romani wasn't on the map. Not that it mattered, but this was the first time she'd seen her travels from this perspective. It was a bit eerie.

"This is Waverly Manor?" AJ pointed to the second circle east of the port where the *Daphne Marie* had docked after leaving Ireland.

"Yes."

AJ retraced the purple line with her finger, following Maire's path. "She was going back to Waverly," she whispered, half in disbelief, half in understanding.

"Possibly."

"She didn't tell Ethan?"

Finn shook his head. "We don't know why. She claimed to be going to Peterstow, but Ethan thought she might be going to meet with Sir Reginald Ratliff near Oxford."

Where had she heard that name before? "Oh. Wasn't that

where the prior sent the Heart Stone when the monastery was pillaged by Sebastian's power-hungry intern?"

Finn nodded and dropped into his chair, pulling AJ with him, but she twisted out of his grasp. She wanted to stay focused, not get caught up in his scent of cedar and hay. She moved beyond the desk and began pacing like Adam. "Didn't Ethan check Waverly?"

"He canvassed the area with Thomas, including the local village. Everyone said the manor had been quiet since Beckworth left for France. No one knew when he would return."

AJ snorted, then turned away from Finn.

Her pacing increased as the silence grew.

"AJ, stop. You'll wear a hole." Finn's words echoed in the room, not harsh, just commanding.

She dropped into a chair and pulled her legs up, wrapping her arms around them. The silence returned, and AJ rubbed her forehead against her knees. Her voice was surprisingly calm when she whispered, "I don't know why I didn't tell you."

When he said nothing, she stared out the window to the front deck. "The first time I saw him, he was just some guy crossing the street. I was meeting Stella for lunch, and I wasn't sure which direction the restaurant was from the antique shop. I was just looking around and caught him out of the corner of my eye. I wouldn't have given him a second thought until he tugged at his sleeves. Then Stella called me, and when I turned back he was gone." She shook her head. "I thought I was imagining it. With the dreams, I don't know. Some days, I feel like I can't breathe."

She hadn't heard him move and jumped when Finn squatted in front of her, folding his hands over hers.

"I knew about the bad dreams, but why have you kept the anxiety a secret?"

She shrugged. "We've been so busy."

"That's not a valid reason."

Unable to pull her hands out of Finn's tight grasp, she rubbed her face against her arm, trying to wipe away the tears that rolled down her cheek. "We haven't talked about anything since we got home. Not really. I know you miss Maire. So do I."

"I haven't asked because I wasn't sure you were ready. I'm not making light of the weeks we spent in my time, but I've been to war. I've seen, done, and lived through much worse than the events at the monastery. We should have talked about what happened, no matter how much it hurt."

He released her hands to wipe the tears away. After kissing her forehead, he dragged her out of the chair and turned to sit, pulling her back down to his lap. "Now look at me and tell me the rest."

She heaved a sigh. "The second time was still just a glimpse, but he knew I saw him and ran." She explained her suspicions about the antique shop, about Stella and her speaking with the store clerk, and the woman's description of a man that fit Beckworth's profile, including an English accent. She finished with the damning evidence that he'd asked the clerk about meeting her.

"Stella told me I was being stupid, not telling you. I knew she was right, especially after speaking with the clerk. I was going to tell you and then Mom called about Adam. When I got home..." She turned away for a second.

"I don't understand why it was so difficult to tell me."

She heard the hurt in his voice, but she couldn't bring herself to express her doubts. Foolish, but there it was. Then another thought blasted her insecurities to dust. Had it been lurking underneath her other misgivings all this time? It seemed easier to admit this new possibility than reveal her inner turmoil about their future. "I was worried about what you'd do to him."

Finn studied her for a moment and then nodded, rubbing

her hands. "That's a fair assessment. You would have cause to be concerned."

Her eyes widened as she gazed at his stern expression, unsure if he was joking. This wasn't the early nineteenth century. It wasn't as simple to dispose of a body. *Although, if no one knew the person existed...* She squashed the idea, as tempting as it sounded.

Finn chuckled and pulled her close. "Don't worry. I wouldn't have killed him. At least not right away."

"Funny." AJ tucked her head under his, listening to his strong heartbeat, the scent of cedar and horses making her mind fuzzy just as she'd predicted.

"I would have thought you were seeing things, just as you expected. But it was still important to tell me."

"I know. I suppose I was trying to keep you safe, just as you did for me in England." She looked up at him, her expression filled with regret.

"Is there anything else you need to tell me?"

AJ stiffened before she could stop herself and inwardly cursed. There was no doubt Finn had felt it. Should she reveal her fear of him returning to his time? With Ethan back and Maire in trouble, it didn't seem to matter. Fate seemed to be deciding their path for them. "I think it's time to learn the bow and pistols."

Finn studied her, and the slight creases in his forehead told her he knew she was evading his question. "All right. First thing in the morning."

She placed her head on his chest again and hugged him tightly. He ran a hand over her arm and kissed the top of her head.

"I could use some help washing the aroma of horse off me."

"I think it smells wonderful."

"Do you?" His voice turned husky, releasing a telltale tingle that coursed through her.

She stared up at him. His kiss was swift, hot, and urgent. She didn't want him to stop. "I missed you."

He stood, his arm on her elbow until she steadied herself. His warm gaze held a strange mixture of anticipation and determination. "We still have things to sort, you and me."

She nodded and reached for his arm, her mouth opening to say something. Before she could utter a word, he clasped her hand and dragged her out of his office.

"Wait, shouldn't we study the map some more?" AJ had no desire to study the map and her heart pounded when she heard his low growl.

"Later."

She raced to keep up as he stormed up the stairs, the sounds of Bach all that remained in their wake.

26

Beckworth enjoyed a leisurely breakfast of eggs, pancakes, and sausage. His smiles came naturally as he bantered with the sisters. Edith and Louise hummed while washing the dishes, seemingly more excited about the minor breakthrough in his amnesia ruse than he was. He should be more careful, but after considering his options earlier that morning, he could squeeze out another two weeks of minor recollections before the sisters became suspicious. That should be more than enough time to complete his plan.

Edith left the house shortly after breakfast, and Beckworth returned to his room to wait for Louise to finish getting ready for an excursion with her knitting circle. He dug behind several boxes in his closet, stopping whenever he thought he heard Louise in the hall.

After opening the safe and finding not only his blunderbuss but a modern pistol as well, his next decision had been what to do with them. He knew nothing about weapons from this era, and after a thorough search of the tiny safe and the shed, he hadn't found his powder flask or shot. What the sisters had made of his pistol, he couldn't imagine, and he'd been surprised they'd never asked. As excited as he'd been when finding the guns, it had been well into the evening before he'd realized neither was of any help to him. One was unusable without powder, though the shot he could improvise. The other he hadn't a clue how to use.

He'd considered leaving the guns in the safe, but after more deliberation, he couldn't remember the sisters ever going into the shed. They did little gardening and kept a tin can on the back porch with pruning shears and a rusty trowel. Once a week, a neighborhood boy came by to mow their lawn.

The closet in his tiny room was a haphazard mixture of both sisters' manner of storage and would be an equally safe place to hide the guns. After careful perusal, Beckworth stuffed the pistols behind several heavy boxes in the far corner of his closet.

Now he wished he'd found a better spot. He was making too much noise moving the boxes around. Once he reached the spot where he hid the guns, he listened carefully, heard nothing, and pulled out the modern pistol. He left his blunderbuss behind for now. He might not be able to use it here, but he'd be damned if he'd go home without it. It was safe for now.

He tucked the other pistol into a backpack, along with his binoculars, a bottle of water, and a few cookies he'd taken from the tin. Then he stashed the pack behind the closet door and hovered near the study.

When Louise rushed down the hall, she smelled of roses and something musty. She almost barreled past him without a word, a sign she was running late. Perfect.

"Louise, dear. I know you need to leave, but could you turn on the computer and show me again where I can search for something? I wanted to find parks I haven't been to yet, and maybe find some residential areas by the coast." He rubbed his forehead. "I keep envisioning a house on the coast."

Her eyes wide, she gave him a hopeful glance. "Are you remembering something else?"

He shook his head. "I'm not sure, but I do feel close to something. Maybe the computer will trigger an area I haven't explored."

She checked her watch. "I can get you started but that's all the time I have. The girls will be mad if I'm too late." She squeezed past him through the door to the study and turned on the computer. "Sit here while it warms up. I need to load some stuff in the car. I'll be back."

Beckworth waited patiently, and when the screen lit up, the sister's earlier internet training returned. He found the search site and began typing in a word when Louise's voice startled him. For two noisy sisters, they had an uncanny way of sneaking up on someone.

"It looks like you're getting the hang of it. You're in the right place. Just start typing the keywords of what you're looking for. Don't forget you can put more than one word or even type out a question." She turned back to the door. "There's a fresh pitcher of lemonade in the fridge and a new batch of cookies in the tin."

"Thank you, Louise. You're a true lifesaver." He waited until he heard the car leave, then typed in "where to buy a gun." He smiled and shook his head. It was just too easy.

"T his may sound silly, but I inherited this pistol, and I don't know the first thing about it." Beckworth scratched his head after placing the sisters' gun on the counter.

The old guy behind the counter chortled. "If I had a nickel..."

Catching Beckworth's questioning stare, he leaned a beefy forearm on the glass display case, his gray, bushy eyebrows forming a bridge over his nose. "Not a week goes by someone doesn't come in here toting a firearm they found in Aunt Betsy's attic or some crazy uncle left them in his will." He picked up the gun, removed the magazine and checked the chamber.

"A Browning Hi-Power. I haven't seen one of these for a while. Not since an old war buddy of mine moved down to California. He'd been in a special forces unit in 'Nam. Hush-hush and all that." He raised an eye at Beckworth. "What were you thinking? Sell it or learn how to use it?"

Beckworth stared at the pistol, unable to keep the excitement at bay. A gun of war. It must have belonged to one of the sisters' husbands. He'd seen modern guns on television, but when he'd held this one, something had felt right. This was everything he needed to even the playing field with Murphy.

"Show me everything you can about it."

The man chuckled, a bit of spit forming at the corner of his lips. "That's the spirit." He picked up the gun and, within seconds, had taken it apart. Beckworth whistled.

"Yeah, not much to it." The old guy ran a finger down the metal of what had been the barrel. "Not as bad as I expected. Someone's been caring for it." Within another few seconds, the pistol was back together. He waved at Beckworth to follow him toward the back of the shop and down a narrow hall. At a door, Beckworth followed the man's example by stuffing in earplugs and donning a pair of plastic glasses.

The old man pushed out to the bright midday sun and continued down a covered walkway. To the right, a dozen wooden tables with attached bench seats ran the entire length of the walkway. Beyond the benches, targets had been placed at varying distances. Beckworth guessed the farthest ones to be a thousand yards out. The faint odor of spent gunpowder flared his nostrils, and his eyes brightened.

The tables were empty except for a lone man bent over a

rifle about halfway down the walkway. The old man stopped just short of the bench and waited while the shooter took his time sighting the target and then fired.

Beckworth turned his head just in time to see one of the farthest targets sway.

The old man yelled, "Pete, I need you to help this gentleman."

Pete nodded as he lined up another shot. The old man walked behind Pete, and Beckworth stepped next to him. Pete fiddled with the scope, something Beckworth had learned about from his early-morning internet research. After a silent minute, a light breeze blowing left across the range, a pop sounded with the barest recoil from the rifle.

This time, the target didn't move.

"Pete's testing a new .223 bolt action." The old man grabbed the binoculars and, after a few seconds, nodded. "Not bad." He handed the glasses to Beckworth.

Beckworth copied the old man's actions and peered through the binoculars. Silently thanking Edith for her lengthy bird-watching lessons, he adjusted the glasses until the target came into focus. Several holes pierced the middle of the target, all closely placed. He released a whistle.

"Yeah. Pete never misses." The old man slapped Beckworth's back, shouted out, "He'll take care of you," and sauntered back to the building.

Pete tucked the rifle under his arm and stuffed a box of shells in his pocket. He picked up Beckworth's gun, which the old man had left on the table.

"A Hi-Power." He slid a look at Beckworth. "And you don't know anything about this firearm?"

Beckworth shook his head.

"Huh." He scratched his balding head, somehow hitched up

his pants with the arm holding the rifle, and limped toward the building.

Beckworth followed, wondering how the expert marksman had injured his leg. Once inside, Pete guided him to a simply furnished room with a table and chairs, a small refrigerator, and a long counter. The only items on the counter were an almost empty coffee pot and the remains of a box of donuts.

"Do you know anything about firearms? Ever shoot one before?"

Beckworth thought about the question. He'd stick to the truth as much as he could. "It was quite some time ago."

Pete nodded. "Okay. First, let's take a few minutes to clean the gun while you learn how it works. Then we'll set you up with the proper bullets and take you to our indoor range to pop a few. Sound good?"

Beckworth couldn't hide his excitement. "It sounds perfect, mate."

An hour later, he left the store with two boxes of bullets, a switchblade that fit nicely in his boot, and a deep appreciation for the advancement in weaponry. What he hadn't expected and eagerly purchased, after a raised brow from Pete, was a small supply of black gunpowder and pellets for his blunderbuss.

As he walked toward the moped, the weight of the gun in his jacket added a bounce to his step. He steered the scooter back toward town, whistling an old sailing ditty he hadn't thought of in years. His spirits hadn't been this high since—well, he couldn't remember the last time he'd been this happy. He could almost smell the wisteria at Waverly Manor.

27

"This seems the wrong time for a dinner party." Finn removed the canvas sheets from the floor and draped them over the construction material still stacked against one wall.

AJ finished setting the table, placing water glasses in their proper places. "It's not a dinner party, but we have to eat, and it's safer talking here than anywhere else."

"It's not that I'm against having Stella and your brother here, but do you think it's fair to get them involved in this?"

She placed two open bottles of wine on the table. "It's not like we can hide Ethan."

Finn strode out the french doors and leaned against the deck railing to stare out to sea. The late-afternoon sun was bright in the cloudless sky and brought out the golden highlights in his hair.

AJ stepped next to him and wrapped an arm around his waist. "Stella and Adam may not be trained in fighting or military strategy like Lando, Thomas, or Thorn, but they have skills. Think of everything they dug up when I went missing. They can help with this."

Finn sighed. "I suppose you're right. They're going to have to be told eventually."

"Exactly." AJ leaned her head against his shoulder, but she could feel the tension coiled in his muscles when he wrapped an arm around her. "What else is wrong?"

"Beckworth. With him on the loose, anyone involved with us is put in danger."

AJ's stomach clenched at the man's name. She'd almost forgotten about the scoundrel after the amazingly pleasant day she'd shared with Finn. They'd each woken with a different plan on how to spend the day. Finn had wanted to go riding again. AJ had wanted to do something that included Ethan and had been surprised when he called them shortly after breakfast. He'd purchased a prepaid cell phone, something he'd never done before, then insisted he wanted the day to himself but agreed to meet them for dinner.

That was when AJ had decided on the dinner party. After confirming dinner with Stella and Adam, she gave in to Finn's request to go riding. She fought butterflies the entire drive to the ranch, making her question the second helping of eggs. It had been months since she'd ridden, and though she managed well enough when she did ride, she was nervous about the horse Finn had purchased for her.

After a quick hello to Mac in the barn, Finn showed AJ the tack room. She'd never prepared her mounts before. Finn or Ethan had always handled that. Finn insisted it was time for her to learn, and the simple activity made her less nervous with Seraphina. By the time he showed her how to brush the mare and clean her hooves, she was more than keen to place the blanket and the saddle. He left her to fuss with the bridle straps while he prepped Hagan, giving her more time with her own horse, who proved to be as gentle as Finn claimed. Once Hagan was ready, Finn checked her bridle straps, showed her a few tricks, then nodded with a large grin that had left her glowing from the inside out.

"You're a natural." He kissed her.

"I don't know about that, but I do feel more like a horse-woman now that I can saddle my own horse."

For the first two hours they simply rode, enjoying the connection with the horses. For another hour they picked through rusted-out farm equipment in an old barn with only two walls left standing. Their last hour was spent in the privacy of a wooded glade with nothing around but the remains of their packed lunch and a few discarded clothes.

When they returned to the ranch, Finn picked grass out of her hair, and she blushed. "You've never pointed out the side benefits to these rides."

"Does that mean I can expect your company more often?"

She laughed heartily. "I think that's pretty much guaranteed."

Everything and everyone had been forgotten for those few precious hours. Reality crashed back when Finn pulled into their driveway. The first thing she did was call Ethan to make sure he was okay. With a slight hint of irritation, he assured her he was fine and would be around in an hour or so.

After a longer-than-planned shower, all activity was now focused on dinner preparations. AJ planned a summer grill, and since Adam was coming, she'd decided to let him cook everything. It would do him good to help with what he did best, and no one could argue with his reputation as grill master. She was wrapping the last of the diced potatoes mixed with onions and rosemary inside tinfoil when the doorbell rang.

Ethan strode in carrying a bag of goodies—two bottles of wine, a bottle of Jameson, and two apple pies from Donna's, the best bakery in Baywood.

"This is how you spent your day?" AJ almost squealed with

delight when she saw the pies. "You didn't have to go all the way to Donna's."

Ethan bent down for her kiss on his cheek. "Of course I did. And no, shopping wasn't my only pastime. Don't worry about me."

AJ noticed the bite to his tone and his false smile, and after his irritation earlier on the phone, she'd had enough. She grabbed his arm and tugged him close while Finn went out to start the grill. Her gaze traveled over the shadows under his eyes and the few strands of gray touching his temples, but she refused to make this easy on him. He needed to listen to her. "Let's get one thing clear. I know we haven't seen each other in a while, but you're family. And family worries about each other. We take care of each other. So if there's something you're not sharing, remember the lecture you gave me yesterday about secrets."

His expression hardened, and he opened his mouth to say something, but AJ cut him off.

"There's nothing for you to say right now. I get that you need your space, time to get used to being back. And I know you're so worried about Maire that you can hardly breathe." Her breath hitched, and the tension in his arm relaxed under her touch. "We need to bury our fears the best we can." She tugged him closer, her voice a mere whisper. "We need to stay focused and trust one another. For Maire's sake."

She stared at him, not giving an inch, waiting to see if she had gone too far.

He stared back, and the intensity of his gaze seemed to pierce straight into her soul, as if he were weighing it. His shoulders sagged, and he dropped his forehead to touch hers. "Forgive me. The only other time I've had such fears was not knowing your fate while in England. I almost wish I'd never left the earl's side for this mad adventure."

"Then we wouldn't have met. I wouldn't have found Finn, and you wouldn't have found Maire. I'm not an expert in love. In fact, I'm pretty sure I'm really bad at it. But whatever happens, I'm better off for having the three of you in my life." She silently cursed her blurring vision, once again hating that she cried so easily. She pressed her fingertips to his cheek and smiled. "This is what happens when we fall in love."

"So you're telling me love isn't all roses and poetry."

She snorted. "Not hardly."

Ethan released a raucous laugh and kissed the top of her head. "Then you better get the wineglasses out. I'm in sore need of some wine, and, if I'm not mistaken, I think I heard Stella's car."

"And it appears Adam is with her," Finn said as he strode through the kitchen. "I'll let them in." Finn stopped when he saw the bottle of Jameson. He picked it up. "Well, it appears I've rubbed off on you."

Ethan shook his head. "I only brought it as a proper guest, but I won't say no if you decide to share."

"Good man. I'll make an Irishman out of you yet." Finn stopped to study him for a moment, then he turned toward the hall to greet the new arrivals, tossing over his shoulder, "I suggest you listen to AJ or she'll greet you at the top of your cliff each morning with a new lecture."

Ethan gave her a critical eye. "You wouldn't."

Her return smile was wicked. "Maybe not every day."

Across the parking lot, hunched behind a tree with Edith's birding binoculars, Beckworth watched with some dismay as the red sports car pulled up to the house. Stella Caldway. Once he'd spotted AJ that first day with the redhead and then followed to see them enter the restaurant together, he'd had an inkling he was onto something. Soon after, he'd begun to notice the redhead's face on signs around town. She was some form of estate agent. It had taken him half a second to realize it might take weeks to find AJ again. His best option had been to follow Stella, assuming their lunch hadn't been a onetime affair.

He'd known a Stella when he'd been a youth scrounging through the back streets of London. She'd been a buxom brunette and tossed him day-old bread and scraps of dried meat from the kitchen of a whorehouse down by the docks. That Stella had saved his life, and he'd bet on the chance that this Stella might be his salvation as well. It hadn't been a sentimental decision but a tactical one to place the first GPS unit on the little red sports car.

But his thoughts drifted, along with his gaze, back to the immense black vehicle parked next to AJ's car. He couldn't believe his bad luck when Ethan Hughes stepped out of it. When had he arrived in this time period, and what did that mean? The last time he'd seen Hughes was on the knoll in France. Had Hughes been standing too close to the fog like him and gotten pulled through time with the rest of them? If so, then it was possible Maire was here too, but he pushed his memories of her away.

He leaned against the tree and considered how Hughes's presence impacted his plan. Everything had suddenly become more dangerous.

Movement at Stella's car refocused his attention, and he raised an eyebrow when another man stepped out from the passenger side. Beckworth studied this new man as he walked to the back of the vehicle and allowed Stella to fill his arms with bags and boxes before they climbed the stairs. He'd need a play-bill to keep track of all these people.

Before they reached the front door, it opened.

Beckworth hissed, "Murphy."

He waited until the door closed, then slumped down to consider his options. It appeared they'd be in there for a while. Was this all a simple social gathering or something more sinister? He'd thought AJ might have seen him. She'd given chase that last time, but had she followed because she'd thought him a stalker or had she seen his face? He cursed his bad luck again.

He scanned the front of the house, watching each window for a long minute before moving to the next. This part of the house appeared to be infrequently used. It would be impossible to discern anything from his current position. Crawling through the tall grass, Beckworth first moved to his right, searching for a better angle toward the back of the house. He could see the edge of the back deck but couldn't get any closer. This side of the house was cut off by a path that curved down to the ocean.

He turned back and slithered patiently to the other side of the house but faced the same dilemma. The landscape offered access to the backyard and a longer stretch of the house, but another path broke off toward the sea. There wasn't cover on either side of the house to hide his approach. All it would take was someone looking out a window at the wrong time and he might not live to see the next day.

Perplexed, he leaned against the tree nearest the house, some thirty yards away, and sighted through the binoculars. He scanned the edge of the house where the deck turned toward the sea and focused on the large bay window. There weren't any curtains and his excitement rose. He glimpsed two dining chairs but couldn't see the table. His jaw clenched when he spotted the back of Murphy sitting next to Stella.

Damn. For every piece of luck, another problem rose. What if he just walked up to the front door and begged them to send him back? He laughed. Yes, they would gladly help him out, right after they put a bullet in his head.

He would learn nothing more tonight, but it hadn't been a complete waste. He'd confirmed both Murphy and Hughes were here. While it wasn't what he'd hoped to discover, at least he knew what he was up against. He scowled as he crept through pine needles into the denser forest toward the moped.

He ran through various new scenarios on his way back to the sisters, but it wasn't until he reached the door to the kitchen that he sighed in bitter disappointment. He should have moved the tracking unit from Stella's car to Hughes's. He stopped. There was still time to do that, and once it was completely dark, it would be safer. He was two steps from the moped when Edith rounded the corner from the garage.

"Teddy, perfect timing. Louise has dinner ready."

He forced his best smile, one that was getting thinner by the day, and turned to follow her inside. He swallowed his dark emotions, reaching instead for the skills that had eventually won him Waverly Manor. Patience had served him well with the long games he'd played in the past. His prize hadn't changed. He simply needed to wait for an opening.

He couldn't help but smile when Maire's sneering image appeared, railing at him as a black-hearted scoundrel. Her silky blonde hair had been tangled, as if she'd just fallen out of bed rather than being tousled from the long ride after being kidnapped. Yes. He could wait.

28

The group pitched in to clear the table, wash dishes, and clean the grill. Stella completed the final touches by restocking the dinner table with a fresh bottle of wine, an open bottle of Jameson, and enough glasses for all.

"What do you think of calling Martha?" Stella asked as she poured wine for herself and AJ. She tilted the bottle toward the men but they shook their head, so she put the wine down and poured the men a healthy glass of Jameson.

"Won't you even try the whiskey?" Finn chided her.

Stella wrinkled her nose. "I'll put up with scotch at times of no hope. We're not there yet. Besides, I'll stay sober longer if I stick with the wine."

"And since she's my drive home, I'll drink to that." Adam said as he lifted his glass of Jameson, getting a chuckle out of everyone.

Except Ethan.

It was becoming harder to find joy. His melancholia wasn't helping the situation, but he couldn't seem to shake himself out of it. After spending weeks searching for Maire and not finding a trace, his only thought had been to try to reach Finn and AJ. At the time, it had made sense.

He hadn't known if they'd made it back to this current time period. If they had, AJ could assist with technology and historical records that might give some indication of where Maire had gone, or at least give him a place to start.

His only other option had been to find a way to France to seek Sebastian's aid. Messages in and out of France were difficult, and his missives to Jamie, the new captain of the *Daphne Marie*, had gone unanswered. The renewed war between England and France made it impossible for him to gain the smallest of breadcrumbs as to Maire's whereabouts.

He'd been at the earl's estate when he'd tossed out the idea of using the stone to find Finn and AJ. He'd laughed after mentioning it, but the earl and Thomas had glanced at each other before pinning their gazes on him. It had taken him a minute to understand they didn't think his suggestion half bad.

The earl motioned for everyone to leave the room except for Ethan and Thomas. "If you think this Murphy and your friend AJ can track Maire from the future, then we must consider it."

"That's mad," Thomas scoffed. But then he ran a hand over his chin, scratching at the stubble. "But everything associated with these stones has been madness." He raised a brow and asked Ethan, "How can you track someone's movements from the future?"

Ethan sat up, not quite believing the earl and Thomas would consider his absurd idea. Now that he'd proposed it, he wasn't sure how to put the notion into words. "One of the first things I did when I found myself in a new time period was to read the papers to find out how much time had passed and understand the current political climate. I also searched libraries and museums. There weren't just changes in politics, medicine, and science. People gained a keen interest in tracing their heritage and lineage, much of it learned through personal journals."

His arm shook and he rubbed his leg to mask it. Was he really considering jumping again? "It's possible, a small chance really, that someone may have kept track of the stones or the book itself. Perhaps enough history has been retained that might point to locations or names. Something that can provide a lead."

Silence filled the room as the three men sat around the hearth. Ethan lost himself in the flames until there was little left but embers.

The earl heaved a long sigh and used the arms of the chair to help him gain his feet. Ethan hated to see the signs of age ravaging the earl's body. *Time takes us all.* And Ethan was quite aware of the irony in the thought. The touch of the earl's hand on his shoulder brought a surge of affection for the old man.

"I know how much Maire means to you," the earl said. "She's a wise and strong woman. I will do what any reasonable man would do to find her. But there is more at stake than just Maire. There's only one reason to kidnap her from armed security."

Ethan nodded. "The stones."

"And for that, we must do more than what reasonable men would do." He turned and clasped a hand on Thomas's arm. "I want you to send three groups of no less than ten men each to where Miss Murphy was last seen. Retrace our steps."

"Thirty men? That will stretch your security." Thomas frowned. "I may know a few others we could use for the search so your own security isn't threatened."

"If they can be trusted, then so be it." The earl turned to Ethan. "You said Maire modified the incantation that leads to the Heart Stone?"

Ethan nodded.

"Then it appears you have your own mission. May it be faster than your last journey."

Everything moved quickly after that. Two days later, Thomas had his thirty men, and Ethan stood in the meadow within eyesight of the earl's estate. The earl sat on his horse, his two bodyguards close to his side, watching him.

Ethan stared at the earl while he spoke the words. He rubbed his finger along the stone set in a pendant the shape of a Celtic protection symbol. As the fog rolled in, the earl's expression changed from concern to something akin to pride. Then the meadow faded away.

Beckworth whacked his head on the bumper of Stella's car and silently cursed. He stilled, listening to the sounds around him. Faint murmurs from inside the house but nothing else besides the sound of waves and a lonely owl. He was sure to hear a door if someone came outside. He grumbled as he crawled from Stella's car, past an old truck, to the black behemoth that Ethan drove. He would have expected Finn to drive something similar.

He'd thought himself clever for figuring out how to leave the house again. The sisters had prattled on through dinner, making him dizzy as they jumped from one topic to the next. He'd tuned them out, nodding occasionally while considering his options. The idea to move the GPS from Stella's car to Ethan's had been eating at him since he'd followed Edith into the house. An opportunity squandered.

If he waited until the sisters were asleep, he'd be too late. Louise fell asleep early but was known to wake in the middle of the night to wander down to her quilting room for an hour before going back to bed. Edith slept like a log, but she went to bed late and rose early. Either way, the party guests at Murphy's estate would be long gone. He shuddered. How could someone like Murphy end up with a mansion on the coast? He snickered. Gambling was the only logical answer.

"Is everything all right, Teddy?" Louise asked as she placed another biscuit on his plate.

"What? Oh, yes. I'm sorry. My mind wandered." He picked up the biscuit and buttered it. They always looked more like scones to him, but it didn't matter, they were excellent.

"What's for dessert?" Edith stuck the last bit of potatoes in her mouth and washed it down with a long, slow slurp of iced tea.

"There's fresh cookies in the tin from this morning," Louise replied in a somewhat indignant tone.

Edith scowled. "That's not dessert. There's always cookies."

"I've had a busy day, and it's not like you weren't home. You had plenty of time to make something. It shouldn't always fall on me to make sure you have a dessert each evening."

Beckworth raised a brow. He must have missed something while he'd been raging over his own stupidity. The sisters were overdue for a good squabble, and he always enjoyed their fighting; it kept them from bothering him. This time, however, he saw an opening.

Before the sisters said something that could destroy his second chance, he cleared his throat loudly enough for the sisters to turn to him. "Do you know what I'm in the mood for?" As soon as the words were out of his mouth, he hoped he hadn't made a mistake. God knew what the sisters had stored in their fathomless freezer.

Louise appeared relieved. "What is that, Teddy?"

"Ice cream."

The sisters stared at him, then Edith smiled. "I think we have some in the freezer."

Damn. Think, man.

Louise lowered her eyes. "I forgot to buy your strawberry syrup."

Edith began to say something, her lips pursed in dissatisfaction, then her eyes lit up. "There's always Frosty's."

That's the spirit, Edith.

"I wouldn't mind driving over to get it." Beckworth jumped in. When the sisters exchanged a glance, he continued, "You've both been so busy today, and all I've done is go for long walks. Let me do this for you."

This time the sisters smiled at each other, and Edith stood to grab a pad of paper and pen from the counter. "Let me make you a list. Jory knows what we like but just in case he's not working tonight."

After she'd scribbled the list down and given him the keys to the Cutlass, he'd raced to Murphy's. He would have to make up some excuse for being a few minutes late with the ice cream, but he'd worry about that later. He could always use his excuse of taking the wrong turn.

Inching his way under Ethan's vehicle, he tugged on the GPS unit. The magnet was strong and would require a strong slam to dislodge it. He only needed it to work for one night. It would be useful to follow Ethan, but he was more interested in knowing where the man was staying.

He crawled out from beneath the SUV and listened. Nothing but a light breeze and soft laughter. The owl had left. He stood, still hiding behind the vehicle, and glanced around. Feeling giddy, and taking a risk that could bite him in the ass, he strolled toward the trees. Halfway across the grass, he glanced back, but no one was there.

He squared his shoulders, lifted his head, and continued his stroll. If anyone had been out front, they would have heard his merry whistling as he wove through the trees.

29

"Ethan, are you paying attention?" Stella's sharp voice pierced his reverie.

"Sorry. I guess I wasn't." Ethan sipped the Jameson and gave her an apologetic smile.

He knew she was going to say something flippant but then her eyes softened, and he wished she would say something that only Stella would say. He didn't want anyone's pity. "What were you on about?"

Stella rolled her eyes and, he was right, it did make him feel better. "We were debating whether to get Martha involved. She was the granddaughter of the last keeper. You knew the keeper, or at least knew of her, Lily Mayfield?"

He shuddered at the mention of Mayfield's name, but he had known her first as Travers. She had been a sly one, and he and Finn had chased her through the years in search of the Heart Stone. He had to hand it to whoever had started the keepers of the stones, making them all women. Definitely the more devious of the species. He smiled fondly at AJ and Stella, and then he thought of Maire. Yes, it had been a wise decision indeed.

"I remember Lily." He glanced at Finn. "She gave us a good chase."

"Aye, she was slippery. Always two steps ahead of us. She's gone now, and you said Martha hadn't really stepped into the role of keeper. Would she know the history?"

Stella shook her head and shifted her gaze to Adam.

He shrugged. "Doubtful. From what Martha said, Lily's mother waited too late to transfer the stone and died shortly after. They never had much time to discuss it or the journals. If there was anything of note before Lily's time, she would have written it down in her own journals."

"Or it's lost forever," Stella mumbled.

"What of this Sir Ratliff?" Finn asked. "Could Maire have gone there? Maybe she hadn't lost interest in the stones."

"Who's Ratliff?" Stella asked.

"He was the one entrusted with the Heart Stone during the Reign of Terror." AJ turned to Ethan. "Did Maire go there?"

Ethan was only partially listening, and AJ had to tap his arm to gain his attention. "Sir Ratliff? Yes, we contacted him. If that was her destination, she never arrived."

"Or so Ratliff said." Finn sat up. "What if he lied?"

"For what purpose?" Ethan's tone was dismissive, but he couldn't help it. He'd been through all this with Thomas, but seeing the frustration in Finn's expression, he relented. "I'm sorry, but the earl claims Sir Ratliff's honor can't be besmirched."

"Did you ask Ratliff about the stone?"

"Again, for what purpose? We know what happened to the Heart Stone."

"Do we?" Finn shook his head, a trace of a grin on his face. "We know it ended up with us, but what if the stone had already been passed to a new keeper before you arrived and Maire found out?"

Ethan went still. Had they missed something so simple? And

more importantly, would Maire have kept it from him? Wouldn't her guards have known, or had she snuck away? That was a skill she excelled at. "To be honest, I don't know anymore."

AJ laid a hand on his arm, but she directed her question to Adam. "Do you think Martha would know the names of the earlier keepers?"

"Maybe. We never discussed that." Adam scratched his head. "I think I know where you're going with this. Something may have alerted Maire to someone else getting the Heart Stone so she may have decided to follow it. Then she got caught up in the middle of something."

Finn nodded. "Possibly. Since Ethan has already performed a thorough check with Ratliff and at Waverly, there are only two other possibilities."

"Someone else has entered the game." Ethan stared at Finn.

"Or someone is lying," Finn finished.

"Or both," Adam supplied. When he received stares from everyone, he shrugged. "Considering the stakes up to this point, it's not unthinkable that a new player might try to get a head start with someone already possessing a stone."

"Then all the more reason to know the name of the next keeper." Finn picked at the label on the bottle of whiskey as silent seconds ticked by. "It would also help to know when the next keeper took over. We need to know the timing."

"Then we need to talk to Martha," Adam said.

Stella snorted. "She'll want the Heart Stone back."

"That's not happening." AJ's statement was met with agreement from around the table. "As far as she knows, we still haven't found it, and we have to make her believe that. The question is whether she's willing to help."

"I'm thinking Professor Emory may be more helpful. At least his friend may be." Adam rolled the whiskey around in his glass, deep in thought.

"His friend in France?" Stella asked.

The other three sat up at the mention of someone in France.

"You mentioned Professor Emory when Finn and I first arrived back, but I could use a refresher."

They turned to Adam, and he sat straighter, pushing his glass of whiskey away. "Did anyone put a pot of coffee on?"

Stella popped up. "I'll do it. I know this part so I can listen from the kitchen."

Ethan studied Adam. He'd been friendly enough when he arrived this evening. The man had put himself in an awkward situation working for both him and Finn. There was something different about him since the last time Ethan had been here, but he didn't think it had to do with the concept of time travel. He suspected it had more to do with the separation from his wife. Finn had mentioned Adam and Stella's investigation when they discovered AJ gone, but that had been the first night he'd been back, and with his thoughts focused on where Beckworth was, he'd only half listened to the tale.

Now Adam and Stella might be the key to discovering Maire's trail. Perhaps he'd been right to return after all.

Adam ran a hand through his hair, glanced at Stella in the kitchen, and turned to the group at the table, his focus on Ethan. "After AJ disappeared, we tried to trace her last steps. Since Finn had vanished at the same time as AJ, and you disappeared shortly after, it seemed obvious the stone necklace was involved, and we had the two matching earrings." As Adam spoke, Ethan could see the lawyer coming out as Adam hit his stride, becoming more animated.

"We went back to Lily Mayfield's house, where I had originally discovered someone had bought the necklace." Adam stopped and gave AJ a sheepish smile. "Of course, we know now that was AJ. We met with Lily's granddaughter, Sarah, and eventually her sister, Martha. They let us read and photocopy a couple of Lily's journals that mentioned the necklace."

Adam paused again and glanced to the kitchen, where Stella watched coffee drip into the pot. "I should have thought to bring the copies I had made. Stella, do you remember the journals mentioning any other keepers?"

"I've been thinking about that," Stella yelled as she pulled cups down from a cabinet. "But no, I only remember Lily mentioning the necklace, of someone looking for it, and how she had to change the setting."

Adam nodded. "That's all I remember as well. Anyway, the journals turned out to be a dead end, at least for what we needed."

"But Martha suggested you speak with Professor Emory?" AJ asked.

"Yes, the professor was the dean of Ancient History at the University of Oregon in Eugene. His specialty was Celtic studies. He's retired now and owns an antique bookstore in Eugene not far from the university."

"And he knew of the stone?" Ethan sat up. The keepers seemed like a dead end to him, but Finn had been correct. He should have asked about the stone itself, but Thomas had cautioned him about revealing too much. He had no idea how this new avenue could help, but if someone had found *The Book of Stones* after all this time, what else might they know?

Adam shook his head. "No, but he knew the earrings had been cut from a larger stone. He didn't believe them to be true stones at all. He was also intrigued by the intricate design of the setting, a protective Celtic shield knot design. He remembered stories of the Druids and their attempts at various forms of alchemy. He contacted a friend of his in France, someplace near a monastery. A book had been discovered a few years ago that spoke of a group of Druids that purportedly turned glass beads into stone and could transport people through time."

The room fell silent and a humming began in Ethan's head. The monastery. A book that spoke of time travel. There wasn't any coincidence here. He glanced at Finn, who twirled his whiskey glass, quietly studying him. They nodded at each other. This was it. This was why he had traveled into the future. It had to be.

"How do we get to this man in France? It has to be the same monastery near Brittany." Ethan pushed his glass of whiskey aside and nodded gratefully when Stella placed a cup of coffee in front of him.

AJ placed a hand on his. "That's not possible. At least not for you or Finn. Or I should say, it's not a trip you could take anytime soon. You need valid identification and a passport to travel out of the country. Adam has been working with some previous clients to secure Finn's identification but we don't have his passport yet."

Stella snorted. "You mean his gangsta friends?" She winked at Adam.

"Not gangsters." Adam pretended to be affronted. "Intellectual freethinkers."

AJ laughed out loud. "You mean hackers."

Adam smiled. "And very good ones, but even they need time to do it right, especially when we're discussing birth records, social security numbers, and passports. But AJ's right. We might be able to push to finish Finn's records in a week, maybe two, but it will take them longer to put something together for Ethan. Although we might be able to give him foreign credentials, but what would be the point?"

"The point is that we would be at the monastery. We'd have the book at our fingertips." Ethan tried to hold his frustration at bay but it wasn't easy.

AJ placed a hand on his. "Adam's right. None of us can read ancient Celtic. I understand how being at the monastery, seeing or even touching the book, could make us feel better. But it wouldn't get us any closer to finding Maire."

Finn poured himself another glass of Jameson and leaned back in his chair, his expression serious. "I'm not sure how *The Book of Stones* can help, but it's an avenue we have to pursue. If Adam and AJ are right, this professor has access through his friend. That's who we'll talk to." He turned his gaze on Ethan, his expression filled with something close to pity and it made Ethan's gut clench. "I know how difficult it is to trust others, to sit on the fringe and wait, but we don't have the time to do anything else. This is why you made the jump, to ask for our help. You have to have faith, and I know bloody well how hard that is."

Ethan stood without a word and strode out the french doors to the deck. He caught sight of AJ starting to rise and quietly thanked Finn for stopping her. A helpless rage raced through him, and he wanted to hit something just to prove he had control over something. He gripped the deck rail instead and stared out into the darkness where a flicker of light came and went, bobbing in the blackness of the sea. The emptiness of the scene somehow dulled his senses, or maybe it simply sucked away all his emotions, which amounted to the same thing. If he didn't care, he wouldn't feel the pain—or the fear.

The day he'd arrived back in Baywood, it had been good to see AJ and Finn again, but the relief he'd hoped to find in meeting up with his old friends had evaded him. When he'd seen the life they were building it had drained him, leaving a hollow husk. Even their squabble over Beckworth had brought an ache of loneliness. They were a couple, two people who would face what came, maybe not in the same way, but their love for each other overcame that.

He knew the unspoken fear AJ held close, her worry of Finn wanting to return to his old life if things proved too difficult here. There wouldn't be anything he could say to convince her that Finn would never leave her. Not voluntarily. Everything Finn had done since stealing her back to the early nineteenth century had been about her and Maire. Yes, Finn had been committed to taking down Beckworth and the duke. Though he'd had to leave AJ and Maire for a short while, there had never been a question about his return.

That was how Ethan felt about Maire. At first, it had been harmless flirtation on both their parts. Months had gone by while he remained close, watching over her and Sebastian while they continued their translations. Maire had insisted he take her on long walks, where they'd shared stories from their childhoods and compared thoughts on books they'd read. Then there were the quiet dinners when Sebastian or the others didn't join them. Through it all something deeper had developed, feelings he couldn't ignore, and a passion neither of them could escape. Then she'd been gone.

Finn had offered Ethan a room at the Westcliffe. They had laughed about Ethan having his pick of any one of the several available in the old inn, but it would have smothered him. The domestic display had been too much a reflection of what was slipping through his fingers. He needed the McDowell house, with its sordid history of obsession and apparent bad luck. It fit his dark mood.

As soon as Finn dropped him off, he'd fired up the SUV that Finn had kept charged and driven to the store, stocking up as if preparing for a storm. He'd barely slept that night, staring out at the dark sea as he did now, the fear eating at him from the inside out. A thin smile forced its way out when he remembered the next morning, sipping his first cup of espresso, staring out to sea again. His thoughts had been on Maire until he'd seen a familiar figure rise like a phoenix from the edge of the cliff. He had shaken his head and laughed.

AJ was still climbing her favorite wall, which led from the beach straight up to his backyard. She'd crawled over to a wind-bent tree and leaned against it, watching the morning sky. He'd almost felt like his old self while they visited, but after she'd left, his melancholia had returned. He'd drunk cup after cup of coffee as he'd sat in an overstuffed chair in his expansive living room, once again staring out to sea, continuing what Stella would call his pity party.

That single dot of light continued to weave through the waves, a ship moving up or down the coast. A breeze rustled his hair, and the chill off the ocean brushed a soft caress along his arms. The soft scent of roses touched his senses and he closed his eyes, trying to recapture one more memory.

Soft laughter drifted through the opened french doors, and he internally railed at the despair that gripped him. He couldn't help thinking he'd made a mistake in jumping again. Time raced by, his target out of reach, and whatever Maire's fate, it had happened two hundred years ago.

He sucked in a deep breath, releasing it slowly. He repeated the effort, counting to ten as he knew AJ did when she needed to refocus. After the third time, he opened his eyes. The spot of light on the waves was brighter, the laughter from the house warmer.

He felt the warmth of her hand. He knew it was AJ, but it was as if Maire herself had touched him. It was Maire's voice whispering in his ear, "Have faith, my love. Trust your family, your friends." The light was moving southward now, and it touched something in him he hadn't felt in a long time.

Hope.

He laid a hand over AJ's and squeezed. The two of them stood side by side for several minutes until Ethan felt AJ shiver from the cold. He rubbed her shoulders as he walked her inside, his steps lighter than they'd been in weeks.

He dropped into his seat at the table, nodded at Finn and the bottle of Jameson, and shared his first heartfelt smile since arriving. "Pour me another glass of that rotgut and tell me your plan."

30

"Are you telling me that time travel is real?" Martha asked.

AJ shifted, a little unsettled by the intensity in Martha's gaze. The woman seemed to be internally picking her apart piece by piece, and somehow AJ felt lacking in some significant way. *Keep focused.* AJ blew out her frustration. "Would it make you feel better if I just said I've been on a long trip overseas?"

"I didn't agree to meet you for platitudes." Martha's irritation lit a match under AJ, who returned an equally annoyed stare.

Stella pulled her chair out of the sun, languidly dragging the legs against the flagstones. "I know it's a bit to take in, but when we spoke about Lily's journals a couple of months ago, you seemed to believe it."

Martha settled back and rubbed her face, suddenly looking bone weary. "It's one thing to say you believe, quite another when someone tells you your beliefs are real." She followed AJ's gaze around the patio, but there wasn't anyone close enough to overhear them. "When you called and said you wanted to meet, I thought maybe you were bringing the stone necklace back."

AJ stiffened. Stella had been right. Thankfully, they had rehearsed responses on the drive down. It still surprised her that the topic of the stone had come up so quickly. Didn't the whole time-travel thing deserve more discussion?

"As I told you, I was forced to turn it over to other people." AJ and Stella had agreed to stick as close to the story as possible. There wasn't any reason to divulge all the details.

"And I'm just supposed to believe you." Martha's gaze darted around the patio. "As if your story isn't a bit far-fetched as it is."

Stella leaned in and lowered her voice. "We can wait and you can discuss this instead with the green-eyed Irishman and the silver-eyed, dark-haired stranger your grandmother mentioned in her journals."

Martha sat back and paled. "I don't think that will be necessary."

AJ suppressed a chuckle. She tried to see it from Martha's perspective, but the woman's misguided need to recover an heirloom she herself had mocked was getting tiresome. "Here's all I can say. The two men your grandmother ran from are two of the most endearing men you'd ever meet. You know, with all that eighteenth-century gallantry and all." She stopped when Martha blanched again, but AJ drove her final point home with a more compelling tone. "But there are other men, not quite as honorable, who would do anything to get their hands on the stone necklace."

"Your sister did you a favor selling the necklace. I know how long it's been in your family, but it was time to dump it." Stella's good-cop routine seemed to settle Martha.

Martha's gaze fell to her lap as she fingered her napkin. All her bluster seemed to leak out of her. "It can be difficult to let go. I realize I never took the journals seriously." She snorted. "Not until you and Adam showed up." She gave AJ a new appraising look. "But I'll admit I spoke to Professor Emory a couple of months back."

Stella laughed. "All this time, you already knew what was happening."

Martha shrugged. "I'm a historian, after all."

"And what did the professor say?" AJ asked.

Martha sighed. "To help where I could, add what I've learned to my own journals, and close this chapter of my life."

AJ startled at her response. "That easily?"

"To be honest, as much as the history itself intrigues me, nothing else does. When Sarah said she sold the necklace, I was angry, finally fulfilling the role of keeper our grandmother had wanted. But another part of me was happy to walk away from it all." Her gaze flitted to AJ but returned to Stella's knowing gaze.

"Your grandmother wasted a good portion of her life protecting the stones," Stella supplied.

Martha snorted. "Apparently from perfectly harmless men."

After a few seconds, AJ laughed. Then all three of them were laughing, which finally caught the attention of the other customers three tables away.

Once the laugher died away, Martha took a shaky breath and retrieved a journal from her purse.

AJ could tell this wasn't Martha's notebook. This journal was decades old, the leather softly scarred, the edges of the pages tattered. A loving hand caressed it, though AJ didn't think Martha realized she was doing it.

"This was Lily's first journal. The first half is what she translated from everything she'd either read from her mother's journals or had been told. What you're looking for is on the first page." Though Stella reached for it, Martha slid it toward AJ.

Surprised by Martha's actions, AJ carefully took the journal and couldn't help but run a hand over it as Martha had. Stella scooted her chair, less dramatically this time, to read over AJ's shoulder.

AJ opened the book to the first page. Eight names were

written on the page. Next to each were dates, and it wasn't difficult to guess these were the years a keeper had held the Heart Stone in her possession. She heard Stella's long sigh the same time she expelled her own pent-up breath.

The first keeper listed was Elizabeth Langdon. 1805 to 1843. Sir Reginald Ratliff had given the stone to someone else two years after Ethan had spoken with the man in his search for Maire.

She stared across the patio, her heart sinking. "The keepers are a dead end."

B eckworth pulled the fedora low across his brow as he pulled the Cutlass along the curb. Edith had given him the hat several days before. The sisters had gathered clothing to donate to a homeless shelter. After seeing both of their closets firsthand, he thought they could have gathered more clothes than the single garbage bag they took with them. Once he'd seen the fedora sitting on the kitchen table, he could give two rats what the sisters gave up. He'd been mesmerized. He prided himself on his knowledge of fashion and had been dismayed by the clothing people wore in this century. The fedora had become a cherished prize.

He knew the fedora was outdated, though Louise said it was coming back in style because of someone or other. He had tuned out most of her prattle. The hat would eventually become remarkable should AJ or Ethan spot him, but until they did, he thought it safe enough to wear for surveillance.

The Cutlass was parked four houses up from the large monstrosity where, according to the GPS, Ethan was staying. The house looked exactly like the picture of the McDowell house he'd found in the town's newspaper.

The hour was early, people were leaving for work, and kids walked to corners where school buses eventually picked them up. He preferred the cover of darkness or busy public thoroughfares. He lifted the collar of his blazer, wishing Ethan didn't live in such a quiet neighborhood. What could be more obvious than a man in a fedora sitting in a decades-old car? He snorted. He could be trying to look inconspicuous on the moped. That would definitely be worse.

He silently watched the street, cars coming and going, and parents saying goodbye to their children. And not one person seemed to take note of him or the car. Deciding this might take a while, he picked up the file folder and thumbed through the paperwork he had collected on AJ.

When he'd first read one of her articles, he had been enthralled with the story. Though it didn't compare with the thrill of finding her work at the *Baywood Herald*. He had collected a few of her articles and cut them out. Now he poked through the newsprints until he found the picture. The McDowell house was what she'd called it, originally built by some old sea captain. He read through the article again and had just begun reading about the Westcliffe Inn when the door of the detached garage began to rise, revealing the black SUV he'd seen Ethan drive.

The vehicle backed out, the garage door lowered, and Beckworth ducked low so his fedora-covered head could barely be seen. He lifted his head the barest of an inch and caught a glimpse of Ethan's profile as the SUV drove by.

He waited a few minutes, watched the vehicle turn the corner through the side-view mirror, then sat up. He checked the GPS and watched the blip move away as he noted the time. He glanced around, saw no one paying attention to him, and returned to reading the article on the Westcliffe, keeping an eye on the GPS.

The signal moved in the direction of the old inn, which didn't surprise him and, after twenty minutes, disappeared from the screen. He smiled. A twenty-minute warning that Ethan was returning gave him plenty of time. He parked the Cutlass a block away and hoped no one would notice. He strolled back to the McDowell house, his hat tugged low and his pace steady as he approached the front door.

He knocked and stood with his hands in his pockets as if he had every reason for being there. After a few minutes, he made a show of lifting the doormat, checking a potted plant as if searching for a key. Like he did this all the time. He scanned the neighborhood and, confirming all was quiet, walked along the side of the house where there were no neighbors to spy on him.

When he reached the back of the house, he stopped to stare at the large bank of windows. AJ had mentioned the windows in the article but it was quite another thing to see them. And then he understood why Ethan stayed here. If he were stuck in this century, this would be the house he'd want. He shook himself and tried the back door. It stuck for an instant before giving way after another nudge.

The soft ticking of a clock pierced the heavy silence. There was a special feeling to an empty house, an infinite emptiness that said no one was home, but he wandered from room to room anyway. Most of the rooms were empty of furniture, though freshly painted. Halfway through his walk of the house, he checked the GPS—nothing. He'd turned up the volume of the GPS so it would signal when the blip returned, though he wouldn't rely on the alarm alone.

He searched through Ethan's room, finding nothing of note. He stopped when he found the scuffed duffel, and when he lifted it to check underneath, a scent hit him that made him tear up. It lasted for a mere second. It wasn't a bad smell, and he couldn't completely place it, other than it smelled of home. His knees went weak and he dropped to the bed, waiting for the intense emotions to run their course. How much longer before he could return?

He stormed out of the bedroom to prowl the kitchen, stopping to stare at the espresso machine, not quite sure what to make of it. He checked the refrigerator, found several beers, considered them, but closed the door empty handed. When he made it to the living room, he screeched to a halt. The view was breathtaking. A single overstuffed chair was the only piece of furniture in the expansive room. He stepped to the windows, nose almost touching, and stared, first down the coast to his left, then back to the coast on his right. The waves crashed on rocks far below.

Now he appreciated the windows and why the sea captain had gone to all this expense. It was worth every shilling.

After a few moments he checked the GPS. No blip. He considered his options.

"The bloody hell with it."

He strode to the kitchen, grabbed a beer out of the fridge, then stopped at the collection of liquor bottles on the counter. The bottle of amber liquid appeared good enough, and he picked it up and kept walking. He dropped into the oversized chair, pleased by how comfortable it was, and stared at the view. If only the skies were charcoal gray, with wind whipping rain against the glass instead of its currently cheery blue color. It would better fit his mood.

He opened the scotch and swallowed a mouthful. "Thank the heavens he paid for the good stuff." He opened the beer and chased the burn in his throat. A soft belch escaped. "I beg your pardon, that was terribly rude."

Then he threw back his head, his laughter echoing through the empty room.

31

Professor Emory studied the men sitting across from him, his elbows resting on the expansive hand-carved wood desk. His steepled fingers tapped a beat against his chin in time with the ticking grandfather clock buried deep within the stacks of books. Cups of coffee hovered around the edges of the desk, having survived the trembling hands of Emory's assistant, Kayla. After passing around the cups, she'd set a thermos in the center of the desk and scurried off as fast as she could gracefully depart. She had given them one last timid glance over her shoulder before the curtains had dropped closed behind her.

No one seemed in a hurry to begin the conversation, but Ethan's jittering leg drew a curious glance from the professor. Finn also watched Ethan, but for an entirely different reason. Ethan's temperament had been slowly degrading. He hadn't been his charming self since his arrival. Finn had begun to see himself as more of a babysitter, making sure Ethan didn't snap anyone's head off. It was the least AJ expected of him.

The pleasantries and ticking clock seemed to be proving his point. Ethan gripped the arms of his chair so tightly, the fragile wood would certainly crack. He considered interrupting the professor's quiet reflection before Ethan did something regrettable.

The professor shifted in his seat, rubbed his hands together, and pushed back his coffee cup. His eyes flashed with curiosity. "So tell me, which of you are from the past?" Behind his thick glasses, his sharp gaze swung between Finn and Ethan. His serious perusal was offset by the edges of a smile.

When neither man spoke, and Adam maintained his silence, Emory nodded and almost squealed with glee. "I see. It's the both of you."

Finn snorted, though he understood why a history professor would be excited—two living specimens. "And you thought, sure, that all makes sense."

The professor shook his head. "If Adam had just blurted it out after one or two meetings, I would have thought him mad, but we'd moved past that when we researched the stones. Besides, whether I truly believe what I'm hearing is neither here nor there. I've seen the stone earrings, have read pieces of Lily Mayfield's journals, and have had many discussions with my friend in France. I'm a student of history who relies on facts, yet the study of ancient lore doesn't always lend itself to facts. So again, whether I believe anything to be true or not, I learned long ago not to cloud my judgment in regards to my research."

"So if we said we were from the stars, you would simply take notes and tell us what you know of space?" Ethan's harsh tone made Finn wince but the professor didn't seem bothered by it.

Emory chuckled. "If I were a scientist or astronomer, I would hope I'd still have an open mind. I think it would be better to say that while a source of information may seem questionable, I'll follow Sir Arthur Conan Doyle's example." He turned slightly and pointed to a sign posted above him, the words etched into a weathered placard.

When you have eliminated all which is impossible, then whatever remains, however improbable, must be the truth.

"I would have thought you'd lean more toward Occam's razor," Adam responded.

Emory raised a brow. "That with all things being equal, the simplest solution tends to be the right one?" He shrugged. "That philosophy removes the idea of the exceptional and the extraordinary. I live in the world of ancient cultures; to remove the exceptional would remove the mystery. Regardless of the facts as discovered, or the stories found in books, or the memories of participants ripped from their journals, no one can truly provide every nuance of the past." His eyes shifted to Finn and then Ethan. "Unless one has lived it."

Finn slid a glance to Ethan, who blinked back at him. It seemed neither of them knew who this Doyle person was, but they'd wait for Adam to explain later. A long afternoon could be spent debating both philosophies. Before he'd ever heard of the stones, he'd lived his life by Occam's razor, yet that had changed after his first trip through the fog.

Emory refilled his cup and held the thermos up to the men. Only Adam nodded, and after Emory poured the coffee and set the thermos down, he settled into his chair. "Before Mr. Hughes breaks the arms of my chair, which is almost as old as he is, let's discuss why you traveled all this way to see me."

Ethan released his grip on the chair but his focus on Emory never faltered.

"We were hoping to learn more about *The Book of Stones.*" Adam glanced at Finn, who nodded.

On their drive down, the men had agreed that Adam would take the lead with the professor since they had formed a relationship over the past few months. Finn and Ethan would assist when needed, but as Adam began their request, Finn kept an eye on Ethan. He understood the man's impatience, but antagonizing Emory would only close their most promising door.

Adam scooted to the edge of his seat, a sign he would be pacing the room before long. "There's some evidence that points to another book. One written by the sole Druid who tested the torc and supposedly traveled to the future. We were curious as to whether your friend might have run across something like that."

Ethan leaned forward, his voice gruff. "And if this Druid book hasn't been discovered, does *The Book of Stones* give any reference to it? Does it state where it might be or where this Druid ended up?"

Emory glanced at Finn, his tone lit with patient humor. "Is there anything you'd like to add to the list?"

Finn smiled. He understood why Adam stayed in touch with the professor, and if they got through this, perhaps they could all share stories. "I may have a request after we hear what your friend uncovers, but the only thing I ask now is that everything we discuss here remains confidential."

It was only a slight movement, a swift change of expression that came and went within a blink of an eye, but Finn had no doubt everyone had caught the shift in Emory.

The silence continued for several seconds and the sound of the clock seemed to grow louder. Emory sipped his coffee, then cleared his throat. "Here's what I'm willing to offer. New knowledge about the book would be difficult for me to forget. It's a well-known artifact that other students of history are examining. It would be impossible to not consider it in my research or speak of it in lectures, though my days as an orator are rare since I no longer teach. However, I do attend conferences. I can agree to not use the information as a general topic of conversation. However, if the discussion in scholarly circles touches on it, I will be compelled to share what I've learned from my friend."

Adam started to say something, but the professor raised a finger.

"Having said that, I would never share a confidentiality to make a point or win a favor. Speaking of the stones from knowledge gained through nonacademic resources wouldn't be prudent or well received. They would be considered stories best told around a campfire."

Finn laughed. AJ would love spending time with Emory. A whole day to wander through the stacks while sharing history with the professor. "That's a thin line, Professor. We're not doing you any favors."

"Ah, the trials of studying ancient history. You'd be surprised at the number of fences we walk."

"We are in a bit of a hurry for the information," Ethan interrupted. "How soon can this information be retrieved?" He wrapped his fingers around the armrest, then relaxed them when the professor frowned at the movement. If this had been Adam, he'd be pacing by now, but Finn believed that Ethan's energy coiled within him, and his frustration was reaching a dangerous level.

In the short time Finn had known him, Ethan had never become frayed in battle. Even when recovering from a sword wound and knowing AJ had been recaptured, he'd held his emotions in check. His current behavior set Finn on edge. He couldn't tell if Ethan was so smitten by Maire that any uncertainty made him crazy, as Finn understood from his own experience, or that Ethan believed Maire to be in more danger than previously admitted.

During the time AJ had been out of his reach in England and France, Finn had never truly worried about her life being in danger. She'd been kidnapped for her knowledge of the future. The only time she'd been in true mortal danger was when she'd infiltrated the monastery to rescue Maire and him. Otherwise, she was too valuable a resource.

In that vein, Maire was more important for her expertise with the book and the stones. That alone should be enough to keep her safe, albeit in captivity. To Ethan's point, neither of them knew the players this time. The duke was dead, and it appeared that Beckworth was hiding in this time period. Without knowing more, Finn couldn't tell if Ethan's deep fears were warranted. Either way, if the man didn't control his emotions, he might do something rash.

Adam scooted his chair closer to the desk. The sound of the legs dragged across the wood floor brought Finn back. He mentally cursed, realizing he'd missed Emory's response to Ethan.

"I know this is a subject that can't be rushed," Adam shot Ethan a furtive glance, "especially if your friend needs to perform further research, but we'd be grateful if he could focus on our request above any others. We could assist with a financial contribution to any research project your friend is involved in."

Finn thought the professor might take offense at the not-so-subtle incentive, but Emory's eyes twinkled. "The field of academic research is always willing to accept donations. So few understand the time commitment and costs of such endeavors. Let me contact him. His name is Gallagher, by the way." He pushed his glasses up and scribbled something on a notepad. "Your earlier questions regarding the book rekindled his interest, but I don't know his current schedule. I'll get back to you when I can, but even if he's available, what you ask will take some time." His stern gaze fell on Ethan. "You'll have to be patient."

32

Isaiah picked up the box of scraps from the dining room of the Westcliffe and almost escaped.

"Take these cans of varnish with you," Jackson mumbled as he bent over to run his hand along the floor trim.

Without a word, Isaiah turned to retrieve the empty cans of varnish, loading them on top of the scraps. He shook his head when he caught his grandfather's quick grin. Two could play that game, and he began whistling an old eighties tune Jackson didn't like. It was sure to stick in the old man's head for the next hour or two.

He jogged down the front steps and had just dropped the box into the back of his grandfather's truck when a quick stab of bright light partially blinded him. He raised his hand and, after blinking for several seconds, searched for the source.

The flash returned for a quick second. His first thought was of the sun reflecting off something. He waited, but it didn't return, and giving the whole episode a lift of a shoulder, he returned to the house. But the more he thought about it, the stranger it seemed.

Instead of heading back to the dining room, he turned right

toward the library. This was his favorite room of this old house. AJ and Finn had done it right. With shelves filled floor to ceiling with books, he could spend days in here lost in other worlds and other times. He ignored the books today and sidled up to the window, staying to one side so he couldn't be seen from outside.

He watched the tree line for several minutes, then caught another flash several yards from where he'd seen it the first time. Almost as if someone might be moving away. He could think of several objects that would catch a reflection, but nothing organic that would be in a stand of woods. And nothing that moved on its own. Maybe a bird carried a shiny treasure. Plausible, but not likely in his opinion.

As he walked back to the kitchen, he considered mentioning it to Finn and Ethan, but they'd been in foul moods since returning from Eugene. He simply nodded to Finn as he walked past the two men on the back deck and continued to the right, the least used part of the deck. It would have a great view of the tidal pools if the terrain and trees were better positioned. Following the path down toward the pools, he cut up through the side hill and ducked into the trees, circling back toward the front of the house.

He stopped for a moment and waited for the reflection. If someone was there, they'd either stopped or were already gone.

He felt a bit foolish, sneaking through the woods on someone else's property. He should have mentioned it to Finn, but if it turned out to be nothing, he'd feel even more ridiculous. His grandfather had told him stories about people breaking into summer coastal homes. Most criminals would wait until winter, when most of the houses were empty, but they held more valuables when occupied. There was one thing he couldn't tolerate and that was thievery.

Worst-case scenario was that he'd spend a few minutes walking in the woods. Something he hadn't done in years, and he made a mental note to hike more. His stealthy steps through the needle-and-twig-carpeted forest came from years of practice. Being the youngest of Jackson's grandchildren, he'd learned from an early age how to sneak up on conversations he wasn't meant to hear. He had gotten very good at it and relied on it to scare his nieces and nephews.

He slipped from tree to tree, pausing every few feet to study his surroundings and listen for unnatural sounds. Within ten minutes, he stopped near a thick Douglas fir and stared across the parking lot toward the inn. His position stood directly across from the front door, just a few feet to the left of his grandfather's truck. He glanced at the sun, took off his reflective sunglasses, and aimed them at the sun. The reflection hit the side of Jackson's truck.

Then he looked down at the base of the tree and grimaced as he shook his head.

The group of men stood around the depression in the tall grass.

Isaiah glanced at his grandfather, who in turn eyed Finn and Ethan. "I don't think this was deer."

Finn shook his head. "No."

"Someone you know?" Jackson's matter-of-fact tone, as usual, gave no insight into his thoughts.

Finn rubbed at his jaw and flicked a glance at Ethan, who barely nodded. "It's most likely an old friend."

Jackson scratched his jaw as if in sympathy with Finn, then ran a hand over the white fuzz on his head. "It seems to me a friend would have come to the door."

Finn sighed. "I'll need someone who can install security

cameras and sensors to cover the yard and as much of the trees as possible."

Ethan responded quickly. "I know someone."

Everyone swung their gazes to him. His smile was chilly when he responded, "Through one of Adam's clients. They'll be discreet."

Finn slapped Jackson on the back. "Let's call it a day and regroup on the deck." He held Jackson's intent gaze. "What do you say, all the iced tea you can drink?"

He waited for Jackson's response, figuring there was a fifty-fifty chance Jackson would just take off. A sane man would thank him but pass, then call the next day to say he couldn't continue working for him. A friend would tell him right now. Jackson was the kind of man to look another man in the eyes when canceling a contract, and he'd have every right to do so. Jackson wasn't stupid, he knew something was a little off at the inn.

So he was surprised when Jackson grunted and led the group back to the house. Finn watched them go, his shoulders relaxing as he released a long breath he hadn't known he was holding. Now came the hard part.

33

Beckworth's body shook, his face and armpits sticky with dried sweat. He parked the moped on the side of the driveway, the barest hint of relief registering when he noticed the sisters' cars were gone. Barreling into the house, he stormed down the hall to his room and locked the door behind him. He paced for several minutes before rushing to the guest bath to douse cold water over his head. He braced the sink with both hands, head hanging, water dripping from his hair as he sucked in deep breaths.

After several minutes, he dropped the wet towels on the floor and stalked to the sisters' stash of liquor. The scotch soothed rather than burned on its way down. He frowned as he tipped the glass a second time. The scotch was the reason for his trouble, but he savored the next swig as much as the first.

He was so stupid.

His days had become erratic, filled with more ups and downs than he could count, today being a perfect example. The discovery of the McDowell house had been a boon. He'd stared out the windows of Ethan's living room for well over an hour.

Once he'd gotten good and bored, and perhaps a bit tipsy, he'd decided to see what was happening at AJ's place.

What a colossal mess. He had no business running surveillance while groggy. Without thinking, he'd checked the time with his silver pocket watch rather than the phone. The second the sun's reflection had hit the man by the truck, Beckworth had moaned in disbelief. All his careful plans had hung on a precipice. When he'd fumbled the timepiece trying to get it back in his pocket, he'd sworn and ducked. The man had looked around and seen the reflection, and Beckworth had run.

He slammed a fist on the kitchen table and drained his glass. Deep in the cobwebs of his mind he knew better, but he shook off common sense and poured another. This time he sipped the drink as it was meant for.

What to do, what to do?

Murphy and Hughes wouldn't find anything behind the tree except for stomped grass, but they were smart. Hughes must have seen him on that knoll before he disappeared into the fog, and with AJ suspecting someone might be following her, it wouldn't take them long to put it all together.

He ran a hand through his hair. At least his hands had stopped shaking. He drained his glass, cleared the table, and strolled to the bath. The hot water soothed him, and he closed his eyes, content to soak while his mind sobered. Sometime later, after the bath had grown tepid, Beckworth laughed. The unexpected sound echoed through the tiny room, startling him. Then he laughed again at his still-drunken state, though not as muddled as he'd thought.

If Murphy and Hughes suspected he was watching them, the simplest recourse was to use that to his advantage. He wanted Ethan to notice the missing beer, wanted them all to know he was out there and had access everywhere—even their homes.

With all the players on the board, his focus returned to the Heart Stone. AJ remained the weak link, his source to the stone. Let them run in circles.

He would become a ghost.

34

"So let me get this straight." Jackson shifted in his seat and removed the unlit pipe from his mouth. "You recite some mumbo jumbo while touching this magic stone and presto, you're somewhere in the future?"

"This was a bad idea." Ethan paced along the deck, stopping every few minutes to grasp the railing tight enough to turn his knuckles white before continuing on.

Finn ignored Ethan and studied Jackson. He couldn't argue with Ethan; the best thing would have been to keep Jackson in the dark. But if Beckworth had been watching them, knew where they lived—the stakes had risen. He'd never forgive himself if something happened to the old man. Jackson had to make his own choice.

He didn't have to tell Jackson about time travel. Some other perilous tale, something more believable, could be invented, but he'd spent the last two years making up stories. He'd be damned if he'd deceive any more friends for the illusion of protecting them.

"Where did the stones come from?" Isaiah's brows scrunched in thought. "Who found them?"

Finn ran a hand through his hair. How many more times would he have to repeat this story before it was over? He slumped in his chair. "They weren't found, they were created."

"Who would do that?" Isaiah asked.

"Druids, from very long ago. There's an ancient book written by one such group that wanted to see into the future. If they could foretell the future of the crops, which marriages were viable, what wars to avoid, they could grow their flock."

"And their pockets," Ethan grumbled.

Isaiah's expression lit with understanding. "It always comes down to money and power." He drained the last of his beer, leaned back in his deck chair, and reached into the cooler to grab another. When he pulled one out, he offered it to Finn, who happily took it. Isaiah grabbed another one and screwed off the cap. After taking a long pull on the fresh bottle, he asked, "You said the stones were created. Do you know how?"

Ethan ended his pacing and reached into the cooler, sitting next to the young man. "The story goes that a group of Druids placed glass beads on a silver plate and spoke their incantations. Over several weeks, they tried to conjure something with no success. Then one evening, during their ritual, lightning struck their fire and hit the silver tray. The force of the lightning knocked them unconscious. When they woke, they found the beads and silver tray had melted together, forming a handful of stones."

Jackson grumbled around his pipe as he gazed out to sea.

"It sounds like an early form of alchemy." Isaiah scratched the beer label until it began to peel away from the bottle. "Alchemy is better known for trying to turn metals into gold but it can be traced to elixirs meant to extend life. It wouldn't be a leap to consider a sect like the Druids trying something like that."

"When did you learn about alchemy?" Jackson asked, his gaze focused on some point on the horizon.

Isaiah lifted a shoulder. "Some college course. Not really sure which one." He scowled at Jackson. "And young people do read."

"Huh." Jackson gave him a sidelong glance.

The men settled back in their chairs, each apparently lost in his own thoughts. Finn hoped their understanding of the world hadn't somehow become diminished. Everything had come out jumbled. Then questions had flown—how did they jump, why did they jump, who was this Beckworth fellow? That had been followed by generic questions about history, Napoleon, and war. But it had been disjointed to the point it had barely made sense to him. Ethan was right, this had been a bad idea. Maybe he should have waited for AJ.

"So your ship was the real deal." Jackson's words came out gravelly, and he spat over the railing. He shook his head and locked Finn with a disappointed expression. "You lied to me."

Finn stared at the old man, unsure whether he'd meant Finn had lied when they first met or at some point that day. When Finn's only response was a questioning look, Jackson shook his head.

"The gun ports. You had cannons on board, but you said they'd been removed."

Finn stared at Jackson for a few seconds, then his sly grin emerged, followed by a bark of laughter that startled Isaiah. He kept laughing until his eyes blurred. "Aye, I did indeed lie, but it was for your own good." His brogue was thick and he finished with another grin and a wink.

"I don't know whether to believe you, but for now, I'll play along while I let this notion of time travel settle for a bit. I can't see a reason why you'd create such a far-fetched story, but people do the craziest things. One thing though, I'll never forget that ship. It didn't look like any replica."

A sharp thud jerked everyone around.

Adam leaned against the french door, a hand grasping the doorframe, a brown bag at his feet. He rasped out, "You told them about the fog?"

35

AJ tossed her pen down and pushed back her hair. After leaving their meeting with Martha, Stella had suggested they work at her real estate office. For two hours they'd combed the internet, starting with Elizabeth Langdon, but were no further now than when they'd started. All they needed was one breadcrumb that might lead to another but AJ had to admit they were in over their heads.

"Maybe Professor Emory would have an idea," Stella suggested as she stretched, then rolled her shoulders. "This could take months." She sat up. "We could call the Baywood historical society. They must have some methods for tracing history."

AJ slumped in her chair. "It's a thought, but it would still take months and Ethan won't wait. He's already impatient. I doubt he'll last several days without blowing up."

Stella picked up her cell.

"Who are you calling?"

"Maybe Adam has an idea." She swiped at the phone and began scrolling. "Huh, he's been trying to reach me. He left a message."

AJ rolled her eyes. Stella and Adam had become so close, they almost talked daily. Pretty soon he'd call to gossip about who he'd seen at the grocery store. She shook her head at the thought, then frowned when she saw Stella's expression.

"What?"

"Adam said a client called about something they overheard in town. He's on his way to your place."

A whisper of a premonition shivered down her spine. "Let's go."

The parking lot at the inn gave the impression it was open for business. AJ had never seen the lot so full.

"Looks like the gang's all here." Stella pushed her sunglasses up her nose and bounced up the steps.

AJ trailed behind and dropped her purse in the entryway. She turned her head to listen, but there'd only be one place to find the gang.

She caught up to Stella after passing through the kitchen, bumping into her at the french doors. Stella had both arms braced on the doorframe, and AJ pushed her aside, already getting a glimpse out a window at what she'd find.

Five men hovered around a table littered with empty beer bottles, glasses of iced tea, and an open bottle of Jameson.

She glanced at Stella, who smirked and disappeared into the house.

Adam dominated the conversation, his arms flying around as if sharing fishing tales. Only one problem with that—Adam didn't fish. The men laughed. They appeared to still have their wits about them, though Jackson and Isaiah looked a bit glassy eyed.

Finn noticed her and beckoned with an outstretched arm. She worked her way around the chairs and eyed the men, some-what suspicious of their jovial nature. She sat on the arm of the Adirondack as Finn wrapped an arm around her waist.

Adam wiped his eyes. "I think I was flapping my arms, but I can't remember. There are probably a few seagulls that haven't forgotten the scene I made."

The men broke out in another round of laughter, and even Ethan had tears in his eyes. Her misgivings were momentarily suspended seeing Ethan free of his worries, at least for a short time.

She studied the men, wondering what story Adam could share they'd find equally funny. Stella had said Adam's message sounded serious, but whatever it was, it no longer seemed to bother him.

"I take it the meeting with Emory went well?" AJ's question held a light tone and her gaze landed on Jackson. He should be the stable one, and it appeared he was drinking iced tea, though he laughed heartier than the rest.

"Sorry, AJ, I was telling everyone about the fog when you all disappeared." Adam circled a finger around his temple, the universal sign for crazy person.

There was a gasp at the door, and everyone turned to see Stella holding a bottle of wine and two glasses, her face pale.

"What do you mean you told them about the fog?" AJ swung to Jackson and Isaiah first, and they nodded. She stood to stare down at Finn. "What have you told them?" Her voice was steady but she wanted to screech.

Finn grabbed her hand and pulled her back down to the armrest. "Easy, lass, we'll explain it all." He glanced up at Stella. "Come sit, Stella, before you fall over. Pour your wine. You have some catching up to do."

For the next twenty minutes, Finn caught the women up on the visit to Emory, the reflection Isaiah had seen, and the depressed grass.

AJ shivered. "Beckworth has been watching us?"

"It's our best guess," Ethan replied. "And it matches with Adam's story."

"What story?" Stella finally found her voice after sitting down and draining half a glass of wine.

"From the message I left you." Adam rubbed his hands together. "Did you put a pot of coffee on?"

Stella nodded.

"So I had to drop some papers off for a client to sign," Adam continued. "While we chatted, she mentioned overhearing my sister's name."

"Where?" Beads of sweat formed along AJ's spine, already prepared for the answer.

"Some antique shop. A man was asking the clerk if they knew you."

"When was this?" AJ glanced at Finn and Ethan, but they waited for Adam to answer.

"About a week ago. She forgot all about it until she saw me." Adam edged up in his chair. "Up to this point, I didn't think anything of it. You were building up your consulting business. When I asked what the man looked like, that's when I knew you had to hear this."

AJ closed her eyes for the briefest of moments. She knew this part, but it seemed worse hearing it from someone else.

"She said he was handsome, had short hair, but it was his British accent that caught her attention. He had an odd, formal way that he spoke, then he'd slip into a Cockney dialect. She'd spent a few years in England, so the diction caught her attention."

"As if he spoke Old English?" Ethan asked.

Adam nodded. "Precisely."

"Beckworth." It was a statement, not a question, and AJ boiled with anger. She didn't know if it was the same store or if he'd been dropping her name all over town. No. That didn't sound right. Most of the shops were her customers. They would have called her, but he must have visited more than one. She turned to Finn. "And this confirms who you think has been watching the house?"

He shrugged. "I can't imagine why anyone else would. Even if people know the inn is being restored, I doubt anyone would take a chance to set up surveillance to rob the place. There's too much activity with the construction and no assurance there would be anything of value to steal."

Ethan agreed. "It's too coincidental."

"How would he have found the house?" Stella asked. "It's not listed anywhere, other than county records, and he'd have to know the address before finding AJ's name on the records."

That quieted the group as they pondered her question.

"He has to be tracking you." Isaiah's comment was met with wide-eyed expressions from Stella and AJ but everyone else shook their heads.

"From what I'm hearing, you have a man from two hundred years ago trying to fit into this future world. It has to be taking him some time to figure everything out, assuming he hasn't gone stark mad." Jackson held his pipe, squinting out to sea. He shook his head. "Unless he's getting help from someone."

That brought the group to another sobering silence.

AJ rubbed her head. She wanted to crawl into bed, sleep for a couple of days, and wake up to find this insane nightmare over. The last three months had been the happiest of her life. Sure, she'd fretted over Finn, but didn't that happen in all relationships? Now it was all gone. Dread filled every corner of her thoughts, slipping in between the cracks of doubt, and grew, breaking the fissures open. If she didn't come to terms with the situation, they would rip her apart.

She stood to lean against the railing, quietly sucking in air so no one would notice the impending panic attack. *What would*

Maire do? She almost laughed. Maire would narrow her eyes and, with hands on hips, verbally kick her ass. All very civilized. AJ turned back to the group, thankful no one noticed her temporary sidetrack into crazy town.

"Let's assume Beckworth found someone to help him." Finn drummed his fingers on the armrest. "He's smart, but I agree with Jackson. Two hundred years is too long for him to have caught up in the three months he's been here." Finn's tone belied his concern. He stopped tapping intermittently to run his fingers along the grain of the chair. AJ knew that tell. He didn't do it often, but when he did, he wanted to rail. There was also the subtle tic in his jaw. He held everything in like a general not wanting his troops to see his apprehension.

"So how would we go about tracking someone?" Adam wasn't asking the group, he was talking to himself, his brow wrinkled in concentration.

Isaiah stood and paused at the french doors as Stella waltzed through with a tray of cups and a pot of coffee.

"It's going to be impossible to track anyone in a town of this size. We have nothing to go on." Stella set out cups and poured the coffee.

Ethan picked up a cup and settled his gaze on AJ. "Why don't you tell us about your trip to visit Martha? We could use something more positive."

She caught his quick glance at Finn and didn't like it. They wanted to take care of Beckworth on their own. While that would be the easiest, Beckworth had proved to be as slippery as he was smart. A trickster. He'd evaded their grasp before, something for which he was well suited.

Stella helped her recap their lunch with Martha, but nothing AJ shared could stop Ethan's growing frown and brooding expression. She gave him a wistful smile. "We tried an internet search on all the earlier keepers but nothing came up."

Adam shook his head. "The internet won't help for names that old, not unless they were famous for something."

"You would think the first keeper would have been a Ratliff if they'd been given the Heart Stone," Finn said.

"Maybe she was." Ethan leaned his head back and closed his eyes. "She might have been married."

"Possible. But I think it returns Ratliff to the list for a more thorough investigation." Finn scratched his jaw, and when no one disagreed, he stood. "Between the drink and the good discussion, I think we need time for the information to simmer. It's been a long day. Why don't we regroup tomorrow?"

Jackson stood and looked around. "Where did Isaiah go?"

36

Finn and AJ led the way to the front door, where they found their missing man. The porch swing creaked as it swayed back and forth with Isaiah, who stared out at the tall stand of trees growing gloomy with afternoon shade. He didn't look up until Jackson touched his arm.

He brought the swing to a stop and scratched at his knee, the soft scrape against his jeans mingling with the sound of chickadees. After a few seconds, he refocused on the group, a crease between his brows. "There's something you need to see."

Finn glanced at AJ and Ethan, who shared troubled expressions. Had it only been two days since he'd shared a day with AJ? Nothing but blue skies, their horses, and lunch with her in his arms. The insecurities in adapting to their new life had seemed petty. Maire gone without a trace, Beckworth in their time period and following them for some unknown reason, and a list of keepers that told them nothing. Everything hung on the professor's friend, thousands of miles and an ocean away. Now Isaiah had discovered something else. There wasn't enough Irish whiskey in the state to work through their problems.

He followed after everyone until they gathered around

Isaiah, who stood behind AJ's car. When Isaiah scanned the woods, the group mirrored his movements as if playing a game of Simon Says.

"Well, get on with it. My patience cup is overfilled at the moment." Jackson grumbled as he crossed his arms.

Isaiah pointed to Finn and then Ethan. "You'll both want to see this."

He knelt down and then twisted to lie on his back before shuffling his shoulders under the vehicle. Finn and Ethan knelt next to him, placing their hands on the ground to duck low enough to see what Isaiah had found.

"Damn," Ethan swore as he stood up.

"What? What's under there?" AJ's voice seemed to search for a middle ground between panic and anger.

"It's not a bomb, is it?" Stella's hand flew to her mouth. When she realized everyone was staring at her, she squeaked, "Sorry. Too many movies."

"It's a tracker." Adam, his hands stuffed in his pockets as he began to rock side to side, sounded sure of the answer.

Finn closed his eyes for a moment. Beckworth was smart, but how had he learned the technology in a mere three months?

"GPS. Pretty rudimentary but it gets the job done." Isaiah brushed off his pants. "That's not the only one." He turned to Ethan. "There's one on your car too."

"You've only been back a few days." AJ stood with hands on hips, her cheeks flushed to a lovely dark pink, but her brows knit as she scanned the forest. "He's been watching us for a while."

Finn had seen the look a dozen times. At one time, he'd been the cause of her angry rants. He was surprised she hadn't run to the house to grab her dagger and search the woods. Just in case.

"That's not all." Isaiah focused on the ground, seemingly unable to look at anyone. When his gaze flicked to Stella, Finn groaned.

Stella caught the glance. "What? Is there one on mine, too?" Her tone increased in hysteria, until Isaiah shook his head, and she blew out a breath. "Thank God."

"Not anymore," Isaiah admitted.

That got everyone's attention, and Adam and AJ both reached out to steady Stella.

"I can't swear to it," he continued. "But something has been rubbing against the frame, and based on the placement of the markings..." He shrugged and rubbed his tennis shoe along the graveled blacktop. "The GPS either fell off or he got the information he needed and moved it to another vehicle."

"Why does he need to know where I live?" The agitation returned and she held her head. "I need to sit down. I think there's some wine left." Then she leaned into AJ, who put an arm around her shoulder.

"Do you want me to remove them?" Isaiah asked.

"No," Finn stated flatly.

"What do you mean, no? That's how he found us. We need to get rid of them." Stella brushed off AJ's arm and placed her hands on her hips, imitating AJ's earlier stance.

It might have been the auburn hair flying about in the breeze, or the deeper shade of red on her face, but Finn was a little afraid of Stella right now. When he glanced at AJ to gauge her reaction, she smirked, and the tension released from his shoulders. She'd obviously seen Stella this angry before.

"The damage is done. He already knows where we are." Ethan agreed with Finn.

"But why my car?" Stella's question was a good one, but Finn would ponder that later.

"He probably knows we're onto him." Finn stared out at the forest while everyone turned quiet. They were missing something. Whatever it was, it hovered just out of sight, like Beckworth. What was he up to? He wouldn't have traveled to the future for mere revenge. From what he could remember, Beckworth had a clear distaste for time travel. Was it as simple as wanting the Heart Stone? What else was there? "For now, let's assume he doesn't know we found the trackers."

"Giving us a bit of an advantage." Ethan nodded.

Adam shook his head. "And putting AJ at risk."

Finn considered the risk and met AJ's gaze. Her fierce expression told him all he needed to know. "She's prepared. The trackers stay on for now."

Stella wrapped her arms around her waist. "I don't like this."

Adam stepped next to her and touched her elbow. "That's all right. I'll drive you home. We'll figure this out."

Stella nodded and let Adam guide her to his car. AJ followed and ducked her head through the side window to whisper something in Stella's ear, then she kissed her friend's cheek. She stood back and watched the car back up. Her frown disappeared when Stella yelled out the window, "Don't let anyone touch my car or there'll be hell to pay."

When they disappeared from sight, Finn turned to Jackson, who was climbing into his truck. "Are you coming back tomorrow?"

The old man stared up at him and after a few seconds shook his head. "We have a contract, son. You think after surviving a war, three sons, eight grandchildren, and two great-grandchildren to date I'm going to high-tail it because of this time-travel nonsense?" he mumbled as he repositioned himself in the truck. "But if any of this destroys the work we've completed on the house, repairs will cost you double."

Finn chuckled, more grateful than Jackson could know.

Ethan was the last to leave, and he gave AJ a swift hug. "I'll see you in the morning."

Finn caught the brief look of worry in his eyes that AJ couldn't see. It was gone when Ethan released her.

"Will you be okay?" AJ asked. "We can make up a place for you to sleep here."

"I could use some time to think. We have quite a lot to sort through."

She nodded and stepped back, but it was clear she wasn't happy with him running off to stew on his own. But he understood Ethan's need for quiet. Planning took time. It couldn't be rushed. Time to consider the details, search for the nuance in each piece of information, follow each trail, poking and prodding, testing which solution might fit.

He slapped Ethan on the shoulder as he opened the door to his Escalade. "Be here at seven if you can."

Ethan raised a brow. "So early?"

"AJ's training schedule has just been fast-tracked. We've begun bow training, but I think it's time to break out the pistols."

37

Adam peered out the window. He scanned the street and noted each vehicle, watching for anyone lurking behind fences or trees before he moved to the next room. After he worked his way around the house, confirming no one lurked in Stella's flower beds, he made his way to the kitchen.

He started the coffee, knowing the aroma would invade the house and stir its owner. He found the bagels and laid out plates and cups. Within minutes of finishing his first cup and another perusal of the front yard, feet shuffled down the hall.

Stella entered the kitchen with lids at half-mast and a scowl on her rosy face. A flowery caftan had been thrown over apple-green leggings and a long pink T-shirt. With her auburn hair pushed back, she resembled a large flower that had been caught in a windstorm.

He thought of how Madelyn looked each morning. She never left the bedroom without her ritual face wash and carefully combed hair. In the summer, she'd throw on a loose dress that couldn't hide the soft curves underneath. The kids would be waking up, still on their summer schedule. The local moms kept the kids on a weekly routine throughout the summer. Was it Madelyn's day to shepherd the kids to a picnic or a museum? He pictured her pushing the kids out the door and then crawling into bed for another hour of sleep. Then she'd make her way to the marketplace, eating a pastrami and rye at her favorite corner cafe while watching the tourists. Was she settling into a new routine? His gut clenched. He missed his family, and he was losing time he'd never recover.

"Why don't you just call her?" Stella returned the coffee mug he'd set on the counter for her and pulled down a larger one. She filled it to the brim before dropping into a chair across from him.

"I don't know what to say." He played with the edges of his napkin.

"Hello. Have you been doing okay? Do you have any more swords I can fall on?" Stella quipped as she grabbed the napkin from him and began folding it.

"I keep forgetting what a cheerful person you are in the mornings," he grumbled. "Her voice mail is overflowing with my apologies."

"That's the problem. She knows how sorry you are. You need to stop highlighting all the stupid things you've done and remind her of what she's missing."

He ran a hand through his hair and stared at his coffee cup. How did he go about doing that? Should he romance her? He may not be sleeping there, but he could still help around the house. His handyman skills weren't legendary, but he tackled most problems that saved them from calling an expert. He should mow the lawn.

Stella finished a swan and set it next to him. "She may still be pissed off at you, but a woman likes to know her man is thinking about her."

Adam grunted.

They sat in silence, finishing another cup of coffee while

Stella folded a second origami shape. Something troubled Stella but he knew better than to prod. Instead, he mentally listed ways to remind Madelyn of his awesomeness when he wasn't being such a doofus.

"AJ's going back, isn't she?" Stella stopped folding, setting down a partially formed creature that resembled a mangled bird.

The question surprised him, and at first he didn't understand. His stomach lurched. No one had mentioned leaving with Ethan, but AJ had been training with her dagger and a bow. The dagger made sense with this Beckworth guy on the loose. But why would she need to learn the bow? It only meant one thing.

His focus had been on Madelyn and work. Even with Ethan's unexpected arrival and the trip to see Emory, he hadn't fully engaged with the new flurry of activity. Between the few stories AJ had shared and his reading of her journal, he'd come to understand the strength of the friendships she'd built. She'd only known Maire a few short weeks, but their excursions had been emotionally and physically challenging. Maire had been her rock, her talisman.

Adam had never been to war or in any situation comparable to AJ's time travel. But he'd lived through his daughter's illness, one that had almost killed her. Then the unexpected loss of their father, and the tough few months supporting Mom. He remembered every single person who'd helped him through those dark days, and always would. He would drop everything to help them in turn. Wouldn't AJ feel the same pull, even centuries away? He swallowed a grim laugh.

He squeezed Stella's hand. "Yes. She's going back. All we can do is support her decision and do our part to ensure she returns. Just like last time."

Stella's hand was ice cold, and she wiped her eyes with the

free one. She stood and grabbed her mug of coffee before stumbling toward the living room.

Adam stared at the half-formed origami shape. He didn't remember her ever leaving one unfinished.

"Did you see this red car out here?" Stella yelled from the front of the house.

Adam's random thoughts vanished and, within seconds, he hunched next to Stella, peering through the blinds. "Where?"

Stella pointed to the left.

He spotted the vehicle across the street, a couple of houses down. "It wasn't there earlier. Did you see anyone get out? I can't tell if anyone is in it."

"No. It was just there. I recognize most of the cars on the street. It's a pretty tight neighborhood."

"Can you tell the model? It looks older."

They watched it for several minutes but nothing happened.

"This is driving me crazy. I can't live like this."

"And it's barely been a day."

"Funny."

"Beckworth isn't interested in you. I think he used you to find AJ."

"How do you figure that?"

He thought about it. He hadn't put it all together, but something about it sounded right. "Don't know yet."

"If you're trying to make me feel better, it's not working."

The silence returned while he struggled with what to do. He couldn't babysit Stella. He had a day job, and she'd chafe with him underfoot. Maybe his PI friend could tail her for a while. Though in his opinion, if the tracker was no longer on her car, Beckworth had lost interest. He'd found other prey.

"Don't take this the wrong way, Adam."

He tensed.

"Thank you for staying last night. I didn't realize how scared

I was, knowing some crazy guy was following me. I wouldn't have been able to sleep if you hadn't been here. I wanted you to know it meant a lot, you know, without it getting all weird."

"Well, now it's just weird."

She elbowed him in the ribs, and as he rubbed the spot, he concluded she'd be all right on her own.

"Hey, look." She nodded toward the street.

A tall man with dark hair and a trim beard jogged down the steps with a young girl and boy in tow, both carrying backpacks. A woman stood at the doorway and waved as they jumped into the red car.

"Just another ex-husband picking up the kids." As soon as he said the words, a tiny prickle ran up the back of his neck. That could be him in another few months. No. He shook his head. That would not be him.

Stella said something but he ignored her as he rushed to the spare bedroom and grabbed his overnight bag.

"I suppose you don't have a to-go cup?" he shouted as he raced to the kitchen.

Stella handed him a tall, covered mug. A swan sat on top.

He grinned. "You'll have to teach me how to make those things." He took a few steps, then turned and surprised them both with a kiss on her cheek. He laughed when she blushed while her eyes narrowed.

He put a hand up. "Don't worry. I won't make a habit of it."

Stella followed him to the front door. "Are you going to buy her flowers?"

"Better than that. A pastrami and rye."

"At nine o'clock in the morning?" were the last words he heard as he raced out the door.

38

The dagger sliced into the board a bare inch within the tight red circle. AJ beamed at a surprised Finn and Ethan. Two days earlier, Finn had modified the targets, reducing the size of the circles to improve her accuracy. She remembered mumbling something about being happy the blade stuck at all. After practicing three times a day since, the blade hit the board with each throw, striking within the smaller circles with an eighty percent success rate.

"You're slouching before your throws. Keep your back straight." Ethan picked up an arrow and faced a second target. "Try throwing from different positions. Run up to your mark and then throw. You won't always have the time to think about your aim." He drew the bowstring, waited, then turned toward her target and loosed the arrow. It struck within an inch of her blade. "It's all in the focus."

"Show off." AJ smirked.

"She's not going into combat." Finn pulled the arrow and dagger out of the board. "I'd prefer her focusing on hand-to-hand." He pointed the dagger at her. "And it isn't so you can engage someone. It's for self-defense only. You were lucky the first time with Beckworth. I want you prepared while I hope to God there won't be a next time."

AJ grabbed her dagger and slid it into the sheath strapped to her leg. She grabbed the bow from Ethan and the arrow from Finn. Standing in front of the target, her body twisted slightly to the right, she pointed the bow toward the ground, nocking the arrow in place. She raised it, relaxed her shoulders, and drew the bowstring. Her arm trembled under the pressure, but she held her ground. She released her breath and loosed the arrow. It sailed past the two targets, striking a board farther away, sticking just a few inches off-center.

Finn whistled, and AJ released the tension in the bow before handing it to Ethan. She smirked at another of his shocked expressions.

"How long have you been instructing her on the bow?" Ethan asked Finn.

"A few days. She does seem to have a knack for it."

"What did the two of you think I was doing down here so often? Playing in the pools, sunbathing in the nude?"

Finn laughed. "If I'd thought that, Jackson would have been working alone."

AJ blushed and dropped her head, digging her toe in the sand until Ethan stopped laughing.

Still chuckling, Ethan took the weapons from her. He returned the arrow to the quiver and leaned the bow against the rock that held their supplies. He picked up the flintlock he'd brought with him and handed it to AJ along with a bag of powder. "Let's see what you can do with this."

Ethan showed her how to pour the black powder into the muzzle, load the ball, ram it into place, then prime the flash pan. With each step, he relayed cautionary tales of all the things that could go wrong before handing her the loaded pistol.

"I'm not sure about this." AJ brought up the weapon, sighted down the barrel, then glanced toward the men. "I'll admit, this seems a bit more questionable."

Finn stood next to her. "That's because Ethan just scared the hell out you." He glowered at Ethan, who didn't appear the least apologetic.

"She needs to understand the dangers of powder. As helpful as it would be to take a modern arsenal, we can't carry enough ammunition. And if anything fell into the wrong hands..." He shook his head. "That's just as dangerous as the jumps."

"I get it," AJ grumbled before looking at Finn. "No problem, right?"

He ran a caressing hand over her hip before raising her arm, his chest resting against her back. He leaned down and whispered, "Keep your arms extended. You don't want your face close to the pan when it fires. It will give you about the same jolt as the Glock. As long as you don't use too much powder, you'll be fine. Accuracy will come with practice."

"We don't have enough powder for more than a couple more shots." AJ dropped her hand, then brought it back up, getting a feel for its weight. "I think I'm ready."

Finn stepped back while Ethan drew closer, both hovering around her. She closed her eyes, restoring the clarity from her solo practice earlier that morning. Finn and Ethan's presence destroyed her concentration but she couldn't argue the benefits of their instruction.

She focused on the sound of the waves, ignoring everything else as her mind cleared. When she opened her eyes, she waited for the adjustment to the sunshine, inhaled deeply, released the air in a slow and steady breath, then pulled the trigger. The sound was loud as her arm jerked, but she'd held the pistol firm until after the spark of ignition. Wood chips flew with the sound of her hitting her mark.

When she glanced at the men, they both grinned, and she laughed. She'd need to find more black powder.

F inn shifted the pillow before leaning back, tugging AJ closer as she pulled the blanket over them. They had gone their separate ways after weapons training. AJ had visited various antique stores, and he'd stained bookcases in the family room. After dinner in their bedroom, there had been wine, a warm fire, and the hot touch of skin on skin. They'd had little time to themselves since Ethan's arrival, and that wouldn't change until this new mission was over.

The sound of waves flowed through the open window, and when he closed his eyes, he felt the roll of his ship, the creaking of her wood. He'd always been able to sense the spirit of the water beneath him. Would she remain calm until they reached port, or would she rage and make them fight for landing? Each wave, each roll, every creak spoke to him, and for so many years the *Daphne Marie* had been the only woman he'd required. There were times he missed her—walking the deck, standing on her bow, climbing the sails.

AJ shifted, her body warm and supple next to his. With each movement she made, the ocean became colder and more distant. His past was just that. He had no desire to return to it, and only Maire's safety could make him step into the fog again. He'd never spoken his thoughts to AJ. He'd never thought he had to, that she would instinctively know there was no other place for him. Maybe she needed to hear the words.

"Did you take care of everything today?" Finn laced his fingers through hers.

"Gwen jumped at the chance to stay in touch with my clients."

"Even without knowing how long you'd be gone?"

AJ's nod scraped his chin. "She can call Stella if she gets in a jam."

She went still, and when she didn't continue, he asked, "Are you worried about Stella?"

"Huh?" Her hair brushed against his chest, the soft curls tickling his skin. "No. I know she'll worry, but she'll have Adam to lean on and keep her sane. I was thinking of Ethan. He spends too much time alone."

"He's doing the best he can. We need to leave him be."

"Maybe." She turned to sit up and face him. The light of the fire created a dusky halo behind her, and for a brief moment, he wished the world would go away. He wanted to leave the past behind, no matter how much it hurt. He felt an uncomfortable foreboding about stepping back through the mist.

"I'd like to practice more with the flintlock. I need to load faster."

He held his groan. She needed to protect herself, but her quickly improving skills didn't come with earned experience. It was one thing to protect oneself from a highwayman, but it was quite different when running into a skirmish with trained mercenaries. He shook his head. "Loading too fast is when mistakes happen. And you don't want to be stuck in the eighteen hundreds with that kind of injury."

She blanched. "I don't want to set any records. I'd just like to reload in five minutes rather than fifteen."

Finn laughed, his shoulders relaxing. He fingered the tip of her hair, gently tugging it. "I think we can accomplish that. But I don't know where to find more powder."

Her eyebrows lifted, a knowing grin on her lips. "Fortunately, I have a know-it-all brother. He claims the gun store over on McCovey carries it."

"Do I even want to know why he knows this?"

"Probably not. But if we pick it up tomorrow, we can put Ethan back to work."

He shook his head. "All the while you had another motive."

"Not at all." Her chin rose, her expression indignant, until she grinned. "I'd call it a two-for-one special."

Always the minx. It had drawn him to her from the very beginning on that first day at the dock. She had witnessed his ship appearing through the mist, and he'd kept her disoriented with his teasing to stop her myriad questions. It hadn't deterred her then any more than it did now.

"Tell me what has you worried." She picked up his hand, turning it over to run her fingers along the lines of his palm. Maire had done the same thing when they'd been children, and she'd read his palm like the Travellers had taught her.

"You mean besides not knowing what happened to my sister, or that I'm training you with dangerous weapons before returning to unknown danger?"

She closed his palm into a ball and cradled it between her hands. "Yeah. There's something else."

"I wish I knew his motive."

Her teeth bit at her lower lip. Lips he'd rather be kissing than having this discussion. He waited.

"You mean Beckworth."

"Why did he travel here? He's always hated the idea of time travel. I'm not sure he believed any of it until he met you. Any time the duke mentioned him taking a stone, Beckworth cringed. It's difficult to believe he willingly faced the fog."

"He might have changed his mind after the death of the duke."

"Perhaps." It didn't feel right. "But he doesn't have the torc or *The Book of Stones*."

"He obviously has one of the two missing stones."

He sighed and pulled her to him, nestling her in his arms. "There can only be one thing he's after."

"The Heart Stone."

"Aye. It still doesn't tell us whether he came here by happenstance, standing too close to the fog, or did he plan on being on that knoll when the mist took us? It's difficult to plan without knowing more. Without having something to hold over him."

"Why don't we find him and ask him?"

Finn shook his head. "It may come down to that. But we've interrogated him before. He won't be easy to crack, and he's a master at deception."

"He'd rather lie than tell us what we want to hear."

"Most definitely."

After a minute, AJ poked his chest. "Let's see what the professor digs up. If he doesn't give us anything, let's go after Beckworth. He might not tell us anything, but I bet we can figure out what scares him most. Is he happier here or does he want to go home?"

"You are a very intelligent woman, Miss Moore."

She pulled his head down to hers, their noses touching. "Why, yes I am, Captain Murphy." When her lips skimmed over his, the heat burst through him. He tried to ignore the question she posed for Beckworth. It was simple enough, and the answer might provide the needed prod. But he couldn't help wondering if the same question wasn't far from her mind when he caught her watching him. He remembered his earlier thought. He needed to tell her there was no other place he wanted to be.

Before he had time to say anything, her tongue licked the corner of his mouth, soft and delicate. Her kiss moved down his neck and all thought disappeared, leaving only the woman in his arms.

39

Ethan walked out the door of Security Masters with a satisfied smile on his face. He couldn't believe his luck. Larry had agreed to start his crew working the next day. The fat envelope Finn had given him to pass along proved that some things never changed, regardless of the century.

He checked his watch. Still early. He drove out to the Westcliffe anyway, but rather than turn down the drive to the inn, he drove a little farther and parked the SUV along the road. He found the path he had walked all those months ago when he had spied on Finn and the *Daphne Marie*. The path, still difficult to find, was being used by someone. Once he pushed past the ferns, the singular path showed its age, but with a practiced eye, Ethan spotted where the grass had been trampled on the edges. Not recently, but within the last couple of weeks if he had to guess.

It might have been Beckworth, but he didn't think so. The path ended at a point overlooking the bay at the inn. Only the edge of the inn's roof could be seen from where Ethan stood. If Beckworth had somehow found the trail, there would be little for him to see but an empty dock and a deep bay.

He sat on a boulder and waited for the salty air to ease the tightness in his chest. There were moments when he fought for every breath, having severely underestimated how difficult this journey would be. Telling Finn and AJ about Maire had nearly crushed him. Though he'd suspected trouble from Beckworth. Where else would he have disappeared to in the fog? But the waiting was the hardest of all.

He wanted to storm across England, tearing through every town and village. And that was why the earl had been happy to see him go. There was nothing he could do in England that Thomas, the commander of the earl's guard, wasn't already handling. Thomas and the earl had both agreed the best solution was jumping to the future to see if Ethan could find something from the past that could uncover what had been so cleverly hidden.

Good God, this could drive the sanest of men mad as hell.

A seagull flew by, landing several feet from him. It squawked and turned its head. Its black, soulless eyes drilled into him. The seagull screeched again before flying off, sweeping past him, close enough to touch. He remembered AJ telling him how she loved the gulls, how they had helped her through her toughest climbs, especially at the monastery.

The thought struck like lightning on a clear day. Even his skin prickled at the idea. How did no one think of that before? Although it would probably lead to nothing. He pulled out his cell phone and dialed the one number he'd programmed for himself. AJ had entered his other contacts.

He had barely reached the stand of trees when someone answered.

"Professor Emory? This is Ethan Hughes, Adam Moore's friend. I was wondering if you could do me a favor."

Ethan pulled into the dirt lot of the gun store. The wooden building, in need of paint and maybe a new roof, was a mile out of town on a narrow side road. Finn had said its location was to keep the shooting range away from neighborhoods. Through the open window of the SUV, he could hear the occasional pop of a firearm.

"I'm surprised AJ didn't want to see the gun shop." Ethan closed the door and glanced at Finn over the hood of the SUV before stretching his body from one side to the other. He should get out and walk more. Sitting and staring at the ocean for days on end was taking its toll in more ways than one.

"If you had promised the shop held dozens of antique firearms, she'd have pushed off her last business meeting before we jump." Finn jogged up the steps to the front door but looked back before opening it. "You seem in a better mood today."

He shrugged. "Just feeling hopeful."

"Something I should be aware of?"

Rather than risking a reply, Ethan pushed through the door in the hopes of closing the conversation before it started.

When Finn closed the door, he kept any lingering questions to himself.

The three men in the store glanced over when the door clicked shut. One man stood in front of the glassed-in, gun-filled counter. The other two hovered behind it, presumably employees or owners of the shop. Two of the men resumed their conversation while one of the assumed employees hobbled over to them.

He was a beefy man but not tall, with woolly gray hair sprouting from his head. One side of his shirt hung loose, the other still tucked inside baggy jeans. The front of his shirt suggested he'd eaten recently, perhaps something with mustard and ketchup. "What can I help you gentlemen with?" His gruff voice was pleasant enough, his eyes clear and curious.

"We need some black powder." Finn took the lead while Ethan hung back.

The two of them had an innate awareness of who should lead a particular conversation. It was a mutual understanding he'd built with Thomas after years of training and battle. With Finn, it had developed quickly, which was unusual for how little they'd worked together. Perhaps the eighteen months of their adversarial search for the stone had created more than simple distrust.

The older man crossed to another glass counter that ran along the opposite wall. "Don't get much call for it, but I think we still have a bottle or two."

He leaned over, grabbed the item in question, and placed it in front of them. "We sell one of these every month or so. Funny that we had someone just earlier this week buy one."

Finn shot Ethan a quick glance. *Beckworth?* It made sense.

"Really?" Finn responded. "We have a private group of flint-lock enthusiasts. I wonder if it was someone from our group."

The old man scratched his chin. "I hadn't heard about that. I know most of the clubs, private or public."

Finn smiled that lazy grin that charmed everyone and allowed a touch of his Irish accent to come through. "It's not really a local club. It's a group of mates from the valley and a wee bit farther south. We don't get together often."

The man nodded. "That explains it. He might have been your friend." He gave Finn a matching grin. "Even had an accent something like yours, but he didn't seem to know much about firearms. Didn't even know how to load the Browning Hi-Power he'd inherited, which is why I remember him buying the black powder. It seemed unusual."

"Sounds like your cousin, Teddy," Ethan confirmed.

Finn's smile broadened. "That it does." He leaned over the counter, confiding in the old man. "He really doesn't have a clue what he's about, but we're trying to teach him. Family and all."

The man laughed. "Well, he's a quick learner. He spent an hour with Pete on that Browning. Pete said he rarely missed the mark before he left."

"Grand. I knew he had it in him." Finn's smile never faded.

"We'll take both bottles of powder." Ethan turned to leave, letting Finn take care of the purchase. His hopeful mood had begun to sour.

40

"And you're positive it was Beckworth?" AJ shoved a fry in her mouth and picked up her crab po'boy.

Joe's was a local favorite and a regular meeting spot with Stella. AJ had spent so much time at Joe's, she knew when the place would be empty and when it would be impossible to find a seat. Today didn't disappoint. She'd arrived five minutes before Finn and Ethan to a pleasantly quiet restaurant. They would have two hours before the happy hour crowd arrived.

"Absolutely. I asked the guy a few more questions, hair color and height, just to confirm he was my cousin Teddy." Finn shot Ethan a grin. "Quick thinking on that."

Ethan shrugged. "Not compared to your secret flintlock club."

"Okay, before the two of you get started, fast thinking on both your parts." AJ licked the dripping tartar sauce off her fingers, then dipped another fry before stuffing it in her mouth. "So what's a Browning?" Ignoring the stares of both men, she sucked down iced tea before taking another bite.

"A high-capacity pistol. Modern." Finn sipped his beer and continued to stare. "Are you in a hurry to be somewhere?"

AJ glanced at Ethan then down at her meal. She knew what it must look like. If Stella were here, she'd think AJ was pregnant. Fortunately, she was more careful than that. "I don't know. I knew from the time Ethan arrived we'd be going back. But in truth, I didn't give it full consideration until I fired the flintlock yesterday." She shrugged. "Then after my final meeting to temporarily close my business, it all hit." She returned to her po'boy.

The men watched her for several seconds.

"All right. I'll bite. What does that have to do with cramming food like one of Finn's uncouth ship hands?"

She couldn't help but smile. Ethan's mixture of old and new diction made her want to pinch his cheeks. She sipped her tea to wash down the sandwich while the men waited patiently. "When I looked at the menu, all I could think was that it could be months before I eat here again. Then I began thinking about the food in your time, and well, let's be honest, there has definitely been improvement since then. I've already been planning out my menu of last meals."

Finn grimaced. "Not the words I would have used."

"Hardly." Ethan gulped his beer. "So where does this leave us besides Beckworth having two guns?"

"Same place. We just need to be more careful."

Ethan grunted, clearly not what he wanted to hear. She couldn't blame him. Beckworth was in the wind with no warning when he'd show again. She scanned the restaurant, and the closest customers were still several booths away. She pushed her plate aside and settled back in the cushioned booth, her hand resting on Finn's leg.

"Tell us about Maire." She caught the immediate hunching of Ethan's shoulders, but she wasn't going to let him off the hook. "I don't mean what she was studying or where she went. Tell us how she was doing. Did she take time to enjoy the people around her? Was she happy?"

She'd felt Finn tense at her questions. He wanted to know as desperately as she, but he'd never ask. Ethan wouldn't want to talk about it, but it would make him feel better, if she could find the right lever.

Ethan turned toward the window, a tic working in his jaw. He was going to refuse, and she rummaged for another approach, but Finn did it for her.

"We all miss her, but she's my blood. Whatever happens, I want to know how she lived after I left."

How she lived.

Finn's words echoed in Ethan's head. He'd heard similar words so often.

Maire had lain in his arms two months after Finn and AJ disappeared into the mist, the golden glow of the candlelight reflected in her light-blonde tresses. She had been curious about the future. "I miss them," she whispered. Then she turned teasing. "Tell me again how they'll live. Tell me about the future."

He told her a dozen times about the decades he'd visited in his chase for the Heart Stone. Then everything he remembered from AJ's timeline. Weeks later, Maire would ask all over again.

He ran a hand through his hair and glanced at his lunch companions. They would wait him out, both needing to hear something, anything that would bring them closer to Maire. He understood. It wasn't that he didn't want to talk of her, had stopped himself several times from saying her name. The tightening in his chest, the emptiness that hollowed out his insides whenever he thought of her. *What if they never found her?*

Ethan gulped down the rest of his beer and Finn signaled

the waitress for another round. They waited in silence for the beer to arrive, and Ethan sipped the fresh one before sitting back. He stared across the room, transported to that other time.

"As I mentioned the night I returned here, we stayed in France for a couple of months after you left. Without the pressure from the duke, Maire and Sebastian focused on *The Book of Stones*. They began from the beginning, reviewing their notes and correcting some of their earlier translations. Thomas, along with Thorn, Dodger, and the rest of the earl's men, helped rebuild the section of the monastery that had been destroyed by the cannon fire from the *Daphne Marie*."

Ethan glanced at AJ. She grinned with no apparent remorse for the orders she'd given Jamie that day to provide a well-needed distraction. Ethan smiled back. He wished he'd thought of it.

"Maire and Sebastian made fair progress until they came across a passage they couldn't agree on. After a day of haggling over the passage, I suggested they leave it and move on. If they read farther, they might find something that would help with the earlier passage.

"They agreed, but the only thing they found was another difficult passage. When Jamie finally returned, they'd read through the entire book but were left with dozens of passages they couldn't agree on. One of the passages included the incantation for the torc itself."

Finn grunted. "Should they even be doing that? Just knowing the book is still out there is bad enough, but if they found Maire's notes..." He shook his head, not finishing his thought.

He didn't need to. Ethan was quite aware how dangerous her notes would be if a more dubious person found them. He spun the coaster. His gaze became unfocused as it centered in the middle of the spinning circle. It drew him in, and suddenly he was back at the monastery.

"The days became rote. Maire, her nose stuffed in *The Book of Stones* all day, and Sebastian hovering around her, reviewing her translations. Some days they'd only complete a single page. It left everyone frustrated. I finally forced her to leave it for an evening in town.

"Jamie returned with a letter from the earl. The fragile peace between England and France had frayed. England was preparing ships for battle. Maire insisted she could weather the war at the monastery. Fortunately, Sebastian believed otherwise. The new caretaker of the monastery was on his way and they couldn't predict his reaction to a woman living at the monastery without a proper sponsor."

Ethan's laugh held a bitter note. "I believe it was Sebastian's constant nagging that made Maire see reason. It was clear she wouldn't listen to me."

Finn laughed, his tone lighter. "Oh, the stories I could share."

AJ's brows narrowed. "I don't think she'd listen to Sebastian any more than anyone else, unless it was specific to the book."

Ethan turned his pint. "You're right. I think she finally realized they'd reached a dead end. She mentioned the first Druid who was said to have transported through time and gone mad on his return. If you remember, there had been mention of another book, possibly written by him. For some reason, Maire believes the other Druids didn't forsake him as originally thought. She thinks the group hid the time-traveling Druid so he could write everything down without interference. They felt this event too important to leave to oral recitals. She believes the 'Druid book,' as she calls it, is related to *The Book of Stones*."

AJ sat up and rubbed her forehead.

"What is it?" Finn asked.

"Something Maire mentioned about another book." She shrugged and dipped a leftover fry. "It'll come to me."

Finn stole a fry from her plate. "I'm sure it will." He turned to Ethan. "What happened to Maire's notes?"

He paused and ran a hand over his face. "She left her journal with Sebastian. He would split it apart and scatter its sections within the lower floors of the monastery as he'd done with *The Book of Stones*. We removed the stones from the torc before Sebastian hid everything, with the exception of the stone he gave me."

"What about the incantations?" AJ asked.

Ethan smiled. "Maire and Sebastian refined the incantations, working them over and over for days until they were satisfied. If they hadn't completed that work, I don't think I'd have gotten here as directly as I did." He shivered at the thought of spending months finding the right year. "It's amazing the impact a missing or incorrect word has on the stones." He glanced at Finn. "It was lucky we got as close as we did when we first searched for the Heart Stone."

Finn visibly shuddered. "As if eighteen months weren't bad enough."

"Did Maire like Hereford? What did she think of the earl?" AJ sat up, elbows on the table, her chin resting in her hands, as if waiting for a tale of knights and beautiful ladies.

Ethan obliged her. "The earl kept her busy for weeks, guiding her around the estate, introducing her to dozens of people. It had been decades since a lady had lived there." He grinned at Finn. "You know your sister. With the earl's permission, she teamed up with Estelle, the housekeeper, and brought out tapestries and other furnishings the earl had locked away after his wife's death. Then she worked with the kitchen staff, adding to the herb garden. With all her tasks, she seemed to have forgotten about the stones. Then I took her to London."

He paused to consider his next words. The memory of their three months in London squeezed his heart to the point of bursting and his breath stuck in his throat. He closed his eyes and forced a smile. Days of staring at the ocean had done nothing to lessen the ache. His days in London with Maire were his own, and if they ended up being the only memories of her he'd have left, he'd selfishly keep them close to his heart.

"As you would expect, she was the darling of the season. But I'll leave the retelling of it to Maire. She'll do it better justice than me." He drained the rest of his beer. "When we returned to Hereford, Maire fell into a routine as if she were the lady of the estate. The earl allowed her a portion of the garden to grow a larger selection of medicinal herbs.

"One day she told me she'd heard of an apothecary in Peterstow that carried special herbs and seeds she couldn't get in Hereford. The timing was bad. The earl had to deliver more men to the war effort, leaving us to train younger men to add to the earl's guard. Maire chafed at being restricted from such a simple trip, though it would require an overnight stay in Peterstow. Disregarding my concerns, she cajoled the earl into sending her with a small contingent of newly trained men."

He stopped, unable to look at Finn or AJ. "You know the rest."

AJ grabbed his hand. "You are not to blame for this. You know that."

He stared at her, saw the pain in her eyes. When he glanced at Finn, his face was turned away, staring at something only he could see. "I'd give my own life this very minute if I could turn back the clock to go with her, regardless of her complaints. I'll never forgive myself for that single error in judgment."

No one said anything, the only sounds the distant clatter from the kitchen and the murmurs from other customers.

After a few minutes, AJ pushed at Finn to let her out of the booth. "I need to run to a shop just a couple of doors down. Why don't you finish your beers and take care of the bill?" She squeezed Ethan's shoulder and whispered, "Thank you." She kissed him on the cheek and was gone.

Ethan stared down at the two empty pints in front of them. "Did I say too much?" He shot Finn a worried glance.

Finn shook his head. "We're all missing her. She just needs some space."

The silence hung between them until the server dropped the bill and cleared the table.

Finn stood and gripped Ethan's shoulder. His eyes burned with defiance, and through his tight grip, Ethan felt the new rage Finn kept reined in. It was the first time since he'd returned that he thought Finn might punch him. It was the least he deserved. He was surprised by Finn's words when they finally came.

"You are not to blame for Maire's disappearance any more than I was when Beckworth kidnapped her." Finn released his grip for a second before tightening down again. "We will find her."

Ethan stood, forcing Finn to step back. "The training helps but I'd feel better if I could hit something."

Finn's lazy grin gave Ethan a chill. "Let's find Beckworth."

41

AJ slammed through the doors of Joe's and raced to the nearest lamppost, gulping in deep breaths. She'd rather hyperventilate than give in to the tears. The more Ethan spoke of Maire, the more she'd felt the woman's presence. She pictured Maire, plain as day, sitting next to Ethan, rolling her eyes at Ethan's vagueness as he replayed the events of her life. Maire dipped her own fries in ketchup, relishing the tastes of the new century. Had Ethan's stories whipped up the lifelike apparition, or was she traveling down crazy town highway all on her own, the specter a happy side effect?

She lifted her face to soak in the heat of the sun and burn away her fear. If they jumped and found someone had hurt Maire, it would break her. She wouldn't have the strength to save Ethan from himself. And Finn? It would take months, if not years, for him to recover from the guilt. The reality of the situation had slammed into her halfway through Ethan's story. Maire was a bewitching thread who had woven them into her tapestry. She was an irreplaceable part of them.

A terrible foreboding seeped into her and the heat of the bright summer day couldn't stop the ice penetrating her bones.

She couldn't shake the feeling that regardless of the care they took in planning their mission, there was something at play they wouldn't see coming. She was reminded of her time at Waverly when she had seen the inlaid chess set in the library. The bishop. Some other player hovered in the shadows, unpredictable and out of reach. Someone new pulled the strings.

She stumbled away from the light post. The smell of the candle shop next door seeped in, the overpowering aroma shaking her back to the present. Rather than avoiding the store, the idea of sensory overload drew her in. Besides, she was supposed to be shopping. She reached for the cell in her purse to text Finn where to find her. When she glanced up—she froze.

Beckworth.

No more than fifteen feet in front of her. He faced her, just another tourist out for a stroll. He appeared as shocked as she was. Time slowed like in a movie, the two of them cocooned in their own bubble while everyone else moved around them. He was a handsome man, beautiful really. A tan sports coat fit snuggly over a long-sleeved turquoise T-shirt that matched his eyes and, in combination with the tight-fitting jeans, showed off his wiry build. In the moment, without his scowl, and disregarding what she knew of him, she understood how he charmed everyone. The wit and the humor he'd demonstrated at his dinner parties might entice her.

Almost.

She snapped out of her stupor, his presence a more powerful jolt than any candle shop. She would have laughed if he didn't terrify her. It was one thing to chase someone who didn't want to be seen, quite another to come face to face with him.

He straightened and tilted his head in a slight bow. With a tug at his sleeves, his smile seemed to mock. "Miss Moore."

Just like that. As if everything that had happened between them had been nothing more than a summer adventure.

"Beckworth." It came out as the sneer she'd intended. She resumed her search, her hand sifting through the purse for an entirely different object.

He put his hands up. "I only want to talk."

"Right. That's why you've been following me and then running." Her hands slipped around the handle of the dagger and she pulled it partway out so he could see it.

"I wasn't sure how to approach you." He nodded toward her purse and absently scratched at his shoulder. "It seems I had a good reason to be concerned."

AJ wasn't sure what to do. She couldn't pull a weapon out in public. He didn't look armed, giving her an unfair advantage. That thought didn't bother her in the slightest, but the chance of dozens of cell phones snapping photos of their altercation stilled her hand. Finn and Ethan would be here soon, if she could keep him talking. Like he wanted to.

"I don't know what game you're playing..." she said.

"I only want to talk. Like I said." He took a step back.

When he stepped back again, she thought he was going to run for it. By the time she stepped forward again, she realized she'd been the first to advance. He was trying to maintain some distance between them, his gaze sliding to her hand and the dagger. Then his expression changed, an almost wistful look before he turned and ran.

Too stunned to move, she stood rooted to the spot. Several seconds later Finn and Ethan dashed past her, and though they were fast, she wasn't sure it would be enough. After a moment of hesitation, she shoved the dagger in her purse and gave chase.

42

They had been out the door of Joe's for less than a minute when Finn spotted Beckworth. He grabbed Ethan's arm and pointed. AJ faced Beckworth, and he couldn't be sure, but she appeared to be holding her purse in front of her. Was her dagger close?

"Beckworth," Ethan whispered.

The chase was on. Finn took the early lead, dodging people and yelling shouts of apologies along the way. Ethan's footsteps sounded loud in his head, mere steps behind him. He passed AJ, not even glancing her way, not wanting to lose a single moment.

Beckworth darted through the crowd, moving fast, nothing more than a shadow. *How did he learn to do that?* It explained why AJ had been unable to keep up with him. There was only one other man he'd ever known capable of blending this easily into a crowd—Thorn.

Thirty feet ahead, a large crowd had formed. Teens, all wearing matching green T-shirts, milled about. His optimism rose. The group formed a solid barrier that was sure to slow Beckworth down.

Beckworth became visible again as he reached the unsuspecting and oblivious kids.

Finn gathered more speed. He had a chance but he'd have to be careful. The last thing he wanted was to hurt the teens by knocking into them. Only half a block away. Ethan's pounding footsteps close.

Beckworth reached the group. Finn expected him to stop or turn.

He didn't.

Beckworth rotated and made a pirouette, molding himself against the first teen—a geeky boy, all arms and legs, and as it turned out, uncoordinated. The boy fell back against his friends, leaving a gap wide enough for Beckworth to slip through.

It happened so quickly, Finn thought he imagined it. Beckworth had barely slowed. The scoundrel had canvassed the crowd, identified the weakest link and pushed through without hesitation.

Finn prepared to race through the same weak point. The poor boy appeared shaken and confused, and he hated to do it. The kid was still the weakest link. The group turned to watch Beckworth. No one saw him coming.

Finn sliced through the teens without missing a step. But Beckworth had gained ground, turning right almost a block ahead. Finn pumped harder, his legs burning. It had been too long since he'd run this hard and this fast. As he reached the corner where Beckworth had turned, he realized he no longer heard Ethan behind him.

He pushed it aside and spotted Beckworth turning left down another street. Only one thought blasted through his head as he kept running.

Don't lose him.

Once he passed AJ, Ethan paced Finn by mere inches. Their prey moved seamlessly through the crowds. He immediately recognized the signs of someone schooled in the art of grab and dash. A street kid. Just as he had been. Beckworth wasn't the highborn noble he pretended to be.

When Ethan spied the large group of kids, all matching in bright green shirts, he slowed to let Finn pull ahead. Beckworth wouldn't stay on this street. Which way would he turn?

Beckworth made his move through the crowd of kids, and if Ethan had any breath, he'd whistle. It was a solid move. Finn would be able to use the opening Beckworth made, but Ethan might not be so lucky.

Then Beckworth steered for the right. His first mistake. He assumed Finn would falter through the crowd, and he got sloppy, revealing his intentions.

Ethan knew better. Trick of the streets—don't let anyone guess your next move. Beckworth should have stayed straight until the last possible moment. And that's what Ethan did just before reaching the block of teens, turning seamlessly to the right.

He didn't know this part of town, but he didn't need to. Beckworth would keep running. His next turn would be a left and most likely another right. Ethan flew by the first street and ran for the second. There was little traffic on the next street, and he ran down the middle of the road, ignoring the gawkers. He'd noticed the attention he was getting and kept an eye out for police. That was the last thing they needed.

When he reached the next street, he passed by without slowing. It might be a mistake. He'd have to hope Finn was still in the chase. He turned left at the second street and pushed for all he was worth.

He ran—one block, then another. He spared only a glimpse

down the side streets. Then from the left, half a block ahead of him, Beckworth turned onto the street. He never glanced Ethan's way.

When Ethan passed the street where Beckworth had come from, he spotted Finn running hard but not fast enough.

He understood. His lungs burned, his legs felt like thick tree trunks struggling through mud. But Beckworth was within reach. He was gaining on him. The knowledge created a burst of adrenaline and his chest burned as he reached out.

---

ootsteps echoed in Beckworth's ears. They'd been receding with each block. Now the footsteps were closer and different. It must be Hughes. They'd split up. Damn his luck. He ran for another block, his mind racing for what to do next. He didn't have much more left. The stitch in his side had started two blocks ago. He'd have to stop, but he wasn't ready to give in.

Scanning ahead, he noticed movement through the glass windows of a building. A group of small children were being led toward the door to the street. Beckworth steered for them, the heavy steps right behind him. He could almost feel the hot breath of Hughes on his neck.

He pushed through the agony, his chest in flames, struggling for each breath. When he was just past the door where the kids were, he stopped and turned.

The move startled Hughes as he'd hoped. Hughes stopped short and scanned the area.

They both wheezed as they struggled for their next breaths. In the distance, Murphy closed but had also slowed, seemingly unsure of the game he played.

As he should be. He had no choice.

Beckworth might not have been in this time period for long, but he'd seen on television what cell phones could do. If the men grabbed him on the street, there would be witnesses. Questions.

Murphy would find some other way to thwart him, so he couldn't play this game for long. He only needed a few minutes.

"Hughes. Thought I left you behind in France." Beckworth's words came out in huffed breaths, and he grabbed his hip, ignoring the painful cramp.

Hughes grinned. Not the same effect as Murphy's evil smirk but close enough. "I thought I'd see what I might be missing."

"Just doing a little shopping." Beckworth waved at the buildings around them, though they'd run far from the tourist district.

"What are you really doing here?"

Murphy closed in, scanning the area, probably checking for witnesses and possibly the guards.

Beckworth didn't bother answering. The doors to his left opened and a dozen blabbering children spilled onto the sidewalk, like baby spiders escaping the nest.

Murphy stopped next to Hughes, both men unable to do anything but stare at the children. Two women and a man followed the children, yelling commands.

"Don't go in the street."

"Stay with your buddy."

Beckworth threw back his head and laughed. The sounds of the children and adults drowned out whatever Murphy was saying. Hughes and Murphy stepped toward him, still behind the kids, and he reached into his jacket pocket. The men stopped.

Would they think he had a weapon? They couldn't be sure. The two men glanced at each other and then at the kids.

Beckworth took a step backward and then another. His

fingers wrapped around the Browning. He knew better than to use it, but did Murphy and Hughes know that? They remained motionless. Beckworth raised his arm as far as the jacket would allow, the gun still in the pocket but aimed toward the children.

A small alley to his left opened to a street on the far side of the building. His luck continued to improve. As if the gods themselves had looked down on him, a bright yellow van pulled in front of the building, and the children jumped up and down in anticipation. Their ride had arrived. They'd probably been promised ice cream or some other tempting treat.

Without another thought, while Murphy and Hughes gazed on, unable to do anything, Beckworth turned and ran.

Several minutes later, as children were being loaded into a van, AJ caught up to Finn and Ethan. The men squatted next to a building. She leaned next to them, her breaths as hard and rasping as the men's had been.

"Where the hell did he learn to run through the crowds like that?" Finn grumbled as he wiped the sweat from his brow.

"The streets. He must have grown up on them. Probably a thief. Either working for someone or maybe just trying to eat." Ethan peered up at AJ. "I don't imagine you brought the car?"

She tried a smile through her ragged breaths. "Sorry. I just ran without thinking."

"Now we know why we never found him at the monastery after the final raid." Finn stood and rubbed his legs.

"Or in town after AJ stabbed him." Ethan glanced up at Finn. "You're getting slow with your easy living."

"Aye. And that changes, starting now." Finn gazed down the street, the children and van now gone. "I've focused on AJ's training and forgotten my own."

"And not much time left for it." Ethan stood and stretched his arms, his gaze tracking to where she'd been in time to see Beckworth turn.

"We'll start this evening." Finn put his arm around AJ. "Runs twice a day, morning and evening. Sword training for us while AJ works on her dagger and bow."

"I'll climb in the mornings, run with you in the evenings," AJ joined in. "I don't want to leave before Mom's party. That gives us a few more days."

"We might not have caught him, but we've learned a valuable lesson," Ethan said.

"What was he doing here in the first place?" Finn asked.

AJ shook her head and rubbed at the stitch in her side. "At first, I thought he might have been surprised to see me, but he must have been tracking me again."

"It doesn't matter. We had him and we lost him. Another dead end." Ethan's tone dripped with bitterness, and he strode off in the direction of the tourist district.

She understood. But her adrenaline pumped, keeping her mind on the chase. She was overlooking something important. Something she'd forgotten in the excitement of the chase. It seemed important, but if it was the key they'd been looking for, it was beyond her reach. Ethan was right. Until the elusive nugget of information presented itself, they were back to square one.

43

Beckworth ran for another ten minutes, randomly turning right then left, right then left, his path leading him away from the center of town. Hughes had surprised him. He'd either worked the streets of London as a guard or had been a street urchin himself. Not many could have anticipated his moves. If Beckworth had known these streets better, there would have been dozens of streets, back alleys, and buildings he could have ducked through.

The children had been a miracle.

He found an empty alley stinking of rotting food and urine. All these centuries later and alleys never changed. He found a spot behind a trash bin and slid down behind it. He didn't think Murphy had continued the chase, but he needed to rest and didn't want to take chances. He would wait an hour, maybe two, before working his way back to the moped.

When he'd woken that morning, his day had been unplanned. The sisters had bickered at breakfast. His usual annoyance with them temporarily abating, he'd been grateful for the time to think through his options without interference from their endless questions. Did he remember anything else?

Did he know AJ's last name? Or maybe where she lived. Blah. Blah. Time was running out with them, but his next step evaded him.

With no other reason than to get out of the house, he'd driven the moped to town. He'd sat on a bench for most of the morning, watching people come and go. He'd brought the GPS tracker as an afterthought and checked it every hour. Nothing. The batteries on the units could be dead but it was more likely no one was in town.

He considered driving out to the inn but after his close call with the reflection, he decided to give it another day or two before returning. This time, he'd wait for the cover of darkness.

When he checked the GPS again and noticed the blip, it startled him. He followed it to AJ's car, studied it, and then scanned the area. After considering his options, a thought occurred to him. He walked the streets, checking the stores to see if he could spot her. If he could just talk to her, explain the situation, maybe she could help him. He snorted. That was too much to ask for, but an attempt at negotiation might distract her enough to give him time. He needed inside the inn. He had to find the Heart Stone.

Then AJ walked out of the restaurant. She was clearly as surprised as he was. And what was the first thing she did when he said he wanted to talk? She reached for her dagger. He smiled. She was predictable if nothing else. He'd find a way for that to work to his advantage.

He picked himself up and wiped off his pants before starting his long trek back. His first goal would be the Heart Stone. If that didn't work, he'd focus on the one person that could get it for him.

Miss AJ Moore.

44

AJ fell into the rattan chair, grateful for the shade of the front porch. The table that separated Ethan on her left from Isaiah on her right held a sweating pitcher of iced tea. She wanted a glass but couldn't seem to move. The walk up from the tidal pools had zapped her energy. There wasn't a bone or muscle in her body that didn't ache.

Isaiah poured a fresh glass and handed it to her.

"Thank you." AJ sighed as she gulped the first swallow.

"It didn't look like you'd be able to lift the pitcher." Isaiah chuckled. "I think Ethan is training you too hard. I heard you're running three miles a day?"

"He hasn't heard of the science that says you should give your muscles a day of rest." She held on to the glass, unwilling to move the fraction it took to set it on the table. They needed a sauna or a hot tub. Maybe both.

Ethan grunted. "Just a marketing scheme to let you off easy. You'll feel better after another couple of days." He returned to staring at the woods.

A man climbed down a ladder just inside the tree line.

Another man returned tools to a white van parked just off the lot.

"Weren't they supposed to be done yesterday?" AJ asked.

"Finn added a few more items." Ethan leaned back and grimaced when he stretched out his legs.

"That's not a sign of sore muscles, is it?" AJ mocked.

"I've just been sitting too long," he grumbled.

Isaiah laughed. "All of five minutes." He ignored Ethan's glare. "Seriously, he's been working with the security people confirming camera placements and learning the software setup. I don't know where he found these guys but this is pretty high-tech stuff."

AJ smiled, thankful for Ethan's ingenuity. If she'd learned anything while being in old England, she'd learned to surround herself with men who knew their business, took it seriously, and planned for every contingency.

When she glanced at Ethan, he pointed up to where the front porch beam met the roof.

She squinted, running her gaze over the ceiling until she found a small circle a bare inch from the beam. She laughed. "Point taken. I think that's the smallest camera I've ever seen."

"Certainly for most residential properties." Isaiah flipped through what looked like a user's manual.

"Where's the monitor?" AJ asked.

"It's all web based. I left the other paperwork in the kitchen," Ethan said.

"You can add their app to your cell. Whenever you leave the house, the security system will alert your phone if anyone comes to the front door." Isaiah's expression lit with enthusiasm.

She glanced at Ethan and he grinned.

"It seems our young Isaiah is a technology guru. Is that what you call it?" Ethan asked.

Isaiah laughed with AJ. "Close enough."

The front door opened and Jackson stuck his head out. "If the three of you are done taking a break, do you think you could come in and help those of us still working?"

Jackson left the door open as he disappeared inside, and Isaiah jumped up to follow.

"Even with all this equipment, I don't think I'll feel safe until Beckworth is locked up or at the bottom of the sea." AJ, feeling restored, refilled their glasses and grabbed a handful of grapes from a tray.

"Either way, it will be finished in a few days."

"What do you mean?"

Ethan shrugged. "We're going back, with or without the information I hoped to find. Beckworth will be left behind. He's not our main concern."

"But he'll still be here when we return."

"Maybe, or he'll give up whatever scheme he's planning and find peace. Either way, Finn will take care of it."

Which meant she'd get her wish and his bones would rest on the floor of the bay.

The door opened and Finn strode out, dropping into the seat Isaiah had vacated.

"Adam called."

Ethan and AJ sat up, speaking over each other until Finn held his hand up.

"Emory has something for us. He asked to meet with us tomorrow."

Ethan glanced at AJ. "Looks like you'll get that day of rest after all.

45

Beckworth had woken early and eaten quickly, then lied to the sisters about attending an event miles north of Baywood. They had stopped questioning where he went after he'd admitted to regaining some of his lost memory. He hadn't given them any additional information on the topic, regardless of how often they asked. Somehow, Louise and Edith had gotten it in their heads that his current adventures involved tracking down his lost fiancée. He had a laugh at that. In a way, he was.

He'd planned on returning to the inn later that evening, but he couldn't wait. If Murphy had discovered his observation spot, there'd be some trap waiting. Time to change tactics. There were other vantage points to observe the comings and goings of Murphy and Moore.

The moped slowed as he approached the inn. Sticking with his new plan, he hid the motorbike ten yards from the driveway. He checked the GPS monitor. Two blips. Ethan had arrived early. He stuffed the monitor in his backpack and ducked through the trees toward the house. When he reached the drive-way, he crouched and ran along it for several feet before stopping to scan the area. The low hum of a vehicle forced him back to the trees.

He caught a glimpse of a silver car and its driver as it passed his hiding spot. It was the same man he'd seen with the ginger-haired Caldway woman. Once the vehicle passed, Beckworth sprinted across the drive, skirting the edge of the tree line. He arrived at the lot as the man and Caldway stepped out of the car.

He scanned the area and found a new hideout far left of his original scouting position. Giant ferns grew around the base of the trees and he nestled inside one. While he lost some visibility toward the other side of the house, he had a better view of the dining room window where he'd previously spotted Murphy. Satisfied, he reached into his backpack, pulled out a thermos, poured a cup of coffee, and waited.

An hour later, the front door opened and several people walked out, including the Caldway woman and the driver. A few chatted, but Murphy and Hughes were quiet, both jumping into Hughes's vehicle without a word to anyone else. AJ spoke with the other two, and after a minute, she climbed into the SUV with Murphy. Caldway and the mystery man returned to their car. Two minutes later, both vehicles left.

Where were they going so early in the day? More importantly, how long would they be gone?

Beckworth shook his head and smiled. Damn if his instincts weren't right on the money. He leaned his head against the tree, sipped his coffee, and waited.

46

The musty smell greeted AJ as she stepped into Antiques & Lore. Her shoulders eased from the long, silent drive and the muscles along her back relaxed. She hadn't realized how uncomfortable the ride had been with neither Finn nor Ethan speaking the entire hour.

She couldn't take her eyes off the stacks and disappeared down the long rows while they waited for the other car. Adam and Stella were late. Stella texted and grudgingly admitted to forcing Adam to stop for coffee. AJ doubted it had required much cajoling. Adam was more of a coffee snob than her and Stella combined.

Twenty minutes later, Finn found her deep in the back of the store and dragged her back to the professor's inner sanctum. She couldn't blame him. She stopped at each bookcase on the walk back, occasionally reaching out, forcing Finn to tug her along.

Once they reached the professor's ornate mahogany desk, she swiped her chin in case she might be drooling. She dropped into a squat and ran her hands over the carved legs. Each leg was divided into four sections of intricate designs—people, animals, and objects, some recognizable, others not as obvious. She inspected the carvings, then moved to the next corner, tracing a finger over an image, unable to discern where the desk originated.

She was still focused on a pair of ravens when the rattle of china announced someone approaching from the back of the store.

Stella, already one step ahead of Emory, cleared an area for the tea service, which earned a gracious smile and nod from the professor. He paused for only a moment when he stepped around AJ, who was still perusing his desk.

"You must be AJ. Did you see this side, my dear? There's a particularly excellent reproduction of Odin I think you'll like."

"Ah, Norse mythology. It was one of my guesses. It's nice to finally meet you." AJ glanced up, but after a quick wave, she returned to searching for where she'd seen the Odin figure.

Emory chuckled and turned to the rest of the group. "Make yourselves at home. I'll be right back with some biscuits."

Stella worked her way around AJ as she set out the cups and poured the tea.

"AJ, please take a seat," Finn chided.

She ignored him. It was one thing to yank her away from the extensive collection of rare books but quite another to fuss over her appreciation for an amazing work of art posing as a desk. He'd become as moody as Ethan since Emory called. They were all anxious to hear what Emory had found, but they could wait five minutes. The tension had built as they approached Eugene, the air so thick with it, the men's worry so palpable, she'd arrived with stiff shoulders and a headache. Her new love affair with the desk had removed the remnants of her anxiety, and she wouldn't relinquish the calming effect until the last possible moment.

Emory returned with the biscuits as Stella finished handing

out the cups. The group quieted taking their lead from Finn and Ethan, who lived in their silent world. The two men sprawled as if this was all some tedious chore, but a quick glance confirmed the tic along Finn's jaw and Ethan's brooding brows. Underneath their calm exteriors, they were as lethal as lounging leopards. AJ hoped Emory had information to share or this would be a difficult afternoon.

The professor leaned back in his chair, fingers steepled in front of him as he studied each person. After several seconds of lingering silence, a slow smile flickered. "Apologies for the moment of reminiscing. Most of you know I used to be a professor at the university. I retired two years ago, and I think you're the largest crowd I've spoken to since."

"We appreciate everything you're doing for us, Professor. Take all the time you need." Adam reached for his second biscuit. "How is Gallagher?"

"Oh, he's quite well. He just received a grant to study a site not far from him. They discovered a cave with paintings they believe to be early Gaelic. He's quite excited for such an opportunity close to home."

"I hope we didn't take him away from that important work." Adam gave Finn and Ethan a quick glance, and AJ smiled. A diplomatic reminder they were here on the professor's good graces.

Finn shifted in his seat but said nothing. Ethan continued to stare at some spot over the professor's head.

Emory chuckled. "It's all good, as the kids say." He directed his next comment to Stella, who watched him with a puppy-dog expression. "It appears your friends are as nervous for what I have to share as Adam was several months ago." He turned to Ethan and Finn. "I won't fill space with additional frivolity. Let's get to it then."

The professor opened a drawer and pulled out a leather-bound journal, opening it to a bookmarked page. He pushed his glasses up and winked at Stella. "I hope you don't mind, but ever since our first chats, I've taken notes on what we've discussed. It helps me remain organized for when I speak with Gallagher. Without it, I'm afraid the two of us would become sidetracked.

"So we know the stones were thought to have been created by Druids sometime before the Romans conquered Brittany. They were made under abnormal circumstances from colorful glass beads, silver, and the hand of the gods, if you will."

"The hand of the gods?" Finn questioned.

"The Druids may have considered the lightning an act of the gods, especially after their apparent success." He sipped his tea, nibbled a biscuit, then steepled his fingers again, seeming to consider his next words. "And of course, there was also reference to the moon going dark, which was most likely some form of eclipse. After the creation of the stones, *The Book of Stones* referenced one of the Druids disappearing for some unknown amount of time. When he reappeared, they claimed he'd gone mad to the point he had to be confined for the safety of the community."

"And he supposedly wrote a book?" AJ winced when Finn squeezed her hand. She wasn't sure if it was a signal to not interrupt or he didn't realize his own strength in his current frame of mind. He released the pressure with a sheepish grin, and she decided on the latter.

The professor nodded, ignoring AJ's pained expression. "There is mention of another book, though Gallagher can't find any other reference except for that single entry in *The Book of Stones*." His gaze shifted to Adam. "If you remember, the book isn't complete. Several sections are missing. If there was more, Gallagher couldn't find it."

Every time the Druid book was mentioned, AJ felt a twitch of memory. Whatever it was still eluded her.

Emory studied the group, his gaze always returning to Ethan, who remained motionless. "Do you have any evidence of another book?"

Seconds passed with nothing but the soft notes of classical music on the store's sound system and the tapping of Adam's fingers on his briefcase.

AJ assumed the professor was trying to get Ethan or Finn to speak but Adam finally broke the stalemate. "We had information that led us to believe *The Book of Stones* would have provided more insight."

"I see." The professor considered the notion as he tapped his glasses. "Gallagher will be very curious to hear that." Emory suddenly broke out with a bark of laughter, startling everyone. "All this time and he missed a lead. He'll spend days scouring over the text again."

"You believe there could be something in his transcription that Gallagher missed?" Ethan's tone sounded strained. He rubbed a finger along the edge of the armrest, worrying at a loose piece of thread.

AJ sensed Ethan's turmoil. They all believed Maire and Sebastian knew what they were doing. If Gallagher missed this piece of translation, it didn't bode well for finding anything useful to help Maire.

The professor nodded. "Why not? *The Book of Stones* was written in ancient Gaelic, and while many people understand the words, how the words are put together can create different interpretations. And with this book, nothing written should be taken at face value. The Druids were clever in subterfuge, writing in their own secret codes. Understanding Gaelic would only be the first step to deciphering the Druid's true meaning. And keep in mind, we don't have all the pages."

Emory leaned across his desk, his attention squarely on Ethan. "It seems someone, or maybe a group of someones, has previously interpreted the book well enough to gain a keen understanding of how the stones work. Gallagher believes he found one possible incantation but nothing more. Perhaps someone with more belief in the power of the book and more insight into the Druids may have uncovered their code. If so, this is a remarkable person."

For the first time since Emory asked for a meeting, Finn and Ethan seemed to relax as one. Emory had just validated Maire's mastery of the book, though they had known this by the improved incantations. The unfortunate result was if anyone in Maire's time period knew about the stones and still lived, they would be a threat to her, especially if she had been asking questions.

"Unfortunately, my friend hasn't reached that level of understanding. While *The Book of Stones* is obviously real, no one has uncovered these stones," he paused and nodded at Adam, "except for the earring you brought me that was chipped from a larger piece. We can only assume these may be the same stones." He glanced at Finn and Ethan. The professor wouldn't quite admit the two men were proof enough of what the stones could do. "No one has recovered the torc. We only have the Druids' words that it exists."

"What about the keeper journals?" Stella asked.

Emory lifted a shoulder. "Journals written by women who had no knowledge of the book and were simply handed a piece of jewelry to protect." He waved a hand at Stella, who was getting ready to pounce. "I'm only saying there's no chain of evidence that the stone they were given to protect had anything do with the book. It's only hearsay."

The professor sighed. "Look at it this way. The book was uncovered a couple of decades ago, and Gallagher began studying it about ten years ago. While that seems like a long time, it hasn't been his main research. He only dabbled at it when he could, until Adam and you showed up on my doorstep. And even without the entire book, the recovered pages would keep a scholar busy for years."

AJ sighed and could almost hear the wind leave Finn's and Ethan's sails. Gallagher would only have a fraction of the knowledge that Maire had of the book. It's possible he might find something Maire had overlooked but it was slim at best. AJ sank back in her chair as the mood in the room shifted.

"You're repeating information we already know, Professor. Is this a way to ease us into telling us your friend wasn't able to garner any more information for us?" Adam's tone was steady and calm, but AJ caught his quick glances at Finn and Ethan. He was probably judging their reactions at driving to Eugene to hear nothing of value.

At this point, AJ wouldn't want to be in Emory's shoes if they were here for a nice cup of tea and an afternoon of pleasantries. Finn and Ethan might be gentlemen, but they'd grown up in a different age and their judgment on this topic didn't lean toward best behaviors.

"Not in the manner you were probably hoping. If you wanted to know more about the stones, or what may have come of them, then no, there wasn't anything more he could tell us. That area, I'm afraid, is a dead end unless more of the book is found. It appears you know more of that area than he does. I'm sorry."

A cracking sound drew their stunned attention to Ethan, who stared down at his hands. Broken shards of a china cup fell from his hands and the remaining tea soaked into his jeans.

47

Beckworth peered through Louise's binoculars. No movement. He checked his watch. An hour since the group had left. He glanced down at the GPS monitor. Nothing. It could be days or weeks before a better opportunity landed at his feet.

He stuffed the binoculars in the backpack next to the now-empty thermos. He stood, stretched his legs, and relieved himself on a nearby tree. One last glance at the GPS monitor confirmed he was alone, and he sprinted toward the house, scanning the upper windows for any sign of movement. He was across the lot, heading for the front door before he veered to the left. Though he was confident he was alone without the prying eyes of neighbors, there was something crass about breaking in through someone's front door. He was unwilling to even mount the front steps.

Staying to the left, he approached the side yard and squatted below the wraparound deck. A few feet farther down, he ran up the stairs to the deck and leaned against the house, next to what he'd earlier assumed was the dining room window. Inching over, he peeked through the window—dining table, a large kitchen, and off to the right what appeared to be the living area. No one in sight.

With a last glance to the parking lot and driveway, he stepped toward the back of the house. When he turned the corner, the ocean view enveloped him. He grabbed the railing, closed his eyes, and sucked in the salty air. For the briefest of moments, the sound of hawkers in the shanties by the Thames and the smell of fresh-baked bread assaulted his senses. Even the gulls reminded him of home.

With renewed desire, he turned and tried the handle of the french doors. He smiled when he heard the click.

He spent ten minutes running through the first floor and up the stairs but he needn't have bothered. The place had the air of emptiness. Returning to the kitchen, he dropped the backpack on the counter and reviewed the place with different eyes.

The décor wasn't to his taste, but Finn had done well for himself. Had this all come from his gaming? Beckworth snorted. Most likely. What more could be possible with an Irishman?

A lord of Ireland, my ass.

Where to start? After a quick run through the inn, he discovered the upper floors were nearly empty. Unsure how long he had, he began a more thorough search on the bottom floor, beginning with the kitchen. The Heart Stone wasn't something they'd just leave out. His worst fear was that it was in a safe like his flintlock had been. He pushed the thought away and got to work. He opened every cabinet, pulled out every drawer, running his hands both within and underneath. He checked behind pictures and mirrors, then moved on to the next room, leaving everything as he found it.

When he walked into the library, he stopped and slowly circled, taking in every inch of book space. He breathed deeply and once again found himself in his own era, this time at

Waverly. The musty odor of the books mixed with the faint scent of cigar was like transporting with the stone. Almost.

He shook himself and returned to his search. He traced a finger along the floor-to-ceiling shelves, reading the titles, pulling out a book here and there. No secrets to be found. The desk proved to be another dead end. He laughed when he opened the closet—Murphy's arsenal. Surprise, surprise. The room held enough weapons to lay siege, and while some of the firearms were modern, most were of their time period. What was Murphy planning? Unable to answer the question, he completed his search. Nothing.

He sped through the rest of the house and had given up hope until he scanned a closet in an empty room on the third floor. He was two steps away from walking out to the hall and down the stairs when he stopped. He turned and stepped toward the closet. A frame with an aged black-and-white photo hung lopsided on the back wall.

Beckworth strode to the frame and straightened it. A woman. He considered her attire and hairstyle and placed the time period somewhere around the second World War, if he remembered the movies correctly. He had no idea who the brunette was. Pushing the photo up from the right side so it swiveled on its nail, a small door revealed itself.

Heart pumping, he lifted the picture from the wall and set it aside.

He glowered at the digital display and keypad.

Damn it to hell, Murphy.

48

The remnants of the broken teacup weighed heavily in Ethan's cradled hands. He sensed the stares, the heat in Antiques & Lore stifling, the walls closing in. All this time, all this wait—for nothing. A sense of urgency filled him. He wanted to dash back to the dock and return home. It didn't make sense. He knew the desire sprang from his baser instincts, but he needed to do something, be someplace where he felt he was making a difference.

He blew out a breath when he realized Stella was trying to take the broken china from him. When he gazed up into her narrowed brows and flashing eyes, he could have kissed her. Anger was better than pity.

"It's a good thing the tea set wasn't a family heirloom, but it was still a beautiful set. Now with one less cup." She leaned next to his ear. "Hold yourself together. This isn't the professor's fault."

"It's only a cup, my dear. Did you injure yourself?" Emory had risen but returned to his seat when Stella shook her head at him.

Ethan looked up, and Stella squeezed his shoulder before

taking the shattered pieces. He heaved a sigh and glanced at the professor. "I apologize for the cup."

"We drove a long way to be told you have nothing for us." Finn's tone disguised what Ethan knew must be brewing inside him. Had they been in their own century, the professor would be dangling against the wall, his feet a few inches off the ground while Finn held him by the throat.

Emory ignored Finn and continued his perusal of Ethan. "I've been researching artifacts on behalf of others for decades. I can spot the difference between those seeking glory versus those happy to hear a good tale. I can also recognize those who seek power, stumbling over anyone they can to grab hold of it. But the ones who touch me the most are those who seek absolution where there's none to be found."

Out of the corner of his eye, Ethan saw AJ grab Finn's hand and bring it to her lips. Ethan looked down, unable to hold the professor's gaze. Was that what he was seeking? Absolution for his mistakes? Maire would have left with or without his permission. No one could have predicted she'd be kidnapped again. Or had they become lazy? He had sent everyone out to search for her, canvasing the countryside, but had he blamed himself when no one found a trace of her? He glanced at AJ. The first time he and Finn had met her, he'd tried to keep her out of their mad search for the Heart Stone. He'd fretted over her getting dragged into their battle, but when she'd returned to her own time with Finn, he had been happy for them both.

When he'd followed them and seen the life they were building, he'd been both proud and jealous. Jealous they had each other while he'd let his happiness slip from his grasp. His mad desire to find Maire had overshadowed everything else. Had he really thought he could jump to the future and find a trace of her? Sitting here in this antiquated bookstore seemed foolish and naïve. Guilt rose when he considered his only goal was to bring Finn and AJ back with him to find Maire, regardless how that might impact their lives.

Absolution. He didn't think there was anyone alive who could provide that relief.

He lifted his head. The professor still studied him, and for the first time since Finn had announced Emory was ready to see them, Ethan smiled. He saw it now. Emory wouldn't have them drive over here for nothing.

Ethan settled back in his chair, the band across his chest loosening. "If your friend's limited knowledge of the book won't be of any help, what else was he able to find?"

"Your call the other day struck me as a shot in the dark." The professor moved his tea aside and turned pages in his journal.

Ethan felt the gazes of the others and shot a glance at Finn. His questioning look pained him, but Ethan had been right in holding back his call to Emory. If nothing was to be gained from his sudden insight, then it had been one less foolish idea to burden Finn. If something came of it, they would know soon enough.

"But it isn't the first time my friend or I uncovered treasure from the most meager of morsels," the professor continued, as if the silence in the room weren't filled with new tension. "I don't know if what my friend discovered will make sense, but now we're both curious.

"Not long after they found *The Book of Stones*, Gallagher searched for other books and discovered a personal journal. It was written by one of the monks who lived in the monastery during the French Revolution and Napoleon's reign."

When everyone leaned forward, the professor raised a brow before nodding and returning to his notes. "As historians, finding someone's diary is like stepping back in time." He gave the group a wry smile before continuing. "They give us firsthand knowledge of how people lived, thought, and felt. Sometimes, if we're very lucky, we gain insight to external forces, such as battles or political instability. Imagine what a find it is when a journal comes from the days of the French Revolution and the Reign of Terror." The professor almost shivered with excitement. "That said, we can't always jump to the projects we want to study when we have pressing matters, such as grants. When I mentioned your request to Gallagher, he had reviewed the monk's notes months ago and found no reference to *The Book of Stones*. But he did run the name you gave me through his notes. The name matched the monk who wrote the journal."

"What name?" Stella asked, her tone perplexed and a bit frustrated. Ethan almost laughed at her eagerness to cut to the chase. He also noted Adam's gentle kick and her returned one.

"Sebastian," Finn responded.

When everyone stared at Ethan, he shrugged. "I probably should have mentioned my call to the professor." He rubbed his forehead. "I'm not sure why we hadn't mentioned the name before. When I thought back to the last days at the monastery and how often Maire and Sebastian wrote in their blasted books, I thought maybe something of Sebastian's remained behind."

"Amazing. But it makes sense." Adam picked up the renewed energy in the room and leaped from his chair to start pacing. "We were so concerned about *The Book of Stones* and the keeper journals, we ignored other possibilities."

Ethan glanced at AJ and Finn. "I know I should have told you. I was frustrated with how long everything was taking. I'm used to taking action, not sitting around waiting for others to solve the puzzles."

"It's all right. I think we all feel like that," AJ said. She asked Emory, "I take it Ethan's call led somewhere?"

The professor shrugged. "Possibly." He turned the pages of his journal.

Adam returned to his seat, but he hovered at the edge. Stella folded her napkin. AJ and Finn huddled closer, their hands entwined as if giving each other strength. Ethan released his breath and settled back, refusing to give any more power to his fear.

Emory tilted his desk lamp. The sound of him turning pages mingled with the soft rustle of Stella's folding and the hushed melody of overhead music that became amplified and grating the longer they waited.

"It may be nothing," Emory eyed the group with a knowing grin, "but let me read what Gallagher emailed me." He pulled the book closer. "As I said, there was never a direct reference to *The Book of Stones* in the journal, but he found two names. Sebastian mentions a friend who spent months with him deciphering an ancient text. He stayed in contact with this friend who was then living in England, despite the renewed war between England and France. However, he only refers to this friend by the initial M."

A teacup rattled and Ethan thought the professor might lose another cup, but AJ caught it before it fell from her fingers. He couldn't blame her. If he hadn't already crushed a teacup, he would have this time.

The professor glanced at her but kept going. "There was interest between this M and Sebastian in reference to a package that had been sent to someone with the initial R during the Reign of Terror." Emory looked up, his focus on Finn and Ethan. "It appears the monk was so nervous about any reference to *The Book of Stones* or this package, he only used initials. I can only assume the initials may carry some meaning to you. Anyway, Sebastian sent a missive to this R person, but with the war, it took several months to receive a response. It appears we have a new name you haven't mentioned before."

Emory flipped the page while Ethan's stomach roiled in

unison. The fire that had begun to burn in his belly dampened at the professor's words. Another name, another lead, and another long path down a winding road that led nowhere. He closed his eyes and waited.

"The response was written by the daughter of our mysterious R. The note wasn't in the journal but it appeared Sebastian copied the words, or at least parts of it."

Emory ran his finger over a passage and began to read.

" 'I'm sorry to inform you that my father is recently deceased. Upon receiving some guests a few months ago from Hereford, he became agitated. He eventually took me aside and mentioned a package he'd received from you several years ago. He said he originally hadn't put much stock in the letter but had stored the package in a safe place. At some point, he turned the package over to someone else. He didn't say to who or why he had done that. But after our guests from Hereford departed, Father left to see an old friend. I can't be certain, but I think he left to reclaim the package. His body was returned to us two weeks after he left. We were told he was killed by a highwayman during a robbery. I do hate giving out this information in a note, with the war and all, but the story of Father's death still seems suspicious to me. What I am willing to share with you is that he was on his way to a town south of Bristol. He was to meet with the Viscount of Waverly.' "

Ethan felt the room spin, he grasped both arms of the chair. He held the arms so tightly he knew they would splinter without their three inches of stuffed padding. Before he could wrench the name from his lips, Finn did it for him in a low growl.

"Beckworth."

49

Beckworth stared at the smooth waves as they broached the shore. He nestled into the Adirondack on the back deck of the inn, a cold beer numbing his hand. The salty breeze caressed his sun-warmed face, but he had to admit he preferred the dour setting of Ethan's living room. It somehow fit his morose mood. He glanced at the GPS monitor in his lap. No blip.

His worst nightmare had been confirmed. Deep in his gut, he knew the Heart Stone had to be in that locked safe. He had no idea who the woman was in the blasted photo, or what if anything it meant, but when he stood in front of the safe, he swore a pulse tugged from the small stone stuffed in his pocket.

In desperation, he'd held the stone against the safe and whispered the incantation he'd heard AJ recite on the knoll in France. He wasn't familiar with the strange Celtic words, and his tongue stumbled over them. Either he didn't remember the words correctly or the stones had to be touching as the duke always assumed.

After five minutes of all-consuming panic that he'd never go home, deep unabated anger overtook him. He wanted to rage. He wanted to tear through every room, ripping and destroying whatever he laid his hands on. In the end, with his forehead lowered against the wall, his arms dangling impotent by his side, the fury had dissipated, leaving him empty and tired.

The beer helped. He gulped it down before carefully placing the bottle on the edge of the railing. He opened the second one and settled it on his stomach while he stretched out his legs. He was beginning to understand what fascinated Murphy and Hughes about the ocean. The beer and languid waves calmed him, focused his thoughts, leaving him with only one other option. The one person he'd always known it would come down to, and he absently rubbed his shoulder.

He needed AJ. His lips twisted in a satisfied grin. Ever since she'd stuck him with that dagger, he'd known they both had an unresolved score to settle.

He glanced at the GPS monitor. Blip. They were coming home.

With what he guessed to be ten minutes to spare, he rose from the chair, drained the beer, and placed the second empty next to the first, then sauntered toward the deck stairs. His pace never altered as he crossed the yard and melted into the forest. He heard the cars as they rolled down the drive, but he was twenty yards into the forest, safely hidden. He began to whistle.

It was time to collect on that debt.

I saiah brushed at the incessant fly, beads of sticky sweat running behind his neck and down his back. His knees were cramped, and he grumbled at his poor planning. To be fair, he'd been making decisions on the run, unprepared for the alarm that had alerted him to someone in Finn and AJ's home. He'd checked his watch for the umpteenth time—ten minutes since the last time he'd checked. He'd been stuck under the cedar for more than an hour.

He'd called Finn and Ethan on the drive to the inn but they hadn't answered, probably already in their meeting with the professor. Isaiah had left a message hoping they would check before driving home.

As soon as he'd seen the image of the man at the back door, and without thinking everything through, he'd rushed out of the house. He parked a quarter mile away and dashed through the woods that ran across the street from the inn. It didn't take long walking up and down the road before he spotted the front tire of the moped sticking out from behind a fern. He checked the security app and flipped through the images from the multiple cameras. He found Beckworth on the third floor, partially obscured by where he stood in relation to the camera. Isaiah chuckled. The man had to be seething about the digital safe. Knowing he had time, Isaiah dropped into the foliage around the cycle's hiding spot.

Ten minutes later, he was tucked beneath the cedar. The branches hung low to the ground, and he was able to sit within the branches and monitor the moped. He wouldn't be seen as long as he stayed still. He stared at the phone app and his long watch began.

He wiped at his brow and considered another location with better airflow. He checked his messages and noticed a text from Ethan. They were almost home. Isaiah checked the monitor in time to see Beckworth rise from the deck chair, drain the bottle of beer he'd been holding, and set it on the railing next to another empty bottle. It angered Isaiah to see Beckworth so cavalier in a home that wasn't his and where he hadn't been invited. Thieves. They disgusted him.

Isaiah noticed that Beckworth held an old-fashioned GPS monitor, so when Beckworth made his slow and gradual egress from the inn, it sent a shiver through him. This man was more than a thief. He was a professional. Isaiah needed to remember that. Finn and Ethan had reminded him several times, but it was another matter to see the man so cold in his deliberations and movements.

Several minutes later, a black SUV, followed by another car, turned into the inn's driveway. Finn and Ethan were home. Moments after the vehicles disappeared, a movement in the trees snapped Isaiah's musings from the driveway. The moped was pushed from the trees by a wiry man with blond hair —Beckworth.

He snapped a few photos from his position in the tree. Beckworth brushed his hair back, glanced up and down the street, pushed the machine onto the road, and was on his way. Isaiah waited until the man and cycle were out of sight before crawling out of the cedar. He itched to follow, but instead he jogged down the driveway toward the inn. Beckworth was no longer in control of the game. He just didn't know it yet.

50

"How could he be in two places at the same time?" Stella repeated her new mantra as she tapped her nails against her wineglass.

"I don't know what makes me angrier, that Beckworth is behind Maire's disappearance or that he's been in our home." AJ paced, grateful they had enlarged the dining room, giving her plenty of space to stretch her legs. She knew her pacing irritated Finn but she was too hyped up to sit.

"Enough with the two of you. You're not helping." Finn reached out and grabbed AJ's arm on her next pass. "Sit. Have a glass of wine. You're distracting and not just to me." His expression softened. "I know you need to walk it off. Do you want to go down and throw a dagger?"

AJ struggled against his hold, but as soon as he asked his question, the fight went out of her. "No. Well, yes, but not right now." She felt her cheeks redden at the admission, a little uncertain about her aggressive behavior. Beckworth certainly brought out the worst in her. She grudgingly took her seat, sitting on the end as if she might need to spring into action. When she noticed

Adam perched at the edge of his chair, she almost laughed. Seeing the similarities to her brother released the tension in her neck. They had come so far in just a few short months. Amazing how quickly a little time travel changed people. She suppressed an urge to giggle. Maybe she was having a breakdown.

Adam returned her smile through a quizzical expression, not having a clue what she'd been thinking. "Let's work through the timeline again. There must be something we're missing." He flicked the pen hovering over his notepad, where he'd drawn out a long horizontal line with two vertical lines intersecting it. He tapped at the beginning of the line. "When you went back with Finn, you arrived in the spring of 1802."

AJ nodded and shrugged simultaneously before turning to Finn for confirmation.

"It was well after the first spring planting, but the crops were still young." Finn tapped a finger on the table, his head bent in concentration before a smile broke through. "I remember my first trip to town, I had to find a way to determine the year without looking like a fool." The smile had turned to a full grin, and he rubbed AJ's wrist where he'd grabbed her.

She remembered that day, now that he was retelling it. They'd had a good laugh over his failed attempts.

"And you stayed in Ireland for about two months?" Adam drew a vertical line and made a note.

"About that, maybe a week or two more."

"From the moment you made England, and your time in France, to when you arrived back here, how long was that?" Adam made some other notation while he waited.

"Maybe another two months." Ethan chimed in.

AJ studied Ethan. He seemed more relaxed since returning from Eugene, though she didn't understand why. Discovering that Beckworth appeared to have once again orchestrated

Maire's abduction made it impossible for her to settle down. Yet both Ethan and Finn seemed calmer than they'd been in days.

Adam made a note under a previously sketched line. He scratched his chin before drawing another vertical line through the bar graph. "Ethan, you stated earlier you'd spent a few months in France after AJ and Finn left. When did you leave France?"

Ethan stared out the window, his expression taking on a faraway gaze. "It was late in the year. We worried about the weather. When Jamie returned, he said a smuggler had given him a route between the French patrols and the Royal Navy blockade, but he worried about the return sail."

He glanced up with a weary, yet content smile, the combination forming a haunted look. "We were in Hereford before Christmas." His tone turned nostalgic. "It was good to see Maire focused on something other than the blasted book."

Finn nodded and gave Ethan his own resigned smile. "She always loved Christmas."

"How long in England before Maire went missing?" Adam unwittingly ruined whatever reminiscing AJ may have witnessed between the men.

Ethan slid his chair toward the table to review Adam's rudimentary drawing.

AJ smiled. How alike the men were. Tempers flared when they felt unable to do anything, yet one morsel of a lead and they grasped on to it like drowning men who'd discovered a piece of driftwood at sea. Even Finn focused on Adam's drawing from the other side of the table.

Ethan pointed to the right of Adam's last vertical line. "We traveled to London in February of the new year and spent a few months at the earl's London house. It was the height of the season and Maire's first trip to London." He glanced at Finn. "You can imagine what an impression she made."

Finn laughed. "Was that before or after she spoke?"

Ethan laughed with him. "Both. But yes, once they heard her Irish accent, the women would have turned her out had it not been for the earl." His eyes were moist and AJ wasn't sure if it was from sadness or mirth because he continued to chuckle. "The two of them made quite an impression on everyone. The gentry and other nobility thought the earl touched, cavorting with an Irish lass more beautiful than anyone London could offer and smarter than most of the men in the room."

Ethan's eyes sparkled when he spoke of Maire, and his story bubbled forth after being locked away for so long. "After that first ball, the invitations poured in, sometimes dozens in a single day. Everyone wanted Maire at their ball or luncheon. She couldn't possibly attend them all so the earl and I helped her sort through the invitations. We advised, as best we could, on which events she'd be truly welcome at rather than shown off as an oddity."

"Balls, fancy dresses, and sharp-tongued women." Stella shivered. "Almost as fun as swimming with a pool of sharks."

Finn and Ethan eyed each other before they both chuckled.

"Aye," Finn replied with a touch of bitterness. "You have the point of it. It was all about who knew who and whose daughter was the best for their son."

"Or vice versa. Partnerships avowed or newly made," Ethan agreed.

"And a good time to hatch plans not so favorable to many." Finn sat up. "Did anyone seem familiar or out of place?"

Ethan rubbed his forehead as if replaying the entire season, searching for anything that appeared out of sorts. "Not that I remember. There were a few acquaintances, but no one seemed interested in anything other than conversation, whiskey, and a good cigar."

"What about Maire? You couldn't have been with her every

moment." AJ knew Ethan wouldn't leave her side for long unless it was unfashionable. Though she'd never had an opportunity to attend a ball, she assumed there would have been rooms where the women gathered that would be out of bounds for the men. Places where they could gossip about fashion and dalliances. Even if Ethan was by her side throughout the party, he wouldn't notice the subtle gestures and quiet stares that only Maire would have sensed. He was as astute as Finn, but men wouldn't pick up on the eyes that followed Maire, the gentle bumps as someone walked by, or a loose hand carelessly brushing against something they shouldn't. And that might have been all that was necessary for someone to set their sights on Maire.

Ethan's forehead scrunched in concentration, his normally well-groomed hair disheveled from continually running his hands through it. "There were dozens of events and they've all become a blur." He blew out a sigh. "Either the earl or I was with her most of the time, but you're right. There were moments when she would have been on her own." He glanced at Finn with an apologetic shrug. "You know how she hates to be smothered, and there wasn't any reason to suspect anything. We were across the channel from the monastery, war was imminent, the duke was dead, and we'd seen Beckworth disappear in the fog. If Maire had been bothered by anyone, she would have mentioned it. But honestly, as much as she complained about the women, I think she had the time of her life."

"Aye, but it's possible she might not have mentioned something out of the ordinary." Finn nodded in agreement before reflecting a second possibility. "It's just as likely she might have heard something that didn't mean anything at the time, but days or even weeks later, it wormed its way into her thoughts. She's a patient one, for all her fire."

"After eighteen months with Beckworth, she'd have to be," AJ quipped. "But Finn's right. Maire is quite intuitive. She could have heard something that she tucked away for future reflection. But if that happened, it's useless to us."

"Her independent nature could have led her to investigate without bothering anyone." Finn filled empty glasses, then stood in front of the bay window to stare at the sea. "Where does that leave us on your schedule?"

Ethan turned to Adam's sketch. "We returned to the earl's estate before the end of the season, sometime in May."

Adam scratched a note under a new line. "That leaves us almost mid-1803."

The group quieted, eyes returning to Ethan to pick up the rest of the tale. AJ glanced at Finn, sensing a subtle change in him. He appeared at ease, his posture relaxed, but his finger tapped against his glass. Something was brewing.

Ethan, on the other hand, had mentally returned to Hereford as he replayed his last days with Maire. "After the constant activity in London, Maire was thrilled to return to the earl's country estate. The peaceful setting revitalized her. After being back a week, she turned her attention to the medicinal gardens. Toward the end of summer, she had prepared a list of seeds she wanted to gather, either to grow indoors through the winter or have on hand for the next planting season. That's when the earl and I agreed she could go to Peterstow."

Adam frowned and scratched his head. "Would that be the end of August?"

Ethan shrugged. "Close enough. The kitchens were busy with preserving the harvest."

As Ethan's reminiscing grew closer to Maire's disappearance, his tension resurfaced. A muscle in his jaw ticked, and his eyes darkened under brows knit together in frustration.

AJ pulled a chair next to him and laid a hand on his arm. "How long did you search?"

Ethan stared down at his arm, but AJ could tell he was still hundreds of years away. His words were a whisper when he finally responded. "About two months. We sent men in various directions, repeating her path, then repeating our own with ever-widening circles. Not a trace or single explanation. Dugan was out there somewhere and the stones were the only thing that made sense, but we didn't have a single lead. That's when Thomas and I went to Beckworth's estate at Waverly, but only the staff was in residence. Then we traveled to Ratliff's with no success."

Finn grunted as he turned from the window to reclaim his chair. "You shook something loose, since Ratliff left for Waverly after your visit."

"So you returned before the new year?" Adam asked.

Ethan patted AJ's hand, his attention back to present day. "It was during the winter solstice." He shrugged. "We determined it couldn't hurt to travel during a spiritual time, and the winter solstice, or Yule as it was called, was important to the Druids." He lowered his head. "It just seemed right."

"And it was. You're here with us now." AJ grasped his hand, feeling his need for personal connection. Something that would validate he'd done the right thing.

"That puts us at the end of 1803." Adam tapped his pen on the pad of paper. "It doesn't make sense."

"That's the truth of the timeline," Ethan insisted.

Adam raised a hand to stop him. "I'm not questioning your facts."

"But it doesn't match what Emory told us of Sebastian's journal. Ratliff left to visit Beckworth in 1803." Finn looked to Adam. "Didn't Ratliff's daughter mention when her father left for Waverly?"

"It was right after Ethan visited." Adam glanced at his timeline, then rummaged in his case for a new pen. He made a new vertical line with the red ink. "That would have been sometime in October."

"All we know is that he went to visit the viscount. We don't know if the viscount was actually at Waverly." Stella placed an origami swan next to five others. Everyone turned to her. "Well, he wasn't there when Ethan stopped by."

Finn grinned. "Leave it to you to keep us all straight."

She beamed at the praise and picked up another napkin.

"Then how did Ratliff end up dead?" AJ asked. The words from the letter had haunted AJ after Emory had read Sebastian's notes. She knew what Ratliff's daughter must have been going through. AJ's memory of being told her father was dead had rushed back, and she'd pushed it away at the time, but she had unconsciously formed a connection to this Ratliff woman.

"Aye, his death is too convenient to be an accident." Finn rubbed his chin, his fingers tapping once again, this time on the arm of the chair. "But if Beckworth is here and didn't find a way to jump back to abduct Maire, who else is there?"

Ethan studied Adam's paper. "It could be Dugan, but what purpose would that serve, unless he had some other backer?"

"So if Maire was abducted, and Sebastian has a letter from Ratliff's daughter claiming he was on his way to Waverly, isn't that our answer?" Stella chimed in, proving that as bored as she seemed with her stack of origami figures, she was still paying attention.

"But Thomas and I had already been there, and there was no sign of Beckworth." The edge in Ethan's tone confirmed his patience was beginning to fray.

"Or that's what they wanted you to think." Finn sat up. "There's a building that Beckworth used as barracks, and plenty of other smaller outbuildings to hide in if he needed to."

AJ nodded. "Even if you spent hours in the main receiving

hall or west wing, the entire east wing would be off-limits. That's where Beckworth hid Maire for months."

"That leaves us only one path as I see it." Finn stood and poured another round of drinks. He turned to gaze at the man sitting in the far corner of the room and raised his glass in salute. "Isaiah. Come tell the group what you were up to this morning. It's time we hunt the only man we know who might have answers."

51

Isaiah unfolded himself from the chair, his gaze flickering to the group, a shaky smile on his face. He strode to a monitor that he'd set up and grabbed a remote control. After pressing a few buttons, the monitor came to life, reflecting six square images—three on the top of the screen and three on the bottom. Each image displayed a different part of the inn.

"As you can see, we have cameras installed both inside and outside of the house." Isaiah clicked on one. "This is the front door." He clicked another one. "This is the back deck where the french doors let into the house, and this one inside the library."

"I didn't know we had cameras inside." AJ turned to Finn. "I'm not sure I'm comfortable having my movements monitored."

He grinned. "The inside cameras are programmable. They're only meant to be turned on when we leave. After the issue with Beckworth is resolved, we can decide whether we want to remove them."

AJ wasn't sure if anyone else caught his quick wink, but she felt the ill-timed blush warm her cheeks. She glared at him but he only grinned wider.

Isaiah cleared his throat. "There were only three areas in the house Finn was concerned with—the library, Finn's office and the third-floor closet.

"A closet?" Stella asked. "I thought the third floor was empty."

"It is," Finn agreed. "Except for a wall safe we installed in the closet when we decided to make the inn our home."

"Wouldn't it have been easier to put a safe in the library or your office?" Stella dug further.

"Aye, and there's another wall safe in my office where thieves would expect one to be."

"So, why..." Stella stopped and shook her head.

"But it's a decoy. At least where the Heart Stone is concerned," Adam finished for her.

"Exactly." Finn turned to Isaiah. "Continue."

"There are more cameras outside and you can click through the images or go to the left-hand navigation to select a single camera to show on the screen. The important thing to remember is that all camera images are being saved and continually backed up so you don't have to be watching the monitor to capture an image."

Isaiah brought up another screen and punched more numbers. "I'm bringing up recorded images from this morning when you were all in Eugene speaking with the professor." Six new images popped up. "As you can see, we have three outdoor images—Beckworth running across the far side of the parking lot, the front door, which he ignores, and the back deck where he made his entry."

"Damn. Why is he coming from that direction rather than where he had been watching us previously?" AJ leaned over, elbows on her knees as she focused on the screen.

"Because he's a smart bastard," Ethan supplied. "He must know Isaiah had seen the reflection and that he'd been discovered. He's too motivated to completely stop watching, so he just found a different spot." He stood and stepped to the monitor, pointing at the screen. "We have cameras at all entry points leading to and around the inn. This includes the paths to the bay, the tidal pools, and the driveway."

Isaiah nodded. "We installed one where Beckworth originally hid. We thought it might be a waste, but we couldn't take the chance. The fact the driveway camera didn't pick him up just tells us he came in from the other side of the woods on the bay side." Isaiah brought up three images from the inside cameras. "Beckworth appears in all three of the inside cameras." He let the images roll so everyone could watch Beckworth move from room to room.

"He's looking for something." Stella scooted her chair closer.

Everyone quieted as they watched Beckworth move through the library, touching the books, then opening the door to the weapons arsenal.

"I'm a little surprised he didn't take any weapons," Adam said.

"Nothing we can see," AJ countered.

"He has two pistols. He's dangerous enough with those." Finn turned to Isaiah. "Fast forward to the third floor."

The camera had been placed above the door of the closet and faced the black-and-white photo on the back wall that hid the safe.

"Who's that in the photo?" Stella asked as she leaned in.

AJ smiled fondly. "Martha mailed it the day after our lunch. She had several pictures of her grandmother and wanted me to have one."

"That's Lily Mayfield?" Adam whistled. "The last keeper."

"Still watching over the stone," Ethan whispered and slid a glance at AJ. "You have a wicked sense of humor."

She shrugged. "It seemed fitting."

They watched the screen as Beckworth came into view. He reached out and the picture swung sideways up the wall, presumably Beckworth pushing it up since he blocked most of the activity. Then the picture slid back and Beckworth kicked the wall.

"Great. Now he's pissed." Stella sat back. "He knows where the Heart Stone is."

"Anger is good. He may not think clearly if he's getting frustrated," Ethan added.

Finn agreed. "But we may have pushed him into doing something foolish. It will make him more unpredictable."

Isaiah returned to his commentary. "The security system alerted me when there was movement at the back door. The alarm came in around ten and I knew you'd be in your meeting with the professor so I drove over."

"That was dangerous," Stella observed.

"I had no intention of going down to the inn. We had another thought." Isaiah glanced at Finn and Ethan before explaining. "Ethan's friend at the security company gave us our own tracker." He smiled as he logged off the security system and opened up an internet connection. He spoke as he navigated to another site. "It depended on him coming to the inn and our ability to locate his vehicle."

"That couldn't have been easy." Adam sat back, arms behind his head as he stared at the monitor. "There aren't many houses on this stretch of road but it has access to the beach and cliffs."

"But no parking areas to speak of. I know from trying to park along the road myself," Ethan said.

Isaiah nodded in agreement. "I parked a good quarter mile away and hoofed it over. I kept an eye on the house monitors to make sure he hadn't left and walked along the road in both directions from the inn. It didn't take long to find a moped hiding in the trees."

AJ snorted. "A moped? Isn't that like a knight coming to battle on a donkey?"

The group laughed.

"Not elegant," Isaiah agreed. "But easy to get around and easy to hide. And most people never notice a moped leaning against a fence. They remember cars, maybe a Harley, but a moped? Not usually."

"Makes sense. I'm not sure I'd have noticed it," Finn remarked.

"A moped isn't very big. Wouldn't he notice a tracker?" Stella asked.

"He would if we had a '90s model like he has." Isaiah turned his focus on the monitor, and a map of Baywood came up on the screen. "Technology has advanced since then. This tracker is about the size of a quarter and fits nicely under the frame." The image quickly changed as Isaiah zoomed into a region south of the inn, still along the coast.

"Horizon Village. That's a retirement community. Do you think he's charmed some old lady?" Adam asked.

"Or found an empty house," Ethan suggested.

"Not this time of year." Stella pushed back her chair and tapped a finger on the table. "If this was winter, I'd say it was very likely he'd find an empty house. But summer season? It's almost unheard of to find something vacant near the coast." She squinted at the screen. "Zoom in and see if we can narrow down the street. I can pull records for the homes, see if we can identify where he's staying."

"What are we talking about doing?" AJ asked.

"We're not sure." Finn nodded at Isaiah. "Thank you, Isaiah. Smart thinking that has given us an edge."

"And now that we have it, we need a simple plan." Ethan

stared down at Adam's timeline. His finger tapped on the page as he studied it. He turned a predatory gaze toward Finn. "We know what he wants."

Finn nodded with what AJ considered his scary grin. "And with ample incentive. He'll try again."

52

The raucous conversations from the kitchen, dining room, and back deck drove Finn deeper into the house. After stumbling over several children racing up and down the staircase, he herded them into the family room. He needed something to capture their attention before someone broke a leg. With help from Adam's oldest son, Patrick, they mastered the remote control and started a movie.

With his sanity restored, Finn made his way to the library, where he collapsed into a chair in front of the unlit fireplace. Behind the closed door and floor-to-ceiling bookcases, the voices became dulled and he welcomed the silence.

It had been two days since they'd placed the tracker on Beckworth's moped. The group had spent the first day arguing over a plan to deal with Beckworth and the second day completing final arrangements for Helen's party. Over twenty people had descended on the inn earlier in the day. Everyone was either related to Helen or were long-time friends, but he thought a good many of them wanted a firsthand glimpse inside the century-old building.

It wasn't that he was averse to crowds or mingling with

people he didn't know—he'd done enough of that in London through the years—but he'd grown accustomed to the solitude of his life with AJ. A few close friends and family were all he needed. These last three months at the inn with AJ had been the happiest of his life.

After Ethan's return, Finn had battled to keep his growing irritability at bay, and it had shocked him when he'd discovered a slow-burning anger. It made sense. Someone had taken Maire. Would her life forever be in torment and fear with her constantly looking over her shoulder? He was able to compartmentalize his impatience, confident that somehow they would find her, but that inner turmoil didn't go away. He kept his riotous thoughts tightly controlled, terrified they would consume him. It seemed a simple enough task when he spent most of his time worrying about Ethan and his mood swings.

Then one morning, when he'd watched AJ make a quiet breakfast for the two of them, the truth of his irritation had overwhelmed him. He was angry at Ethan. Angry at Maire for being obstinate and not exercising more caution. He'd found the perfect life here with AJ, and through two hundred years, trouble had still found him. Would his past continually haunt them? He wished he'd never seen one of those blasted stones, but if he hadn't, he wouldn't have found AJ. What a conundrum.

A light rap on the door deflected his harried thoughts.

"Come in," he yelled so he could be heard through the solid maple door.

He was surprised when Helen took a hesitant step inside. She gave him a warm smile, and after peering around the room, slid in and shut the door behind her.

"I hope I'm not disturbing you." She strode around the room, gazing at the books as if it were her first time though she'd been in the room dozens of times. Stopping at one of the cases, she rolled the pearls of her necklace between her fingers, considering an Armani figurine AJ had picked up at an estate sale in Astoria. After a moment, she dropped the pearls and turned, running her hands down the sides of her yellow summer dress.

"We don't spend much time talking, just you and I." She turned the chair next to him around so she could face him rather than the fireplace. After sitting, she pondered him, her warm smile still in place.

When it didn't seem she was going to continue, Finn prodded, "And that has been a waste of precious time and something we must remedy."

She laughed. "I do love when you get formal. How about you just come over every once in a while and tinker with something on my to-do list? It seems to grow longer every year."

Finn chuckled with her. "I think that could be arranged as long as we can share lunch together."

"It's a date." Her expression changed, and her gaze became more contemplative. "AJ can sometimes be headstrong."

"Aye, and stubborn and impulsive."

"So you've seen all her blemishes."

"And they don't compare to her generosity, her intelligence, or her passion."

Helen cocked her head. "I was expecting you to say her beauty."

He grinned his lopsided smile. "I thought I had."

After a moment, Helen patted his hand and leaned back in the chair. "You are a keeper."

Finn almost laughed at her words and the double meaning only he understood. "Tell me about Joseph."

Her smile turned melancholy. "Hasn't AJ told you about him?"

He nodded. "She's shared many things about her father, but she doesn't have the same stories to share."

"No, she wouldn't."

To Finn's surprise, Helen kicked off her shoes and repositioned herself so she could tuck her legs underneath her, a similarity with her daughter. "AJ tells me you were a sailor."

Finn nodded, curious as to whether it was AJ or Helen who considered his role as a sailor just a past memory, something to be left behind.

"Joseph never sailed. Never even stepped foot on a boat, but he always dreamt of seeing the world from a ship."

"AJ never mentioned that."

Her laughter changed when she spoke of her husband, becoming more musical. "No one knew, except maybe Adam, but if his father ever told him, he never mentioned it. Adam has that same spirit. Loves boats although I doubt he'll ever step foot on one either."

Helen shared several stories and she glowed with her fond memories. After thirty minutes had passed, she unfolded herself from the chair and slipped on her shoes.

Before she stood, she reached for his hand. "Promise you'll always protect her."

Finn studied her for a minute and shook his head. "Your daughter can protect herself, but I'll always stand beside her. I'll always be there for whatever she needs."

He stood with her, and she leaned in to kiss his cheek. Before pulling away, she whispered, "You are definitely a keeper."

When she slipped out the door as quietly as she had come in, Finn fell back into his seat. Would he and AJ ever build similar memories? Knowing he'd hid himself away for too long, he crossed the room to shut the window against the early-evening chill.

He left the library and stopped in his study to shut another window. As he made his way around the house, closing windows and stumbling over children who'd gotten bored with the movie, he thought about his future and the cloud of sorrowful history that hung over the inn. He didn't believe in an object having good luck or bad luck. The old stories of the inn didn't scare him, nor were they a precursor of the future. This was his home, and whatever happened when they stepped through the fog wouldn't change that. If nothing else in his life was ever certain, this he knew to be true.

As he guided Adam's youngest child, Charlotte, back toward the kitchen, he spotted AJ talking with a group of women from Helen's gardening club. Her brows were knit as someone spoke demonstratively, hands waving about. Then she threw back her head and laughed, her eyes sparkling. The love of his life.

He knew what needed to be done before they left. He would make good on the promise he'd made to Helen.

AJ leaned on the railing and gazed at the silvery clouds brushed with strips of rose hues. A late summer storm brewed, she could smell it. She turned to her left in time to see her niece and nephews race around the outdoor tables on the lawn before they ran for the front of the house. Several groups of people gathered chairs to watch the sunset, her mother's garden club mixing with her friends from the women's shelter. Jackson and Isaiah mingled with a group that had been more Joseph's friends but kept in touch with Helen on a regular basis.

She hadn't thought Jackson and Isaiah would come to the party. Jackson had meant to bring his wife, Olivia, but she'd already made other plans that hadn't included Jackson. He'd decided to accept the invitation to join the party, and as it turned out, had a green thumb and knew most of the flowers in the garden by their Latin name, which endeared him to the gardening circle. The man was a mystery, and once Finn and she returned from their mission, there would be a huge Jackson family party at the inn. She desperately wanted to meet the woman who had captured Jackson's heart.

"It's going to be a perfect sunset. I couldn't ask for a better day." Helen slid next to her at the railing, her gaze roaming over the sea.

"Where have you been? Janet's been looking for you." AJ wrapped an arm around her mother's waist.

Helen leaned into her. "I've been avoiding her most of the afternoon. She has some crazy notion for a garden Christmas party."

"So you're hiding from her."

Her mother's laugh came out in a rush. "Who wants to discuss Christmas during a summer party?"

"Janet has always been pretty focused."

Her mother squeezed her daughter and turned toward her. "That's a kind phrase for her obsessive personality."

"So where were you hiding?"

"In the library with Finn."

AJ pulled away to stare at her mother. Helen leaned with her back against the railing. The light breeze rustled her mother's summer dress and locks of hair that had escaped from her updo. She noticed the increased laugh lines around her mother's eyes and sensed a calmness that hadn't been there before.

"He's a good man," her mother said. Her smile reminded AJ of family picnics when her mother had laughed all day long. "He loves you."

"I know." AJ blinked. She avoided her mother's scrutiny and glanced at the lawn full of people. Adam and Madelyn sat across from each other at a picnic table, and she was surprised to see his hand resting within Madelyn's palm.

She turned toward the ocean, gripping the railing while the sea air dried her eyes.

Helen slipped an arm around AJ's waist. "Your father would approve."

AJ rested her head against her mother's. The scent of her mother's favorite perfume, light floral with a touch of spice, flowed over her, filling her with sweet memories of a loving family.

"I cherish every moment I have with him. Sometimes when I wake and he's not in bed with me, I think he might have disappeared." She heard her partially strangled voice, and she laughed. "It's so silly."

"Nonsense. I know exactly how you feel." She gripped AJ's hand and dabbed at her own eyes. "And I know it more so now. Don't ever waste a day with him, and never go to bed angry with him. If he feels the need to protect you, let him. It's a small thing to grant him."

AJ didn't know why her mother would have said that. It seemed strange, or perhaps prophetic, and a cold chill rode in with the breeze.

"And what if I feel like I need to protect him?"

Helen averted her gaze for several seconds. When she turned to AJ, her eyes were bright and fierce, and they caught AJ in a powerful hold. Her hands tightened on AJ's, more strands from her updo flew about her face, and for an instant, she reminded AJ of an ancient warrior queen. "Then do it. Do whatever it takes to keep him safe, to keep him close. You're a fighter. You have your father's spirit, his intelligence, his courage. You always have. You and Finn are equal partners in everything, and sometimes it will be up to you and your strength, your power of conviction to be there for him." Her grip softened. "But there will be times when you have to let him go so he can be who he is. You can never take that away from him."

AJ pulled her mother in for a long hug. "You are so wise, Mom."

Helen's tinkling laugh lightened the mood. "I always tried to tell your father that."

AJ grinned, wishing they had more time before she faced the fog. "He knew, Mom. He always knew."

They held hands and talked about the yard. Helen promised to bring her gardening club out to help prepare the yard for winter. They'd just begun discussing container gardening when the scent of cedar touched her nose.

A strong arm circled her waist, and Finn rested a hand on Helen's shoulder. "And how are you lasses fairing?"

Helen smiled up at him, giving him a long appraisal.

AJ felt Finn shift as Helen's perusal continued before she finally responded, "We were talking about gardening and men." Her brow lifted. "It seems they have a lot in common."

Finn grinned and replied with a strong Irish accent. "Aye. They both require tending or they get a bit unruly."

Helen laughed and patted his hand.

Finn released AJ. "Now I must go see if Jackson requires rescuing from your ladies club, but I have a feeling it's wasted effort."

Helen kissed AJ's cheek and had turned to go inside when Charlotte grabbed her grandmother's hand and tugged her down the deck toward the yard.

AJ scanned the guests. Adam still sat at the picnic table with Madelyn, their hands touching, their legs brushing together under the table. Finn stood next to Jackson's chair and laughed along with the circle of women, who seemed entranced by Jackson's stories. Stella's fuchsia blouse stuck out of the middle of the group like a flare.

AJ had everything she needed, everything a normal person could wish for—a man who loved her, a family, and the world's best friends. And yet, in a couple of days, she'd risk it all for another friend, another family. She would be stepping back into virtually unknown circumstances during a very dangerous time. She prayed the events Ethan had laid out were true and accurate, and that their plan for Beckworth would be successful. Trust was all they had, and in the past, it had proved to be a very fine line indeed.

53

After checking on his guests, ensuring everyone seemed to be enjoying themselves, Finn strolled back to the house, nodding with his infectious smile at those he passed. A warmth enveloped him as he watched AJ sit next to Ethan, who had somehow gotten caught in a web of older women. He wasn't sure if she was rescuing Ethan or getting a front row to his discomfort at being the center of attention.

He wandered through the rooms again, this time without having to dodge children, and took note of the changes AJ and he had made to turn the inn into a home. When he stepped into his study, he sat at the desk and stretched his legs atop its surface, arms behind his head. He stared at the picture on the wall—a stormy sea with a tall ship riding it out. Helen had given it to him as a housewarming gift. The painting had been a favorite of AJ's father. He knew AJ wasn't fond of it being here, that the ship reminded him of the *Daphne Marie* and all he'd left behind.

When he'd made the decision to follow AJ back to her time-line, it wasn't a choice he'd made lightly. He'd had a good life when he was on a mission, but he hadn't had a place to call home. Not really.

He could have gone back to Ireland and cargo runs on the *Daphne Marie*, but it was a lonely life. A loneliness he concealed behind evenings at a gentlemen's club or in a rowdy pub. His family estate, though much smaller than it had once been, had been a viable option, but the thought of being a farmer, his days stretching to infinity, had terrified him. Hensley would find another mission for him, and while it would also entail running cargo—illicit or otherwise—it was a front for a spy network in service of the Crown. His life wouldn't be his own.

A moment of melancholy dampened his spirits. He had to admit he missed his friends, especially Hensley, who had seen something in Finn when they'd first met, not long after Finn had left the ship he'd crewed with Lando. It hadn't taken long for Hensley to see Finn's potential as a new recruit. Though Finn was Irish, which would be a challenge for infiltrating London's finer society, Hensley was convinced it could work. He built Finn a background that connected him to an unknown peerage, trained him in comportment at social gatherings, and taught him the high-stake games of gentlemen's clubs.

Finn learned quickly, and with his natural charm and quick wit, he found most doors open to him—Irish or not. It was a life he was proud of, and while he worked for England, most of the money he made went back to help those who worked his family estate. He originally thought he'd go back to Ireland one day and fight for her independence, but after careful deliberation, he determined he could better serve his country by remaining close to England's inner circles.

Years later, after Finn had won the *Daphne Marie*, Hensley moved Finn up the chain in his network. Having a ship was the best cover they could have hoped for, and it put Hensley on the trail of the Duke of Dunsmore, who had previously owned the ship. When Hensley heard of Beckworth's outrageous request to speak words over a rock and magically transport Finn to the future, they both had a good laugh. Yet Hensley considered it the best path to rescue Maire and support their mission to protect England. Hensley and his contacts asked Finn to try the Celtic incantation.

Finn had hated the first few months of time travel, but when he had time to think about those months, those days had been good ones. He marveled at the changes in society and technology with each jump. And if it weren't for his worry for his sister, he would have explored more of each period. He learned a great deal each jump, built his nest egg on the off chance he might never find the Heart Stone to take him home, discovered books that spoke of war and strategy, and witnessed the good and bad of humanity. But his worry for Maire overrode everything. Eventually the time travel became another lonely extension of his life. Until his last jump to Baywood.

He gazed at the photo on his desk. It had been taken when they'd first opened the door to their new home at the inn. Helen had wanted to be there, specifically to take photos. She had a talent for it. She'd captured her daughter's face perfectly. The large brown eyes that he'd seen through every possible emotion. Those luscious lips had thinned in frustration when they'd first met. He'd been concerned when his ship had appeared through the fog and he'd found her at the dock. The way she'd touched the ship, as if testing to be sure it was really there, had made him worry about explaining how he'd arrived.

He grinned as he remembered purposely keeping her off-balance so she wouldn't dwell on his ethereal arrival. He hadn't known it at the time, but he had found his touchstone. The one thing in his life that meant more than anything, and the one person who could end his loneliness. So when she made the decision in France to return home, there was no question he'd follow, for she was his home, wherever that might be. And though he still had to work out what he'd do after the Westcliffe was completely restored, he hadn't lied when he'd told AJ they'd work it out.

"Am I interrupting?"

Finn turned to find Adam staring at him from the door with a bit of a grin.

"No. I'm afraid you've caught me musing about my past."

"It must have been a good one. You're grinning like you discovered that pot of gold at the end of the rainbow."

Finn's grin grew wider. "Aye, and I believe I have. Sit. Can I get you something more to drink?"

Adam shuddered. "I think I'll take a pass. I still need to drive home."

Finn's grin faded. "How goes it with Madelyn?"

Adam brightened as he dropped into a stuffed chair and looked around the room. "We're talking. She hasn't said anything about me coming home, but she sometimes slips and mentions plans that seem to include me, so I think that's a good start."

"Have you asked to go home?"

Adam swiveled from gazing at the portrait of the ship, his eyes wide as if the thought had never occurred to him. "No."

Finn laughed. "Sometimes we men forget the obvious. Maybe she's forgiven you but isn't sure you want to go home."

"Why would she think that? She's the one that kicked me out."

"Maybe, but you don't appear to be suffering." Adam's brows furrowed, and Finn caught the fire brewing behind his eyes. "You're not sleeping at the office or a hotel. You have a nice apartment that you've begun to furnish. You tiptoe around

Helen." He shrugged. "On the surface, it appears you've set up a new life. Next thing you know, you'll be making up a spare bedroom for the kids to visit."

Adam's fledgling anger faded and he wilted into the chair.

"If you want to go home, just ask. It's been long enough."

"It never even occurred to me. I thought she'd let me know."

Finn laughed. "Sooner or later she will, but why wait?"

Adam jumped up and began to pace, hands in pockets. "I could have been home weeks ago. Well, maybe days." He ran a hand through his hair and stopped in front of the portrait. "This looks good in here. It fits."

"Aye. Your mother was kind to share it with us."

"Dad would have thought it a perfect setting." He scratched his head as he continued to stare at it. "It's almost prophetic." He glanced over his shoulder. "Does it make you homesick?"

Finn considered the question that he'd been mulling over earlier. "No. But I do miss my ship."

"I hate to do this at a party, but I wanted to update you on the power of attorney. Stella will represent AJ's business, finances, and the Westcliffe. I'll act on behalf of your other investments." Adam lowered his head before leveling his gaze on Finn. "Are you sure you're comfortable with me holding the reins?"

Finn raised a single brow. "You haven't been thinking of gambling again?"

Adam's face dropped.

Finn raised a hand and chuckled. "I'm sorry. That wasn't fair. But honestly, who else is there?"

Adam shrugged but still appeared hurt by the comment.

Finn stood and placed a hand on Adam's shoulder. "I trust you, Adam. I wouldn't have said that three months ago, but I have no doubt today. I can't think of two people better qualified to look out for our interests until we return."

"In case you don't return." Adam's voice hardened. When his

expression changed to match his tone, it confirmed what Finn already understood—how difficult it was to have family walk into danger and maybe never come back.

Finn held Adam's glare. "We have every intention of coming home."

Adam turned away from him, his gaze turning back to the portrait, but he didn't respond.

"This is my home now. Where AJ wants to be. It's as simple as that, but I have no illusions. We'll be going back at a time of war, with unknown adversaries. It's why Ethan and I have been training AJ in self-defense. I don't plan on sending her into danger, but she needs to be prepared."

"While Stella and I wait."

Finn nodded. "The power of attorney will go into effect when we leave and will stay in force until AJ and I return—or if only AJ returns." His voice trailed off because they both knew what it meant if AJ returned home alone.

"What about the Westcliffe?"

"Jackson has agreed to manage the property again. I've given him a list of work items that will keep him occupied through the rest of the year. Ethan claims Maire has improved the incantations for the stones, but I don't know what that means for us. When AJ and I jumped, only a week had passed in this timeline, but for a reason I can't explain, we spent months in 1802. I have no idea how long we'll be gone this time. Maybe a month but it could be several."

Adam nodded. "The papers should be ready in a couple of days."

"Right on time."

Adam walked away but stopped when he reached the door. "And you really plan to return?"

"Why would you ask that?"

Adam's expression went blank, and he dropped his gaze to the floor, his hands back in his pockets. "No reason. Just making sure."

After Adam left, Finn returned to his chair and stared at the painting of the ship. If Adam questioned his motives, did AJ? Did she really think he could ever leave her? That the call from his past was stronger than his love for her?

He knew he was melancholy at times. He missed Maire and worried about how she had lived her life, and now it seemed with good reason. But AJ had been right. They still grieved for the people they'd seen only months ago but who, in reality, had been long dead.

Except for the door that remained open. They still had the Heart Stone.

For AJ to think he would leave and not return was unacceptable. He considered his earlier discussion with Helen, then jumped up, tired of his journey down memory lane. When he reached the kitchen and saw Stella opening a bottle of wine, he smiled.

He took the opener from her. "Let me help you with that."

Stella reluctantly released the bottle of wine and glared up at him. "I'm perfectly sober enough to open another."

He leaned down and kissed her cheek. "Aye, I know lass."

"Okay. What's up?"

He gave her a shocked gaze. "What do you mean?"

She pushed back her hair and placed her hands on her hips. "Don't give me your Irish brogue and think you can pull one over on me." She squinted up at him, ignoring how easily he removed the cork or that he was pouring her the first glass. "You're up to something."

She seemed surprised when he poured a second smaller glass. He set the bottle aside, handed her a glass and lifted his own. He tapped her glass with his own. "I have a little project I was hoping you might help me with."

She studied him for a second before her own grin slipped out. "Am I going to like this project?"

"I think you might."

She tapped his glass. "To special projects."

54

Beckworth scowled as he watched the cars continue to arrive at the inn. The light breeze wasn't strong enough to keep the gnats away and a stream of sweat inched down his back. Murphy had posted two men around the parking lot. They appeared to be assisting with parking, but unless he'd invited the entire city, there was more than enough parking. The two men continually swept the forest with hard gazes, and Beckworth easily recognized them as security.

He almost laughed, somewhat pleased Murphy thought him a large enough threat to protect his precious guests. The music blared from the house and he shook his head. A party. Was Murphy sending him some signal that they weren't afraid of him? Was he flaunting the fact they had the Heart Stone and there was nothing he could do about it?

The only thing he knew for sure was that he couldn't remain here any longer. When an older woman got out of her vehicle and stumbled on her way up the stairs, forcing both security men to run to her aid, Beckworth slid from the ferns and snuck back through the trees. When he reached the moped, another car approached. Not wanting to be seen, he pushed the cycle through small breaks in the foliage, moving farther south, still hidden from the road. The going was slow, but when he determined he was far enough away, he caught sight of a narrow, well-worn path.

Playing a hunch, he leaned the moped against a tree and followed the path. Within minutes, the trail left the trees for a bluff opening to the coast. A spectacular view of the coastline stretched before him, and the cooler air dried the sweat from his brow, driving the flies away. He sucked in a deep breath and almost sighed.

His gaze flicked to the right, and he discovered he was able to make out what had to be the edge of the inn's roof. A low rise and trees blocked the rest of the building and the parking lot. The trees appeared to be the grouping he'd just been hiding in. A path ran down from the inn to a dock nestled within a private inlet.

Beckworth dropped to the ground, leaned against a rock, and stretched out his legs. He scrounged in his backpack and pulled out an apple and a long, single-edged, thin-bladed knife. He sliced a piece of apple and plopped the juicy tidbit in his mouth, gazing at the workmanship of the knife. He'd found it in the safe with the Browning Hi-Power and his flintlock. It had probably been owned by one of the sisters' husbands. It was finely made, and he had spent several evenings honing it and then polishing it until it sparkled.

He chewed the apple, savoring its tart sweetness, and considered the current state of affairs.

The sisters. What to do. What to do.

It had started with Louise and her innocent and continual questions about the mysterious AJ. Then he'd overheard Edith telling Louise that she'd been asking her friends at bingo if they knew anyone with the name. Baywood was a populous city but one of them would eventually discover something.

He didn't relish the idea of having to do something harsh if they got too nosy. He didn't see a reason to be mean.

Oh, he knew he could be dangerous, even deadly. He'd spent most of his life struggling to get one step ahead. To rise one more rung from where he'd been born. He hadn't become viscount by playing nice, but he had a limit. Some may think it a blurry line, and he had to admit he found the line faded at times. Yet there was a difference between callous and just plain evil.

He shuddered. The duke had been evil. Dugan was evil. Beckworth hadn't considered his actions toward Finn to be evil —kidnapping his sister, manipulating him, torturing him. That had all been in the name of claiming the Heart Stone. Then he'd discovered the duke's motives went far beyond the magic of the stones, and he'd begun to understand the duke was a bit mad.

He'd had no choice but to follow the duke's orders. He owed his title to the man, daft or not, and even from the far reaches of France, the duke had the power to strip him of it. When the duke had ordered the kidnapping of Maire and sent Beckworth the stone to give to Murphy, he'd had no choice but to comply.

He tossed the apple core over his shoulder and cleaned the blade before shoving it in his backpack. His own predicament pushed away his musings, leaving him to consider what he was willing to do to return home. With the duke dead, he could live the rest of his life as the viscount with nothing and no one to threaten him. He had enough money to live the life he deserved to have. Had been born to have.

He watched the waves splash against the dock. The bay appeared deep, and he wondered if Murphy had docked his ship here. He'd heard that Murphy had been able to transport his ship through the fog. He shuddered at his own memory of the mist.

His best option remained with AJ. If he could catch her

home alone, where he didn't have to worry about witnesses or her calling for help, he might be able to force her to open the safe. The Heart Stone would be his.

He absently reached into his pocket to touch the smaller stone. For the first time since he'd arrived, he felt close enough to his objective to allow himself to think farther than he had. The fog would probably take him back to the knoll in France where he had left all he knew behind. His first step would be to find a ship to England. He would need money, and while he had access to the sisters' money, it would be worthless in his time. What he needed was gold or silver. He laughed. That wouldn't be a problem either.

For the first time since the chase through downtown, he felt in control again. He stared down at the dock, silent and ignored in the big empty bay.

55

The black SUV slowed and parked along the curb under a Sitka spruce. Baywood was busy with tourists and Ethan was lucky to have found a parking spot in an older neighborhood a block from the center of activity. His blood pumped. After days of alternating between self-imposed solitude and training with AJ, he'd barely been able to keep the dark thoughts away. Images of what he'd done, or worse, what he hadn't done, were never far away.

Armed with a plan and a target, his mind was the sharpest it had been since his arrival. Energy coursed through him, firing every nerve, and he sensed the same intensity from the others in the vehicle.

Finn, who sat next to him in the passenger seat, turned around to face AJ and Isaiah in the back seat. "Is it still there?"

Isaiah nodded. "Hasn't moved."

Finn glanced up and down the street, his fingers drumming on the console separating him from Ethan. "I wish we'd been able to see which way he went."

Ethan turned off the engine and settled his back against the door so he could face everyone. "That was a great idea, moving the tracker from my SUV to Adam's car. If Beckworth is monitoring, he should be wandering the streets several blocks away. We shouldn't have to worry about him coming back too soon."

Isaiah, his eyes glued to his phone app, chuckled. "I'd love to see his face when he can't find either of your vehicles but his GPS says one of them should be right in front of him."

"Let's see where Adam and Stella are." AJ typed a message on her cell. After a minute, she nodded. "They're in place. About three blocks from the moped. They haven't seen anyone fitting Beckworth's description. I still think I should have gone with them. I'd be able to confirm it's Beckworth."

Finn shook his head. "I know that seemed the reasonable approach, but it's enough of a risk with Stella in the car. I don't want him spotting anyone."

"You're not saying Stella sticks out, are you?" AJ appeared shocked and a bit injured.

After two seconds of silence, boisterous laughter filled the enclosed space.

Ethan swiped tears of laughter from his eyes. AJ's response hadn't been that funny but the momentary reprieve from the building tension made him feel like his old self. "She's definitely the rainbow in our group."

Another short burst of chuckles followed until AJ's phone chirped. The laughter instantly drained from her face, leaving her a lighter shade of pale.

"What's wrong?" Finn asked, a grimace replacing his grin.

Ethan sensed the mood shifting again, and his hackles went up. AJ typed furiously and it was all he could do to not rip the phone from her hands, which, if he had to guess, was the same thing Finn planned as he hunched over the back of the seat.

"Tell us what's happening." Ethan reached for the door handle, ready to sprint wherever he needed to go. Driving to

Adam and Stella's location would be problematic with the tourists, and he envisioned another race through the streets.

AJ shook her head. "Stella got out of the car."

Finn slammed his hand on the dash. "Damn it all."

"Adam's texting. Beckworth turned back, like he was giving up and going back to the moped." AJ's voice cracked. "Stella tossed Adam the phone and was out the car before he could stop her."

"Flamboyant and brave. She's luring him back." Ethan had to hand it to Stella. She had quick wits and a bravery that went beyond stupid.

"Then let's not waste her gamble." Finn nodded at Isaiah.

Isaiah took a last look at his phone and stuffed it in his pocket. He ran a hand over his short-cropped hair. "I'll text you when it's done."

Finn gripped his arm before Isaiah could exit. "Don't take any unwarranted chances."

"Aye, Captain." Isaiah smirked before he exited, closing the door quietly behind him.

"He'll be all right." Ethan watched Isaiah hustle down the street wearing a simple black T-shirt and black jeans.

"Yeah, the only ones that'll notice him are the women," AJ quipped.

Her comment made Finn's brow rise, and Ethan laughed, the earlier tension slowly fading. They now played the waiting game.

AJ kept her eyes on the phone, occasionally glancing out her window. Finn seemed glued to the GPS app Isaiah had added to his phone. Ethan monitored the street, his instincts and training kicking in to stay alert. With Finn and AJ running surveillance, the role of scout fell to him. He cracked the windows, the sounds of cars and tourists racing in with the warming morning air. He breathed deeply as the mixed scents of salty air and cooked fish filled his senses. He could almost be in London, the loud noise of the bustling city similar to the chatter of tourists.

"Stella went into a store, and Beckworth is a couple of stores down. Oh God..." AJ's voice hushed to a whisper.

Finn's head popped up. "What?"

"Adam said he'd be right back." AJ glanced up, her expression hard to read. Ethan could swear that was a touch of pride mingling with her worry.

"Didn't we tell them not to get out of the car?" Finn ran a hand through his hair. "I've had less trouble with a ship full of drunken sailors."

Ethan barked out a laugh.

"And why are you laughing?" Finn scowled, his gaze continuing to flash back to the phone, never one to drop his guard.

"It feels good to be on a job again."

Finn stared at him for several seconds before a grin lit up his face. "Aye, that it does."

Adam tapped his fingers on the bottom of the steering wheel while he studied every face in the crowd. Most of the people he immediately ruled out—first women, then short men, old men, and then the heavier ones. When time ticked on, he began to worry that maybe Beckworth would disguise himself.

"You're not planning something stupid, are you?" Stella twirled her coffee cup, her fingers probably itching for paper or a napkin to fold her origami.

He grunted. "Why would you say that?"

"Your forehead is all wrinkly."

"And that tells you I'm thinking something stupid?"

"That tells me you're worried we're missing something." She glanced around. "You're thinking too hard."

"Not planning anything, but you're right. I'm wondering if he's wearing some disguise."

She shook her head and repositioned herself, turning toward him. "I considered that already. I don't think so."

Adam snickered. "So, tell me, oh great one, how did you come to that conclusion?"

She shrugged and played at the edge of her pink and orange silk cape. "He's too arrogant." She tossed her head as she scanned the streets, her auburn hair falling easily back into place. "He's been sneaking into homes, hanging out, drinking beer, watching the frickin' sunset. He's not worried about being seen when it suits him."

Adam had to agree and was thankful she'd steered him back on course. He couldn't understand how cops ran stakeouts without going nuts. Sheer boredom had his imagination running off target.

"Oh my God. That's him." Stella's voice rose an octave and Adam flinched when her fingernails gripped his arm.

He pulled his arm away, rubbing where her claws had penetrated as he followed her gaze. "You're right. That looks like him."

Stella turned in her seat to face the windshield, then scooted down. "He seems to be looking for someone."

"Yeah, and he looks frustrated."

"I thought Finn said he was a patient man," Stella said.

"Patient, maybe. But nothing is making sense to him. He knows Ethan or AJ should be around here but there's not a sign of them, and he hasn't found either vehicle."

"But he's getting close to yours."

"Maybe we should have parked AJ's car over here earlier so he'd find it and stay in the area."

"Isaiah seemed confident Beckworth could get close with his

GPS but wouldn't be able to zero in on the exact location of the tracker."

"Close is feeling a bit awkward right now."

They both melted into their seats, lowering themselves until they could barely see over the dash. Beckworth came within twenty feet of Adam's car before turning around.

"Shit. I should have texted AJ to go." Stella woke her phone and began to type.

"Hold on."

They both watched as Beckworth walked away, heading back toward his moped. He kept glancing down at the GPS.

"Well, crap." Stella tossed him her phone. "Tell AJ now."

"Where are you going?" Adam hissed as Stella jumped from the car before he could guess her plan. "Now who's being stupid?" His hoarse holler either didn't reach her, or as he suspected, she was simply ignoring him.

She ran down the street toward Beckworth, then jerked to a stop to look in a store window when Beckworth turned around. Beckworth's expression changed and a slow smile emerged. He'd spotted Stella.

Adam typed as fast as he could. He ignored AJ's all-cap reply. He refused to lose his partner in the crowd.

Beckworth watched her, and for a moment, Adam thought he might actually approach her. He gripped the door handle, ready to burst out. He took a deep breath and held it before slowly releasing it. There were too many people on the street. Beckworth wouldn't cause a scene. Would he? AJ said he'd run when she'd encountered him the last time, but that was only after Finn and Ethan had shown up.

Adam felt the blood drain from his face, and his breath hitched. Beckworth wore a jacket and had access to a gun. No. He had two guns and it wouldn't require much effort to steer Stella to a quiet location.

Adam opened the door, leaving it ajar in case he had to get out quickly. He shouldn't have worried. Stella must have sensed Beckworth getting too close. She'd probably caught his reflection in the storefront window because she stepped back just as two men began to pass her. She ran right into the men, stepping on one of them by the way the man lifted his foot as if in pain. She wore stiletto heels. Adam laughed.

Beckworth fell back to stand by a lamppost.

Stella made a show of apology, the men moving away as quickly as they could, then she followed two women into a clothing store.

56

Beckworth wanted to scream with frustration. He studied the monitor and rubbed his eyes, ignoring the first signs of a headache that had plagued him since his arrival. The blip hadn't moved in the last forty minutes. AJ's or Ethan's car should be within sight of where he stood. There had been a few that looked similar, but this time he had the plate numbers. A suggestion from Louise that had surprised him. For all her nonsensical banter, she occasionally revealed a crafty side. He might miss the sisters after he got home. Then he laughed out loud, startling a woman walking by, which only made him laugh harder.

The laughter died quickly when he glanced down at the monitor and his frustration returned.

After circling the block for a second time without success, he tapped his finger against the monitor. He glanced around. The crowd grew as the morning waned. It was getting warm, and his jacket stuck to his back, the weight of the gun reminding him why the lightweight coat was necessary. He stopped under a tree, a small reprieve from the sun. Five more minutes and one final slow walk around the block before he'd call it quits.

He scanned the cars again without success. His focus turned to the crowd, first on body type and then hair color. While it wasn't necessarily true with tourists, most people walked with their head down, so he found hair color to be the fastest way to single people out. Between AJ's brown hair and Ethan's black hair, he could ignore the fair-haired people.

When nothing flagged his interest, he walked a few feet, then decided the hell with it. Perhaps lunch was in order while he considered his options. He turned around and walked several feet before someone bumped into him. Beckworth cursed when the man strolled on without one word of apology. He was still fuming over the inconsequential nudge when he spotted the red hair. Not the bright ginger that was more common, but the darker, richer hue of auburn that he preferred.

She walked with her head up, her gaze following the store windows, but he didn't need to see her face. The bright orange and pink wrap that hung to her knees would have been enough to give her away. The cape flowed around her, showing off the lovely curves underneath her sunflower yellow dress. Something stirred in his loins and his earlier irritation vanished. She was a vision. His unexpected bodily response to her shocked him. A memory, buried deep inside where he had mentally locked it away, seized him and he shook it off.

Stella Caldway. Her name rolled off this tongue. He hadn't given her much thought even with her picture plastered on real estate signs all over town. Nor had he paid attention to her when he'd seen her with AJ or the time he'd noticed her arrive at the inn. Yet there was something in her casual stroll and the way she flicked back her hair that excited him. He shook his head when he realized he'd started walking toward her. What would he say? Should he ask after AJ? Would she scream and bolt? He didn't think so. Something told him she'd have more spine than that.

Her back was toward him. He glanced into the window

where she stood, wondering which article of clothing had caught her eye. He was only a few feet away when she stepped back without looking and ran into two men. One yowled and picked up his foot, a curse flowing from his mouth.

Stella appeared concerned as she tapped the man's arm, asking if he was all right in between her quick words of apology.

Beckworth backed away. *What had he been thinking?* He scanned the people before quickly checking the GPS. If Stella was here, AJ had to be close. When he looked up, he caught Stella walking into the store.

He should follow her. Then he saw the man. The same one who had arrived with her the last time he'd seen her at the inn. Her husband? Disappointment fluttered through him for a reason he refused to examine. Beckworth didn't know where the man had come from. Was he with her for protection or was it just a coincidence? The man appeared in decent shape but didn't have the predatory bearing of Murphy or Hughes. He could still be a worthy opponent.

The man appeared concerned with his brows knit together as he followed Stella into the store.

I saiah strode down the sidewalk of the less traveled side street, hands in pockets, just another tourist stretching his legs. His heart pumped like a racehorse, and he drew in a deep breath to settle his nerves. Stella seemed more than capable of distracting Beckworth long enough for him to complete his part of the plan. *Stay cool.* His grandpops would knock him back to apprentice if he knew he'd gotten this involved in Finn and AJ's business. The old man was still fussing and growling about the whole time-travel thing.

When Isaiah had arrived in town to help with the inn, he'd

been over the top to see his grandpops working on his favorite building. When Isaiah was younger, Jackson would tell the story about how he came to manage the property. Then he'd share tall tales about the first owners, the civilian plane spotter during World War II, and the crazy man who had lived in the inn.

The old man's dream of refinishing the old building came true when he met Finn Murphy. He'd been given the chance to restore it like he'd always imagined. They followed Finn's final designs, but Finn depended on his grandpops's wisdom and insight, easily agreeing to many of his visions. The more the old man grumbled, the more Isaiah knew Jackson wouldn't want to be doing anything else.

Isaiah stopped at the corner of Eighth and Main, where the tourist shops lined both of the busy streets. He leaned against a building next to two other men who were probably waiting while their wives shopped. He scanned people as they roamed the busy intersection, locals in a hurry and tourists with all the time in the world deciding what to do next. No one fit Beckworth's description. He dropped his head and slipped into the crowd, moving toward his target.

Two blocks later, he stopped again and stood in the long line of a food vendor. Across the street of a quieter intersection and a couple parking spots off the main drag, he spotted the moped. He studied the tourists and took a deep, calming breath that did nothing to settle his heart rate. The aroma of rolled tacos and empanadas made his stomach growl. After waiting another minute and with a last look around, he stepped out of line and followed a couple as they crossed the street.

Halfway across, he noticed the coffee shop on the corner with large windows that ran along both sides of the building. *Perfect.*

When he reached the corner, a slender man brushed past him, tugging at his sleeves. Isaiah stopped. His heartbeat thundered in his ears and sticky sweat coated his armpits. When the man strode past the moped without a pause, Isaiah wiped his forehead and, before he could talk himself out of it, followed the man. As he approached the cycle, Isaiah pulled a folded note from his pocket. Two strips of double-sided tape ran down one side of the note. With his head partially bent, his gaze racing from one person to the next, he peeled the paper from the tape. When he reached the cycle, he slammed the note in the middle of the handlebars, gave it a good solid rub to ensure the tape stuck, and kept walking. Twenty yards later, he turned to cross the street and leaned against a large maple. No one followed or paid any attention to him. He saw no one resembling Beckworth.

Breath rushed out of him like he'd been holding it for the last five minutes. He wiped his brow and could smell the mixture of terror and excitement soaking the air around him. Feeling exposed, he hustled back toward the corner, past the moped across the street, note still in place.

He entered the coffee shop, and though there were plenty of customers, the cashier wasn't busy. He picked up a bottle of water, handed the cashier some money, and found a seat at the bar that ran along the window. From his seat, he could easily see the slight rustle of the note where he'd left it. Now it was time to wait.

Beckworth ducked behind a lamppost and a colorful sandwich-board sign. A few minutes later, Stella and the man walked out. They seemed to be arguing, and Stella had her arm on the man's bicep, steering him down the street.

Beckworth grinned. She was a feisty one.

The two walked several feet before Stella released her grip on the man, and he rubbed the spot where she'd held him. They slowed their pace, seeming to have settled whatever difference they had.

He turned away from the domestic scene and walked back to the moped. He'd had enough for one morning. Nothing made sense with the tracker, and he was confused by his unexpected response to seeing Stella. Nothing good could come of that.

He sighed with relief on seeing the moped until he got closer and noticed the piece of paper fluttering in the light breeze. He glanced around as he pulled the note from its perch, his fingers sticking to the back of the note.

It took two seconds to read it, and his earlier confusion turned to rage. They had played him. He wanted to lift his head and howl with frustration, but they might be watching. He hadn't felt it before but now he sensed someone out there. While still within the safety of tourists, he crumbled the note and stuck it in his pocket.

He jumped on the moped and turned onto the busy street, thankful for the comfort of a crowd. Once he'd driven several blocks, his breathing slowed, and the sweat dried.

They had turned the tables on him. The war was far from over, but he'd lost this skirmish. He didn't know where he'd gone wrong, but the excitement of the chase made his blood race.

Fair enough, Murphy. Game on.

57

Beckworth stared at the crumbled note, now stained from beer rings and grease from his basket of fries. After finding the paper stuck to the moped, he'd felt the thrill of the chase, but it had soon worn off, and rather than go back to the sisters, he'd just ridden down the coast. An hour later, he'd driven back in a darker mood and circled the streets of Baywood before ending up at the marina.

Sparrows jumped back and forth from a nearby table to the ground, feasting off leftovers from a family of five who had left their trash behind. The birds twittered with happiness over their newfound treasure.

He traced a finger over the edges of the note. The more he read the words, the less sense they made.

Tomorrow. Two p.m. The safe will be open. Take it and leave.

This was their plan? Did Murphy take him for a fool? It was such an obvious trap, he began to wonder about Murphy's sanity. He sighed and rubbed the sting from his eyes. He was so weary of the game. If he were honest with himself, he'd prefer to walk up, knock on Murphy's door, and beg to be sent back to England. The only thing preventing him from jumping on the moped was the fear of them simply shooting him and dumping him in the bay. He understood their fear about relinquishing the Heart Stone.

He glanced around. He'd been at the marina a few times before to stare at the fishing boats and listen to the gulls screech for food. If he sat on the bench in between the fish-cleaning station and dock ramp, he could close his eyes and breathe in the combination of salt air and rotting fish guts while the boats scraped against the side of the dock. It was the closest he could get to the sounds of home. Not of Waverly, for that he needed gardens and the sweet trill of songbirds, but of London. The only thing missing was the shouting of hawkers, but if he arrived at the marina at the right time, the fishermen could be just as boisterous.

It was time to stop hiding. He'd taken the game to them, but he would never master the technology of this era. He knew when he was beat. And, truth be told, he couldn't take one more day with the sisters. They ran hot and cold, browbeating more information from him, and Edith appeared more suspicious with their increasing questions. It was probably his imagination, but it no longer mattered.

He picked up the note, holding it so tightly between two hands that it ripped where the beer stain had weakened the page.

A scuffle at the nearby pier drew his attention. Two men argued over something, one pointing a finger at the other man's chest. The other man, hands planted on his hips, shook his head. Beckworth couldn't make out the words, but he almost laughed when the man who'd been stabbing his finger stepped into the boat with too much haste. Unable to correct his footing, the boat rolled from the uneven weight. When he landed on his ass, the other man jumped in to help, which caused another jostling of the boat, and soon, both men were down. They began to laugh.

Beckworth stared at the sleek little sailboat, and then smiled to himself as the men tried to stand. Each time they tried to help each other, one would pull the other back down, creating additional barks of laughter. But Beckworth was no longer interested in the men.

If Murphy wanted him at the inn, he would be happy to oblige. If it was a trap, so be it, but he wouldn't play by Murphy's rules, the man should know that. If Murphy didn't, that would be his loss.

Fate might be a cruel mistress, but she certainly has a timely sense of humor.

Beckworth drained the last of his beer and tossed the rest of his fries to the ground for the sparrows and gulls to fight over. He dumped his trash, then returned the plastic tray to the fish stand as he'd seen others do and winked at the lovely lasses working the counter.

He stopped to talk to the harbormaster, then wandered down to another small building. Fifteen minutes later he jumped on his moped.

Regardless of what happened tomorrow, he'd only have to endure one more night with the sisters. He could only hope they didn't plan on poisoning him.

58

AJ leaned into the Adirondack, savoring the last of her wine, the taste of grilled salmon and rosemary risotto still happily lingering on her tongue. Not only had Finn made a superb dinner, but he'd whistled as he'd washed the dishes. While phase one of their plan had gone off without a major disaster, Finn's lightheartedness seemed counterintuitive to their morning or the waiting game they now played.

Stella's last-minute decision to get out of the car had put the plan in jeopardy, but without her quick thinking and bravado, the mission could very well have been a failure. They had all gathered at Joe's after the event, lucky enough to snag a large corner booth on a Saturday, and whispered about how things had gone.

Finn had patiently waited for the first round of drinks before turning to Stella. "I thought we agreed you and Adam would not leave the vehicle." His tone was even, but his gaze held cold shards of emerald.

Stella either didn't notice the edge in his voice or, more likely, didn't care. She had long ago stopped being scared of Finn, regardless of the mood he was in. She waved a hand at him as she sipped her martini. The fact she was drinking vodka at noon rather than wine spoke volumes. Stella was excited and terrified by what she had done. When she gave Finn one of her shit-eating grins, AJ held her breath. While Stella might not be afraid of Finn, AJ knew how angry he was underneath his carefully controlled manners.

"Beckworth looked frustrated, running his hands through his hair and constantly tugging at his jacket sleeves. He had turned to go back to the moped. We were losing our opportunity." She huffed and sat back, a slim finger gliding around the rim of her martini glass. "What was he going to do in a crowd of tourists? Besides, Adam was there."

Adam nodded. "I have to admit, at first I was as irritated as you when she jumped out of the car. But she's not exaggerating. Beckworth was walking away."

Finn studied Stella, then let out a large sigh that seemed to release all the tension he'd built throughout the morning. After another moment, he nodded and raised his beer. "Then thank God for your quick thinking." Then he turned to Isaiah. "And to Isaiah for his tracking skills and confirming Beckworth got our message."

Everyone raised their glasses and that was that. The rest of their lunch was spent reviewing their plan. While everyone considered the morning a success, the next phase was the trickiest, and everyone agreed there were too many things that could go wrong. Yet, it was the only plan that reduced collateral damage. After they reviewed their roles for the next day, Finn excused everyone. There wasn't all that much to review, and Finn wanted everyone rested and not worrying about tomorrow. While that might work for seasoned mercenaries, AJ doubted it would work for this particular group, but everyone seemed eager for time alone.

Finn surprised AJ with an outing to the ranch. While visiting with Hagan and Seraphina, they decided to take the horses for a short ride. It had been more than a week, and she could use some time in the saddle before they returned to England. Neither of them expected they'd be spending time in many carriages in their pursuit of Maire. AJ had to be ready for anything. After their ride, while AJ brushed down the horses, Finn spent time discussing a modified version of their travel plans with Mac.

When he jumped into the truck, he looked haggard.

"Why don't we pick something up for dinner?" AJ suggested. When he didn't respond, she asked, "Is everything okay with Mac?"

He nodded and gazed out the window. "She was surprised by how long it might be before we return from our European vacation." He snorted an abrupt laugh. "But she promised the horses would be exercised, and she has Adam's contact information." He reached over and squeezed her knee. "I was actually thinking about whether I should cook salmon or steak." His grin offset the concern in his eyes, and his thumb traced a circle on her skin, a sensation that at any other time would have elicited a tingle. "It might be some time before you get any more of my home cooking."

The missing tingle became a quick bolt of fear that shimmied up her spine, and not for the first time, she questioned what they were doing. But they had come too far to turn back now. They had to know what had happened to Maire, and leaving it like this would haunt them the rest of their lives. She shook her head, pushing away thoughts better left for tomorrow.

She gripped the hand on her knee, using her thumb to rub against his little finger, embracing the hint of a tingle that found its way to her. His eyes softened, the creases around them lightening, and she leaned over to kiss his cheek. "I love your grilled salmon."

Now with dinner over, AJ watched the sun creep toward the horizon and tried not to think of what the next day would bring. She pulled her wrap tight around her shoulders. This might be the last time the two of them watched the sunset together from this deck. She shook her head, forcing herself back to more positive thoughts. They might be going back two hundred years, but it wasn't as if it were medieval times. The Georgian period was civilized under a single king, and as long as they stayed in England, they didn't need to worry about the war with Napoleon.

Before she could revert back to mentally listing all the things that could go wrong with their mission, she felt warm hands on her shoulders. Finn removed the empty wineglass from her hand and leaned down to whisper in her ear. "Now that dinner is over, would you mind drawing us a bath? I want to spend the rest of the evening with you in my arms."

The telltale tingle nipped at her sensitive spots while his whisper melted into her skin, drawing in the heat of his words and flooding her senses. She couldn't think of a better way to spend the evening. He helped her stand and gathered her in his arms for a hot and way too brief kiss. When he finally released her, he turned her toward the door and softly slapped her backside. "I'll be up once I finish the last bit of cleanup."

AJ winked at him. "I so love to see a man in the kitchen. It gets me all hot and bothered."

He grinned and pushed her through the door. "Keep it up and you'll never make the stairs."

"I would be okay with that."

"Aye." His eyes smoldered with intent. "But I have other plans. Now go. I'll only be a minute."

59

AJ flew up the stairs grinning like a blushing bride. The last few nights, between the stress of unexpected events and the twice-a-day training, they'd fallen into bed, a tangle of arms and legs, bodies too tired to do anything more than cling to the warmth of the other. If he was thinking bath, she would make wicked plans for what to do after.

Steam rose from the bubbles, and candles cast warm shadows as she stripped down and stuck her toe in the tub, grimacing at the heat. She let her body acclimate to the temperature inch by inch and was neck deep in the scented froth by the time Finn entered the room.

He was naked, and she couldn't help but let her gaze trace down his lean, muscular frame. With their busy schedules, this was the first time she'd had to fully appreciate what the last couple weeks of training had done to his body. Her body had changed as well. She climbed faster and wasn't as tired when she reached the top. Her clothes fit differently, tighter in some areas, looser in others. As she continued her slow perusal, she noticed the cut edges to his biceps, the light shadows between the hard ridges of his stomach, and the lean muscles of his runner's legs.

A simmering heat darkened his emerald eyes, and he patiently held a tray with two glasses filled with their own bubbly liquid. He had to be the best damned waiter she'd ever seen, and she giggled as she motioned him closer with one curled fingertip.

He handed her the two glasses before placing the tray behind her. He stepped in, ignoring the heat as he immersed himself, grabbing the bottom half of her leg and pulling her closer. She slid easily with only a drop of champagne slipping from the glasses. They clinked glasses before taking their first sip.

"What are we celebrating?" AJ watched him carefully. He was up to something. It wasn't the first time they'd shared a glass of wine or bubbly in the tub, and he loved a good soak in a hot bath. He was beginning to enjoy showers more and the thought made her cheeks burn. Yet, if she didn't know better, he seemed a little nervous underneath all his suave seduction.

"Can't a man have a soothing bath with the woman he loves without it being a special occasion?"

She smiled. "It's not something we've done much lately."

Finn frowned. "Aye. We've definitely had other priorities." Then his lopsided grin appeared, and she felt her earlier blush creep lower until it met the skin where the water skimmed her shoulders. The tingle coursed through her, as intoxicating as the first day they'd met, when all she'd wanted to do was shove him in the bay. "But we've got time now, and lost time to make up for."

He set their glasses aside and pushed her back against the tub, lowering his head until he was so close she could hear him breathe her in. His lips were gentle at first, tasting, and then the explosion of heat became an earth-shattering kiss. She gave back with just as much abandon, grabbing his hair to pull him closer, her tongue moving with his in some sensual dance.

She wrapped a leg around him, tugging at him. He followed her command, his arm curving around her waist as the kiss deepened. Before she knew what was happening, his arm tightened, and he twisted, flipping them around so he was underneath her. Water splashed over the rim, and they laughed at the mess they'd made.

He slid back and pushed himself into a sitting position, pulling her onto his lap. The water settled around them, and he ran a finger over her breasts before leaning in for another kiss. When she met his lips, they were softer, almost hesitant.

The kiss warmed quickly but when she pushed for more, he pulled away. He placed a chaste kiss on her forehead, then twisted around and fiddled with something on the tray. When he turned back, AJ couldn't take her eyes off the small black box tied with silver ribbon. She couldn't move, couldn't breathe. The only sound was a slight rushing in her ears and the whoosh of the bathwater as it settled from Finn's movements. The light scent of lavender cascaded around them, but through it she could still pick up the slight aroma of cedar from his heated skin, and she remembered their first time on the *Daphne Marie*.

When she glanced up, his eyes held the same fire as when he'd first stepped into the bath. His signature grin remained but seemed a faint memory of its original glory just moments ago. If she bent her head to his chest, she knew it would be beating as fast as hummingbird wings. Her heart skipped a beat. Then she inwardly cringed. Maybe it was earrings.

His voice was rough and somewhat hesitant. "This isn't what I had originally planned. To be honest, I'm not really sure what I'd intended. And if you want something grander, I'll search for something more fitting once we're back home, but I hope this will do until then."

He handed her the box. She knew she must have taken it because it was suddenly in her hands, but it wasn't the box that made her speechless. It had been his words, *once we're back home*. She could have cried. Nothing could be more cherished than hearing he wanted to come back. That this was his home. With her.

Sucking in a deep breath, she slipped the knot from the ribbon, cracked the box open, and stared. She didn't think she could be more surprised by everything that was happening, unless of course they had been earrings. They were so much more. Two Celtic promise rings burrowed within the soft velvet. They weren't the traditional Claddagh rings, but a simple silver design of two clasped hands etched with tiny Celtic knots.

Tears sprang as she remembered the ring Maire had almost bartered away when they'd escaped from Dugan. It had been her mother's promise ring, and Finn had held on to their father's so each would always remember their parents' undying love for each other. He'd made his own promise to always watch over Maire.

Now AJ held similar rings in her trembling hands.

"They're promise rings. I know the timing is wrong with us leaving and your mother's party. I didn't want to overshadow it." He caressed her thighs, and as good as it felt, AJ didn't think he was aware he was stroking her. His thoughts seemed miles away.

When he finally met her eyes, they were bright and full of love. "You think I haven't noticed you watching me? That I don't see the worried look in your eyes when I'm contemplative? I've told you before that I sometimes miss my time line—my sister, my friends, and, aye, even my ship."

When she turned her head away, he touched her chin, bringing her gaze back to his. "But with as many friends as I had, it was a lonely life. I never thought I'd find the kind of love my parents had for each other, and now that I've found it, I won't squander it. I won't let it go. I'll follow my heart to my dying days as long as I have the ability. I'm going nowhere without you. And this life," he waved a hand toward the house, "this is what we make of it. Fate brought me to you. I won't question it."

AJ struggled to get her mouth to work. All she wanted to do was kiss him and keep kissing him until there was no one in the world but the two of them. "When you took me back to your time, it wasn't by my choice. Then I had to make a terrible decision to return home without you." Her gaze locked with his. "I'll never be left with that choice again. I'd prefer to live in this time and in this place, but the truth of it is, I'll live wherever you are. I never want to be separated from you. So yes, I'll marry you, Finn Murphy. Tonight if I could, before we step into the unknown. You are my past, my now, and my future."

He squeezed her upper arms and kissed her forehead before taking the box from her. "My father married my mother with promise rings. Do you know the history of them?"

AJ cleared her throat, and her voice rasped, "I know something about them."

He nodded and smiled. "They're similar to fede rings, and their meanings have changed over time. In Ireland, the more common practice was handfasting. But my mother preferred the promise rings because they announced their commitment to the world."

"That's beautiful."

"You're beautiful." His tone turned serious. "I don't mean for these to be engagement rings, AJ."

"What do you mean?" The words stuck in her throat, and she blinked to decrease the pressure forming in the back of her eyes.

"You said you'd marry me tonight if you could. I'm saying you can."

She stared at him, lost in his gaze, not quite sure how they had gotten to this moment. So many things had fallen into place for the two of them to be here, and she worried that if she blinked, she'd be back in her old apartment, everything some distorted dream.

"Do you trust me?" His words were as tentative as the first time he'd said them.

She couldn't help but smile. That had been his question when he'd pulled her into the past. She'd spent weeks wondering if she'd given him the wrong answer then. She didn't have to wonder tonight.

"Until my dying day."

He handed her the large band while he took the smaller band. He stared at her and released a slow breath. His grin lit his eyes, and AJ felt that familiar tingle sending a shiver up her spine and sprouting goose bumps along her flesh. It might have been from the cooling bath water, but she didn't think so.

"Repeat what I say and do." He kissed the tip of her nose. "Are you ready, love?"

She nodded as he took her left hand.

As he slid the ring on her finger, he said, "You are blood of my blood, and bone of my bone. I give you my body that we two might be one."

After a short pause, he nodded at her. With trembling hands, she took his left hand and slid the ring into place. "You are blood of my blood, and bone of my bone. I give you my body that we two might be one."

"I give you my spirit till our life shall be done. You cannot possess me for I belong to myself, but while we both wish it, I give you that which is mine to give."

She repeated the words in a soft rush, mesmerized by their endearing meaning. When she was done, he clasped her left hand with his left, took the ribbon that had been tied around the box, and with her help, fashioned a loose knot around their joined wrists.

"From this time to the last, will you stand by my side?"

"Always."

His kiss was long and full of devilish temptation. The ribbon fell loose as he reached down and his fingers dug into her hips, closing any gap that prevented them from becoming one. The cool air of the room prickled her skin in defiance of the sensuous heat melding them together.

He slowly released her and his full, heart-stopping grin reappeared. With a motion so fast he set the tub water splashing over the sides, he stood and picked her up.

As they crossed into the bedroom, AJ spied the bottle of champagne he'd left on the dresser.

"Wait. Go back so I can grab the champagne."

He raised a brow but turned as directed. After she grasped the bottle, he turned toward the bathroom until she whispered in his ear, "We won't need the glasses."

60

AJ played with the necklace, a silver box chain she had strung through her promise ring. She rolled the ring between her fingers. She couldn't stop smiling every time she touched it.

"I've caught you daydreaming again." Finn stepped behind her and wrapped an arm around her middle, pulling her against him as he nibbled her ear.

"And if you keep doing that, we'll never get on with our day." She leaned her head to one side to give him more access to her ear and neck.

"You tempt me, woman." His murmured words created a shiver along her spine. "Do you need help cleaning up?"

She shook her head and looked down at the small breakfast of fruit and croissants they'd barely touched. It seemed the prospect of their afternoon had marred their first morning of wedded bliss. She turned around and played at the black cord around his neck that held his promise ring. "Do you really not mind that we're wearing our rings on necklaces?"

He kissed the tip of her nose. "It makes sense we keep this between us for now. We don't need the distraction."

"I don't know how I'll keep it from Stella."

After a minute, he sighed. "You won't have to."

A brow rose as she studied his face. No. He hadn't. "You told her." She wasn't sure if she was hurt at not being the one to tell her best friend or shocked Stella had been able to keep this type of secret.

He chuckled and grabbed a strawberry as he moved away. "She picked up the rings. If it helps, she only thinks we're engaged." This time his kiss found her lips and whatever hurt feelings she had disappeared. He seemed to be reluctant to let her go, his grin melancholy. "You can tell her as much as you want. It appears she can keep a secret."

She thought about it as she fingered her ring, rubbing a thumb over the Celtic etchings. "You never said where you got them."

"I had them made." He picked up plates and placed them next to the sink before pulling her to him again. "Do you remember the last day we were in France and Maire melted down the Heart Stone setting into a new one?

AJ nodded. Maire had created a Celtic cross setting similar to the one Finn had worn with his stone.

"After she removed the smaller stone I carried, she gave me back the original silver setting. I asked a local jeweler to melt it down and create our rings. She had a special knack for engraving."

When AJ couldn't find the words to respond, he bent his head until their foreheads touched. "In a way, it was part of what brought me to you."

A shaky breath escaped and AJ wrapped her arms around him until she heard his soft grunt. She chuckled and held on tighter. "I love you so much, I'm not sure I can breathe."

He laughed in turn and tried to pry her away. "I know the feeling."

She stepped away and gave him a wry smile. "Guess I don't know my own strength."

He rubbed his ribs and grumbled, "The training must be working."

She tucked her ring under her blouse and patted his backside before clearing the rest of the table. "We have a long day, husband. Best we get to it." She tried to hold her stern expression, but she couldn't stop grinning when she passed by.

He stopped her long enough to kiss the top of her head, and she thought she'd enjoy married life if he felt the need to kiss her every two minutes. "Aye, wife, and I expect you to be quick about it." He checked his watch. "Ethan will soon be wearing a hole in the floor." He shoved water bottles into a duffel.

The reality of their day almost spoiled the sound of Finn calling her wife. Yet thoughts of Beckworth couldn't overshadow her happiness, and still giddy from their impromptu ceremony, she hoped it didn't distract her from completing their plan. She picked at a slice of cheese, nibbling at it before sliding it into a plastic bag. "Are we doing the right thing? Will he take the risk of coming here?"

"There aren't many sure things in life."

"Except us?"

He lifted his head from his tasks, his lopsided grin reassuring her. "Aye, except us."

After storing the fruit in a tub and placing it and the cheese in the fridge, she turned and ran a hand through her hair. She fidgeted as she stuffed the croissants in another bag. Shaking her head, she blurted out, "Something just doesn't feel right."

Finn nodded. "It's sometimes like that before a mission. Doubts. Have we thought of everything? What is he planning?" He shrugged. "It's normal to be a bit nervous. The only thing we can do is follow our plan but stay vigilant for any surprises."

"What if he doesn't come? He has to know it's a trap."

"Aye, he'd be a fool to think otherwise. But he wants this over as much as we do."

AJ thought about it. She had suspected it herself. "How can you be sure?"

Finn shrugged. "You can never be sure. Always remember that. But in this case, I saw it in his eyes after the chase through downtown. Besides, didn't you say yourself he wanted to talk? You seemed to believe him."

AJ slid the croissants in the freezer and submerged the empty plates into the sudsy water. She tried not to think of last night's bath and the hours after. It was going to be difficult to stay focused today. After a minute she said, "Maybe we should have met him in a public place or even at this house he's staying in with these two older women." She shook her head. "Even that seems wrong. Why would these older women take in a strange man?"

"Didn't Adam say they were widowed sisters? Perhaps they thought they were taking in an injured bird."

"More like a snake."

"You've seen Beckworth in action at Waverly. He can be charming when he needs something."

She shivered, trying not to remember. "I suppose you're right."

"If this doesn't work, then we might have to risk taking him at the sisters'. But if we can do this here, where other people aren't put in danger, it's worth the attempt."

She nodded and returned to the dishes.

Finn stepped behind her. "I wish you'd come with me. I can drop you off at Stella's."

She rinsed a plate and set it in the draining basket. "I won't be more than five or ten minutes behind you." She laid the last dish in the basket, released the sink stopper, and let the soapy water drain away. Wiping her hands, she clutched him and hugged him until she thought she might crack his ribs. She couldn't stop touching him and knew it was as much from nerves as the need to hold her husband. "You have your part to play, I have mine. I'll meet you at Stella's like we planned."

"And after the large pot of coffee I'm sure she's already brewing, you'll both be buzzing like angry bees."

She laughed. "Enough. Grab your duffel and begone with you."

"Careful, wife. I might be forced to drag you upstairs and remind you of what that word means."

Her brows knit into a frown but it was difficult to repress her smile. "Not if I use some of the moves Lando and Ethan taught me. I'll have you on your back before you can say uncle. Then I'll show you what it means to be my husband."

He laughed, his eyes bright with mischief. "What a life we'll have together." He kissed her, but his expression turned serious as he backed away. "Ten minutes. No more. I don't want you in this house alone."

"We have hours before he's supposed to be here."

"Never underestimate your enemy, AJ."

The statement sobered her instantly. She nodded. "Ten minutes, then I'm gone."

She followed him to the front door and watched him climb into his truck. She waved as he drove off, and after glancing at the trees surrounding the property, she turned to finish her tasks.

61

Isaiah crawled out of bed after an early morning call from Ethan. He schlepped down the hall, slippers slapping against the wood floor of the apartment, eyelids drooping. He turned on his monitor as he passed by the kitchen table on his way to the coffee machine. After the coffee began to brew, Isaiah stared at down at his monitor. The GPS displayed Beckworth's moped at the marina again.

After a quiet grunt, he scratched his head and stretched his arms as he stumbled down the hallway. Fifteen minutes later, after brushing his teeth, running through three sets of sit-ups and push-ups, and taking a quick shower, he strolled back to the kitchen a new man. All he needed was coffee.

His class schedules for the fall semester lay strewn across the table, and he slid the papers into a pile before turning his attention to the monitor. Glancing at the GPS, he frowned when he saw Beckworth's moped still at the marina. He checked the history, which confirmed the moped had been there since four a.m. He brought up the security cameras at the inn. When he saw AJ's car in the parking lot, he scrolled through the outdoor cameras and ignored the inside cameras, not wanting to invade her privacy. Nothing out of the ordinary.

Still bothered by the location of the moped, he texted Ethan an update.

E than dropped his bag by the front door and shuffled through a final walk of the house. He ended the tour in the living room and fell into the stuffed chair in front of the massive windows that overlooked the ocean. The sun hadn't quite reached the water, leaving the sea a somber shade of blue. Puffy white clouds dotted the morning sky and promised another hot summer day.

Though the view was breathtaking, he hoped this would be the last day he'd ever have to gaze at it.

He hadn't slept well since arriving at Finn and AJ's door. His dreams had begun simply. One dream—Maire dressed in one of her finer gowns, one of such a deep shade of blue it seemed spun from sapphires. She stood at the other side of a large ball-room. Dozens of other guests milled about. Ethan strode toward her, but with every step, the crowd closed in on him, and she floated farther away.

The nightly visions quickly turned to nightmares. Maire spirited away in the middle of the night—scared, alone, and spitting mad. She would come to him, a silent plea on her face, before she disappeared into a smoky haze, and he'd woken screaming her name on more than one occasion.

When he'd woken this morning, something had changed. He'd dreamt of her walking the gardens at Waverly, pink flowers threaded through her flowing, wheat-colored hair. He guessed the dream was Waverly, though he'd only caught a brief glimpse of the winter landscape when he'd traveled there with Thomas. When they had confirmed she wasn't there.

Now that he knew Beckworth was somehow involved, Waverly made sense. Perhaps they'd held her someplace else before moving her to Waverly. He clenched his fists. He'd discover what had happened to her once they had Beckworth hog-tied with nowhere to run.

Once they were back home in his century, it wouldn't matter what army Beckworth had amassed. With the king's attention turned toward France, Ethan would bring the hammer of Hereford down on Waverly. If that wasn't enough, the earl had friends with enough men to lay siege like their ancestors before them.

A low growl ripped from this throat seconds before he heard the honk. Broken from his daydreams, he launched himself from the chair, ready to get this day done. After one last glance at the ocean, the rays of sunshine skimming the surface, he turned, grabbed his bag, and locked the door behind him.

Finn's old, battered truck hummed softly in the driveway.

When he climbed into the passenger seat, Finn just nodded as he backed into the street. He'd driven a few miles before Ethan asked a perfunctory question. "Adam has the papers ready?"

"Aye."

They rode in silence for several more miles.

"Is Isaiah monitoring?" Finn asked.

Ethan stared out the window, his mind centuries away, still seeing Maire walking the gardens. "Since this morning. He texted before you arrived. Beckworth was at the marina."

Finn shot him a look. "The marina?"

"We don't know why. He was there last night as well."

"Damn it."

"What's wrong?" Ethan found it strange that Beckworth had

begun visiting the marina. He assumed Beckworth had heard the call of home as he had. A nagging feeling slammed him in the gut. He'd been mooning over Maire instead of keeping his head in the game. Foolish.

Finn slammed the brakes, swerving to miss an oncoming car as he made a U-turn in the middle of the street. Horns blasted and Ethan grabbed the dash as Finn urged the truck faster.

62

AJ folded the dishcloth and left the dishes to dry while she ran upstairs. She changed from jeans to a knee-length summer dress with deep pockets. The jeans were more practical but a nagging feeling warned her to keep her dagger close. She listened to those little voices now, something both Finn and Ethan had encouraged during her training.

She was on her way downstairs when she popped into her office with a last-minute thought. If she was going to Stella's, she might as well clear another to-do off her list. She grabbed files for two fussy clients she wanted Stella to coddle while she was gone. It wasn't that she didn't trust Gwen, the shopkeeper covering her clients, but Stella had a knack for the difficult customers. After emailing the files to Stella, she stuffed her notes in a satchel.

The ten minutes she'd promised Finn stretched closer to fifteen, but she couldn't see how it mattered. Beckworth shouldn't arrive for another few hours, assuming he bothered to fall for their trap.

Ethan had wanted to storm the house where Beckworth lived with the sisters. She had worried he would go without them in his rush to get home, but Finn had convinced him to back off. Each time she thought about the sisters, she couldn't understand their reasoning for taking in a stranger. Then she remembered Beckworth in action at Waverly. Finn had been right. Beckworth was quite the charmer when he wanted to be, and if he had bewitched the sisters, she wouldn't forgive herself if innocents were hurt. Not yet. The sisters would be plan B.

She caressed her necklace and a rush of deep contentment enveloped her as she strolled down the staircase. Married. Husband and wife. It was all so surreal. An unexpected stab of icy fear stamped out the warm emotions. Before long, the fog would come. She wanted to help Maire, but she had doubts about stepping back into the mist. At first, she'd thought her reticence stemmed from fear of what they'd find when they returned. The truth was, she worried that fate wouldn't appreciate the way they played with destiny, and as the saying went, she could be a cold bitch.

She dropped the satchel next to her purse on the hallway side table. A sound from the kitchen made her turn. Had Finn returned for something or had Jackson forgotten he wasn't scheduled to work today? Maybe he'd forgotten his tools. She glanced back and caught the edge of the dagger sticking out of her purse. An itch made her want to grab it but she scoffed at her silliness. It was just a matter of time before she'd start seeing the boogeyman lurking in the shadows.

She took two steps before stopping. She'd rather be a paranoid fool than a smart-looking corpse. Sticking the dagger in the pocket of her dress, she tiptoed to the kitchen.

"Finn, is that you? Jackson?"

When there was no response, she hesitated as she reached the entry to the kitchen. Her skin hummed with electricity as she eased into the kitchen.

And froze.

Beckworth sauntered toward her. Not in a rush but with the steady stride of someone who knew he had the upper hand. She backed up, her mind racing. *Why is he here so soon?* He must have been sleeping in the shrubs based on the small cluster of leaves that clung to his disheveled hair. So unlike his usual suave persona.

A sickening thought struck home. He must have seen Finn leave.

She quickly calculated her options. She could run for the bedroom, or more accurately, the bathroom. While it was on the second floor, it had a reinforced door, but so did the closet in the library.

Finn would eventually build a panic room, but until then, the two rooms filled a niche. She hoped she'd be able to test that theory.

Without another thought, she raced for the hall. She'd barely made it past the stairs when he caught her hair and the pain snapped her to a halt. A hand, firm as steel, grabbed her upper right arm to hold her in place.

"And where do you think you're running off to?" Beckworth snarled in her ear. "You did invite me, didn't you?"

AJ winced at his pincer grip and the burn of her hair being ripped out by the roots. She spit out through clenched teeth, "I really hate early guests. I haven't vacuumed yet."

He chuckled. "I always enjoyed your spirit." His hot breath at her ear made her shudder. "Where is it?"

He shook her head as he asked the question and the pain was so intense, stars formed at the edge of her vision, followed by tears that blurred the rest of it. The tight grip on her right arm dug into a nerve, cutting off her ability to reach for the dagger.

"Where's what?" she managed to spit out. She tried to

concentrate but with his relentless pressure on her arm and hair, all she wanted to do was beg for mercy.

"The Heart Stone, Miss Moore. Stop being obtuse. I saw Murphy drive away. He's getting sloppy with this fine living." He sneered. "My luck seems to be changing."

Her eyes focused on the hallway. The library was so close, but Beckworth dragged her backward toward the staircase.

"Is it still in the safe?" The growl reverberated through her skull.

Stay calm. Think it through.

The closet with the safe was a good place to be, but she preferred the library. It would give her more time.

She relaxed enough to let Beckworth continue his direction. She needed an advantage and the only idea she could grasp on to was the stairs. He might have a good grip on her now, but navigating the stairs would be a different story.

"You could have made this easy. All I wanted to do was talk," he hissed.

His breathing became labored and they'd only managed four steps. He must have been sitting around, letting the sisters fill him with crumpets while she'd trained twice a day. She wasn't the weak little tulip he'd first met.

Her body relaxed with each step they took, and he reciprocated by loosening his grip as he tried not to trip up the stairs.

When they reached the halfway point, she'd waited as long as she dared. When he raised his foot to the next stair, AJ slammed her foot down on the one bearing all his weight. He screamed and his leg buckled. When he grabbed for the railing, he was forced to release her. She kicked his knee, and he dropped. He rolled down the stairs, arms flailing.

She waited a split second to gauge the cadence of his fall. Grabbing the railing, she leaped over him and ran for the library. A few terribly short seconds later, she heard the stomping of his feet on the wood floor.

The little shit was more spry than she gave him credit for. She could turn on him with the dagger, but Finn had trained her better than that. She needed help and had to trust that her team had her back. It didn't stop her from reaching to feel the handle of the dagger.

The library was only steps away. If she could make it to the closet, all the better. She would have an armory at her disposal, but that wasn't her main goal. She just needed to cross into the library.

His footsteps pounded in her ears and she could almost feel his breath on her neck. He was unbelievably quick. Terrified he might be within grasping range, she threw herself into the library, sliding across the carpet like a baseball runner sliding home.

"Damn it, woman. Why can't you ever cooperate?" His breaths were ragged, and she considered letting him get closer so she could kick him where it counted.

She rolled over to face him. Her fingers grasped the handle of the dagger before gently releasing it.

The coward stood over her with just enough distance between them to keep him safe. And he held a gun pointed at her head.

I saiah retrieved the plate of bacon from the microwave, his nostrils flaring at the tasty aroma that filtered through his apartment. He moonwalked back to the counter, then dipped into an electric slide move while Aretha blared from the tower speakers in his living room. With his college schedule confirmed, he felt the first jitters of homesickness with half the summer still left to enjoy. The sounds from his grandfather's playlist reminded him of family picnics at the beach and holidays around an old stone fireplace.

As he assembled his egg-and-bacon sandwich, bopping to the classics, two faint knocks reverberated from the wall that separated his apartment from Mrs. Kowolski. He smiled, opening the fridge to grab the orange juice. Two knocks meant she enjoyed the music, three knocks meant she was being tolerant, and he would either lower the volume or turn on his wireless headset.

He'd begun what he considered another impressive moonwalk back to the counter when a faint ping from his computer snagged his attention. He dropped the orange juice container on the counter and ran to the computer. He had programmed each of his software applications to ping with a different tone so he'd instantly know how critical the alert.

He glanced at the clock above the corner desk. AJ and Finn should be out of the inn by now. His fingers sped over the keyboard in a blur and the monitor enlarged the picture that had created the alarm.

A chill ran over him when he spotted the two figures in the library—one on the floor and the other standing over her with a gun in his hand. He fumbled for the cell phone as a call for respect rang from the speakers.

Finn thrummed his fingers on the wheel. The traffic slowed along the coastal route. He should have waited and left with AJ. How could he have overlooked the bay? Did Beckworth know how to handle a boat or had he paid someone? What other skills did the man hide?

He glanced at his watch. They were only five minutes from

the turnoff to the inn but with this traffic? He couldn't just sit here. Ethan hadn't said a word since Finn had turned back for home, but his fingers tapped a staccato rhythm on the window frame.

Ethan's cell rang and it filled Finn with dread. After he quietly listened, Ethan stared out the window. His reply sent chills down Finn's spine. "Wait for us at the top of the drive and call Adam."

Ethan's anger-filled expression turned Finn's chills to ice.

"Beckworth is at the inn. He has AJ."

63

Beckworth paced the room, his mumbles growing louder with each pass. He'd been at it for several minutes, but the gun remained trained in AJ's general direction.

She didn't think he'd shoot her, but pulling a dagger against someone with a gun wasn't the brightest idea. The closet door, only ten feet away, glared at her like a beacon in the darkness. If she were standing, it would be worth running for it, but she had no advantage sprawled on the floor. If he was desperate enough, he just might pull the trigger.

"All right. Let's do it this way." Beckworth glanced around the room, tapping his foot. "Lie face down and don't make a move."

She glared at him and stayed where she was.

He advanced so quickly, she flinched back. He kept his distance, and while he might not shoot her, he appeared mad enough to take a swing.

"Why must you make everything so difficult? You can either let me tie your hands or I'll be forced to knock you out." He waved the gun in her direction and smiled. "Your choice."

Worry crept across his features when she hesitated. He didn't want to hit her. That had to be a good sign but she capitulated. She didn't want to be tied up, but unconscious? That was unthinkable, and she'd still end up bound.

She spit carpet fibers out of her mouth and watched his shoes move around the room. Drawers opened and slammed shut. She guessed he was searching for something to bind her hands, and she almost choked out a laugh at the absurd situation she found herself in. *Take as long as you want, you fool.* The more time they spent in the library, the more chance she had of Finn finding out she was in trouble. She stopped herself from skipping down the dark path and letting negative Nancy have her way with her. She would stay positive and have faith that Isaiah was monitoring and Finn would be on his way.

All those weeks of training, and here she was, caught out of the first gate. It would be difficult trussed up, but she wasn't out yet. Finn had taught her patience, and that included drawing Beckworth's game out as long as she could.

She closed her eyes and pressed her cheek to the warm floor. After several minutes, he knelt next to her, his knee pressed against her hip. He was surprisingly gentle when he tied her hands together. Her head faced the door of the closet. Ten feet. She'd shake her head if she could. So close.

While she lay face down, Beckworth strode to the closet and disappeared. She'd managed to get to her knees and was creeping toward the hall door when Beckworth pulled her up.

His pistol had been replaced by a rifle. A modern one that didn't require powder.

A bolt of fear ran down her spine. Why did he need a rifle? She struggled at her bindings.

He grinned at her. "I know you have a dagger in your pocket. If you promise not to use it, I'll let you keep it." He laughed as he dragged her out the door.

She struggled all the way to the staircase, where Beckworth stopped and pulled her close. "I'd ask if the Heart Stone was still in the safe. I'd ask when Murphy will be returning. But we both know you won't tell me anything, so let's play a game. First, we need to get to the third floor." He stopped and tucked the rifle under his arm. "I should have a clear view of the parking lot from there."

AJ's eyes flew wide with understanding. Finn and Ethan would be target practice for Beckworth. A sudden bolt of true fear shot her with adrenaline. She tore free. It took only three steps before Beckworth grabbed her.

His breath skimmed along her neck when he whispered, "We're going up the staircase. If you fall with your hands tied, you'll likely break your lovely neck. Be a dear and hold your struggling for when we reach the top."

As much as she wanted to fight him, she knew he was right. With her hands behind her back, one wrong sway would push her off-balance. That didn't mean she didn't resist with each step, soaking up every minute she could to slow him down. Halfway up the stairs, he picked up a backpack that had been shoved to the side. She hadn't noticed it earlier and he must have dropped it when she'd stomped on his foot.

When they reached the top, he ignored the room with the safe and pushed AJ into a room across the hall that faced the parking area. Tiny beads of sweat broke across her upper lip, and unable to wipe her face, she licked at the salty wetness. Finn would be blind to their location in the house. He would walk right into Beckworth's trap.

Beckworth pointed to a corner on the front wall. On shaky legs, she used the wall to slide into a seated position.

"Just stay." Beckworth left the room and returned a minute later with two boxes he set by the window. He peeked through the sheer curtain and, seeming satisfied, gave her a smug grin. He retraced his steps, this time returning with one box that he set on top of the other two. With infinite care, he perched the rifle on the stack of boxes and sighted down the barrel. He stepped back and cracked the window just enough for the barrel of the rifle to poke through.

After a few minutes, he turned toward her. "Anything to say?"

AJ glared at him until he glanced away. He picked up the backpack and pulled out an old pocket watch. Any other time, the antique would have her asking questions about the maker and year of manufacture. Now all she wanted to know was how much time had elapsed since she'd first slid into the library. It seemed like hours but it was probably no more than ten, maybe fifteen minutes.

How far would she let him take this before she gave up the Heart Stone? When she heard Finn's truck pull in? Maybe she could distract him by asking him about Maire.

Beckworth laughed. "I can see the wheels turning in your head, my dear, but I've got all the time in the world and a bird's-eye view."

They sat in silence, Beckworth staring out the window, the minutes ticking by until he snapped. He growled as he turned on her. "You need to tell me the combination to that safe."

AJ flattened herself against the wall until she realized the dynamics had changed. Her eyes flashed with such hatred, she was surprised he didn't spontaneously combust at the heat rolling off her. "I thought you had all the time in the world."

His hands balled into fists at his sides and then he tapped them against his head. He looked like he wasn't sure what to do, like he'd never thought through the rest of the plan. He whispered, "I just want to go home."

She tilted her head, unsure she'd correctly heard his simple plea.

"What about Maire?"

Confusion filled his eyes, punctuated by down-turned brows. "Who?"

She rolled her eyes. "Please. You know. The woman you had as a *guest* for almost two years." She put a special emphasis on the word guest since she didn't have her hands to add the air quotes.

"Miss Murphy, you mean? What about her?"

AJ hesitated, not expecting a denial. "We know you have her at Waverly again."

He snorted. "And how would I have accomplished that since I'm obviously here with you? You've all become daft."

Her anger sparked. "We're getting pretty tired of your games. Just like this one."

He strode over and squatted in front her so they were eye to eye.

She noticed he'd left the rifle by the boxes.

"I don't play games, Miss Moore. But I do play for keeps. One way or another, I'm going to get that Heart Stone."

"We'll see about that."

Beckworth and AJ turned toward the door as if on cue.

Finn stood just inside the door, Ethan behind him. Both of them were sweating and breathing hard.

Beckworth's gaze flicked to the rifle, then back to Finn. In a split second, Beckworth leaped for the rifle.

Finn must have been expecting the move because he was lightning fast. He tackled Beckworth as the rifle went off.

64

Ethan groaned and leaned away from Stella.

"Sit still. It's barely a scratch." She sounded angry and her hand shook when she dabbed at his arm with a cotton ball dowsed in antiseptic.

"That's what he gets for not moving fast enough." Finn glanced over Stella's shoulder. "She's right. It's just a scratch." He turned back to AJ.

She'd sunk into a dining room chair and now stared out the window at the ocean, absently rubbing her wrists. Thin red marks showed where she'd struggled against the restraints. He wanted to punch something. The marks would be gone by morning but that wasn't nearly the point, and he cursed himself for the hundredth time for not making sure she'd left with him earlier.

He crouched in front of her chair and grabbed her hands, running a thumb over her wrist. "How are you doing?"

"I didn't hear your truck pull up. That's what he was waiting for."

"Aye. We parked at the top of the drive and came in from the south. We used some of his own tactics."

Her gaze turned to him, her expression unreadable. Then he noticed the spark of gray rimming her brown eyes. She was angry. He couldn't blame her. He'd spent the last hour wavering between paralyzing indecision and needing to rip someone's head off.

She forced her thoughts out in a rush of breath. "I don't like Isaiah and Adam up there with him."

"They'll be fine. It's a minor precaution. Beckworth is tied up and locked in the closet with a bar across the door. They're only up there because Ethan refused to come down without someone watching the door."

Her eyes blurred for a moment and then she blinked. "When the rifle went off..." She shivered and a grim smile appeared. "I guess I need to toughen up."

He kissed her forehead. "It was a scary situation and you did well. That was great stuff, keeping him distracted and talking."

She glanced at Ethan before leaning into Finn. "Do you believe what he said?"

It took a moment for him to understand what she was asking. Beckworth and his denial that he knew Maire's whereabouts. Finn didn't know what to believe, and until he had a chance to speak with Beckworth himself, they could only go on the information they'd uncovered. AJ wanted a safe answer, a pleasing answer. He couldn't give her one. It wouldn't be fair. She had to prepare herself for whatever they got Beckworth to reveal.

In the end, he just squeezed her hands and stood. "We're about to find out."

Ethan waited for Isaiah and Adam to leave and closed the door behind them. The room was bare with the exception of the stacks of boxes against one wall. Two folding chairs sat open next to the boxes. A wooden, straight-backed chair sat in the middle of the room, its back to the window that overlooked the ocean, ropes laid across the seat.

The time he'd waited for was at hand. He nodded to Finn, who pulled up the board braced against the closet door.

"You have a fine sense of irony to lock him in the same closet as the Heart Stone." Ethan picked up the ropes from the chair.

Finn shrugged. "If he wants it so bad, he should at least be near it." He grinned and opened the door. "Let's have some fun."

Beckworth sat with his arms tied behind his back. He leaned against the wall with the safe, the picture of Lily Mayfield several inches above his head. Ethan would have laughed but he was beyond the ability to find humor where this man was concerned. In fact, he'd become someone he didn't recognize, and he wondered if Maire would ever look at him the same way. It bothered him. He wanted to find himself again, but not until Beckworth answered their questions.

Finn moved in and picked Beckworth up by an arm. Ethan waited for Beckworth to fight back and found it unsatisfying when he didn't resist. Ethan braced again when they untied his arms and settled him onto the chair. Beckworth only squirmed to find a more comfortable position before Ethan retied the ropes.

"If you want to beat me for breaking into your homes, it seems fair. But all I want to do is go home."

"Worried the sisters might be missing you?" Finn asked.

Beckworth snorted. "Those women are deranged. I need to get away from them before I do something I'll regret." He glared at Finn. "I'm talking about Waverly. I want to go home to Waverly."

"Why don't you just pop over there like you've been doing for the last couple of months?"

"You're talking in riddles. You know what I want."

Beckworth sounded tired and his confused expression surprised Ethan.

He slid a glance at Finn.

"Why don't we start at the beginning." Finn pulled over a metal folding chair and sat with one leg crossed over a knee.

Ethan leaned against the wall, too emotionally charged to sit. He wanted to prowl the room, but he held himself in check. His eagerness to hear Beckworth's tale kept him focused on the man he planned to bloody before the afternoon was through.

"How did you get here?" Finn started.

Beckworth thought about it. "I assume you mean in this time?"

Finn nodded.

He shrugged. "I don't really know." He hurried to continue when Ethan shifted his stance. "I don't. I remember being at the glade in France."

"Why were you there?" Ethan asked.

"I wanted to know if the stones worked. I didn't believe the stories." He glanced at Finn. "You were gone for so long, everyone else became a believer. Then you returned with Miss Moore. There was something off about her, but I couldn't put my finger on it. Well educated, yet she seemed out of place. I'd met people from the colonies, and she didn't quite add up." He paused and lowered his voice. "I'd been watching you with that monk, and when the lot of you headed for the knoll, I followed. I wanted to see what would happen."

He closed his eyes, then fidgeted against the ropes, seeking a comfortable position. "When the fog came, it was as if Miss

Moore had called for it with those strange Gaelic words. When you vanished, I couldn't move. I couldn't fathom what had happened. Then something tore through me, like someone or something had reached inside to pull out my guts."

He stared at Finn. "It was the worst feeling in the world. Nothing but a bright white light. My stomach cramped, then the fog seemed to toss me out like yesterday's garbage. I was delirious and my shoulder hurt worse than when the Moore woman stabbed me. Next thing I knew I was living a nightmare."

Ethan stared at the floor. The story was plausible. Finn knew it as well as he did from the dozens of times they'd traveled themselves. He didn't like the way the discussion was going, and when he glanced at Finn and noticed the firm set of his jaw, he knew Finn didn't like it either.

Could Beckworth's jump have been nothing more than a mistake? Had Beckworth simply been drawn along with the stone, as Ethan had been from the dock when Finn and AJ had disappeared?

"You have one of the stones?" Finn asked.

Beckworth nodded. "I took one before the duke packaged them for travel. He never noticed. He was too focused on escape."

"Why would you take one?" Ethan asked.

Beckworth shrugged. "I was never a favorite of the duke's. No matter what I did for him, it was never quite good enough. I thought if I had a stone, I'd have a bargaining chip."

The man wasn't a complete dolt after all. Finn was right. It was his arrogance that had done him in.

"Why were you following AJ?"

Ethan groaned. It didn't matter anymore. He wanted to know where Beckworth had hidden Maire.

Beckworth shook his head. "It's not what you think. I wanted the Heart Stone so I could go home." He sneered, some of his hubris returning. "How can you stand this time period?" He nodded at the room they were in. "The traffic and tourists, foul-smelling air from tin boxes you call cars, and constant noise. Don't you want to return?"

Ethan's gut clenched at the truth of what he heard, that instinct to go home, to complete their mission, and forget everything they'd seen during their time travels. When he glanced at Finn, similar thoughts were written across his expression.

Was it all a simple accident of fate and nothing more than Beckworth wanting to go home? It made sense Beckworth would look for AJ. It was simple to deduce this was her time period.

"If all you want to do is go home, why do you travel back and forth between this time and our own?" Ethan's question snapped Beckworth's head up.

He stared at Ethan as if he were addled. "What are you on about, Hughes? Has one too many time jumps cluttered your brain?"

Ethan stood over him after toppling his chair with one swift kick. In a flash, Beckworth stared up at the ceiling.

Ethan leaned into Beckworth's field of vision. "Tell me how you're traveling back and forth in time without the Heart Stone. Did you somehow get your hands on the torc?"

Beckworth's eyes bugged, and he lifted his head to scream at Finn. "The man's daft. What the hell is he talking about?"

"Don't play us for fools, Beckworth," Ethan continued. "We know you were at Waverly in 1803. There were witnesses. How were you able to jump back and forth in time?"

Beckworth stared at Ethan as the seconds ticked on. Then he dropped his head to the ground and laughed. It was a hysterical, high-pitched sound that grew into a strong belly laugh. Tears streaked his face before he began to choke.

Ethan and Finn jumped to raise his chair so the man could breathe, and Finn slapped him on the back for good measure.

"This is your one chance to speak the truth." Finn pulled his chair closer and sat, his menacing grin in place. "Maybe you're spinning a tale. If you have the torc as Ethan suggests, the Heart Stone would make it very powerful indeed. Maybe when you jump back and forth, the timing isn't as accurate as you hoped for, or you don't arrive in the right location." He leaned in until Ethan was sure Beckworth could smell Finn's breath. "Maybe we need to find the torc and force you to remain in this time period."

Beckworth's gaze widened with each word Finn spoke. "No. No. It's not a lie." He tossed his head toward Ethan. "I have no idea what he's on about. I've been here for almost four bloody months now. I'm losing my mind. All I wanted was the Heart Stone so I could go home. 1802, 1803, who bloody cares." The last sentence rushed out as a shout.

It was the most frighteningly honest thing Ethan had ever heard, and the worried expression from Finn confirmed he believed Beckworth's rants as well.

Finn nodded toward the door, and Ethan followed him.

"Do you believe me?" Beckworth called out as the two men closed the door behind them. "I could use some food."

Neither man spoke as they tramped down the stairs to the kitchen. Ethan mentally ran through everything they'd learned from Emory. Beckworth claimed he wasn't time jumping. If he wasn't lying, then what of Sebastian's journal? And more importantly, where the hell was Maire?

65

AJ shoved the clean pan into the cabinet and slammed the door. She watched Stella, Adam, and Isaiah out of the corner of her eye, glancing at each other with encouraging nods, desperately searching for a change of topic. The silence continued as she finished putting away the dishes from a hastily prepared lunch.

Stella had attempted to help with the cleanup, but AJ had unfairly bitten her head off, not wanting to be consoled or managed. Finn had been right that she shouldn't participate in the interrogation, but damn it, she'd been the one Beckworth had dragged around the house by the hair.

"Enough," Stella declared. "We've watched enough of your pity party. You know you don't belong up there."

AJ scowled at her but when Stella's shoulders dropped, her anger dissolved, yet she couldn't quite admit defeat.

Stella wrapped her arms around her. "There are so many other things we need to do. Is your duffel ready?"

AJ wiped her hands on the jeans she'd changed back into and nodded. "It's in the library with Finn's bag. He just needs to add the weapons." She touched the dagger she'd strapped to her leg. As long as Beckworth was in the house, it wasn't coming off.

"Let me go give it a once-over while you finish paperwork with Adam." As Stella turned to leave, AJ grabbed her hand.

"I'm sorry, Stella."

"I know." Stella glanced at Adam before she left the room.

AJ turned to the bay windows, hands on hips as she stared at the ocean. There really wasn't much left to do. They'd eaten most of the perishables at lunch. Dinner would either be frozen dinners or a meal out of a can unless someone ran to town.

"I just need your signature on a couple of pages." Adam pushed a chair around for her. He spread out the papers and laid the pen on top of them.

A loud crash reverberated from upstairs and everyone glanced at the ceiling.

"They'll be down soon to tell us what's going on." Adam pointed at each line where AJ needed to sign, handing over power of attorney for her business and finances to Stella. Finn and Ethan had signed similar pages before they'd started questioning Beckworth.

Isaiah placed three mugs on the table and poured coffee. "It must be going well. There's hardly been any screaming."

AJ glanced at Adam and they both laughed.

Isaiah's face went blank, then realizing what he'd said, he smiled. "It's official. My ass must be as crazy as the rest of yours when I think a good interrogation is anything less than three screams."

"If we don't count the thumping coming from the room, then we're only at two screams," Adam seemed to agree.

AJ shuddered, wondering why she'd been so angry at missing out on the beatings, although she'd like to take a swing or two at Beckworth.

When Stella returned, Isaiah grabbed a mug for her, but she took the pot from him. "Weren't the two of you going to take a look at the boat? Someone should take it back to the marina."

"If it's a sailboat, Finn will be the only one qualified to sail it." Adam picked up the legal documents and stuffed them in his briefcase.

Stella grinned at AJ. "I recall Finn teaching you to sail."

AJ snorted, then smiled fondly at her memory of Finn's failed attempt. They'd hardly known each other, and she'd been too interested in a getting a story. "I don't think my short-lived drowning session counts."

When the men looked at her, she waved her hand. "A story for another time."

Isaiah held her gaze. "I'm counting on that."

AJ was genuinely touched by his concern. He wasn't alone in hoping she and Finn found their way home again.

"You can tell us about it tonight over one last blow-out meal before you all leave." Adam sipped his coffee while listing out dinner possibilities.

Another thump, louder than the rest, was followed by the slamming of a door.

"Assuming they finish with Beckworth. Sounds like whatever they're doing could take all night," Stella quipped. AJ thought Stella would have walked away from the sounds coming from the third floor, but she hardly batted an eye. Not until AJ had wanted to participate, then Stella had been Team Finn in agreement to squash that idea.

"As long as we find out what's happened to Maire," AJ responded. "It will be worth the wait."

"Then I'm afraid you're going to be disappointed."

Everyone turned at Finn's words as he and Ethan stormed in. Their expressions said it all. Not even a few more screams would give them what they wanted to know. Then a cold realization dawned as icy fingers squeezed her gut. Was it possible everything they'd learned at Emory's was worthless? Had the information in Sebastian's journals somehow been wrong?

"He's sticking to his story that he hasn't left this time period since his unfortunate arrival." Finn thanked Stella for the fresh coffee and took a long drink, not seeming to notice the heat as it burned its way down.

"And you believe him?" AJ asked but didn't need to. She could see their acceptance on both their faces.

Finn dropped into a chair. He ran a hand over his face, then rubbed his eyes. Beyond his fatigue, AJ noticed the hard set to his jaw. His calm reserve was starting to fray. "He's scared, and I can honestly say it's not something I've seen in the man before. I thought he had ice in his veins, rarely showing a sign of weakness. Even in France when we had him trussed up like a Christmas goose, he showed backbone." He glanced at Ethan. "Aye, I believe him."

"His story of getting caught in your stream, or whatever you call what the fog does—" Ethan waved off the mug of coffee Stella offered him. He pointed to the bottle of Jameson, and she fetched a glass. "It matches what happened to me when you and Finn jumped the first time. The Heart Stone seems to drag any stones within a certain perimeter along with it. We don't know what that distance is, but it seems to still work that way, even with Maire's updated incantations."

"Stella, sit down and stop waiting on us," Finn commanded. He got up and gave Stella's shoulder a quick squeeze before pulling a bottle of wine from a rack. He opened it and poured two glasses, sliding one to Stella and one to AJ. "Keep the coffee for later. We have some thinking to do."

"So, what do we make of Sebastian's journal entry?" Adam's question caught them off guard, but the truth of it hit the group hard.

No one responded, and Finn poured himself two fingers of Jameson before pushing the bottle toward Isaiah. He declined, having retrieved a fresh bottle of beer.

AJ racked her brain for another solution. She knew Sebastian better than any of them, had spent time under perilous conditions at the monastery, and through it all, the monk had been steadfast. Not just in keeping them safe, but in his role as protector of *The Book of Stones*. He'd held it as seriously as any knight. He wouldn't write something in his journal he didn't truly believe.

Was it possible something had happened that had changed history? AJ didn't think so. After returning home safe and sound with Finn, she'd had time to think about her experience while Finn healed from the jump. Her father had talked about time travel. She hadn't remembered until the stress of her trip began to fade. One of the concepts she remembered was that the universe insisted on order. Small changes would flow like shallow ripples through time, fading the farther time progressed, restoring everything to how it should be. Another theory was that time was fluid. Could it really fold back on itself? She'd tried to read about quantum fissures and quantum flux but had become lost within the first few pages.

"Something isn't right," AJ finally said, pushing away the wine.

"I think that's fairly obvious," Ethan replied.

"No. I mean there isn't anything wrong with Sebastian's journal." She picked up an origami swan from the pile Stella had completed earlier. She picked at the tips of its wings, bending one before releasing it, then she flicked at its head. "Sebastian wouldn't have written something he didn't know for fact. Maybe this Ratliff girl didn't know what she was talking about, but why would she lie? If she didn't receive Sebastian's letter until after her father had already left for Waverly, he couldn't have encouraged her to lie in her response. So why would she share anything but the truth or bother writing back at all?"

Finn rubbed his finger along the wood grain of the table. A

sign he was thinking through the possibilities, strategizing. "So that piece hasn't changed. Ratliff traveled to Waverly assuming he was meeting with Beckworth."

Ethan nodded. "It's still plausible."

"Then if Beckworth wasn't at Waverly, who did Ratliff meet up with? I have to say, while the story of meeting a thief on the road is equally likely, the timing bears scrutiny." Finn poured another two fingers and sat back.

Ethan stood. "There's only one way to find out."

When Finn started to get up, Ethan placed a hand on his shoulder. "This might go faster if it's just the two of us."

Finn studied Ethan with a hard gaze before nodding and settling back down. No one offered another suggestion. This was Finn and Ethan's area of expertise. AJ had no qualms with Ethan handling the next round of questions on his own. In fact, she was fine with him using whatever means necessary to get at the truth. She wondered if she should be bothered by the senti- ment. She rubbed her head where she could still feel the burn of Beckworth grasping her hair and decided a little payback was in order. If she couldn't be the one to deliver it, she'd leave it to the professionals.

The room remained silent when Ethan left the room. His boots stomped up the two flights of stairs, and no one lifted their gaze when the door slammed shut a minute later.

66

Ethan leaned against the door, arms folded across his chest. Beckworth glared at him, his lip cut, nose bloodied, and he'd be sporting a bruise along his jaw in a day or so. They'd kicked his chair over a couple of times but other than a punch or two in his ribs, he was markedly untouched.

Finn was right. Beckworth didn't have the fire in his belly that he'd had in France. He seemed worn down, like a modern-day clock whose battery was slowly dying. Ethan believed if Beckworth didn't get back to his own time, he'd eventually cave in upon himself until he withered into a dried-out husk.

Then a thought occurred to him.

He strolled around the room, and Beckworth followed his movement with a curled lip and steady glare. There was a kindling of a spark in there. When he'd made a full circle, he dragged the metal chair close to Beckworth, so when he sat, their knees almost touched. He smiled when Beckworth leaned back.

"Why did Ratliff go to Waverly?" He let the question hang there, hoping for something to register on Beckworth's features. The man had stopped talking halfway through their last interrogation. It was a smart move on his part. With enough time and no food, Beckworth would change his tune, but Ethan refused to give Finn the two days needed to wear Beckworth down. After the first few hours though, Finn had agreed there would be little more to be gained from an extended interrogation. They would leave in the morning, with or without Beckworth's cooperation.

If Ethan had expected Beckworth to be surprised by his question, he was out of luck.

Beckworth's blank expression seemed genuine, and he shook his head as if trying to clear it. "Ratliff? I haven't seen him in years." He didn't seem to be talking to Ethan. He had a faraway gaze, as if thinking back to the last time he'd seen Ratliff.

"Then why would he travel to Waverly? Did you ask him to come?"

Beckworth appeared confused. "What are you on about, Hughes?"

"We know he was on his way to Waverly. We want to know why."

Beckworth shook his head and stared at the floor. His leg began to twitch. "I don't know. It's been four months, almost five, since I've been to Waverly."

"So you try to convince us." Ethan spoke in a bored tone. He leaned toward Beckworth, elbows on his knees, head perched on his knuckles. He studied Beckworth like a bug under a glass. "Did Ratliff have business with the duke?"

That got the surprise he'd anticipated. Beckworth's leg stopped bouncing, and he slammed against the ropes, forcing Ethan to sit back. A sneer marred his face and spittle formed at the corners of his mouth. "Ratliff and the duke despised each other. They didn't circulate among the same people." His laugh was hoarse from lack of water. "If they ended up at the same party, one always took their leave early." He rolled his head, stretching the muscles in his neck. "So no, they didn't have any business with each other."

Ethan narrowed his eyes and tapped his finger against his chin. "Yet they had you in common."

Beckworth sighed and sat back. "As I told you, it's been years since I've seen Ratliff. It was before I became the Viscount of Waverly. If he knew I was the viscount, it wasn't from me."

It was Ethan's turn to be surprised. There had to be a connection, maybe one Beckworth wasn't even aware of. The man had leaned his head back to gaze at the ceiling, and his left leg began to jiggle again. The confinement was wearing him down.

"You're going to try and convince me you didn't have a reason to kill him?"

Beckworth's head snapped forward. "Kill him? He's dead?" His questions were shrieks. There was no doubt this had come as a surprise, which only made Ethan more confused. What the hell was going on?

Ethan studied Beckworth as he continued to fidget—leg bouncing, another neck roll, a tug at the ropes. Ethan decided on one last attempt to retrieve something useful. He stood and stretched, holding his arms high above his head before pulling them behind him. He paced across the room in long, slow strides. After several minutes, he turned on Beckworth.

"If you're going to continue to lie to us, you have no value. Do you know what that means?"

Beckworth snickered. "That you'll let me go?"

Ethan smiled. "Exactly."

Beckworth stared at him, mouth partially slack.

"You don't believe me? I can call Finn up here right now, and we'll walk you to the road. It will be a bit of a hike back to where you live, but it's turning into a nice evening."

Beckworth paled. "Aren't you going back? If Maire is missing, you want to find her. If she's at Waverly, like you said, I can get her out of there."

Ethan waited, his finger tapping at his chin again, as if he were truly giving it some thought. "No, I don't think so. You don't have even the simplest of answers. I don't know what help you could be."

"You can't leave me here. I need to go home. I promise I'll find a way to help you." He looked crazed, and Ethan almost felt sorry for him.

He understood the terror of never going home. Remembered those first few months of jumping when it had hit the hardest. He felt it now, worried about spending days here that might be weeks or months back home, and Maire, still lost wherever she was.

Ethan stood over Beckworth. "Then tell me something I don't already know."

"The last time I saw Maire was on that knoll. I have no idea what happened to her."

"Then like I said, you're no good to me." He balled his fists, ready to strike, but instead of hitting, he swung out his leg and kicked the chair over. Beckworth fell back, hitting his head on the floor with a grunt.

Ethan kicked at the chair, the sounds of splintering wood obscured beneath the blood pounding in his head. Beckworth was supposed to have all the answers. Instead, he was another dead end. Ethan wanted to scream until the roof caved in.

Beckworth simpered as he rolled his head back and forth.

Ethan turned away, tired of looking at him. Finn was right. Beckworth hadn't been traveling back and forth in time. He'd been stuck here all this time. As far as Ethan was concerned, he could stay and live out his days in misery.

He strode to the door, deciding to leave Beckworth trapped on the floor like a turtle stuck on its back, legs waving in the air.

He was reaching for the doorknob when something hit him in the back of the head. He dropped to his knees, and turned in time to see Beckworth slam a fist into his jaw and down he went.

———

"Do you need to help Ethan?" AJ rubbed Finn's shoulders.

He patted her hand, then pulled her around to face him. "No. I'll finish packing the duffels. We wouldn't want to forget your favorite bow."

She kissed his cheek. "They're in the library waiting for you."

"I think it's time to get the Heart Stone. The plan is to leave in the morning, but we should be prepared. If Ethan gains something useful out of Beckworth, there will be no reason to wait." He glanced at Stella. "I'm sorry. I know this isn't easy for you."

Stella attempted a weak smile. "As they say, the sooner you leave, the faster you'll return."

"Adam hoped you'd be able to take the boat back to the marina." AJ disappeared into the pantry and returned, dragging a two foot-by-two foot bin across the floor.

"Did he go down to the dock?" Finn asked.

She nodded. "He went down with Isaiah. They should be back in a few minutes."

"We'll wait until Ethan is done. If we aren't leaving until morning, I'll return the boat tonight. Otherwise, either Adam or Isaiah will need to talk to the shipmaster about retrieving the boat. Adam can use money from the operating funds to pay for the extended rental."

He pulled her close and whispered in her ear. "You look beautiful, wife."

She would never get tired of hearing him call her wife. She hugged him and kissed his nose. "I love you, husband. Now finish packing." She pushed him away and yelled at Stella, "Come help me with this."

He left the room with a smile on his face and his whistling floating back to her.

Stella stood in the pantry. "What are you doing?"

"Getting the Heart Stone."

"Did you put it in the flour?"

"Funny." AJ knelt on the floor where she'd pulled the bin of wild birdseed away. Using her knuckles, she rapped on the floorboards. When she heard a hollow response to one of her taps, she ran her fingers along the board to a notch and, with her fingernails, pried the board loose.

"I thought it was in the safe." Stella peered over her shoulder.

"It was until Beckworth's surprise visit." She pulled a small bag from the empty space and replaced the board. "What did you do with the earrings?" The earrings were made from small pieces of stone that Lily Mayfield had chipped from the Heart Stone. Because they were made from the Heart Stone, the pieces were attracted to each other like magnets. The incantation Maire had deciphered from *The Book of Stones* forced the Heart Stone to seek out its missing parts—the earrings. That was how they'd returned home from the last jump.

"I put them in a box in the back of my closet."

AJ laughed. "Are you sure you'll be able to find them again?"

"Now who's being funny? When you've been gone for more than a day, I'll put the earrings back in the hiding spot down by the dock." She shut the pantry door and watched AJ add the Heart Stone to the necklace around her neck. The poker-chip-sized stone had been set in a silver Celtic cross, and AJ's promise ring lay on top as if they belonged together. "Will I be calling you Mrs. Murphy soon?"

AJ rubbed the promise ring that lay on top of the Heart

Stone. She tried for stoic but she couldn't hold back the wide grin that became infectious.

Stella laughed and hugged her. "I wasn't sure when to say something. I thought it best to wait until we were alone."

"And we appreciate that."

"Ah." Stella stepped back. "You're waiting until you return."

"Now that's something to keep you busy while we're gone."

Stella's eyes widened. "I get to plan the wedding party?"

"I can't think of a better person. But leave something for my mother to do. I obviously can't give you a date, but let's plan on having it here so we don't have to worry about renting a place."

"I'll just sketch a few ideas for you. I promise not to order anything, but what about...," Stella stopped talking, her eyes growing wide.

AJ's hand dropped to her dagger but not before a hand grabbed her arm. The same grip as earlier that day.

Beckworth.

A J tugged at his grip. The few hours tied up and beaten hadn't lessened his strength.

Stella leaped at him. He turned to block her and kicked her legs out from under her. She dropped like a limp doll, hitting her head on the cabinets.

AJ shoved and twisted but his arm snaked around her waist, reducing her struggles.

Beckworth dragged her away. She tried to pull her right arm free but he seemed stronger than before. His eyes were wild in his desperation to leave the house. He pulled her out the front door before AJ remembered to scream, which she did with gusto, her one free hand clamping on the doorframe. He used the same technique he'd used on Stella and kicked her legs, forcing her to let go.

He dragged her down the steps, then picked her up when she tripped. He moved quickly, even with her continual squirming. How had he gotten away? Where was Ethan? They were halfway across the parking lot when Beckworth stopped, his breath ragged as he scanned the area. She managed a backward kick, which forced a grunt and curse from him.

She twisted until she could see the front door. Finn must have heard her screams. Beckworth stared at her with a savage sneer. She wasn't sure if he'd flipped his lid or simply had no idea what to do with his hostage and no place to run. When his gaze traveled lower, a maniacal grin lit up his eyes.

AJ glanced down to see what had caught his attention.

The Heart Stone glistened in the sun.

Her struggling increased. He tightened the arm he'd wrapped around her and used his left hand to reach into his pocket. When he opened his fist, he held a small stone.

"No." She pushed against him but his arms were like steel. She could smell his sour breath and sticky sweat. What had she been thinking, putting the necklace back on? She should have kept it in a drawer until it was time.

Beckworth wasted no time in grabbing her necklace, which forced the stones together. When she heard the thick Gaelic words spewing from him, she began to kick out wildly. Then she stopped and relaxed, hoping he'd respond and give her an opening. His grip only tightened. Fool him once, but he remembered her tricks.

Panic seized her. She swept her gaze to the front door. She thought she saw someone in the hall. Would they make it in time? Beyond the house, the sight froze her for an instant. The fog was coming.

Her heart raced. "Let me go. You have what you want. Take the stone."

"You should have just given it to me in the first place."

She heard yelling. Adam and Isaiah had crested the path leading up from the bay. They were running toward her. She glanced back at the house and there was Finn, struggling to get out the door at the same time as Ethan. He breached the doorway, the combination of terror and anger clear on his beautiful face.

All she needed was another minute, but the fog was overtaking the house, hungry in its need to devour them. Stella stumbled from the house, her arm gripping Ethan, who'd stopped at the top of the stairs. He held Finn back, yelling something at him she couldn't hear.

She only had a second to wonder why he did that. When she swiveled her head toward the bay, Adam held Isaiah. They backed up as the mist overtook the inn.

The rushing in her ears competed with the pounding of her heart. Yet over it all, Beckworth's laughter rang in her ears. His grip loosened, but not enough to let her go. His hand still grasped the necklace around her neck.

This wasn't the way it was supposed to happen. Then she remembered Finn's reaction when they'd returned from the past and how he'd fallen at her feet after the fog had dropped them on the dock.

Her gaze turned to his. She would remember his look of defeat for a long time.

Finn.

She mouthed the words "I love you" and thought he nodded in understanding.

Then she did the only thing she had left to do. The one thing that might save her on the other side. With his grip loosened, she finally wrenched an arm free.

Beckworth tightened his grip but it was too late.

A rolling burst of anger spread through her. She reached for her dagger.

As the mist thickened, she swung with all her might and buried the knife in his shoulder as the bright light consumed her.

Keep reading for a glimpse of AJ's journey to find Maire in *The Druid's Stone*, Book 5 of the Mórdha Stone Chronicles.

A DRUID STONE

1804 - February

AJ Moore was going to be sick. Passionately and thoroughly ill. The fog swirled around her, its thick white tendrils reaching out like skeletal arms in a horror movie. She doubled over, clenching her middle. Her stomach twisted like someone was squeezing every drop of moisture out of an old dish rag.

The dead weight of Beckworth, the Viscount of Waverly and deceitful bastard, hung over her left shoulder. Somehow, even through the horrible nausea, she felt his sticky blood staining her shirt.

She smirked. If she survived the jump, she'd stab him again —just for good measure.

Then all thought vanished as the pain intensified. The brightness of the mist overwhelmed her senses before she fell into blessed darkness.

When she opened her eyes, the heavy body sprawled across her triggered a claustrophobic attack. She shoved against it until she was able to twist away. She managed to crawl two feet before the remains of her lunch returned. That was when she noticed it was raining. Correction. Pouring. The vomit instantly melted into a pool of water, turning it into an ugly gruel.

She backed away before she gagged and scraped aside the wet bangs that dripped water down her face.

Where the hell were they?

She crawled back to the body and turned it over. Remembering who it was, she hoped he'd drowned in the puddle of mud he lay in. Unfortunately, Beckworth stirred.

When his eyes fluttered open, she screamed at him. Partly to ensure he could hear her, but also because, short of repeatedly stabbing him in the neck, it was all she could think to do. "What the hell were you thinking? Why did you do that?"

He either couldn't hear her or didn't care to answer.

She grabbed his shirt, heedless of the blood still seeping from his wound, and shook him. "Why couldn't you wait? We could have all come back together."

Tears mixed with rain and her chest heaved as she cried out her anger and frustration. When it didn't appear Beckworth would answer her, she beat on his chest, then fell back to pull herself together.

The landscape was difficult to make out through the steady rainfall, yet it seemed familiar. She had expected to arrive in England at the Earl of Hereford's estate. Realization dawned. That would have required Ethan's incantation. The new and improved version from Maire's more recent translations. Instead, Beckworth had interfered and grabbed the Heart Stone she'd foolishly worn around her neck. Although he'd whispered an older incantation, it hadn't mattered. Just the act of him touching the stone he carried with the Heart Stone was enough to carry them back to the location of the torc.

They were on the knoll in France. The only question was the

year. At least the monastery would be close. That was something. Full of despair, she sank back in the mud. What would she find when she went to town? Would Ethan and Maire be at the inn as she'd last left them?

Finn.

Her heart filled with longing and a deep, aching sense of loss. Less than twenty-four hours ago, they had married and promised never to leave the other. Now he was two hundred years away. Or was he?

Ethan still had a stone. They never discussed Maire's updated incantations, but Ethan would have the translation to follow the Heart Stone. AJ had no idea how accurate the travel would be or the timing. It could take months for them to connect, assuming they arrived in the same time period.

Distorted mumbling drew her attention back to her current dilemma.

"You."

She crawled over and rose to her knees so she could stare down at him.

"You." His head rolled from side to side. He paused after each word, waiting for his labored breathing to subside. "You," he attempted for the third time. He heaved and almost gagged. A line of spittle formed at the corner of his mouth, and even scrunched in pain, his soaking-wet face was beautifully handsome. His normally cornflower-blue eyes were dulled, his face pasty as he forced out the word, "Stabbed." He sucked air but couldn't seem to squeak out the next word.

"Me." AJ finished for him. "You stabbed me. Is that what you're trying to spit out?" When his half-crazed eyes rolled to her, she nodded, her eyes narrowing, her voice spitting with controlled rage. "Yes. I did. And I've a mind to stab you again. So lie still while I think."

There were dozens of reasons to stab him. For kidnapping

her months ago, for holding Maire hostage for two years, for torturing Finn when he was held in the duke's dungeons, for blindly following them back to the future, for stalking her and then kidnapping her again. Hell, he deserved to be stabbed just for being an asshole.

She considered the real reason she'd stabbed him. In those last few seconds before the fog had claimed them, she'd remembered Finn having difficulty after their jump back to the future. He'd been injured from torture before they'd left, and though he'd mostly healed, Finn had said injuries made the travel more difficult. Finn had been in and out of a delirious state for hours upon their return. It took a day before he had the strength to walk and two days to fully recover.

Beckworth had confessed to being unconscious for two days after the sisters had found him. His injury, the first time she'd stabbed his shoulder, also hadn't completely healed before he was pulled into the vortex of AJ's and Finn's jump home. The two days of Beckworth being out cold might have been from medication the sisters had given him. But AJ she didn't think so.

Tired of being wet, she scanned the area. The bushes where closer than the trees and would be sufficient for her plan. Standing somewhat awkwardly, she took advantage of his partial moments of awareness. After several false starts, and an equal amount of time waiting for Beckworth to regain consciousness, she dragged him to the underbrush. It wasn't entirely dry, but it provided some reprieve from the torrential rain. She discovered the backpack during their long crawl. He must have grabbed it as he raced to get away from the inn with her in tow. She pulled the pack from him and pushed her arms through the straps, allowing it to fall against her back.

If her suspicions were correct and they were in France, she had some options. The only question was the year. Based on the rain and the leafless trees, it was winter or maybe early spring. Then she remembered the war and groaned.

Beckworth had passed out again. She left him as he lay. It was doubtful anyone was walking about in this weather. She considered stabbing him again, just to be sure, or maybe just because. Instead, she stood, kicked decayed leaves over his legs to completely cover him and turned toward the direction of town.

She followed the trail until she reached the main street. The docks were to her left and Guerin's Inn to her right, just as she remembered it.

She was almost to the inn when she noticed the first soldiers. Two of them leaned against a building. If they spotted her, they didn't care, but it confirmed one thing—it was no longer 1802.

When she knocked at the back door of the inn, she tried to remember the innkeeper's name. She didn't remember anyone calling him Guerin.

The door opened and a gruff voice spoke in French. She panicked. She could only guess what the innkeeper thought of the drowned rat that stood before him. No words came to her. She didn't know French. Everyone had spoken English when she was last here. If they were at war, it made sense that French would be the first words spoken.

She stood there, struggling with what to say, when the man grabbed her by the arms and dragged her in. He yelled, "Sofi." AJ almost cried with relief. Sofi was the innkeeper's wife.

Before she knew it, she was pushed into a chair in front of the kitchen fires. A minute later a blanket was thrown over her drenched summer blouse and jeans. She shivered. Another minute later, a towel fell over her shoulders. Another was wrapped around her head as someone vigorously rubbed her hair in what she assumed was an attempt to dry it.

"Miss Moore. Is that you?" Sofi's worried question made AJ sigh in relief. They remembered her.

She nodded and pushed the women's hands away so she could look up. Husband and wife stared down at her before glancing at each other.

"This is a very dangerous time to have returned. It looks like you swam across the channel." The innkeeper shook his head and wiped flour from his hands. He'd been baking bread. That explained the heavenly aroma that filled her nose and made her stomach grumble.

"I can explain. But first, I have a large favor to ask." She spoke slowly, trying to change her speech to match the current era. When the pair glanced at each other again, AJ added, "And I can pay you."

An hour later, Beckworth lay on a bed in the smallest room possible, a fire blazing in the hearth.

AJ sat in front of another fire in the room next door. Her clothes dried over the back of a chair. Her shoes and socks sat on the warm stones in front of the hearth. Sofi loaned her a dress, and though it was short at the ankles and arms, the rest fit well enough. Beckworth's backpack perched next to her on the couch as she slowly went through the contents.

Her concerns about finances were immediately relieved when she found the silver coins and jewelry they had planned to return to the sisters. She'd save what she could, but her survival came first. She'd never met the sisters and didn't know why they'd taken in Beckworth, but everyone paid for the risks of their decisions. She would require transport to England, and with the war, which the innkeeper confirmed had begun last summer, the price would be high.

Her second request of the innkeeper, after retrieving Beckworth, was to send a message to Sebastian at the monastery. Henri, the innkeeper, promised to send someone as soon as the rain let up. All she could do was wait.

She'd expected to see several soldiers at the inn, but there were only three. Henri said the soldiers took turns visiting the inns. Two dozen troops stayed in the barracks by the dock at any given time. Most of them preferred the inn across the street which Henri was grateful for. The soldiers discouraged customers.

Feeling secure for the moment, she stared into the fire and considered her plight. If Ethan had used the stone, and Finn and Ethan arrived in France, they shouldn't be too far from town. Her greatest fear was them landing in the middle of French soldiers. The one thing she hated most about this time period was no cell phones. Communication with England could take weeks, and with the war, possibly months.

Her mind raced with possibilities until a headache crept up her neck and pounded at the back of her skull. She couldn't jump back home without the proper incantation. She'd written it on a piece of paper that she'd stuffed in her duffel. The one she'd left in the library at home. She could get it again from Sebastian, but for now, she had a different mission. She was here to find Maire and there was only one place to start. Hereford. When Ethan and Finn arrived, she was certain that would be their destination.

She closed her eyes, unable to focus. The backpack fell to the floor when she stretched her legs across the couch. A short nap and she'd be good as new.

When the knock sounded at her door, she groaned at the stiffness of her body. She pulled the dagger still strapped to her leg. When the knob began to turn, she scurried to stand behind the door before it opened. Was Beckworth awake? She couldn't imagine him knocking. The soldiers had ignored her when she went down earlier for hot water.

A figure emerged, and she swung the dagger to bring the hilt down on the stranger's head, but she pulled back at the last minute. The figure was her height with a larger girth. She recognized the hooded cloak.

When the man turned, AJ almost leaped into his arms.

Sebastian stared at her with his whimsical smile, and she fell into his arms with a sob of gratitude.

Thank you for reading *A Stone Forgotten*.

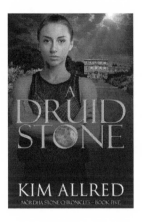

Stay connected with Kim to keep up with next releases, book signings, and other treats by joining her newsletter at www.kimallred.com.

ABOUT THE AUTHOR

 **Kim Allred** lives in an old timber town in the Pacific Northwest where she raises alpacas, llamas and an undetermined number of free-range chickens. Just like AJ and Stella, she loves sharing stories while sipping a glass of fine wine or slurping a strong cup of brew.

Her spirit of adventure has taken her on many journeys including a ten-day dogsledding trip in northern Alaska and sleeping under the stars on the savannas of eastern Africa.

Kim is currently working on the final books for the Mórdha Stone Chronicles series and a new paranormal romance series - Seduction in Blood.

facebook.com/kim.allred.52831

instagram.com/kimallredauthor

amazon.com/-/e/B07CQY2J8Y

bookbub.com/authors/kim-allred

pinterest.com/kimallredauthor